# *Romantic* Suspense

## Danger. Passion. Drama.

### Colton's Secret Stalker
Kimberly Van Meter

### Hunted Hotshot Hero
Lisa Childs

# MILLS & BOON

DID YOU PURCHASE THIS BOOK WITHOUT A COVER?
If you did, you should be aware it is **stolen property** as it was reported
'unsold and destroyed' by a retailer.
Neither the author nor the publisher has received any payment
for this book.

Kimberly Van Meter is acknowledged as the author of this work
COLTON'S SECRET STALKER
© 2024 by Harlequin Enterprises ULC
Philippine Copyright 2024
Australian Copyright 2024
New Zealand Copyright 2024

First Published 2024
First Australian Paperback Edition 2024
ISBN 978 1 038 90266 5

HUNTED HOTSHOT HERO
© 2024 by Lisa Childs
Philippine Copyright 2024
Australian Copyright 2024
New Zealand Copyright 2024

First Published 2024
First Australian Paperback Edition 2024
ISBN 978 1 038 90266 5

® and ™ (apart from those relating to FSC®) are trademarks of Harlequin Enterprises
(Australia) Pty Limited or its corporate affiliates. Trademarks indicated with ® are
registered in Australia, New Zealand and in other countries.
Contact admin_legal@Harlequin.ca for details.

Except for use in any review, the reproduction or utilisation of this work in whole or in
part in any form by any electronic, mechanical or other means, now known or hereafter
invented, including xerography, photocopying and recording, or in any information
storage or retrieval system, is forbidden without the permission of the publisher,
Harlequin Mills & Boon.

This book is sold subject to the condition that it shall not, by way of trade or otherwise,
be lent, resold, hired out or otherwise circulated without the prior consent of the publisher
in any form or binding or cover other than that in which it is published and without a
similar condition including this condition being imposed on the subsequent purchaser.

All rights reserved including the right of reproduction in whole or in part in any form.
This edition is published in arrangement with Harlequin Books S.A..

This is a work of fiction. Names, characters, places, and incidents are either the
product of the author's imagination or are used fictitiously, and any resemblance to
actual persons, living or dead, business establishments, events, or locales is entirely
coincidental.

MIX
Paper | Supporting
responsible forestry
FSC® C001695

Published by
Harlequin Mills & Boon
An imprint of Harlequin Enterprises (Australia) Pty Limited
(ABN 47 001 180 918), a subsidiary of HarperCollins
Publishers Australia Pty Limited
(ABN 36 009 913 517)
Level 19, 201 Elizabeth Street
SYDNEY NSW 2000 AUSTRALIA

Cover art used by arrangement with Harlequin Books S.A.. All rights reserved.

Printed and bound in Australia by McPherson's Printing Group

# Colton's Secret Stalker
Kimberly Van Meter

# MILLS & BOON

**Kimberly Van Meter** wrote her first book at sixteen and finally achieved publication in December 2006. She has written for the Harlequin Superromance, Blaze and Romantic Suspense lines. She and her husband of thirty years have three children, two cats, and always a houseful of friends, family and fun.

Visit the Author Profile page
at millsandboon.com.au for more titles.

Dear Reader,

When I was asked to be a part of the new Colton continuity, I was humbled and flattered to be included in such an incredible lineup of talented authors.

I hope you enjoy *Colton's Secret Stalker* as you delve into a suspenseful story nestled within the complicated dynamics of a large family filled with secrets.

Hearing from readers is a special joy. You can always find me on social media or you can email me.

Happy reading!

Facebook: Facebook.com/Kim.VanMeter.37

Email: alexandria2772@hotmail.com

*Kimberly Van Meter*

# Chapter 1

Frannie Colton had a sixth sense about things. She wouldn't go so far as to call it a genuine psychic gift—but she had a feeling in her gut when a bad wind was blowing.

Today seemed to be one of those days.

A shiver tickled her spine as if the July sun wasn't doing its best to break seasonal records in Idaho. She hustled into her bookstore, Book Mark It, thankful for the air-conditioning that hit her face and cooled her skin.

Usually, Idaho had mild summers but brutal winters. However, this year, Mother Nature seemed interested in pushing boundaries. Today, the temperatures were pushing 90 degrees, which was practically like setting the state on fire.

She waved at her friend Darla, who'd held down the fort so she could make a quick run to the post office, and helped herself to an iced tea from the attached café.

Finally able to breathe, she joined Darla behind the counter. "Thanks for covering the store for me. I had to get those certified documents mailed before the end of the day."

"No problem. It's not every day something that beautiful wanders into the veritable bore factory known as Owl Creek."

Puzzled, she looked to Darla, who then covertly gestured

to the man sitting in one of the comfy high-back chairs, sipping a mocha while thumbing through a table book on ancient Greek architecture.

Frannie chuckled. He was definitely worth a second glance, but he wasn't new to the shop. In fact, he'd been in a few times, but Darla must've missed him.

"His name is Dante Sinclair and he's really nice. Don't go scaring him off," Frannie warned playfully, reminding Darla, "Also, you're about to be married. Keep your eyes in your head."

Not for nothing though, Dante was the kind of man you'd have to be blind to miss. He was tall enough to make the oversize chair appear modest, and his short, cropped hair and the beginnings of a beard were flecked with gray. She didn't know much about him, just that he was polite and courteous and enjoyed a quiet moment with a new book. He definitely wasn't from around these parts. Whether that was a good thing or not remained to be seen.

Darla pouted as if suddenly remembering her fiancé, Tom, was still in the picture. "Fine, but if I can't, you have to promise me you'll try to flirt with that incredible specimen. I'm serious, that right there, is an import. That's no corn-fed farm boy. He looks…dare I say… European?"

"Flirt? That's unprofessional," Frannie scoffed, "Just because he's not wearing mud-caked work boots doesn't mean he's from Europe. And what's wrong with a corn-fed farm boy? Honest work builds strong character."

"Mmm-hmm. Tell that to the Higgins boys. All raised on a dairy farm and all criminals at some point or another."

"The Higgins family has issues. That's not a fair comparison." She sipped her tea while surreptitiously stealing another peek at the stranger. Okay, he wasn't hard on the eyes, and there was a certain air about him that seemed more distinguished, more polished than the local men who called Owl Creek home, but he was probably married, and Frannie wasn't looking for drama.

Besides, men that handsome were trouble—they couldn't help themselves.

"He's probably just on vacation."

"Who in their right mind would vacation here?" Darla quipped.

"Why are you hating on Owl Creek?" she teased. "Blackbird Lake is a popular destination for boaters."

"Does he look like he spends a lot of time on a fishing boat?"

"I try not to judge a book by its cover," Frannie replied with a saucy grin. Darla rolled her eyes, and Frannie pointed finger guns at her playfully, adding, "See? There's a benefit to being a bookworm. Makes you delightfully witty."

"Don't quit your day job, kid." Darla popped from the stool and grabbed her purse. "If you don't need me for anything else, I need to run. I'm supposed to meet Tom at The Tides to go over the wedding details, sign contracts, pay our deposit…you know, all that fun stuff."

"It'll be beautiful," Frannie assured Darla. "And you'll be the most gorgeous bride this town has ever seen."

"We'll see about that. I'm starting to wonder if we should've eloped. I'm over all this wedding crap. What a huge headache. But Tom insists on doing it up big, so here we are. I mean, honestly, who are we trying to impress? Let's just head to the courthouse, sign documents and then spend all that wedding money on an epic honeymoon."

"Stop being a sourpuss and enjoy the moment," she told her best friend. She shooed her out the door, smiling as Darla drove away. Bless Tom for being a saint. Although she loved Darla with everything in her heart, the woman was difficult on her best days.

But she was also intensely loyal and would chew anyone to pieces if they dared to hurt someone she loved. Frannie found that level of commitment reassuring. Not that she wanted Darla to commit a felony in her honor or anything, but…it was nice to know that Darla had her back.

Her gaze strayed to the handsome newcomer. What would it hurt to be friendly and say hello again? Not flirting, of course.

Being neighborly was good business.

But she held back even as she contemplated walking up to the man and interrupting his quiet time. He probably didn't want to be disturbed. Being interrupted while reading was one of her biggest pet peeves, second only to people calling mayonnaise MAN-naise. She always argued, "You don't say, 'Hold the MAN-O,' you say, 'Hold the MAY-O.'"

Darla said Frannie needed to let that peeve die because it made her sound like a card-carrying member of the grammar police.

*So be it.* Words—and their proper pronunciation— mattered. Hence, her love of books.

But the man was intriguing, sitting in a small-town bookstore in the middle of the day as if he had nothing but time on his hands. He was older than her, she thought. If the gray flecks in his beard weren't enough, the subtle weathering of his skin gave him a rugged, if not sophisticated, look that she found appealing.

Frannie sipped her tea, contemplating the handsome stranger's back story as if he were a character in a novel.

People-watching was one of her favorite pastimes, mostly because she enjoyed creating narratives for her amusement.

He was safely engrossed in his reading, which gave her

the perfect opportunity to watch without being weirdly off-putting.

Maybe Darla was right. He did have a vibe that wasn't quite American.

International spy? James Bond–type right here in Owl Creek? What were the odds? Highly unlikely but not impossible.

It seemed everyone had secrets these days. A sour note threatened to ruin her good mood. The thing about painful breakups was that the pain popped up at unexpected times, even if you've convinced yourself that you're over the cheating jerk-face.

Three months was plenty enough time to move on from a bad boyfriend.

Except…there remained an emotional bruise beneath the skin that hurt like a sonofabitch when she poked at it.

Solution? Don't poke at it.

Instead, enjoy the imported eye candy and remember that books would always be better than boyfriends.

As the thought zipped through her head, the handsome stranger swiveled his gaze straight to hers and smiled.


Being sharp and observant was his bread and butter at work. The minute the cute young woman entered the shop, her cheeks flushed from the heat, her blond hair damp at the hairline, he'd been aware of her every move.

He unintentionally caught a whiff of her skin—a blend of coconut butter and citrus—and his senses prickled with interest.

He'd been coming to the bookstore for a while, but today seemed to be the first day the woman had taken more than a cursory notice of him.

He liked the quaint bookstore and café. For one, books

had a calming effect on his nerves, and two, the mocha blend with cream was nearly as good as the one at his favorite café back home in Italy.

Owl Creek was suitable for his needs—small enough to be unremarkable and big enough for him to blend into the scene without drawing too much attention. But he'd abandoned all hope of finding a coffee shop capable of making anything remotely palatable.

And then he'd stumbled on Book Mark It.

That first tentative sip had flooded his mouth with joy. He missed Italy, but not enough to go back. Not that he could.

And the woman had stunning hazel eyes that sparkled with curiosity and intelligence.

Collecting the book, he rose and approached the counter. "If I haven't said it already, you have a lovely shop," he said, pushing the book toward her. "And I'd like to purchase this."

"Oh! Yes, thank you." Was it the heat, or had he caused that fluster? She quickly rang up the purchase. "So… I have to ask, are you on vacation or something?"

He ignored her question yet extended his hand. "I'm not sure if I've formally introduced myself… I'm Dante Sinclair."

"Frannie Colton. Likewise."

Her hand had calluses on the palm like she was accustomed to working with her hands. Was she the handy sort? Lugging hardware and hammering nuts and bolts for her business? Didn't she have a man to do that for her? He had to remind himself that American men weren't like Italian men, and women here were far more independent. "Is this your shop?"

"Yep. Every nook and cranny. My love affair with books

is an obsession that will never end. I figured I ought to try and monetize it so I can at least use my book purchases as a tax write-off."

He chuckled. "We share a similar love. Whenever I travel, I always seek out the bookstores first."

"Me too! I thought I was the only person to do this anymore. It seems everyone's nose is so stuck in their phones most days that reading an actual book is a foreign concept. My friend Darla, the woman who just left, she's always saying that I was born in the wrong generation, though I don't think I would do very well in a corset with these sturdy hips."

Her self-deprecating humor made him chuckle. Although he didn't see anything wrong with her build. He liked what he saw. *Careful. You're not here to make connections.* He straightened, collecting his book with a short smile. "It was a pleasure to meet you."

"Same to you. You didn't say whether you're here on business or pleasure…"

"A little of both," he answered. "Colton…any relation to the Colton hardware store I saw earlier?"

Frannie's little bashful laugh was adorable. "Um, yeah, my family's been here for generations. There are plenty of Coltons running around this place. You can hardly walk down the street without bumping into one. Made it difficult to get away with anything when we were kids."

"I can only imagine. Probably makes it hard to date, too."

"Oh, yeah, forget about dating," she agreed, chuckling, though there seemed a strained quality to her humor. "Especially with three older brothers who think their baby sister should be kept behind glass. They were a little overprotective."

"Brothers are good for protecting sisters." He paused before asking, "Any older sisters?"

"Yep, two of those. We have a big family. You?"

"No, I'm an only child," he answered without elaborating. Talk of his family was a bad idea. Especially if he wanted to glide under the radar. He supposed no matter where he landed in the heartland of America, he was bound to draw some attention, but he'd needed a place where his family wouldn't think to look.

"So, I hope it's not offensive or anything, but my friend said you have this look about you that's…I don't know how to say…not from around here, which I think is a good thing! Don't get me wrong, you're like a breath of fresh air but was she totally off-base to guess you're from…?"

She was fishing. He ought to lie. But it seemed harmless enough to share a small truth. "Italy."

"Oh damn, she was right. She said you were European."

He smiled, reluctantly charmed, though a frisson of alarm followed. "Is it that obvious?"

"Um, well, a little bit, but I like it. We don't get many international visitors around here." Her cell chirped to life, and she grabbed it quickly, apologizing as she glanced at the message, a frown gathering on her face. "Sorry… I… have to make a call. It was nice to meet you," she said hastily before disappearing into her office.

The door was thin, but her voice was muffled enough only to catch a word or two, and it didn't seem like good news.

He was inclined to wait and see if she returned, but whatever was happening wasn't his business.

He had his own troubles, and he didn't need to add the cute bookstore owner's woes to his plate.

Dante exited the bookstore and hoped whatever had stolen Frannie's smile worked itself out eventually.

Lord only knew he held on to no such hope for himself.

# Chapter 2

"I don't understand," Frannie said, still trying to wrap her brain around what her oldest sister, Ruby, was saying. "Aunt Jessie is saying *what*?"

Ruby's voice on the other line was strained as she repeated, "She's saying that...well, that she and Dad had a secret affair for decades and...that she has kids that are owed consideration in his will."

Frannie's mind was spinning. It was hard to decide which bomb to prioritize first. "Okay, give me a minute to process, this is wild. I mean, I know Mom has a twin sister, but we've never heard from or seen Aunt Jessie for pretty much our entire lives. And now she pops up out of nowhere to lay claim to Dad's assets? What does Mom say about all of this? Oh my God, she's probably devastated. Has anyone checked on her yet?"

"I thought we could go see her tonight, maybe bring her dinner or something? I don't know, Mom is so private... even if she did know about this alleged affair, I doubt she would've shared."

"Yeah, it's not like that's something you'd want to shout from the rooftops," Frannie quipped with a rare burst of understanding for her mom. She and Jenny Colton had never been terribly close, but Jenny had been reserved with

most of her children. "I shouldn't even find this shocking…
It's not like she and Dad had a stellar relationship."

"Well, they got along well enough to have six kids,"
Ruby pointed out dryly.

The thought of her parents getting biblical ruined Frannie's
appetite for the foreseeable future, but Ruby had a solid point.
"All I learned from our parents' relationship is that marriages
are complicated." She drew a deep breath and peered out of
her office to the bookstore, disappointed to see the handsome
Italian had left. She returned to her conversation with Ruby.
"Okay, I'll pick up a brisket family meal from Back Forty
Barbecue. Mom always said food helped bad news go down
easier, though I rarely find myself interested in eating when
I'm already choking down something terrible."

"Can you rally the troops? I'm swamped with patients
today and my break is almost over."

"Sure," Frannie agreed but secretly she didn't want that
job. Her siblings were ridiculously hard to wrangle, and she
didn't like chasing them down. The easiest to get to agree
would be her brother Fletcher because he frequently popped
into the shop to say hi, and they were fairly close. The hard-
est would be her oldest brother, Chase, who was now running Dad's property business. And to be honest, sometimes
Chase didn't want to carve out time for family stuff because
everything else under the sun was more important.

Maybe that wasn't nice or kind to say, but the truth often
stung.

Family dynamics were complicated. Just like marriages.

"So, how did you hear about this?" Frannie asked.

"Dad's attorney called to let me know Aunt Jessie had
marched into his office demanding a copy of Dad's will.
When questioned, she dropped her little scandal bomb."
Ruby groaned. "God, I hope she didn't do this in front of

people we know. I can only imagine how quickly that little nugget would roll around town."

"Small towns love gossip," Frannie agreed, wincing. "Well, I guess we'll cross that bridge when we come to it. See you around six?"

"Yeah, thanks for picking up the food. I'll call Mom and make sure she's home tonight."

"Sounds good."

They clicked off, and Frannie took a minute to breathe through the chaos swirling in her head. Was it possible Aunt Jessie was lying? Maybe she and her kids were trying some desperate money grab? No one knew the woman's financial situation. Maybe there was nothing to Aunt Jessie's claims, and all of this would go away once she realized no one was buying her story. But it sure was a whopper of a tale to tell without proof.

A DNA test would immediately prove whether or not her kids were owed something from Robert Colton's assets.

*Eww.* Just saying that in her head made her want to vomit.

And how old were these supposed half siblings? Younger than her? It would be unsettling to discover her place as the baby of the family had been usurped by these mystery kids.

She groaned. Two more siblings? *Our family is big enough as it is.*

Frannie rubbed her rumbling belly. Her stomach had always been sensitive to drama. The conflict made her stomach yowl in protest. Imagine being the youngest in a loud, boisterous family, the only one who preferred peace and quiet with a book somewhere far away from the shenanigans of her siblings.

Her bookstore was not only her happy place but a reminder of how books had always been her safe place growing up.

Chase had teased her mercilessly whenever he'd found

her nose in a book, and Wade, desperate to impress his big brother, had almost always chimed in. Fletcher, on the other hand, had always defended her. It was probably why they'd remained close and why Fletcher continued to be so protective. When Fletcher had discovered how dirty her boyfriend had done her, it'd taken a reminder that he wasn't cut out for prison that'd saved Bobby Newfield's worthless hide.

But Lord knew Frannie loved him for it.

Releasing a deep breath, she sent a quick group text to the gang:

Important meeting at Mom and Dad's @6 p.m. Aunt Jessie blew into town with a potential scandal. I'm bringing a brisket meal. Feel free to bring a dessert or drinks.
Frannie

Texting was better than a phone call, anyway. It wasn't like anyone liked to answer the phone anymore.

As expected, Chase's response was cut, dry and impersonal.

Sorry, out of town, but I'm already aware. Handling it.

He probably didn't mean to sound that way, but he did. And, wait a minute, if he already knew, why did Ruby have to find out through Dad's lawyer? *Damn you, Chase, always acting like the gatekeeper. So annoying.*

Hannah quickly apologized.

Sorry, Lucy's got that bug going around, so I'm going to stay home with her. Let me know what's happening after you talk to Mom. Love ya, Han.

Wade didn't respond at all. *Typical.*

Fletcher's response made her smile.

I'm around the corner. Be there in five.

He knew how to make her smile and, somehow, feel less agitated.

Thankfully, it was almost closing time. She started her closing routine, and Fletcher walked in moments later, just as he'd promised.

The look on his face pulled at her heart. "What the hell is going on?" he asked, hands anchored above his law enforcement utility belt. "Is this for real? Aunt Jessie? What kind of scandal are we talking? Has a crime been committed? Is this something that should be reported?"

Frannie sent Fletcher an exasperated look, glancing meaningfully at the last straggling customers left in the store, and Fletcher caught her drift, reluctantly waiting as Frannie closed and locked the door and flipped her sign. "Sorry, your text got me all riled up," he apologized. "But what the hell? I need more details than that."

"Honestly, I don't have much to go on. Ruby said Dad's lawyer called to say that Aunt Jessie showed up in his office demanding a copy of the will. When he asked who she was and why she was entitled to the documents, she said that she and Dad had been together for decades and that she had two of his children, who, by law, are entitled to a portion of Dad's assets."

"What?" Fletcher exploded. "That's some bullshit if I ever heard any."

"Well, maybe? I guess a DNA test will clear up that mystery real quick, but what if she's telling the truth? I can only imagine how hurt Mom will be by this news. I mean, her own sister? Her *twin*? That's cold by any flick of the channel."

Fletcher softened at the mention of their mother. "Yeah, that's a crap sandwich if it's true…but do you really think Dad would—hell, I don't even like to think he was capable of being that big of an ass."

They'd long suspected their dad wasn't faithful to their mom, but no one liked to talk about the elephant in the room.

However, to cheat with Mom's sister? Frannie pushed down the wave of disappointment. Everyone thought Frannie had been their father's favorite, but Robert Colton hadn't exactly been involved in any of his kids' lives. He'd been a solid provider, but as far as emotional support went, he'd been sorely lacking.

Even so, Frannie and her dad had shared some commonalities that had created a bit of a bond, which made the current news sit uncomfortably.

"Is it bad to hope that Aunt Jessie is mentally unstable or lying through her teeth?" Frannie asked.

Fletcher sighed, shaking his head. "Hell, I don't know but I feel the same. Guess we'll find out."

"Yeah, I guess so. Do you think I should pick up a bottle of wine or something? Feels like alcohol might help settle the nerves."

"For you or for Mom?"

Frannie laughed. "Maybe just for me."

Fletcher chuckled. "All right. I've got to finish my shift. I'll see you in a bit."

Frannie nodded and followed Fletcher, pausing to lock up the shop and head to the barbecue joint.

It might've been a misplaced attempt at distracting herself from current events, but as she placed her order, Frannie thought of Dante, the Italian stranger. As Darla pointed out, Owl Creek wasn't a huge draw for international travelers. Sure, it was quaint, and it had its charm, but it was hardly a mecca of touristy attractions, no matter what the Chamber of Commerce tried to assert with their splashy local commercials.

So why would a man like Dante, who was sophisticated, well-spoken and sticking out like a sore thumb, pick a place like Owl Creek to hang out?

Maybe she'd read too many true-crime novels because she was already formulating less-than-legal reasons why.

This was one of the downsides to being a voracious bookworm—the what-ifs were endless.

"Lord knows, Francesca, your imagination is enough to fuel an entire literary career," her mother had once said to her in a moment of exasperation. And she'd used her *given* name, which always made her cringe. Not that *Frannie* was much better, but she had to deal with the hand and the name she'd been dealt.

"Order for Frannie C," a voice rang out, and Frannie snapped out of her random thoughts to scoop up the order with a brief smile.

As she climbed into her car, the aroma of fresh barbecue filling the cab, she thought ruefully that at least the food wouldn't disappoint.

But she had a feeling tonight was going to be rough.

Dante stood on the porch of his rustic rented cabin and listened to the wind whistle through the trees. The warm air caressed his cheek and ruffled his hair. The temperate summer was similar enough to his native country, but that was where the similarities ended.

There was a comforting simplicity to the ebb and flow

of Owl Creek. He'd been here almost two weeks and had begun to get a feel for the vibe. The countryside was breath-taking, and the rental was fitting for the area. The A-frame log cabin was built to withstand bitter winters with plenty of snowfall, but he didn't know where he'd be come winter.

He wasn't accustomed to the quiet.

Dante breathed in the clean air, closing his eyes as birds twittered from the branches while unseen forest floor crea-tures rustled from beneath the ground cover, but something was soothing about the fact that out here, nature ruled su-preme.

Not his family.

Being part of the Santoro family—one of the most pow-erful and dangerous in Italy—was a double-edged sword. It was only a matter of time before you got cut somewhere.

It would be disingenuous to say the money and prestige didn't have its perks: the fine clothing, expensive cars and the privilege that came with the association. But nothing came without a cost.

And he was done chipping off pieces of his soul to pay the toll.

Dante straightened, rubbing his arms as an errant chill popped goose bumps along his skin. The paranoia never left him. No matter how random Owl Creek seemed on a map or how remote this cabin was, he couldn't shake the tension that eyes were on him.

His uncle Lorenzo wasn't the kind of man to let any per-ceived slight go unanswered.

Not even when it was family committing the offense.

His only insurance policy until he could figure out a better solution?

Something his uncle would kill to have returned.

For now, it was locked away in a safety-deposit box under a fake name.

But sometimes, he worried not even that would keep him safe from his uncle's reach.

Dante pushed away from the railing and went inside, locking the door behind him.

## Chapter 3

Jenny, always calm during any crisis, was no different when faced with the possibility that her husband had fathered two children with her twin sister. Just saying the words in her head made Frannie want to sink into the floor.

*Damn you, Dad.*

If he wasn't already dead…

"Frannie, can you please get the plates out," Jenny said, moving on autopilot as she unpacked the brisket meal Frannie had brought. Of course, Frannie was there before any of her siblings showed up because even when she tried to drag her feet, her need to be on time took the reins.

"Mom, we don't need to use the real plates. Paper plates should be fine."

"Not for brisket, dear," Jenny replied without missing a beat. "Also, did you manage to talk to Mrs. Gershwin from the Garden Club about those dead azaleas in the planter berm in front of your store? It's such an eyesore and takes away from all the lovely work you've done for your little shop."

Dead azaleas were the least of Frannie's concerns at the moment. "Mom, I know what you're doing. It's okay to admit that you're upset. We're all here for you. What Dad did—"

"We don't know anything yet," Jenny cut in, her soft

voice with the slightest reproachful edge, as if Frannie were the one acting out of pocket for even mentioning it. "I don't believe in building bridges for rivers we don't need to cross just yet."

"But that's just it, Mom, we do have to cross that bridge, the river is here and it's about to wipe out the aforementioned bridge. We have to face this head-on."

"What's to face? If it's true…" Jenny paused, revealing a minute crack in her reserve before pushing forward "…then we deal with it. It is what it is."

Frannie hated that saying. Not only did that phrase feel like a cop-out, it also felt like defeat. "Do you think your sister could be lying?"

"I haven't seen or spoken to Jessie in decades. I haven't a clue what she might be capable of at this point in her life."

"Yeah, but you knew her as a kid. What was she like?"

Jenny blinked as if Frannie had viciously poked a bruise to see if it still hurt. It took a minute, but Jenny recovered, saying, "It was a long time ago. I hardly remember. Besides, no one is the same person they were as a child. I know I'm certainly not. Life changes people. Circumstances, choices, all those variables go into the mix, and you pop out a different version of yourself when it's all said and done. It happens to everyone. It's just the way of things, Frannie."

Frannie heard the hidden pain in that statement. As a mother, Jenny had been competent, solid and appropriately present. Even as a full-time nurse, Jenny had been the one to oversee her children's schooling, sports and home needs, though Frannie had never felt that Jenny loved being a mom. It felt contradictory to admit that truth when the woman had given birth to six kids. But Frannie always wondered if that had been some attempt to keep Robert interested in staying, not so much an interest in being a mother to a large brood.

It always hurt to stare hard truths in the eye.

But it also made her sad for her mother. "Mom…did you and Dad ever actually love each other?"

Jenny stilled, her back to Frannie. "In the beginning, very much." She slowly turned, exhaling a long breath as she admitted, "Well, at least for me, anyway. I've spent a lifetime trying to make something better than it was for the sake of my children. The truth of the matter was, Robert and I…well, maybe we were never a good fit at all."

Jenny's revelation stunned Frannie. Intensely private by nature, her mother would rather lick a dirty sidewalk than share the depth of her feelings on any particular subject. The fact that Jenny was sharing even a smidge of her business with anyone was jarring.

And Frannie didn't know how to respond.

Jenny seemed to understand and returned to unpacking the brisket meal.

But Frannie had to say something. "Mom…if it turns out to be true… I'm really sorry. You deserved better than what Dad gave you."

Jenny accepted Frannie's sentiment, sniffing back what may have been a tear or two, and then excused herself to the bathroom with a reminder that the sturdier napkins were in the pantry.

Sighing, Frannie sank into the chair at the kitchen island and mentally prodded her siblings to hurry up and get their happy asses to the house. She wasn't sure how much more she could absorb on her own. She needed the buffer of her brother and sister, or she'd end up stress-eating everything in sight.

Her gaze wandered around the home she'd grown up

in, seeing memories in a different light. It was funny how kids could be incredibly intuitive yet miss obvious clues staring them in the face.

Their home was aesthetically beautiful. Jenny had refined tastes that she used to shape Robert's rough, masculine edges into something strong yet elegant. Frannie had never known the sharp pangs of hunger or gone without anything she needed. Between Jenny and Robert, their six kids had enjoyed the privilege of an upper-middle-class upbringing. Christmas had been a favorite holiday, with the smells of holiday baking permeating the house and plenty of gifts beneath the tree.

As a kid, she remembered her dad sitting in his chair, watching the chaos with a small, satisfied smile, like the proud papa enjoying the fruits of his labor. And she remembered the hushed arguments behind closed doors and the strained smile of her mother as unspoken words between them created an invisible tension.

But even on Christmas Day, Robert only hung around for a short time, always with an excuse or reason to cut out. Now it made her wonder, had he been rushing off to spend time with his other family?

Frannie groaned, hating every syllable of that question. Even worse, had her mother known the reason he was leaving? The thought of her mother suffering such emotional agony in silence was more than she could bear.

Fresh anger at her father washed over her in a wave, and tears stung her eyes.

The front door opened, and Frannie muttered, "Thank God." She quickly wiped at her eyes, relieved that the troops had finally arrived.

Ruby lifted a brown paper bag, announcing, "I brought the wine," and Fletcher, right behind her, said, "And I brought peach pie and beer, because I don't drink wine and peach pie is good for any occasion."

"Mom's freshening up," Frannie said, motioning to Ruby. "I'll take a glass, if you don't mind."

Ruby's eyebrow rose as she reached for the wine glasses. "Already? What'd I miss?"

Frannie didn't have the words. "Just pour the wine."

"That means I'll start with the beer," Fletcher quipped with dark humor, but they all felt the heaviness in the air. How could they not? As if their dad collapsing from a stroke hadn't been a big enough shock to the family. Now this? Well, if this situation had taught Frannie anything, it was…sometimes the secrets of the dead didn't stay in the grave.

It was a dream and a memory morphing into one another to create a hellish movie that Dante couldn't escape.

"I'm not doing this anymore," Dante shouted at his uncle Lorenzo. "I'm done being the club you wield to ruin lives. I'm out."

"Who do you think you are?" Lorenzo's thick Italian accent deepened with florid anger. "I made you—I will end you. I decide when you're finished, and that time is not now."

The Santoro trust had paid for Dante's law degree, but Lorenzo acted as if the check came from his personal account. As the executor, Lorenzo knew he held a certain power over the entire Santoro family, and he wasn't shy about reminding anyone who stepped out of line.

But Dante wasn't afraid of his uncle. Maybe he should be, but Lorenzo had exhausted Dante's endurance, and if he didn't get out now, his soul would never recover. "You've gone too far. I won't be a party to this level of corruption. You'll have to find a new attorney to represent the family."

"For a smart man, you make stupid moves," Lorenzo said. "I've destroyed men for less than what you dare right now. I'll allow this one moment of insanity because I have a softness for you, nephew, but don't press your luck. My patience only stretches so far."

Dante held his uncle's stare without flinching. "I'm out."

And he left Lorenzo's office, his uncle's shouting still ringing in his ears.

One truth about Lorenzo, and perhaps why the family was obscenely wealthy—his ruthlessness was exacted with purpose.

The scene shifted, and he was at Belinda's apartment, waiting for her shift to end at the hospital. A pediatric surgeon, Belinda was at the top of her field. Hospitals worldwide courted her services, but she loved her home country and refused to relocate, no matter the offer.

Belinda made Dante realize he couldn't keep doing what he was doing at his uncle's command if he wanted a life with a woman like her. She was kind and generous and believed in the inherent goodness of people. If he married her and inevitably dragged her into his world, it would ruin everything he loved about Belinda.

And he couldn't do that to her.

Besides, he could start fresh. He didn't need the Santoro money to make his way. He'd have to start small, but he could build something he could be proud of from scratch.

Something his father would've approved of. There'd been a reason his father had moved away from his brother and the entire Santoro legacy.

If he hadn't died…maybe life would've been much different for him and his mother.

*May she rest in peace.*

The loud ticking of the clock reverberated in his head. Belinda was late.

The scene shifted again.

Belinda, broken and bleeding, beaten within an inch of her life, barely alive after the attack.

But the brutal destruction of her fingers made Dante realize with horror that someone had specifically targeted the very thing that made Belinda special in her field.

The tendons in her right hand had been severed, the bones in her left, crushed. The reality that she may never operate again struck his core, lodging a permanent stone in his stomach.

And then the note, delivered with a brilliant spray of flowers to Dante while he spent every hour at Belinda's beside, praying desperately for a miracle that chilled his blood.

The Family is here for you and Belinda. Arrangements are already prepared for Belinda's care when you return.

His guts twisted in agony. Lorenzo had done this. *That sick bastard.* He'd crushed an innocent woman to get Dante to return as a warning to get back in line, or else the consequences would be severe.

Dante had foolishly believed he could handle whatever Lorenzo threw at him.

He'd never imagined Belinda might be the one to pay the price for his actions.

His hands curled, shaking with impotent violence.

How could he prove it? He couldn't.

Lorenzo's strength was his ability to protect himself from legal ramifications. Dante had spent his legal career doing that for the Santoro family—enabling them to ruin people from behind the safety of legal might.

And Lorenzo had just ruined Belinda.

Belinda's eyes popped open, bloodshot, and rimmed with tears. "You did this to me!" she screeched, holding up her gnarled and broken fingers, the unnatural bend of her digits like something from a horror film. "This is all your fault, and I will never forgive you until you die!"

With Belinda's scream ringing in his mind, Dante shot up, his heart racing, staring blindly into the dark of his bedroom. *Where am I?* Sweat dampened his body and made the sheets tangled around his legs feel like cling wrap. *Idaho.* Not Italy.

*Just a nightmare. No, not just a nightmare, a terrible memory.* Six months later and the same nightmare chased him wherever he went.

Kicking off the sheets, he rose on unsteady feet to splash water on his face. Pale moonlight bathed the rustic bathroom, creating unsettling shadows where anyone could lurk. His heart was still beating hard against his chest.

A million apologies would never fix what Lorenzo had taken from Belinda.

What Lorenzo had taken from Dante.

And if Dante was right…that tally was far bigger than he could've imagined.

Pushing away from the sink, he returned to the bedroom and quickly dressed.

It didn't matter that it was only three in the morning. There'd be no more sleep for him tonight.

# Chapter 4

Frannie would need all the coffee to keep her eyes open today at work. She tried to get Darla to come by the shop to help her do inventory, but wedding details had her busy all day. Frannie's request probably wasn't entirely based on her need for help but rather on someone to talk to about her current family situation, someone she knew she could trust.

It wasn't like she wanted to share her family's embarrassment all over town. But the news was likely circulating in hushed whispers, because the gossip hotline in Owl Creek was second to none.

The usual customers milled about, enjoying their lattes and browsing, or sitting in the big, comfy chairs while reading, which gave Frannie a chance to decompress from last night's meeting.

She supposed it went well enough, but only because Jenny Colton wasn't the type of woman to weep and wail, no matter her tragedy. If there was one thing her mother excelled at, it was internalizing emotional trauma. Marrying Robert had given her plenty of practice, if the rumors were true.

"Mom, we just want you to know we're here for you," Ruby had assured their mother, trying to get their mom to open up. But Jenny, as always, had kept her emotions in check and smiled at her daughter, suggesting that Ruby get a trim because her split ends were starting to show.

Frannie had shared a look with Ruby, feeling her sister's frustration but appreciating her restraint when she just accepted their mother's mild reproach with a tight-lipped nod. Even if she were bleeding out in the street, their mother would never admit to needing help. Maybe that was why she'd never talked about why she and her sister stopped speaking to each other. The emotional pain was private, and no one needed to know. Frannie was fairly sure her mom saved her tears for the privacy of the shower. She could recall one instance when she thought she'd heard her mom crying in the bathroom, but when Jenny emerged an hour later—dressed and ready to start the day—it was like Frannie had imagined it.

What kind of life was that?

Frannie winced as her gut cramped. She pushed away the half-eaten croissant and blew on her coffee before sipping. What she wanted to say to her dad if he were still alive to listen would make her childhood Girl Scout leader gasp.

"Frannie…a good woman minds her business," Robert had once told her when she'd dared to ask why he never bought his wife flowers on any occasion despite knowing that Jenny loved flowers of any kind.

"But Dad…"

"Your mother gets what she needs."

Even at a young age, Frannie didn't believe that. A sadness pulled on her mother, even though Jenny did a bang-up job hiding it beneath a veneer of efficiency and practicality.

But Robert Colton never made mistakes and therefore hadn't felt the need to entertain the opinions of others on the subject. Even those of his "favorite" daughter.

God, her dad had been such a prick.

And then there was her Aunt Jessie, too. What kind of woman not only slept with her twin sister's husband but then carried on a decades-long affair with the man? That was almost sociopathic.

There were also her supposed half siblings to think about, which caused an involuntary shudder.

She didn't want to be salty to innocent people—Jessie's kids didn't ask to be part of this drama—but it was hard not to feel some standoffishness when it felt like interlopers were trying to cram their way into her family.

If her Aunt Jessie was telling the truth, that meant these new cousins were her siblings—the thought gave her an instant headache. Never in a million years had she ever thought her family might have scandal lurid enough to land a guest spot on some tell-all TV show.

The front door opened, and the handsome Italian walked in. Even though she wasn't much in the mood to smile, the urge tugged at the corners of her mouth. Her heart did a little jig when he walked straight to the counter instead of perusing the shelves.

"Good morning," he said with a brief smile before going straight to business. "I'm going to be in town for a little while longer and I wondered if you'd be able to order some books for me?"

Frannie stood a little straighter. "Oh! Yes, of course. I'd be happy to. What did you have in mind?"

"Well, a combination of legal works and fiction." He slid a prepared list toward her, including his cell number. "Just call me when they come in, and I'll come and pick them up right away. I'm also happy to pay in advance."

"You don't have to do that. I trust you," she said, the words popping from her mouth before she realized she had nothing to base her assumption on. Was this her problem? Always assuming people were inherently good? Look where that had gotten her. For all she knew, he could be an incredibly attractive swindler. She hastily replied, "But if you'd feel more comfortable paying in advance, that works, too."

"I'll just go ahead and pay now," he said, smiling as if somehow privy to her mental conversation. He pulled cash from his wallet as she rang up his purchase. Hadn't she read somewhere that someone carrying a lot of cash was a red flag nowadays? Or was her overactive imagination running away with her?

"Is everything okay? I couldn't help but notice you got an upsetting call yesterday," he said.

Surprised but inordinately touched that he noticed, she answered with a smile. "Just family stuff. You know how that goes."

"Of course."

Dante had ordered legal tomes, different from the usual purchase for the average reader. Was it possible he was an attorney? She might not want to share her family drama, but Dante might have some tips on handling the situation with her Aunt Jessie. *Ten seconds ago, you questioned his moral integrity, and now you're considering asking him for legal advice?* Fair point, but what were the *actual* odds that he was a bad person? She was going to risk it. "I'm sorry if this is none of my business, but I wondered, might you be an attorney?"

He hesitated for the barest moment before confirming, "I am. Why?"

"Oh, no reason. I mean, the books you ordered suggested you might be connected to law in some way, and I could really use someone to talk to who has some understanding of certain legal things."

"Are you in trouble?" he asked with a concerned frown.

"Me? Um, no, not exactly, but my family might be."

"Do you mind sharing?"

She hesitated. Was it wise to talk to Dante about this stuff, or was she tripping headlong into a muddy puddle by asking him for advice? There was no way to explain it logically, but she felt she could trust him and needed someone to talk to.

"I should warn you, it's very 'Maury Povich' level."

His expression deepened in question. "What is… Maury Povich?"

"Sorry, it's a saying when something is scandalous and geared toward 'revealing taboo secrets.' From a daytime talk show host. Anyway, it's embarrassingly scandalous." Was that a slight smile? He must be like most people who thought nothing bad happened in small towns. *You sweet summer child.* Frannie was about to ruin his illusions. She chuckled ruefully, "No, trust me, it's next-level embarrassing. Shocking, even."

"Now you have to tell me. To leave me hanging would be cruel."

Frannie glanced around her shop. The nearest customer had left, and the only other was deep in the Self-Help aisle farthest from them. She felt safe enough to share. "I might as well just rip off the bandage. My dad died of a stroke a few months ago—it was a shock, but then again, not so much. He didn't do much to safeguard his health, so it was either going to be a heart attack or a stroke, and in the end, it was the stroke that took him out."

"I'm sorry for your loss," he murmured appropriately.

"Thank you. It's been hard but we'd started to adjust to life without Dad. Until my aunt Jessie—my mom's twin sister whom I've never met, by the way—showed up demanding a piece of my dad's assets for her children because, surprise, she and my dad were having a decades-long affair beneath my mom's nose."

Dante absorbed the information without reacting, which lawyers were trained to do, but she appreciated the mature response. It was hard enough to get the words out without having to navigate big reactions, too.

"Does this Aunt Jessie have proof of her children's paternity?"

"Not yet but that's the first thing I suggested. In this day and age, if you're going to make a claim like that, you'd better have proof."

"Yes, indeed. Your family has legal representation?"

"Um, well, we have my dad's attorney who facilitated the will and stuff like that."

"But you haven't retained him for this specific purpose?"

"No, not that I'm aware but I didn't think to ask my mom about that specifically. For all I know, maybe she already has that handled. It's hard to know the appropriate way to deal with something like this," she admitted forlornly. "Honestly, it feels like an out-of-body experience just hearing the words come out of my mouth."

Dante was kind but firm, saying, "You need to find out if you have an attorney safeguarding your father's assets. It'll be important in the future. The burden of proof is on your aunt to prove paternity. That's the first hurdle. If she fails to produce evidence that your father is in fact her children's father, then she has no case. But a good attorney will be able to smother that spark before it has a chance to cause any damage."

She didn't know if her father's attorney was good, but her brother Chase might have a good attorney on the job. Chase might be distant and preoccupied, but he wasn't stupid. He'd do whatever it took to protect the family's assets. "I appreciate the insight," she said. "My brother is probably already handling all the business side, but I can't help but worry this will unravel my family. I'm more worried about the emotional shrapnel."

"The consequence of infidelity is often destructive," he agreed with empathy. "Have you met these alleged half siblings?"

"No, my aunt and mother had some kind of falling out before we were even born. I've never met my aunt or her kids. I don't know if that's a blessing or not. I don't know how I'd feel if I found out cousins I'd known my entire life turned out to be half siblings. Blech, the whole thing is gross."

He chuckled, then apologized. "It's not funny, but I've never heard anyone characterize a family trauma as 'gross' before. I suppose you're right, though. If it's true, very gross, indeed."

*I like him.* Frannie smiled, biting her lip. Was she flirting? *Well, that's inappropriate as hell.* She let the smile fade, shaking off the warmth Dante's attention created. "Anyway, I don't mean to bore you with all this stuff. I'm sure it'll work out in the end, somehow."

"You're an optimist."

"Yeah, I guess so. You're not?"

"I'm a realist."

"Sounds depressing," she said with a laugh. "Reality often sucks, which is why I prefer books."

"Fair enough. Maybe that's why I prefer books, too," he agreed, flashing that million-dollar smile again. Did all Italian men have that subtle twinkle in their eye? Like a flash of banked mischief just waiting for the right opportunity to flare up?

"So, subject change, have you read the books I'm ordering for you?"

"Yes. When I left Italy, I didn't have room in my luggage, so I planned to buy new copies when I landed."

"Not that I want to talk you out of a purchase, but you know you can just download these onto your phone?"

"I prefer to hold a book in my hand. Helps me to absorb the information," he said, shrugging. "It's more of a comfort as well."

"I'm the same way," she said, tickled that they shared the same preference. She loved all access to literature but truly loved settling into a cozy chair with a printed book in her hand. Reading was more than absorbing information—it was an experience. "Well, I'll let you know when they arrive."

"Thank you," he said. If it seemed he was looking for a reason to stick around, it passed, and with a small wave, he left the shop.

Frannie wasn't looking for a date, but if she were... Dante would be at the top of a very short list.

*You're playing a dangerous game*, a voice warned Dante as he climbed into his car. Frannie was a sweet young woman—and he wouldn't put her in harm's way just because he found her sharp mind intriguing.

*That's not the only reason you can't stop thinking about her*, the voice added.

All right, there was a wholesome sweetness about Frannie that he found alluring, but that was precisely the reason he had to keep his distance.

Even though he took precautions to remain under his uncle's radar—he paid cash wherever he went and maintained a low profile—the second his diligence started to slip, he only had to remember Belinda's gnarled hands, and he snapped back to reality.

He couldn't risk Frannie falling into Lorenzo's sights.

Besides, what did he think could happen between him and Frannie Colton? If she thought the potential of her father stepping out on her mother and creating another family was scandalous, the crimes of his own family would put her into a coma.

Financial extortion, intimidation, hostile corporate takedowns...all skirting the letter of the law, but the lives ruined at the expense of his uncle's greed was nothing short of emotional bankruptcy.

*What one can convince another to do with manipulative persuasion is amazing.*

In the beginning, his uncle had greased the wheels with praise, pride, and familial attachments. Then it had progressed to outright bullying whenever someone pushed back.

The movies helped perpetuate the myth of the Italian mob family, but you didn't have to be toting guns and blowing up cars to intimidate people into doing your bidding.

Lorenzo wasn't a mobster, but he'd done things that should've been criminal.

And Dante had helped him.

*God save my soul.* It was bad enough that Dante felt he'd never be free of the stain on his soul, but after Belinda's attack, he suffered the sickening realization that maybe his uncle's crimes went farther than white-collar financial greed.

And he had to know.

Speaking of...

His cell rang with the number of the private investigator he planned to hire. The man had a reputation for having a sharp mind, discreet tactics and international contacts. Dante needed a ninja who wasn't afraid of the Santoro name.

"Dante," he answered.

"This is Nicholas Gladney, but you can call me Nick. You left a message."

"I did. I want to hire you."

"What would Dante Santoro need a private investigator for?"

The man had already done his homework. *Good.* It would be the first time verbalizing his suspicion, but after what happened to Belinda, he was done speculating.

Cutting straight to the point, he replied bluntly, "I suspect my uncle had something to do with my mother's death—and if it's true, I need proof."

## *Chapter 5*

Frannie felt as if she were doing something wrong. She didn't know why she'd agreed to this meeting with her estranged aunt Jessie. Morbid curiosity, perhaps? Maybe she was a glutton for punishment? Who knew.

Purposefully asking for a table in the back, she chewed her cheek while waiting for the woman trying to rip her family apart. She wondered if she still had time to bail before her aunt arrived.

This was ridiculous. At the very least, she should've asked Ruby or Fletcher to come with her—safety in numbers. Not that she thought her aunt would jump over the table and stab her with a dinner fork, but she didn't know this woman from Adam. Who knew what she was capable of?

Just when Frannie's anxiety was about to hit the roof, a woman rounded the corner, and Frannie instantly knew it was her aunt Jessie.

She was the same height as her mom, but her hair was a brittle blond as opposed to her mother's dark blond with streaks of gray, and Jessie's sharpness almost seemed hawkish.

Frannie knew her mother and sister had been known around town as great beauties. Small towns loved to cling to the memory of someone's past. Whereas Jenny had aged gracefully, allowing time to soften the edges and claim its due, her sister seemed determined to cling to her youth with almost palpable desperation.

"Darling, sweet Frannie," Jessie cooed, coming straight at Frannie to fold her into a hug. The woman was so thin that Frannie could nearly count the bones in her spine. "Goodness gracious, you've grown into such a beauty."

As Frannie had never met Jessie, she didn't know how her aunt would know anything about her. Unless her mother had contacted her sister unbeknownst to anyone else, but that didn't seem likely.

Especially when Jenny had maintained that she hadn't seen or spoken to her sister since Aunt Jessie divorced Uncle Buck.

What was the etiquette for this kind of situation? She took her seat and waited for Jessie to take the lead. After all, Jessie had asked to meet.

Jessie signaled for the waitress and ordered an iced tea without sugar or lemon, which, as far as Frannie was concerned, was just bitter dark water, but that seemed appropriate given the circumstances.

"My dear, I can only imagine how confused you must be—how confused you all must be—and I want to assure you, I never wanted things to happen the way they did."

Which part? The part where she had an affair with her sister's husband or demanded some of Robert Colton's assets after he died? Frannie didn't want to be sharp but found Jessie's comment disingenuous. Frannie chose her words carefully. "Aunt Jessie… I don't want to be rude, but I can't make head or tail of anything that's happened recently. I have so many questions but don't even know where to start."

"Of course," Jessie said, flicking her napkin and placing it on her lap. "I understand. I always wanted to tell the family, but for obvious reasons, your father had adamantly opposed my ardent desire to be honest with Jenny. It was one of our more frequent disagreements."

Frannie was grateful they hadn't ordered any food. She doubted her stomach would allow for anything beyond a breadstick. "I'm not a fan of placing all the blame on a woman when infidelity is involved but I gotta say, you're coming off as real cold to do what you did with your sister's husband. You knew he was married. How could you do that?"

Jessie's smile froze, and her gaze frosted. "It's easy to stand in judgment, darling, when you're not involved."

"But I am involved, aren't I? You're my aunt, he's my dad…kinda involved by default. And now my cousins are my half siblings? It's all very Jerry Springer, you know what I mean?"

"I told your father it was best to be honest," Jessie returned, narrowing her gaze. "But your father wasn't a man who listened to any opinion above his own."

That much was true. "I'm sorry," Frannie murmured because it felt like she should, but it was hard to feel compassion for a woman who'd purposely had another life with a married man on the sly. "So what happens now?"

"Well, as distasteful as my request may seem, the ugly truth remains—Robert and I may not have been married but I was his wife in all things except on paper. My children deserve their fair share of their father's assets…as do I."

"You?"

"Yes."

"How so?"

"As I said, I was his wife as much as Jenny. The only difference—"

"The big difference was that he was *actually* married to my mother. Legally," Frannie pointed out, her temper rising at her aunt's audacity. "I fail to see how you can think that you're owed anything when you knew what you were doing was wrong."

"When is loving someone wrong?" Jessie countered. She seemed to be trying to appeal to Frannie's sense of romanticism.

"When the other person is already married to someone else," Frannie answered flatly.

"Yes, I suppose that may be true but what's done is done. Your father isn't here to bear your judgment, so that leaves only me. Whether you agree or not, legally, I'm assured I have a solid case." It didn't look like Jessie was going to go quietly.

Frannie stilled. "You have an attorney?"

"I wouldn't have stirred the pot without ample assurances that doing so would be worth the trouble."

*Worth the trouble of blowing up my family's life.* A blithe statement for such a terrible action.

Frannie swallowed the sudden lump in her throat. "Did you think of your sister at all? How this might hurt her? You're twins…surely you must've cared for her at some point in your life."

"I loved your father, and he loved me. It may be hard to hear but your father never truly loved Jenny."

Maybe it was the subtle shrug or the feeling that Jessie didn't actually give two figs for her sister, but Frannie saw red. "You're a piece of work. How dare you. Who do you think you are? You were my father's *mistress*, not some great love—and I hate to break it to you, but I doubt you were the only one."

Jessie's cold smile matched the chill in her eyes. "Darling, I knew your father better than anyone. Fidelity was never his strength, but he always returned to me."

"No, actually, he always returned to my mother."

Something flashed in Jessie's eyes—rage, perhaps?— and Frannie sensed this entire meeting had been a ruse to try to feel out the family's disposition about her claim. As if they were going to hand over a portion of Robert's assets with a smile and an apology for her trouble. "Your loyalty is admirable, but the law is on my side."

"And what do your kids say about all of this?" Frannie fired back, wondering if her half siblings/cousins were cut from the same cloth as their mother. "Are they okay with what you did?"

"I wouldn't dream of speaking for my children."

"Yeah, well, I can't help but wonder if they're anything like you."

Jessie drew a measured breath though the strained smile never faltered. "So full of fire and brimstone, just like my Robert."

That was a purposeful dig. Frannie rose stiffly. "I think we're done here. Please don't contact me again. I have nothing to say to you."

"No worries, dear. I'm sure the lawyers will sort the details soon enough."

With nothing left to say, Frannie left the restaurant beyond thankful she hadn't ordered anything. Sharing a meal with that woman would be enough to turn the strongest stomach.

Dante intended to keep a professional distance from Frannie, but fate seemed to have other plans.

He seemed to sense the minute Frannie entered the brewery, his pint half raised to his lips when his gaze zeroed in on the blonde woman. In an instant, the bustling chaos of a popular place faded to a low hum.

But even as he watched, privately soaking up everything about her—the way her hair lightly dusted her shoulders, the stubborn tilt of her chin—he could tell something was bothering her.

A heavy weight dampened her usually sunny disposition. Likely more of the family troubles she'd been telling him about earlier. Even though their family issues were apples to oranges, he understood the stress of familial drama.

*Just mind your business*, a voice inside his head warned.

And yet, he was drawn to say hello at the very least. Nothing wrong with being friendly, he argued with himself.

Making eye contact, he waved to Frannie, letting fate decide the direction. If she waved and kept on her way, that was the way of it, but if she came over to say hi, then he'd enjoy the friendly company.

Warmth spread across his chest and excitement followed when she brightened and headed his way.

"Mind if I join you?" she asked, hopping beside him at the bar.

"Not at all." He motioned for the bartender. "What'll you have?"

"I'll take a pale ale," she said, reaching for her purse, but he waved away the need. She raised a brow with an uncertain but appreciative, "Are you sure?"

For a man raised in Italy with staunchly Italian roots, it was a foreign concept for a woman to pay for her drinks in a man's company. "I'm happy to pay for your drink," he assured her.

Her smile widened, and his mouth curved in response. She had this infectious way about her that was hard to ignore. After everything he'd been through last year, he craved the sunshiny warmth Frannie radiated effortlessly. She probably didn't even realize how she lit up a room.

The bartender set down her ale, and she gratefully took a drink, instantly relieved. "God, I needed this. It's been a day."

"Everything okay?" he asked, not wanting to overstep but genuinely curious.

She drew a deep breath, shaking her head. "Honestly, I don't even know. I don't want to bore you with my family stuff, though."

"I don't mind listening," he said.

"Really?"

He gestured with a generous smile. "Please, I'm all ears."

Frannie chuckled. "Okay, well, just remember you offered."

"Go for it."

"Against my better judgment I met up with Aunt Jessie a bit ago and as you might imagine it was about as enjoyable as a poke in the eye. For one, she's a horrible human being and doesn't seem to understand that having a decades-long affair with a married man is a bad look. Two, she doesn't acknowledge how hurtful her actions were to my mom, her own sister. I was flabbergasted at how blatantly selfish she was, and I guess I was hoping that maybe there was some kind of explanation that would make sense but there's nothing that could excuse what she did. And yes, I realize it takes two to tango, but I can't help but judge her more for being such a horrible person to her sister."

"I'm curious…why did you agree to meet with her?"

"Excellent question—one I kept asking myself when it all went to crap. I'm not sure what I'd hoped for or what I thought might happen, but it surely didn't end happily. Let's just say, the word *lawyer* was used instead of a friendly goodbye."

"Always a sign that negotiations have reached a stalemate," he agreed.

She nodded. "The thing is, she seems pretty confident that she's got a legitimate claim. I get that the kids would be entitled to something if it turns out they are my dad's, but can she claim anything? They weren't married."

He didn't want to worry Frannie, but there could be grounds for compensation for the aunt if Frannie's father had been the woman's sole source of support for more than ten years. He didn't want to insert himself where it wasn't appropriate, but he hated to see her weighed down by the situation. "People can make claims. Doesn't mean they'll win in court," he said. "However, if possible, it might benefit the estate to offer a lump-sum settlement to encourage the problem to go away without dragging the family through the courts."

"I can't imagine giving that woman a dime," Frannie said with a shudder. "I don't want to be mean but she's the one who made the choice to carry on with a married man. I don't have a lot of sympathy."

"It's not so much about sympathy as it is efficiency. Settlements make problems go away."

Frannie's subtle frown as she considered his advice reminded him that they came from different worlds. She had relatively normal problems, even if they were emotionally distressing. The crises he dealt with as Lorenzo's right-hand legal muscle would turn your hair white. As if summoned by his memory, the hairs on the back of his neck prickled, making him quickly look around the brewery out of habit.

It was Frannie's turn to ask, "Everything okay?"

He forced a chuckle, shaking off the paranoia. "A goose must've walked over my grave."

"Oh, I hate when that happens," Frannie commiserated with a shudder. "Every time my grandma said that, I got the heebie-jeebies."

"The *heebie*-what?" he asked with an incredulous laugh.

"Heebie-jeebies," Frannie repeated with a grin. "You know, the creeps."

"That might be my new favorite word."

Frannie's laugh could chase away any lingering fears. It didn't feel right to enjoy this time with her, but he was selfishly unwilling to cut the night short.

He needed a mental break from the constant stress of looking over his shoulder.

And Frannie was precisely what he needed tonight.

# Chapter 6

It felt good to laugh. After her disastrous meeting with Aunt Jessie, she didn't think anything could lighten her sour mood. But seeing Dante across the crowded brewery had instantly chased away the clouds.

There was something about Dante that calmed and soothed her nerves. People tended to make her fidgety, which was probably why she preferred the quiet company of books to actual people. She had a tight-knit group of friends but often kept to herself.

However, with Dante, she didn't feel fidgety or out of place.

His eyes, sharp yet compassionate, held her stare without being off-putting, and he listened when she rambled, which in her experience was rare.

Frannie often felt set apart from her peers and family, even though no one was mean. Well, her brothers used to tease that she was "weird," but that was only because she'd preferred her nose in a book than anywhere else when given a choice.

But there was something about Dante she couldn't quite put her finger on—a wariness to get too close, perhaps?—that probably should've put her off but instead intrigued her more.

Had he been hurt in the past? A harsh breakup, maybe? If so, she could relate. Also, why did he pay cash for every purchase? He walked around with a clip of money, which in this day and age seemed unusual, but to ask why felt too personal. Of course, it wasn't any of her business why he paid cash for everything, but her curious, okay, nosy mind pressed for more details.

"So, you're from Italy, and you mentioned being here for business and pleasure... What drew you to Owl Creek?" She hesitated to mention that he didn't seem the type to spend all day on a boat like most tourists who flocked to the area during the summer, but she also didn't know much about him, so it was possible he loved boating.

"I spent ten years in the States before relocating to Italy with my family. There's something wholesome about American small towns and I needed a break from my usual scene."

Frannie snorted. "Wholesome? That's a stereotype that needs to die a grisly death. We have our share of terrible stuff. I mean, I hate to be the bearer of bad news but drug use in small towns is on the rise. For some reason, the Chamber of Commerce is reluctant to put that on the brochure, though."

He grinned. "Seems like a lost opportunity."

"Absolutely." She laughed, sharing, "Oh, here's something else—last year Blackbird Lake had a red algae bloom that killed tons of fish and sections of the lake had to be cordoned off to keep people from getting sick. But no one mentioned that."

"Are you always this passionate about your lake health?"

She shrugged. "I'm not obsessed with it, but I do feel not enough attention is being put on the right things. It's a beautiful place but too many people on the water with their boats and garbage pollutes the natural ecosystem. You can't deny that there have been so many ecological disasters that have been directly attributed to human interference."

"No argument from me. Keeping the balance between

the carbon footprint and nature is a constant battle that we often lose," he admitted. "Italy faces similar issues with pollution as the rest of the world. There are always going to be people who champion the environment and those who fight any change that threatens inconvenience."

"Do you practice environmental law?"

*If only.* His predatory uncle was his own kind of human pollution. "No, sadly, not my area of practice but I appreciate anyone who goes into that field. It's a tough one to chase. Too much collective greed to truly affect demonstrable change. But we need warriors out there fighting the good fight."

She met his gaze, her insides warming, tingling with awareness. He had the most expressive eyes. How was he single? She wanted to ask, but it seemed so personal, and she didn't want to ruin the moment, but her mouth had other plans. "Why don't you have a girlfriend or a wife?" she blurted out.

Her abrupt question threw him off-guard—*shocker*— and he waited a minute before answering with a short yet restrained smile. "Uh, too busy, I guess. Up until recently, I was a workaholic. Never seemed to have enough time to do both."

Relief flooded her. That made sense to her. For a moment, she was secretly afraid that he had some dark secret he was protecting. Reading too many crime novels had warped her brain. "I understand," she said. "There's a comfort in the routine of work. I love my little shop, but my best friend, Darla, keeps reminding me that there's more to life than work. She's actually getting married in a few months."

"Your friend is a smart woman."

"Yeah, probably smarter than me for sure, but there's another thing about living in a small town that no one talks about…"

"Which is?"

"The dating pool is excruciatingly small." When he

chuckled, she explained with a laugh, "No, seriously! I've known everyone in this town my whole life. It's hard to see guys I went to kindergarten with in a romantic light. I know too many things about them." She glanced around the brewery, spying on someone she knew. She gestured discreetly. "See that guy over there with the ball cap talking a mad game with his buddies like he's some kind of baseball stud? That's Johnny Rogan. He peed his pants in the third grade, and when I see him acting all macho, that's all I remember."

Dante regarded Johnny. "He seems a good-looking enough adult. Has he ever asked you out?"

"Multiple times. I can't think of more creative ways to turn him down at this point. He's nice, I guess, but I literally feel nothing for him in that way. Besides, he isn't a big reader and I can't see myself tied to someone who thinks books are a waste of time."

"So a man interested in taking you out for a date…should share your love of books?"

"It's a great start," Frannie said, holding his gaze, adding, "and I wouldn't mind a foreign accent, either…"

It was bold of her—and entirely out of character—but she wanted to kiss him, and she sensed that he wouldn't make a move without her obvious interest.

Besides, being coy? Never her strength. She was either clueless or awkward, and sometimes both, when it came to approaching guys she was interested in, and that wasn't likely to change anytime soon.

*Shut her down, don't encourage that kind of involvement*, that infernal voice urged again, but Dante felt caught in a whirlpool dragging him ever closer to Frannie. He knew why he ought to politely set her straight, to tell her that he wasn't interested in her romantically, but it would be a lie.

He wanted her.

He thought of Frannie in ways that crossed the line, even if he knew he shouldn't. He wanted to taste her lips, touch her skin and feel her beneath him.

The smart—responsible—play would be to make some excuse, pay the tab and end the evening, but the idea of walking away was physically painful.

And he couldn't do it.

But his hesitation cost him.

"Oh, I'm sorry, I just made it weird, didn't I?" Frannie said, her cheeks flaring with pink. "I… Oh, man, this is awkward. Forget I said anything. Actually, I think I should probably go. I've taken up enough of your time whining about my problems. I'm sure you have plenty of your own, you don't need to listen to mine." And before he could say anything, she jumped from the stool and practically ran from the brewery.

*Damn it.* He tossed down a wad of cash and hurried after her. He couldn't stomach the thought of Frannie feeling rejected when it was a lie.

Even as he ran after her, that voice in his head countered that this was a blessing, but he couldn't let her go like that.

"Frannie! Wait!" he called after her, catching her seconds before she climbed into her car for a quick getaway.

He skidded to a stop, breathing hard. The woman could run like a track star, getting a surprising distance before he caught her. "Jesus, you're a good runner," he said, sucking in a big breath. "It's been awhile since I hit the treadmill. You reminded me that I need to return to my exercise routine."

"Sorry, I ran track in high school and the habit kinda stuck," she said, unsure of why he'd chased after her. "Are you okay?"

He wiped at the bead of sweat on his brow, admitting,

"Aside from feeling a little sheepish, yes. However, I couldn't let you go with this misunderstanding between us."

"No, it's my fault, I shouldn't have made such a forward comment. We barely know each other."

"Frannie, I like you but—"

"Oh, God, the dreaded 'I like you, but.' Thanks but I think I know where this is going and it's totally okay. We can just pretend that I never said anything, okay?"

This was going from bad to worse. "Frannie, that's not what I was going to say."

She frowned. "What were you going to say?"

"I like you, a lot. More than I should. But you deserve complete honesty. I'm not in a position to start anything real or meaningful and I respect you too much to suggest something casual, if you catch what I mean."

"You mean, sex?"

"Well, yes."

She surprised him with a chuckle. "Dante, I think you're getting ahead of yourself. I'm not looking for anything super serious either. My life is a mess right now. But we're both adults and I like you. Is that so bad?"

Frannie was giving him the green light for something casual between them. Did he want that? Was it possible to entertain a casual arrangement while he was in Owl Creek? It wasn't exactly his style, but if he couldn't offer much more, he liked the idea of spending more time with Frannie.

But was it safe?

Perhaps if they were careful…even then, it was taking a risk. He didn't know if Lorenzo had spies looking for him, but it would likely happen sooner or later. Dante had something Lorenzo wanted back. That much wouldn't change, which could put Frannie on Lorenzo's radar.

And how much should he share with Frannie about his

circumstances? He wanted to be honest but couldn't see that conversation going well. If he wasn't a red flag, he didn't know what was.

He'd underestimated his uncle's reach in the past, and he swore he wouldn't do that again. Yet, here he was, his brain clouded with desire for a woman he had no business wanting.

It was so damn selfish of him to want more with Frannie knowing that getting too close to him would put her in danger.

And yet, he still reached for her.

*Was he really that much of a selfish bastard?*

The answer was immediate and humbling.

Dante pulled Frannie into the cove of his arms. She nestled against him, gazing into his eyes with a shy smile. "Does this mean you're down for some casual adulting?"

"I think it does," he murmured, brushing his lips across hers, his tongue darting to taste hers. She sank against him with a sigh, and he knew he'd made a mistake immediately, but it was too late to turn back now.

She felt like a dream he didn't have any business enjoying. There was a sweetness to Frannie that felt like stolen treasure in his hands. But as before, when the voice warned him to keep his distance, he ignored every bit of good sense and tightened his hold around her waist.

"My place or yours?" she murmured against his mouth, her lips curving in a flirty smile.

"Mine," he answered, pulling away to slide his hand into hers but not before giving the parking lot a glance to check for anything that shouldn't be there.

Frannie grinned, unlocking her car. "I'll follow you."

And Dante knew there was no turning back from this decision.

He'd sealed his fate—and hers.

## Chapter 7

Frannie's heart thundered in her chest as she followed Dante out to his place. Who was she? What was she doing? Listening to herself boldly offering a casual relationship with the sexy Italian when she was a serial monogamist was a surreal experience.

Darla always said she needed to put herself out there more, but this felt so far afield that she didn't know how to navigate the unfamiliar terrain.

But this was exactly what she needed. Another thing about small towns—if you weren't careful, they would keep you thinking small.

Frannie didn't want to fall into that trap.

Also, something about Dante set her blood on fire in a way she'd never experienced.

And she wanted more.

She pulled up behind Dante and exited the car, immediately recognizing the rental property. "This place used to belong to Gavin Pritchard's family. They moved away a few years ago." Frannie smiled at Dante's amusement, adding with a shrug, "Another one of those pro/con arguments for living in a small town."

"Did you and this Gavin date back in the day?" Dante asked as he unlocked the front door and waited for her to pass through before closing the door and locking it behind them.

"No," she answered, tickled by his chivalry and sense of protection. "My mom and Gavin's mom used to sell Tupperware together and would host Tupperware parties." Of course, he had a higher chance of being surprised by a bear in his kitchen than a burglar, but she liked that he cared about her safety and watched as he quickly checked doors and windows.

Satisfied they were secured, Dante asked, "Can I get you something to drink? Wine or...juice? I don't think I have beer stocked."

"Water is fine with me," she answered, taking in the surroundings. It looked different from when the Pritchard family had lived there, but she remembered the house's general layout.

Dante returned with two bottled waters, cracking hers open before handing it to her.

She smiled: there was that chivalrous nature again. "Are all Italian men as considerate as you?" Then, when he seemed puzzled, she pointed to the bottled water, adding, "And the opening of the door. It was very old-school and charming but not what I'm used to."

"Do men not open doors here?"

"In my generation? Not really. I mean, some do, but it's not common. I can't remember the last time a guy opened the door for me, much less opened my water for me."

"Would you prefer I not?" he asked, furrowing his brow.

"Oh, gosh, no, please don't stop. I like it. I'm just not used to it, that's all."

"If that's the case, American men have lost the art of appreciating women."

"It could just be here. Other states might have different traditions. All I know is Owl Creek, Idaho, though."

Dante smiled, reaching for her hand. She accepted, allowing him to pull her gently toward the bedroom. Her heart rate immediately picked up as anticipation wiped away all thoughts of anything but what was happening between them.

Dante clicked on the small bedside lamp, illuminating the room in a soft glow.

A large, rustic bed framed in rough-hewn oak and covered with a Midwestern-style comforter dominated the room. The faint aroma of Dante's cologne clung to the space—a spicy masculine scent that was both sophisticated and brawny—and Frannie immediately felt at home. But there was still the awkwardness of being in a relative stranger's bedroom after only sharing a kiss in the parking lot of the Tap Out brewery.

"Can we sit and talk for a few minutes?" she asked, hoping he didn't mind.

"Of course," Dante said, following her lead with grace. She sat gingerly on the bed, and he sat beside her. "If you've changed your mind—"

"I haven't," she assured him quickly. "I just need a few minutes to get my bearings. It's probably not very cool of me in the hookup era but I'm not in a habit of going home with someone like this. Usually, my sexual relationships happen within the framework of an actual relationship, so this is new territory for me. But I definitely haven't changed my mind."

"If it makes you feel any better, I'm not accustomed to this sort of thing either."

It did make her feel better. She smiled. "Can you tell me about your last relationship? What was she like?"

A curtain closed behind his eyes, and Frannie knew in

an instant that question was probably off-limits. She knew the signs of a painful breakup when she saw one and felt like an idiot for dragging him into the deep end of the pool before finding out if he could swim.

"Actually, that's way too personal, I'm sorry," she hastened to add, letting him off the hook with a rueful chuckle to share, "One thing about me? I have a tendency to ask all the wrong things at the absolute worst time. Either you'll find it endearing or terribly off-putting. Just let me know where you land on that score, and I'll try to adjust accordingly."

"I find you…enchanting," he admitted, gently pushing an errant strand of hair behind her ear with such tenderness she almost melted. "However, my last relationship is one I'd rather not talk about, if you don't mind."

"Of course, I understand," Frannie said quickly, her breath hitching as he leaned forward to brush his lips across hers. "We could…stop talking all together…if you like…"

"I'd like that very much," he murmured, deepening their kiss.

In an instant, Frannie forgot everything—potentially even her own name—as her senses exploded.

Beneath Dante's masterful touch, Frannie's anxiety drifted away, leaving her free to sink into the pleasure of discovering one another.

Dante pushed away all thoughts of anything before Frannie. He didn't want to contaminate the moment by allowing memories of the past to color the present.

Frannie's skin was like silk against his fingertips. Her soft moans ignited his desire like embers alighting on tinder.

She was beautiful and unfettered by an ugly past. He

didn't deserve her trust or sweetness, but his bitter soul needed it.

Dante pressed soft kisses along the column of her neck, drinking in her subtle shivers as she gave him complete access to her body.

When he came to Owl Creek, he'd never imagined meeting someone like Frannie. She was the variable he couldn't have planned for, which would probably end up being his Achilles' heel. But he couldn't stop what was happening between them.

The second he felt her body against his, something inside him shifted, and that need to protect her at all costs made the idea of something casual between them laughable.

But keeping a safe emotional distance between them was for Frannie's protection.

Even if all he wanted to do was hold her close.

"You're an incredible woman," he said, rolling onto his back, trying to catch his breath.

Frannie grinned, wiping away the sweat as she rolled to her side to regard him playfully. "No complaints on this end either."

He chuckled, grabbing his water bottle for a long swig. The pale moonlight bathed her form, giving her the glow of a reclining goddess, like something from a Renaissance painting.

Dante returned to the bed, lying on his side, facing her. He didn't have a lot of experience with "casual." He had a feeling snuggling afterward wasn't the general way of things, but he liked the idea of Frannie curling into his arms and falling asleep together.

Frannie must've had the same thoughts as she reluctantly rose and dressed. "Well, this was fun," she said, sliding on her jeans and buttoning them up quickly. "I should probably

get going. Tomorrow is inventory day. I have a big shipment of books coming in— Oh! And the books I ordered
for you might be in that shipment, too."

"You don't have to leave," he said, going against the advice in his head. "You could stay."

"The night?"

"Yeah."

She paused as if thinking over his offer but ultimately
declined because at least one of them was thinking straight.
"The thing is, I'd really enjoy sleeping over, but I'm sure
that's how lines get blurred, and if we're trying to keep it
casual, we probably shouldn't push boundaries at the very
start."

"Of course, you're right," he agreed through his disappointment. "As long as you feel okay about our arrangement."

"I mean, I don't love the idea of calling this an 'arrangement'…but yeah, it's better if we don't get too comfortable
with each other's personal space."

Solid advice. Why did it feel wrong? Maybe he wasn't
cut out for this kind of situation. Or maybe he should've
followed his good sense and buried things in the "casual
acquaintance" zone.

But now he knew the sound of her breathy moans and
had learned how her body responded to his touch. The taste
of her skin was stamped on his memory, and her throaty
laughter made his insides hum.

Yes, helluva way to keep things light and easy between
them.

Maybe it wasn't ideal, but it was necessary, he reminded
himself as he walked her to the door.

"A kiss for the road?" she asked, gazing up at him with

a playfulness in her smile that immediately made him want to scoop her up and carry her back to the bedroom.

But he obliged her request, ending the kiss when his resolve weakened.

"You are the best kisser, and I'm not just saying that to butter up your ego. Honestly, it would be better if you weren't so good," she said against his mouth, giggling at her assessment. "Would make it easier to leave if you slobbered like an enthusiastic puppy."

He laughed at her odd humor and finished with one last kiss before sending her on her way. "Drive carefully. As everyone has been fond of telling me since coming here, 'Watch for deer—and if you see one, there's more.'"

Frannie saluted with a "Will do!" and climbed into her car. He watched her drive away until he no longer saw her headlights and then returned inside the house, locking the front door as was his new habit.

Back home, he hadn't been as diligent about his safety, feeling insulated against harm because of his name and stature. Now he knew that feeling of safety had been an illusion.

And danger could lurk around any darkened corner.

Had he made a major mistake in allowing Frannie into his life, even peripherally?

His satiated body tricked his mind into thinking it might be okay. He was thousands of miles away from Lorenzo, and his trail was well covered as far as he could tell.

Maybe it was possible to enjoy his time with Frannie, even if it felt like borrowed time.

# Chapter 8

Frannie had spent the day humming lightly beneath her breath, replaying her night with Dante in her head ad nauseam. It was her current favorite memory. She'd just finished her inventory toward the end of the day when Darla walked in, looking harried and the opposite of the blushing bride.

"Tell me I'm doing the right thing by marrying that man," she said as she huffed in the chair opposite Frannie. "I swear, if he lives to breathe another day, it'll be a miracle."

"What's poor Tom done now? Aside from the audacity of not wanting to elope," Frannie said with a small grin at Darla's pique.

"As my best friend and maid of honor you're obligated to be on my side," Darla warned with a glower. "And don't give me that look. Tom has crossed the line this time."

"How so?"

"He's insisting on a half chocolate cake when I specifically told the baker we would have vanilla and strawberry. It's ridiculous to have three flavors in one cake. Everyone knows that!"

Frannie shrugged. "Who doesn't like chocolate?"

"If we have a third flavor tier, people are going to get all picky about the slices and the next thing you know, we'll have a lopsided amount of leftovers and that's just wasteful. Strawberry and vanilla, people choose one or the other and that's it."

Frannie knew she ought to commiserate with Darla, but she could only giggle at how ridiculous it was. She was in too good a mood to see anything but the lighter side. However, Darla was unamused and suspicious. "Why are you in such a good mood? Isn't it inventory day? Usually, you're stressed out and grumpy on inventory day."

"No, I'm not," Frannie disagreed, wondering if that was true. She loved inventory day—*new books, what's not to love?*—but it could be a little stressful logging everything in while still running the front desk. She was a one-woman army, after all.

But before Frannie could adequately defend herself, Darla gasped, "Oh my God, I know that look!"

"What look?"

"The look that says someone got lucky last night!"

Frannie's cheeks flared with immediate heat, and she shushed Darla. "Oh my God, keep your voice down," she said, embarrassed. "And what makes you say that?"

"Because I'm your best friend and I've known you our entire lives. Since your breakup with that douche monkey, you've been depressingly celibate for reasons I can't even fathom. But you have the look of a woman who has been deliciously taken care of, if you know what I mean."

Good Lord, nothing got past Darla. "Okay, fine, yes, I had a date last night," she said, gesturing for Darla to keep it on the down-low, "but it's nothing serious. Just casual."

"You? Casual? Do you know how to do that?"

"Of course I do," Frannie lied, hating that Darla knew her that well. "I mean, I can learn. Besides, I'm not ready for anything more serious anyway."

"Okay, with *whom* did you knock boots last night?" Darla asked, needing to know all the details.

Frannie almost didn't want to say, but there was no way Darla would be satisfied with anything but the truth, and she'd get it out of Frannie at some point anyway. "You have to promise to keep this to yourself," she warned. When Darla motioned to zip her lips, Frannie shared. "Last night I ran into Dante at Tap Out. One thing led to another and the next, I was at his place."

"The hunky, mysterious Italian?" Darla exclaimed. "Oh my God, please, I need to know…was he…"

"Darla!" Frannie glared. "I'm not about to kiss and tell those kinds of details. Suffice it to say we had a nice evening."

"Nice?"

"Okay, it was amazing," Frannie corrected with a tiny swoon at the memory. "But please, we agreed to keep it casual and it's not a thing, like we're not dating or anything like that."

"And why is that?" Darla was immediately suspicious. "Is he married or something?"

"No, he's just…well, he doesn't plan on staying in Owl Creek. He's here for a short while and it doesn't make sense to start something serious when we both know he's not staying."

"Are you sure he's not married?"

"I didn't ask Fletcher to run a background check if that's what you're asking."

"Not a terrible idea, though," Darla said, believing the idea had merit. "First of all, he's not local and he could be making up any sort of story and how would you know any different?"

Frannie frowned at her best friend. "When did you become so suspicious of everyone?"

"You need to be more suspicious of people," Darla countered. "You're so accepting of everyone's motives, and I love that about you. But I worry that you're a perfect target for people who have bad intentions."

Remembering her meeting with her aunt Jessie, Frannie scowled. "Speaking of people with bad intentions... I went against my better judgment and agreed to meet with my aunt Jessie yesterday."

Darla's eyes bugged. "And why did you do that?"

"I don't know, I was hoping that maybe she was going to call the whole thing off and admit that she'd made it all up as a poor attempt at connecting with her estranged family."

Darla grimaced. "Yeah, if that were a bet in Vegas, I wouldn't take those odds."

"Yeah," she sighed, "it went about as well as you could expect."

"What did she want to talk about?" Darla asked, ignoring Dante for a moment.

"I think she was fishing for information. She's doubling down on her claim, and I have this bad feeling that she's actually telling the truth. If that's the case, I have two more siblings and I don't know how I feel about that."

Darla's expression softened. "I'm sorry, Fran. What your dad did...it's just not right. How's your mom holding up?"

"Mom is Mom. She's acting like she's fine but there are cracks in her veneer. Sadly, even if she's brokenhearted, she won't let us in. Too many years pretending like everything is fine to let the gates down now. I don't know how to help her."

"Your mom is the sweetest person I know. She doesn't deserve this."

The funny thing about Jenny Colton…to everyone else, she seemed sweet as pie, always with a smile, generous and compassionate to everyone in need. And she was that person—but there was more to the woman than met the eye.

And that was something only her children knew.

Jenny Colton was intensely private and guarded her secrets well. It was as if she prided herself on hiding her cuts and bruises from the world, no matter how she might be bleeding inside.

And Frannie could only imagine how many cuts and bruises she carried after being married to Robert for all those years.

"I do wonder if my mom knew about her sister and my dad all along but chose to ignore it because he always came home to her at some point?"

"Like the mentality of a stereotypical fifties-era housewife?" Darla suggested, pursing her lips in thought. "That generation was definitely cut from a different cloth. If I found out Tom was carrying on with another family, I'd end up in an orange jumpsuit for the rest of my life."

Frannie chuckled. "See? If you're willing to go to prison over the idea of Tom cheating, it's definitely love. Let the man have his chocolate cake," she said.

Darla huffed a short breath. "Fine. But don't say I didn't call it when I end up with an entire uneaten tier of vanilla cake."

After a beat of reflective silence, Frannie noted it was closing time. "I think I'd better go see my mom tonight. She might not want to open up to any of us, but it might be a good idea to let her know we're here for her all the same."

Darla smiled, nodding. "I think so. She needs her family, whether she wants to admit it or not." Then, as she rose, slinging her purse over her shoulder, she added, "Also, not a terrible idea for Fletcher to run lover boy's name through the system. You'd hate to find out too late that your hot, international stud muffin is a cheating bastard."

"I will do no such thing." Frannie rolled her eyes, gesturing, "Go on, get out of here."

But as she went through her closing routine, Darla's advice stuck in her brain. If Dante had nothing to hide, nothing would pop up.

There was no harm in peeking, right?

Maybe she'd talk to Fletcher about it tomorrow.

In the meantime, time to do her daughterly duty and check on her mom.

With permission from the property management, Dante spent some time installing video cameras on the front and back of the house, though it'd been a hard sell.

"Mr. Sinclair, Owl Creek is very safe," the plump lady behind the desk had assured him, regarding Dante with faint confusion at his request. "We've never had any complaints from renters in the past. Did something happen to cause concern?"

He couldn't exactly share that he needed to ensure his uncle wasn't sending henchmen to break his fingers in the dead of night, but he also couldn't set off alarm bells with the property manager.

The fat stack of cash he'd put down for the deposit when he rented the property was the only reason she was even considering his request.

"It'll be at my expense, and I can either take them down when I leave or donate them to the property, whatever the owner prefers. But I would feel more at ease if I knew there was proper surveillance around the house."

"I…that's very considerate of you, but I still don't understand the reason. Was there something that made you feel unsafe at the property?"

Yes, the fact that his unscrupulous uncle would stop at nothing to reclaim what Dante had stolen.

"In my line of work, I require a higher level of security," he'd explained with a slight, apologetic smile. "I'm truly happy with the property and I don't want to have to move but the security must be upgraded while I'm renting out the space. I'm sure you understand, and I hope my request can be accommodated."

"Oh, yes, of course." She stopped short of asking what he did for a living, but he could see the question on the tip of her tongue. When she sensed he wouldn't budge, she'd said, "I'll ask the property owners how they feel about it and let you know."

"I appreciate your attention to the matter," he'd said, adding, "The sooner the better."

Thankfully, the owners had been amenable to a free surveillance system, and within a day, Dante had purchased the system and installed it himself, not willing to trust anyone he couldn't vet with his current location.

Satisfied, he returned to the house in time to hear his cell phone ringing. Only two people had this number: Frannie and his private investigator. He would be lying if he didn't hope it was Frannie calling, but it was his private investigator.

"Hello?"

"Nick Gladney. I have some more information you might find of interest, and it's about your father."

"Go on."

"It wasn't easy, but I had a friend pull the records from your father's accident. Not a lot to go on—pretty cut-and-dried from the report—and not a big incentive to dig any deeper, if you know what I mean."

"How so?"

"You said you were a kid when your dad died, right?"

"Yes, around ten."

"Well, do you remember your dad being a drinker or anything like that?"

"My father never drank," he answered, wondering where this was going. "Why?"

"According to the records, your dad had a blood alcohol level way over the legal limit. If the report is to be believed, your dad was drunk as a skunk when his car crashed into that tree."

"That's bullshit. My father hated the smell of alcohol. Neither of my parents drank." Which made his mother's subsequent death by a drunk driver cruelly ironic. "The report has to be wrong."

"Well, through official channels, the report says your dad was drinking the night he died. I mean, you were a kid, maybe your memory is distorted of who your dad was. It happens. Kids want to believe the best of their parents."

"No—" Dante cut in sharply. "Believe me when I say, I know my father wasn't a drinker. Dig deeper. Go beyond the official channels. Find out who signed off on that report. Find out if they suddenly came into a large sum of money. Someone lied about how my father died and I want to know who."

The information nagged at his brain, deepening his suspicion of his uncle. Lorenzo had always been willing to go to great lengths to get whatever he wanted—even if it meant removing a brother who threatened his position within the family.

Dante remembered bits and pieces of conversation between his parents behind closed doors, hushed voices always coated with a sense of urgency. His father, Matteo, kept them on the move, always hyperalert and ready to hit the ground running for reasons he never shared. His sweet mother, Georgia, always tried to hide the worry in her heart by covering it with a sunny smile and pretending they were on a grand adventure.

But Dante remembered details from his childhood that most would've happily forgotten.

And he knew with certainty that his father wasn't drunk that night.

# Chapter 9

Fletcher surprised Franny when he walked into the bookstore the following day.

"Aren't you supposed to be working?" Franny teased, though she was always happy to see her brother.

Fletcher smiled and kissed her on the cheek. "That's a funny way of saying, 'Hey, bro, always a pleasure to see you.'"

"I'm not saying I don't love when you drop in, I'm just saying that I'm not sure Owl Creek PD is getting their money's worth if you're constantly popping in here for a latte. Because I know that's what you're here for."

Franny and Fletcher had always enjoyed the kind of relationship where they teased one another mercilessly, but it was their closeness that enabled them to poke at each other without injury. Unlike Chase, with whom she didn't feel close enough to even enjoy small talk about the weather.

"Actually, I'm kind of glad you're here, because I need to talk to you about something."

Fletcher was intrigued. "I'm happy to listen while you whip me up that aforementioned latte. I mean, since you mentioned it."

Franny winked as she walked over to the café side of the shop. She made a quick latte, just how he liked it and handed the frothy drink to him. "Although I think it's kind of bizarre that you can drink something so hot when it's warm outside. When will you let me talk you into trying a nice herbal iced tea? They're quite good if you give them a chance."

Fletcher grimaced. "That sounds disgusting, no thank you. So, what did you want to talk to me about?"

Franny straightened, remembering. "Yeah, about that... so last night I went to drop in on Mom and see how she's doing and when I got there, Uncle Buck was there, too."

Fletcher shrugged. "And?"

"I don't know, they just seemed...there was something odd about the way they were talking to each other. I might be imagining things, but it seemed like they were *close*. I don't know how to say this without it being more than it is, but it seemed like there was a vibe between them."

"A vibe? As in a romantic vibe?"

Franny understood Fletcher's confusion because that was exactly how she'd felt when she saw it. She nodded with a grimace. "And I'm reluctant even to mention this because what if I'm wrong, but they took like two steps away from each other when they saw me walk in like they got caught or something, which seemed weird."

Fletcher seemed to mull over the information before ultimately rejecting the speculation. "Here's the thing. Uncle Buck and Mom have been close for years, but I think it's more of a brotherly/sisterly thing because Mom helped Uncle Buck when Aunt Jessie left him high and dry with the kids. We've spent how many summers out at the ranch? He's family, there's nothing more going on there."

Franny wanted to believe that, and if it weren't for the fact Aunt Jessie was currently in town telling anybody who would listen that she was Robert Colton's long-term lover, it would be easier to swallow. But the reality was that her aunt had maintained an inappropriate relationship with Robert Colton, so was it out of the question to wonder if Jenny Colton had decided to do the same with her sister's husband? *Yuck*, the whole thing made Franny want to vomit. Still, she saw what she saw. "I'm the last person who wants to think about this stuff, but I'm telling you, there was a vibe."

Fletcher grimaced at the idea as well. "They're both adults. I guess we don't really have room to say anything to them if it's true. Dad's gone, so it's not like Mom would be cheating on him. Even if it were true, it kind of feels like, maybe, payback? I don't know, the whole thing sucks to think about, and I'd rather just push it out of my brain."

"Hopefully, I'm way off base and I'm imagining things because I don't think I can take any more family surprises."

"Amen to that." Fletcher said with happiness as he sipped his latte. "You make the best lattes hands down."

Franny smiled. "Thanks, bro."

"Was there anything else you wanted to talk about? Because as much as you tease me, I do have a job to get back to."

"Actually, yes. My second reason for wanting to talk to you is a little more complicated."

"How so?"

"There's a new guy in town. His name is Dante Sinclair, and I was wondering if you would be willing to take a peek into his background."

Fletcher's demeanor changed, morphing into that of a protective brother. "Is there something I should know about this guy? Has he hurt you?"

"Good grief, no. He seems like a really great person but Darla mentioned that maybe I should ask some questions because he's not from around here. Honestly, even saying it out loud feels like I'm overreacting and makes me cringe."

"I can't run a background check on someone for no reason. That's illegal."

Franny's hopes fell. "Oh, I'm sorry I didn't know that. I wouldn't want you to do anything that compromises your job."

"I said I couldn't do it for no reason," he clarified. "Maybe this guy gave you a weird feeling? Or maybe he was asking for you to order some materials that felt a little suspect?"

Franny wanted to laugh at her brother's suggestions because they were all ludicrous. Dante seemed like the straightest arrow she'd ever met, but she also didn't want Fletcher to do anything that would get him in trouble.

She supposed a small white lie wouldn't hurt in this instance. "Maybe you could run his license because he went over the speed limit or something like that."

"What does he drive?"

"A Toyota sedan, a Camry I think? A rental."

"Color?"

"White."

"What else can you tell me about him?"

"Um, well, he's from Italy."

Fletcher's brow rose. "Italy? What's he doing here?"

"I don't know. He said it was a combination of business and pleasure."

"And you didn't ask any more questions?"

Exasperation colored her voice. "Fletcher, it was none of my business. I wasn't going to grill the poor guy when I just met him."

Guilt pinched at Franny. Why did it feel like she was selling Dante out somehow? "I don't want to make a big deal about this, okay? Just a peek. Don't go getting the FBI involved, okay?" At the mention of the FBI, Fletcher perked up, and immediately Frannie shot that idea down. "Don't you dare go bothering Max over this. He's doesn't need us pestering him with something as frivolous as this."

"No promises, sis. It all depends on what my little peek turns up. Besides, Max wouldn't mind. Hey, how about while I'm doing my little peek, you keep your distance until I can give you the all clear? Just to be on the safe side?"

She didn't like the idea of involving her cousin who worked for the FBI at all. In fact, she was looking forward to seeing Dante tonight. "I think you're going a little overboard. I'm sure Dante has no big, dark secrets. I was just curious because he's not from around here. I don't want you to get freaked out over nothing. I probably shouldn't have said anything."

"Look, not that I would ever want to find myself agreeing with Darla, of all people, but I think she's right. It's best to err on the side of caution nowadays. What is he even doing here? It's not like Owl Creek is a haven for international travelers."

Franny had had the same questions but framed in a far less suspicious manner. "You're going to feel real bad for thinking so poorly of the man when you find out Dante is a normal, friendly person."

"We'll see." Fletcher smiled, scooped up his latte and waved as he walked out the door.

*Brothers.*

She wasn't worried. Dante was exactly who he said he was.

At least, she hoped he was. Or else Franny would never hear the end of it.

Dante opened the front door, smiling when he saw Frannie, who was holding the books she'd ordered for him, looking like a sugary confection in a white sundress with pink accents. "Special delivery," she said, smiling up at him. "They were in the shipment that arrived this morning. I thought you wouldn't mind me bringing them to you personally."

He should mind—but he couldn't bring himself to care.

"I don't mind at all," he said, accepting the books and stepping aside so she could come in. "That's some top-tier service. Does everyone get this level of customer service or is it just me?"

Frannie's flirty smile as she shrugged nearly stole his breath. Goddamn, the woman was beautiful. "Can I get you a glass of wine or something?" he offered, trying to get his bearing before he threw her down on the sofa and devoured every inch of that smooth, succulent skin.

"I'm not much of a wine drinker but if you have something on the sweet side, I'll give it a go."

"Americans and their sweet palate," he teased, placing the books on the table before heading to the kitchen. "But I think I have something you'll enjoy. Make yourself comfortable. I'll be right back."

Dante pulled a chilled Riesling from the fridge and quickly poured two glasses. It wasn't a Moscato, but it was the sweetest wine he had to offer. He'd planned to spend a quiet evening researching, but Frannie's unexpected visit kicked those plans to the curb. He shouldn't encourage her popping in unannounced, but he'd be lying if he said he wasn't happy to see her.

She accepted the wineglass, took a delicate sniff, pretending to be a connoisseur, then sipped the wine, nodding with approval before giggling, admitting, "I have no idea if this is a good wine but it's yummy."

"That's all that matters," he said, amused at her playful nature. Frannie was unlike anyone he'd ever met. Somehow, she'd retained that sense of whimsy and wonder that most adults lost as they grew up. The part of him that needed goodness in his life soaked up her energy like a dying man. Clearing his throat, he shared, "I'll let you in on a little secret—wine snobs like to go on about a wine's properties, but at the end of the day, people like what they like, and that's what's important."

"Works with people, too," Frannie murmured, catching his gaze with a mischievous look that immediately made him forget about the wine. "I mean, from what I see… what's not to like?"

"Miss Colton, I get the impression you did not come here just to be neighborly and deliver my books."

"You might be right," she admitted, setting her glass down and climbing into his lap, straddling Dante with a boldness that ignited a fiery need between them. Her strong legs bracketed his hips, and the soft swell of her breasts caused his eyes to glaze over as he struggled to remember his name. "The thing is, I like you, Dante. I like you a lot, and I know we're doing the casual thing, but there's something about you that I can't get enough of. So, in the spirit of keeping it casual…would you like to 'casually' get naked?"

He grinned. "Right now?"

She nodded. "Right now."

He surged against her hot center. "I don't have a problem with that request," he said before she sealed her mouth to his. She tasted of sweet wine and heavenly temptation. That internal voice of reason faded to a whisper as his hands cupped her behind, drawing her close.

Their tongues tangled, and he anchored her hips against him as she ground against the hardened ridge beneath his jeans. Her little moan pushed him over the edge, and he lifted her up and onto her back, rising above her. She curled her hand around his neck, drawing his mouth back to hers.

He would lose control right then and there if he didn't

slow down, but Frannie decimated his self-control in ways that should've been a red flag.

There were many good reasons to keep a healthy distance between them, but his thoughts were hazed, and all he could focus on was the exquisite torture of Frannie writhing beneath him.

Dimly, he heard his cell phone going off. It took a minute to realize the call had to be coming from his private investigator because Frannie was the only person with the number. He hesitated, torn, but when the phone rang again, the urgency of a double call made him stop and grab his phone with a muttered apology before disappearing into his bedroom and closing the door.

He answered on the last ring before it transferred to voice mail. "Hey, Nick, this isn't a good time," he said in a low voice. "What have you got?"

"I knew you'd want to hear this right away. It's pretty significant. After you shared that your father wasn't a drinker, I did some poking around and got lucky. The investigating officer of your father's accident has since passed away, but I managed to talk to his widow. I don't have an amount, but she remembers her husband coming into a lump sum of money around twenty years ago when he still worked on the force. He bought a boat, a source of contention between him and the wife because she said it was too expensive."

"Did she say where the money came from?"

"It was hard to get specific details without coming off as suspicious for asking. I made up some story about a financial audit. She's old and trusting, so she bought it, but I couldn't dig too deep without producing some kind of documentation proving the audit."

"A boat…" he repeated, thinking over the information. "That all she said?"

"Taking into account that she was frail and nervous, she seemed real keen on protecting her old man's name. Talking about what a decorated officer he was on the force and how much pride he took in protecting his community."

"Sounds like a woman trying really hard to make sure her husband didn't sound like the kind of man to take a bribe," Dante murmured.

"Yeah, I think it's safe to assume that that boat wasn't purchased on his small-town cop salary."

When Dante's father died, they lived in a tiny town in Wisconsin. They'd only been there for two months when the accident happened. He remembered his mother's screams when the officer came to deliver the news.

Then, he remembered his mother receiving a phone call late at night, and the following morning, they were packed and on a plane for Italy. He knew Uncle Lorenzo was on the other end of that call.

His life had changed forever with that phone call.

Lorenzo had seemed the knight in shining armor at the time, swooping in at his mother's time of need, placing them under his protection, and taking Dante under his wing.

It wasn't until later that he learned nothing came without a cost.

And now? He had reason to believe someone had killed his father, making it look like an accident.

Had the same thing happened to his mother two years ago?

Was it possible his uncle had been the one behind their deaths?

Before Belinda, he never would've imagined Lorenzo to be so cruel...but now...

He couldn't deny the possibility.

# Chapter 10

Frannie didn't know what to think when Dante disappeared into his bedroom. Whatever needed to be said was clearly private, but it felt wrong to stay when he didn't return.

The moment went from sensual to awkward. Now Franny wasn't sure if she should stay or go.

She could hear the muffled conversation, a low, urgent hum that felt ominous even though she couldn't exactly make out what was being said—not that she was trying.

Frannie attempted to occupy herself to avoid accidentally eavesdropping, but she couldn't do much but fidget and wait.

After another five minutes, Frannie collected her purse, preparing to quietly leave, when Dante emerged from his bedroom with an apologetic expression. But there was something about his demeanor that was far different than before.

"I'm sorry about that, a business call that couldn't wait."

"Of course, I understand," she said, feeling awkward. "Actually, it was insensitive of me to drop in on you without checking to see if you had plans for the evening. I should probably go."

She had hoped that he would ease her concerns, but her feelings were hurt when he accepted her offer.

"I think tonight I might not be the best of company. I

have a lot of work that I need to finish and we should probably just call it a night."

"Right, sure, no problem," she said, feeling foolish. "I'll just see you around, I guess."

Was this what a casual sexual relationship felt like? She had no idea. She'd never been in one before. But she didn't like this feeling, and if this was how casual was supposed to work, maybe she wasn't cut out for it.

Dante walked her to the front door, polite and considerate as always, but she could tell he was a million miles away.

The urge to ask if he was okay overrode her bruised feelings. "I know I'm probably breaking all the rules, but I can tell whatever was said on that phone call upset you. Do you want talk about it? I can be a good listener."

Dante paused as if torn between wanting to share and keeping her at arm's length. She held her breath as hope kindled in her heart, but when he ultimately shook his head, she knew that he was determined to keep private whatever was eating at him.

"I appreciate the offer. It's very kind of you, but I think I need to handle this on my own. You needn't worry. It's business and I don't want to bore you with details that aren't necessary for our relationship."

*Ouch.* If that wasn't a brush-off, then she didn't know what was. How could they go from nearly tearing each other's clothes off to a wall of ice suddenly going up between them?

She faked a bright smile. "I guess I'll see you whenever it's convenient. I don't know how this works but whatever. I'll see you around."

Frannie didn't mean for that to come out as sharp as it had, but Dante seemed to realize that she was wounded and tried to make amends. He reached for her hand. "I've offended you. It's not my intention to hurt your feelings. I probably should've sent you home when you first showed up, but I was really happy to see you. You aren't intruding. Due to the nature of my business, it's probably a good idea to give me a heads-up the next time you want to come out. That way, I'm fully prepared to give you all of my attention."

It was reasonable, and yet his request stung. Just one more example of how whatever was happening between them was superficial at best. He had never promised anything more, so why was she disappointed?

"Yep. Sounds good," she said, eager to get out of there before embarrassing herself further. "I will see you around. Bye."

"Frannie—"

But listening to Dante dance around the obvious would only further her excruciating humiliation for practically throwing herself at him, and that was where she drew the line.

She left so fast that she probably looked like she was running to her car. But she had to get out of there because if she had stayed a minute longer, she would've started crying, ruining the appearance of being fine with the situation.

Because she wasn't. God, she really wasn't.

See? She didn't do casual because she was terrible at it. She wasn't the kind of woman who slept around and engaged in hookups. She was the kind of girl who got invested, cared about her partner and liked feeling part of a team.

What was happening? She had to get her head back on straight and her feelings in line with the reality of the situation. Dante wasn't her forever guy. He was a man passing through town who'd been honest about his situation. So why was she hurt that he was putting up boundaries?

Because she really, *really* liked him. Damn it. That'd happened fast.

Whatever this was, it was bound to end badly—for her.

Dante swore under his breath for handling the situation like a jackass.

Frannie's feelings were plain as the nose on her face. He'd wounded her by sending her away. If the situation were different, he would've loved to spend the evening together, but that wasn't the situation he was in. The phone call from Nick had only reminded him.

Reality checks were rarely kind.

He never should've encouraged anything with Frannie because she was bound to get hurt at some point.

*Like tonight.*

She might think he'd rejected her, but he was trying to protect her. He'd never forgive himself if anything happened to Frannie because of him.

Still, hurting her didn't feel right.

If he left the situation as it was, Frannie would probably ghost him, which would be a blessing in disguise. Then, at least, he'd know she was safe from him. But even as his brain offered the solution, he violently rejected it.

He had to make amends.

Letting Frannie think that he wasn't interested in her, to let her marinate in that kind of emotional rejection, was more than he could stomach.

Hell, he knew the right thing to do would be to let that door close, but he couldn't bring himself to do it.

*That's a problem for tomorrow.*

His thoughts were a maelstrom as he processed the new information about his father's death.

He needed more information. Sitting on his hands and waiting patiently wasn't in his nature. Even though he'd hired the private investigator to do the heavy lifting, he wanted to do his own digging around. It wasn't wise, but he couldn't escape the feeling that he could be doing more.

The answers were out there—he just needed to ask the right questions.

The memory of his father's death was crystallized in his brain. Emotional trauma had a way of imprinting like no other.

Of course, experts said memories were a shaky foundation to build a case on, but sometimes a memory was a good springboard.

He remembered the bitter cold of that night. A terrible storm had blown through the state, dropping temperatures to thirty below. Weather forecasters had warned residents to prepare for dangerous conditions. Stay home, bring in your livestock and avoid the roads if possible. Of all the places they'd lived, Dante hated Wisconsin the most because of the extreme cold.

After that night, he'd had another reason to hate the place.

His cell phone chirped for an email received. His private investigator had sent a file. He opened the file to find a scanned copy of the police report.

Matteo Santoro, 32, DOA, from blunt force trauma sustained from a motor vehicle accident on Greger Road at 2200 hours. Testing revealed a Blood Alcohol Content of .30. Impaired driving and poor road conditions led Mr. Santoro to lose control of his vehicle and collide with a sugar maple tree. Mr. Santoro was ejected through the windshield and died on impact.

Report: Ulysses Weisel, Detective, Hawthorne Police Department.

In all the years since his father's death, Dante had never thought to get a copy of the police report. No one had ever told him that his father's accident had been attributed to drunk driving. Ice on the roads had been blamed, which had seemed plausible because that storm had been a doozy.

Now, as he read someone's lie in an official document that his father had been drunk, rage percolated through his veins. Why the lie? Someone had gone to great lengths to ensure that no questions were asked, that Matteo's death was written off as an unfortunate consequence of some poor sap making a bad choice.

But his father never drank. Surely his mom had to have known that was a lie? Why would she go along with something she knew to be false?

Looking back on his memory, he was willing to bet his uncle Lorenzo had somehow persuaded his mother to let him care for them. She would've been vulnerable, lost, and grieving—a perfect target for Lorenzo.

Only now did Dante realize how his mother might've been lured into a trap. She was never able to escape, which made him feel complicit in keeping her in a golden cage, unknowingly participating in what had kept her silent and cowed.

In truth, when they first arrived in Italy, his uncle had seemed a kind blessing after a lifetime of struggle and confusing instability for a young Dante.

Lorenzo had spent time cultivating a bond with him, nurturing a place in his young heart that his father should've filled.

But even in life, Matteo had seemed too preoccupied to spend time with his son. There'd been no tossing the ball back and forth in the backyard for the Santoros. At the time, Dante had resented his father's distractions, but now, he saw things differently.

Maybe Matteo had been doing his best to keep his family safe from a threat that only he understood.

Dante had only known the struggle of surviving as they'd hopped from one place to another, his dad unable to hold down a job for too long, and his mother trying to make ends meet with barely enough resources to keep them alive.

He couldn't imagine being so terrified of his brother that he kept his family far enough away to avoid all contact—walking away from a veritable fortune because of a rift that couldn't be mended.

But he now understood his father's motivation better, and it shamed him that he'd never thought to dig deeper until it personally affected him.

Even as disgrace and guilt ate at him, there was grief in the mix, too.

For all his faults, Lorenzo had become his father figure, and for a long time, Dante had trusted him implicitly.

Lorenzo had put Dante through school, seen to his needs, and put a roof over his and his mother's heads when they needed it most.

There was a time when Dante had thought the world of his uncle.

But the thing about misplaced hero worship was that the facade eventually crumbled, leaving nothing to hide the rot lurking beneath the shell.

Now he understood why his father had been adamant

that his family would have nothing to do with the Santoro name or legacy.

What had Lorenzo told his mother to convince her to leave everything behind and accept the family's help?

Had she been coerced? Or had she been tired of hiding? Struggling and too lost in a sea of grief to see the shark's shadow closing in?

Either way, it was too late now. Both his parents were gone. Lorenzo was determined to bring him back into the fold by any means necessary, and the only thing keeping Lorenzo at bay was locked in a safe-deposit box.

An old piece of paper might seem a flimsy protection against the Santoro might, but that little slip of paper had the power to go off like a bomb in his family—and Lorenzo would do anything to keep that from happening.

However, that didn't mean Lorenzo would quit. He'd get sneakier in his efforts.

Because that was Lorenzo's superpower—getting what he wanted without getting his hands dirty.

# Chapter 11

Frannie tried to put the fiasco at Dante's house in a locked box and forget about it, but the feeling of being rejected remained with her, lodged in her brain like a poky sticker burrowing into her sock.

The shop door opened, and one of her favorite people, Della Winslow, walked in with her black Lab, Charlie. It was an instant mood saver.

"I need the biggest, strongest cup of sweet tea you can manage before I fall over," Della said, flopping down in the nearest chair and wiping her brow. "I cannot handle this heat wave. We're not built for this kind of torture. Give me snow and ice any day, not Satan's armpit." She gestured to her dog, who was panting. "Look at poor Charlie, he's practically hyperventilating."

Frannie laughed, setting down a bowl of water in front of the parched dog before making Della's tea. "It's not that bad. I kind of like it. I can pretend I'm living somewhere beachy and warm. Like California."

"That's a myth about California. I spent the summer with an aunt who lived in a town called Planada. Definitely no beach. Just a lonely strip of highway, some mountains off in the distance, and a 'saloon' that offered twenty-five-cent root beers. That part actually was kind of nice but other than that…zero stars, do not recommend."

"And to think you gave up a promising travel guide career for that of a dog trainer," Frannie quipped with a teasing smile.

"Um, not just any dog trainer. Charlie is one of the best cadaver dogs in the state. It's not like his factory settings defaulted with that skill."

"My apologies," Frannie said, winking. "No, you're right, Charlie is pretty amazing and you're an incredible resource to our little town. Honestly, I know you can probably get hired someplace else and make a lot more money but I'm glad you're here with us."

Della appreciated the compliment, reaching down to rub Charlie's dark head. "So, I heard a rumor yesterday—"

"If it's about my dad and my aunt…as much as I'd love for it to be trash talk, it very well could be true," Frannie said, knowing that dancing around the issue would only delay the inevitable. People were already talking. The only way to kill a fire was to deny it oxygen. "We're going to ask for a DNA test proving paternity, but I'm not holding my breath that she's lying. If it's true, we'll deal with it like adults. I mean, what choice is there?"

Della pursed her lips in commiseration, admitting, "I guess that's the only way to handle it. Still, it sucks for your family."

"Yeah, it's a crap sandwich. But clearly, Jessie isn't going away anytime soon." She paused, curious, "Where did you hear about this?"

Della exhaled a breath, embarrassed. "I overheard a conversation that I probably shouldn't have been listening to, but to be fair, the woman was being very loud."

Frannie rubbed her forehead. "Yeah, it appears my aunt Jessie has a flair for the dramatic."

"I think she was talking to her attorney, or I don't know, he was dressed nice but there was something smarmy about him. Like a used car salesman vibe. I didn't recognize him, though. I don't think he's from around here. Anyway, she was going off on how much money your dad had, and she was entitled to a piece of it. Then, she said something that was really out of line—"

"Yeah?"

"She said that she deserved more than your mom because she was his *real* wife, no matter what a piece of paper said. That's when I'd heard enough, and I left the restaurant."

Frannie tried to keep her temper in check. The amount of sheer audacity flowing through that woman's veins was nothing short of narcissistic. "She can run her mouth all she wants, doesn't change the fact that my mother deserves every penny she inherited from my dad's estate. My dad wasn't an easy man to live with and she put up with more than her share of bullshit."

An impotent well of frustration sloshed in the pit of her stomach for her father's actions, but he was dead, and even if he weren't, it wasn't as if he would've allowed himself any accountability.

"The worst part? It doesn't surprise me that Dad had a mistress—it's that he chose to carry on with his own sister-in-law. That feels particularly low."

"Were you close with your dad?" Della asked with a subtle grimace, as if she were apologizing preemptively for the question and Frannie's answer.

Frannie sighed. "For a time, yes. We got along the best, I suppose. But as I got older and started having opinions of my own, we were less close. By the time he died, we barely saw each other, and I didn't miss his company. Sounds sad to say that, though. Like, I should've felt worse when he passed. A part of me was…relieved. Just saying that out loud…makes me feel like a terrible person."

"Feelings are complicated. Sometimes they don't make sense and we have to leave it at that."

"How is that you're younger than me and so much wiser?" Frannie teased, wiping away the sudden gathering of moisture at the corner of her eyes. "Look what you've done. I'm leaking."

Della chuckled softly. "I didn't know your dad well but sometimes we have to make a mental agreement with ourselves that when it comes to family, we're going to accept them as they are, good and bad."

"That's a tall order," Frannie said, thinking of Aunt Jessie. "Some family aren't worth claiming."

Della nodded, knowing exactly whom Frannie was referencing. "My personal opinion? I think it's in really bad taste that your aunt would come into our town and start mouthing off like that for anyone to hear. It's personal business and it should stay that way."

Frannie appreciated Della's stance even though she knew plenty of people were probably eating up the fresh gossip about her family. With a family as big as hers and as connected in the town, there were bound to be people who didn't like them. Frannie tried not to dwell on the people who were eager to see the Coltons fall.

The front door opened, and Dante walked in. Before she could temper her expression, her eyes widened in surprise, and her breath caught. He was so damn handsome, and it immediately irked her how her heart rate seemed to jump a beat the minute he appeared. Why was he here? After last night, she assumed their little "casual" adventure was over.

Charlie sensed the tension and cocked his head, licking his lips as he looked to Della for direction.

Apparently, Della could feel the same energy in the room as Charlie and took that as her cue to leave. She rose from the chair, patting Charlie's head for reassurance. "Thanks for the tea and the water for Charlie. I better get going. I'll talk to you later."

"Sure thing." Frannie waved, and Della and Charlie left. Now it was just Frannie and Dante, and the awkwardness was epic. Maybe she should tackle and be done with the elephant in the room. "Dante…"

He surprised her by going first. "No, I want to apologize for last night," he said, shaking his head firmly. "I was caught off guard by the phone call and I needed to deal with a few things. I wouldn't have been good company and I didn't want you to see me like that. But I should've handled it better."

Frannie softened. "Oh…" Well, that felt different than what she had been imagining. "I'm sorry for whatever you're going through. Sounds serious. Do you…want to talk about it?" she asked.

"It's complicated and I wouldn't want to bore you. Suffice it to say I would much rather have spent the evening with you than think about what was said in that phone call."

That was cryptic. *Red flag, much?* True, but it wasn't like Dante was a criminal or anything like that. *Cue the nervous internal laughter.* Frannie didn't know what to think. All she knew was that Dante apologizing for his abrupt change in demeanor made her feel less standoffish and more willing to try again.

Was that a bad idea?

\* \* \*

Dante had had his out, but he didn't take it. Sure, walking away without further entanglements was wise, but he couldn't bring himself to do it.

And he was about to go deeper into the realm of bad decisions.

"I'd like to make it up to you. Are you busy tonight?" he asked.

She hesitated, and he didn't blame her after last night. He was surprised she was still willing to talk to him. "What did you have in mind?"

"A nice dinner with my favorite person in Owl Creek."

"Well, that's not a great endorsement. You don't know many people."

He chuckled. "You're right. I can do better than that. How about dinner with the most *beautiful* woman in Owl Creek?"

She grinned in spite of herself. "You're definitely getting closer to success. And what would we do after dinner?"

"I would leave that up to you. But I would definitely like to take you back to my place and really make up for my poor behavior last night."

Franny's smile brightened. "Now, that sounds like a plan. How about you pick me up at my place around six?"

This time it was Dante who hesitated. He wanted to keep Frannie as safe as possible. Even though he was technically putting her in danger just by spending so much time with her, he didn't like to think that any eyes on him would follow Frannie. But he also didn't want her to think he was hesitating for the wrong reason. He finally answered, "I would be happy to pick you up," with a warm smile to chase away doubt.

"Careful, Dante, this almost sounds like a real date," she teased.

"I suppose it is," he said, fighting against the knowledge that he had no business encouraging her affection. "Text me your address and I will be there promptly at six."

"Promptly?" Her grin deepened. "A man after my own heart. I was raised to believe on time is already late, so that gives you a glimpse into my secret quirks."

It was silly, but somehow knowing that Frannie prized punctuality the same as he did only made him desire her more.

His hands itched to touch her, to wrap her in his arms and make up for all the kissing they didn't get to do last night, but he restrained the impulse. He didn't know who might be watching.

"Aren't you going to kiss me goodbye?" she asked coyly, striking with unerring accuracy at his secret desire.

"Tonight, you'll get all the kisses you can handle and then some," he promised, going to the door. "Gives us something to look forward to."

"Tease," she laughed as he left the shop to run errands.

He hadn't planned to stop at Frannie's bookstore, but he couldn't regret his choice even though it was all wrong. He couldn't deny his mood felt considerably happier than when he left the house, and he was selfish enough to enjoy it.

But now he had things to get done, such as paying the biweekly rent, which he did in cash.

Dante stepped into the property management office, expecting a quick transaction, but the property manager was feeling chatty.

"How are things with the rental?" she asked with a wide smile. "How's the heat treating you? It's not always this warm here but we're getting a real sizzler this year."

"The heat doesn't bother me, and the fans work well enough to keep the temperature down," he answered, being polite. "How about you?"

She fanned her face for emphasis. "Oh, I can't hardly handle this heat. I feel like I'm about to melt. But I'm glad to hear that you're still enjoying our little town. Do you know how much longer you'll be staying with us?"

Dante was purposefully vague. "It's hard to say. I appreciate the biweekly payments. My work is unpredictable. However, just to show I appreciate how accommodating you've been, I'll pay for the month even if I end up leaving."

"Oh, that's real considerate of you. It's not very often that we get long-term rentals like you popping into town."

"Like me? What do you mean?"

"Honey, you're practically a celebrity in this town. Seems everyone's talking about two things. The handsome Italian with the sexy accent and, of course, that terrible gossip that's going around about Robert Colton and his supposed lover who just happens to be his sister-in-law. Sordid business, that."

So, both he and Frannie's family drama were the talk of the town. Not a great combo for either of them. "I suppose all places have their secrets," he murmured, trying to downplay it for Frannie's sake.

"I feel so bad for Jenny. She doesn't deserve what her sister's done to her. Let me tell you, Jessie Robards has always been nothing but trouble all her days. It doesn't surprise me at all that she's come back just to stir up trouble."

Dante didn't like the feeling that he was participating in gossip about Frannie's business and felt mildly protective. "I'm sure it will all work out in the end. These things usually get sorted out somehow."

"I suppose so," the property manager conceded, but she

looked dubious. "All I know is that if Jessie is back in town that bodes real bad for Jenny."

"How so?"

"Oh, that woman has always wanted anything that was her sister's. It doesn't surprise me none that she went after Jenny's husband. That woman has no shame. It's hard to believe Jenny and Jessie are twins. They are night and day. Good and evil, if you ask me."

He felt terrible for Frannie. He knew something about toxic family members. "I hope it all turns out okay," he said, signaling the end to the conversation with a polite reason to leave.

Toxic people were like cancer. Sometimes it took a while to realize the insidious destruction they were doing behind the scenes. He didn't know this Jessie woman, but her intentions could hardly be good.

*Stay out of Frannie's business*, the voice warned. The last thing he needed was to draw unnecessary attention to himself. Engaging with a greedy woman was likely to do that.

Besides, Franny seemed capable of handling her aunt and whatever she had up her sleeve.

He might be unable to solve Frannie's family issue, but he could show her a good night.

For now, that would have to be enough.

# Chapter 12

Frannie was humming under her breath the following morning as she tidied up her shelves, still thinking about last night with Dante. Dinner at The Tides—*exquisite*—followed by quality sexy time at his place—*addictive*—and she couldn't stop the giddy smile that kept curving her lips.

The man was everything she'd never realized she wanted.

Kind, considerate, funny, thoughtful—oh, and so handsome she could stare at him until the day she died. But she knew nothing about him, which was starting to bug her.

She'd begun to notice that he was skilled at dodging personal questions, but he did it so well that it wasn't until much later that she realized he never really answered anything of substance about himself.

She didn't like to create problems where there weren't any, but she also couldn't help but wonder if she was overlooking a major red flag.

People who didn't like sharing details about themselves usually had something to hide.

Like a wife or a girlfriend.

Or worse.

No, she told herself sternly, Dante was a good man who was just a little private. Clearly, he'd suffered a terrible breakup and was still healing from the emotional trauma.

That much she'd surmised when he'd admitted he didn't want to talk about his past.

Wasn't he entitled to his privacy? Of course he was.

Besides, their relationship was created within certain boundaries, which didn't encourage deeper connections, so Dante's reluctance to share details seemed to fit within those parameters.

*Ugh.* That level of circular justification had just made her dizzy.

Frannie already wanted to break the rules of their "relationship."

She wanted more.

It felt strange to allow someone access to her body yet receive so little of the person.

Her intrusive thoughts threatened to kill the sweet high she'd ridden all morning as the questions and insecurities started to pile up.

Grabbing her phone, she texted Fletcher.

Any luck finding anything of interest on Dante?

Even sending the text made her feel guilty, like she was doing something wrong and sneaky, but she rationalized that once Fletcher came back empty-handed, she could relax knowing that Dante was exactly who he said he was, and he wasn't hiding anything.

And if Fletcher discovered Dante was lying about something?

What then?

She pushed that thought aside. *Don't build bridges for rivers you don't have to cross yet.*

Frannie hoisted a box of books and started to walk toward the display table when the front door opened, and a delivery-man with a massive spray of flowers walked in.

"Frannie Colton?" he asked hopefully.

"Yes?"

"Delivery for you."

Frannie accepted the beautiful bouquet, flabbergasted and tickled at the same time. "Thank you!" she called out after the man as he left the shop. Dante must have some kind of telepathy. How else would he have known she was fighting her thoughts about their connection? She smiled, placing the flowers on the counter to find the card, but there was none.

"You sly dog, playing secret admirer," she murmured, gazing at the expensive blooms, approving of his choices. "This is gorgeous."

She grabbed her phone and quickly sent a text to Dante.

They're beautiful, thank you!

Her phone dinged almost immediately in response.

What is?

She giggled at the game. Sure, he had no idea what she was talking about. She liked this playful side of Dante. Frannie texted back.

How did you know I love white lilies?

Dante ditched the text and called seconds later. "Frannie, I didn't send you flowers," he said, his tone nothing like the loving and sensual man she'd spent last night with. "Whoever sent you flowers, it wasn't me."

His denial splashed water on her happiness. Then, straightening with confusion, she pressed him. "What do you mean you didn't send them? Are you being serious? You truly didn't send them?"

"No, I did not," Dante said, his tone clipped. "Who else might've sent them?"

Was he jealous? If he knew her, he'd understand how ridiculous he was being. Frannie wasn't the type to date multiple people at once. She was very much a monogamous person. She tried not to take offense, but it hurt. "I have no idea who might've sent them. I'm not seeing anyone but you."

That should've put him at ease, but if anything, he seemed more tense. "Perhaps family? A friend?"

She shook her head, baffled by his reaction and the subtle urgency in his tone. "Dante, maybe it was a mistake. There wasn't a card attached. Maybe the flowers were meant for someone else."

"Who delivered the flowers?"

"A random delivery person. I didn't pay attention."

"A local florist company?"

She paused to think. "Maybe? Like I said, I wasn't paying attention. I was so tickled by the flowers I didn't notice anything else because I thought they were from you."

Admitting this private truth felt more revealing than standing naked in the town square. She wasn't supposed to have feelings so quickly for a man who was only meant to be casual fun.

Damn it, she'd told Darla she was terrible at this stuff.

"Forget it, it's probably a mistake. I'll call the local florist and find out who the flowers actually belong to and then we can move past this awkward phone call."

The silence on the other end was unnerving. Why was he freaking out over a flower delivery likely meant for someone else? And why was she hurt that the flowers weren't from him?

"Yes, please let me know as soon as you have more information," he said as if they were discussing a business transaction that went awry.

"Yeah, sure." She blinked back stupid tears. She wasn't going to cry over this. Wiping at her eyes, she lied. "Okay, well, I have customers, so I better go," she said, hanging up so she could get off the phone and be pitiful in private.

Why did it bother her so much that Dante hadn't been the one to send her flowers? Last night had been perfect—romantic, fun, sensual—and she'd floated home on a cloud. She knew she wasn't supposed to be thinking of Dante as her boyfriend, but it was hard not to daydream about a life with him.

*Too soon! Red flag!* Except she was the red flag in this instance. She had no business fantasizing about a man who'd been up-front and honest about not being available for anything more than casual.

She was starting to hate that word.

Sighing, she blotted her eyes with a tissue and grabbed her phone to call the florist. The lilies were lovely, even if they weren't meant for her. Someone out there had a secret admirer with discerning tastes.

If only it had been her.

Dante stared at the phone after Frannie clicked off, his thoughts racing.

His knee-jerk reaction had been a flare of jealousy, but he could hear the sincerity in her voice when she claimed he was the only one she was dating.

Under normal circumstances, that would've been enough to calm his nerves, but more was happening behind the scenes than he could share.

If she wasn't dating anyone else, and he hadn't sent the flowers, who had?

An unexpected gift could be an ominous portent, depending on its origins.

It could be a message to Dante that no one in his life was safe—anyone could be reached.

Intimidation and manipulation were his uncle's bread and butter.

With luck, the flowers were inadvertently delivered to the wrong address.

But the warning tingle in his gut told him that the flowers weren't an innocent mix-up.

Dante started to pace while he waited for Frannie's call. It was hard not to jump in the car and start asking questions himself, but that would only make him look like a jealous jackass or a paranoid fool, and he wasn't keen to embrace either look.

Especially not with Frannie.

He knew it was too soon, but he had feelings for her. The way she laughed, her quirky sense of humor, her sense of compassion, and her levelheaded demeanor—everything about Frannie lit up his insides like a carnival.

Which was why he had to know where those damn flowers came from.

He'd never forgive himself if he'd selfishly put Frannie in danger.

He'd made the mistake of underestimating his uncle's ruthlessness once, and he couldn't afford to do it again.

Not with Frannie's life.

Maybe he ought to level with her, share with her why he was in Owl Creek, hiding from the man who'd essentially raised him after his father died.

The man he was afraid had something to do with both his parents' deaths, years apart.

He shoved shaking hands through his hair, willing the

phone to ring with good news, but staring at the phone only ramped up his anxiety as silence followed.

Finally, Frannie called back.

"Hi, it's me." She sounded standoffish, but she went on to say, "So, I'm officially confused. I haven't a clue who might've sent these flowers. The florist said they were commissioned through one of those internet companies and don't have access to any booking information. The order just shows up on the computer with proof of payment. Then, the florist fulfills the order. The only information provided on the order was my name and the shop's address."

Dante felt a cold chill dance on his spine. An internet commission could come from anywhere—even another country. "You should close up early today."

"Why?" Frannie asked, confused.

"Because your location is compromised."

"Compromised?" She forced a chuckle as if he were being ludicrous. "You sound like a spy or something. I'm sure there's a logical explanation for this, and I won't get worked up over a flower delivery. Besides, they're quite pretty and dress up the shop nicely."

Dante wanted Frannie to throw them in the trash, but he knew asking her would only create more questions and an even bigger gap between them.

"I'm sorry...maybe you're right," he conceded, forcing himself to sound less anxious than he felt. "I apologize if my reaction was inappropriate."

"Well, it hurt my feelings," she admitted. "But maybe that's the cultural differences between us. I keep forgetting you're from another country."

"Yes, perhaps."

"So...were you a teensy bit jealous?" she asked.

It was easier to admit to jealousy than to admit he had a

murderous uncle on his tail who could be targeting anyone Dante got close to. "Yes, it's possible."

"I mean, that's not so bad to be jealous… Sometimes it means you really care for someone."

"I do care about you," he said without hesitation. *More than I should.*

"I care about you, too."

He couldn't let his suspicions go, though. "There's no one that you can think of who might've sent them? Not even your ex? Perhaps he is trying to win back your affections."

"No. My ex didn't believe in sending flowers or doing anything remotely romantic. He once told me flowers were only for men who craved validation from the women in their lives. Just saying that out loud makes me embarrassed I ever thought he was The One. He was an insensitive asshole with zero emotional intelligence. So, no, I don't think he sent them."

"Yes, but manipulative men often use methods that previously would've been uncharacteristic of them, to seem changed."

She paused before admitting, "Well, that might be true, but I know he didn't send them. He's engaged to someone else and it's unlikely that he gives me a second thought."

Dante heard the quiet hurt in Frannie's voice. It was irrational, but he felt the urge to punch this ex in the face for stupidly losing an incredible woman, even though the only reason Dante had the opportunity to know her was because of this jackass's actions.

"He's an idiot," he assured Frannie. "His loss is my gain."

"Dante…when you say things like that, it's hard to remember that we're keeping things simple between us."

She was right. He was sending mixed signals. "I know. I'm sorry."

"It's okay. Just wanted to point it out."

But without solid proof that there was no dangerous intent behind that mysterious flower delivery, there was no way he'd let Frannie out of sight now.

He'd made the mistake of assuming his uncle would never stoop so low to get what he wanted—he couldn't afford to make that mistake again.

Not with Frannie.

"How about I cook you some authentic Italian tonight?" he offered.

"Are you sure that's a good idea? Somehow dinner always ends with us naked in bed."

"I'm not complaining."

She chuckled. "I'm not either, but maybe we need to put the brakes on what we're doing for a while."

*Absolutely not.* "Do you prefer Tagliatelle al Ragù or Rigatoni alla Carbonara?"

"I don't know what either of those are, but it sounds like pasta, and if that's the case, I love all pasta. I'm lactose intolerant, though, so nothing with dairy."

"Trofie al Pesto it is then. Bring a beverage of your choice."

She laughed in spite of the seriousness between them. "I haven't said I'll come."

"You will always come with me, that's a promise," he said in a sultry tone.

Frannie's breathy "I'll bring the wine" was all the confirmation he needed. At least when Frannie was with him, he felt secure in his ability to protect her.

If anything happened to Frannie—he'd tear his uncle apart.

And that was a different kind of promise.

# Chapter 13

Frannie planned to meet with her mom for lunch at a small park within walking distance from one of Jenny Colton's private nursing clients. Despite having enough of a nest egg to retire comfortably, Jenny preferred to work part-time to keep her mind sharp and her body in shape.

Frannie thought her mom kept working because the idea of being stuck in the house with the ghosts of the past was too much to bear. But on the more practical side, Jenny prided herself on being helpful and needed, and nursing fit the bill.

She waved as her mom walked toward her. After that disastrous meeting with her aunt Jessie, Frannie couldn't help but compare the two women.

Jessie was thinner but brittle, as if she punished herself by restricting her calorie intake, whereas her mom was thin but fit. Jenny Colton didn't have a problem indulging in a slice of cake or a glass of wine, but she also stayed active at the local gym, enjoying her water aerobics and yoga classes.

"Hi, Mom," she said, kissing Jenny's cheek in welcome. "I brought sandwiches from the brewery. I hope that's okay."

Jenny approved, "I love a good sandwich." She slid onto the picnic bench opposite Frannie. "This is nice. What's the occasion?"

"Do I need a special occasion to spend time with my mom?" Frannie teased, although there was some truth to Jenny's inquiry, and that stung a bit. The recent passing of her dad was a stark reminder that her parents weren't getting any younger, and sometimes past squabbles needed to be put to rest to enjoy what time you had left.

Of course, easier said than done when the past showed up barking about wanting a piece of your inheritance.

"I love the garlic aioli they put on their sandwiches," Jenny said with an ecstatic appreciation of her bite. "I tell you, the main chef at the brewery can put a five-star restaurant to shame. It's like a little pocket of high-end cuisine hiding in an unassuming brewery."

Frannie agreed. They just enjoyed their sandwiches for a moment, soaking up the sunshine and scenery. The park was mostly empty today, which was nice because sometimes the youth soccer teams used the grassy fields for practice. Frannie had made plenty of memories in this park, some of which would remain private. She smothered a small smile and took another bite.

Jenny broke the silence first. "I heard your aunt Jessie is creating a stir in town."

Frannie was grateful her mom had brought up the topic first, but it still made her cringe. Going straight to it, Frannie nodded. "Yes, she's saying all sorts of things, and I wish she'd just shut her trap."

Jenny chuckled ruefully. "One thing Jessie does not do is silence herself for the sake of others' convenience or comfort. I used to be envious of her ability to do and say whatever she wanted regardless of how others felt. Now it seems less of a positive quality."

"Yeah, especially with what she's saying about our family."

Jenny sighed, wiping her mouth with a paper napkin.

The sadness in her mother's eyes made Frannie want to march up to her aunt and punch her in the mouth, or at the very least give her a scathing piece of her mind.

"Are you okay?" Frannie ventured, hating the position her mother was in. "It would be totally understandable if you weren't."

"Oh, I'm fine," Jenny answered with a quick smile that seemed rehearsed. "It's one of those things that you just have to accept and move on. No sense in crying about spilled milk."

She disagreed. "No, Mom, this isn't something you have to accept, and you don't have to pretend to be okay with it. How could your sister do this to you? I hate to put too fine of a point on it but aren't twins supposed to be ultra close?"

"I'm sure she had her reasons."

Frannie couldn't stop the aggravation from creeping into her voice, even though she tried to be compassionate. "Mom, please stop being so accommodating. She stole your husband and now she's trying to steal our money. It's not like Dad was an oil tycoon. Sure, he did pretty well for himself with investments and whatnot but he wasn't a billionaire. The piece of the pie is already being split seven ways, and now we have to figure out how to include three more people? It's not fair."

Jenny tried to use logic instead of emotion. "According to Chase, nothing will change until the DNA tests on the two adult children are completed. As far as Jessie is concerned—" she lifted her hands, unsure "—it's a bit more complicated, legally."

"Yeah, I heard. I will puke if she's awarded one red cent."

Jenny's small laugh reminded Frannie of when she was a kid, and she'd said something outlandish.

Frannie didn't want to laugh, but a reluctant chuckle escaped. "It would be awesome if I could manage to time that so it landed right in her greedy lap."

"Jessie can't stand bodily fluids, so that would be a perfect way to ruin her day," Jenny shared. "She couldn't even handle her own. Once she threw up when she got a bloody nose. That was a mess."

It was hard to imagine that brittle woman as anything other than the hard woman trying to ruin their family. "What was she like as a kid? I mean, what happened between you two? Weren't you ever close?"

Jenny swallowed as if pushing down a sudden lump in her throat. "Yes, we were close at one time. And I don't know what happened," she answered sadly. "Or maybe, I do know and I don't want to say because I would never want you to feel differently about your father. For all his faults, he was a good father."

*Eh, that's being generous.* "Mom, I love how you want to create a positive memory out of something that was crap, but he doesn't deserve that kindness right now. I loved my dad, but I'm not sure how I can forgive him for this."

Jenny accepted Frannie's frank admission and didn't try to change her perspective. How could she? The facts were hard to rearrange. "In high school your dad was quite the catch. Very popular, charming, and an incredible athlete. When you ask what happened between me and Jessie? Well, the answer is your dad. We were close until we both fell for Robert—and we both dated him."

"Ew. Gross." Frannie made a face. "I definitely feel sick to my stomach. Hadn't you two ever heard of the term 'sloppy seconds'?"

"Francesca," Jenny admonished with a grimace. "Should I continue or stop?"

"No, go ahead. Might as well hear the whole sordid story so at least I'll know the backstory of this reality TV episode."

Jenny exhaled a short breath as if praying for patience, then continued. "Yes, he dated us both but at the time, I never really thought Jessie was in love with Robert. We'd always been competitive with each other, but never maliciously, until after Robert. In the end, he chose me, and it created a deep rift between my sister and me. Your father and I got married shortly after graduation, and soon after, Jessie married Buck and I thought we'd moved past the hurts from high school. But our relationship was never the same, strained at best. Then, when Jessie divorced Buck, she took off, leaving the kids for Buck to raise alone."

Jenny's kids were close to Uncle Buck's, having spent countless summers at the Colton ranch, but Jessie had bailed on her first family while Frannie was still a baby, so she had no memory of her aunt until that horrid meeting the other day.

Speaking of, might as well share that information, too.

"I need to tell you something... The other day, against my better judgment, I agreed to meet with Aunt Jessie."

"Why on earth would you do that?" Jenny asked with a mild frown.

"Because...morbid curiosity, perhaps?" Frannie admitted, cringing. "I'm sorry. I shouldn't have met up with her. It was stupid and all she did was make me mad. Now she's running her mouth all over town saying how she deserves a portion of Dad's estate because she was more of a wife to him than you and I'm just about at my limit of patience with her. I mean, I guess there's nothing we can do about it if her kids turn out to be Dad's, but I'll be damned if that piranha should get any of Dad's estate."

"Well, we'll just have to put our faith in our lawyer's expertise," Jenny said, gathering their trash just like she would at home, as if on autopilot. "The sandwiches were delicious, darling. Really hit the spot, but I need to get going. I have a hair appointment in an hour."

Frannie nodded, mildly disappointed. Her mom was intensely private, and that wasn't likely to change, but for once, she wanted her mom to feel safe enough to be open and vulnerable with her kids. Even if she were devastated by the revelation about her sister, she wouldn't dare show the true depth of her pain.

Not even to her grown children.

One of the worst parts about being a nomad in a strange land was the lack of creature comforts, and the lack of creature comforts inevitably led to too much downtime with nothing but the thoughts in his head to keep him company.

And that was a scary place to be.

With the troubling mystery of the recent flower delivery, the tension in his body was enough to break bone. He couldn't seem overly anxious without seeming off to Frannie, who was already ready to dismiss the mystery, but he also couldn't let it ride, knowing the real threat out there.

After Belinda's attack, Dante had moved quickly to get her to safety. Once she could travel, he had arranged for Belinda to be transported to a private rehab facility in Switzerland. He didn't want Lorenzo to have easy access to Belinda in any way as she recovered, but moving her out of the country had been the only way to keep her profile low.

It hadn't been easy.

But he'd convinced her of the danger she would be in if she remained in Italy, and she'd agreed to go.

She'd left behind everything she'd built for an unknown

future in another country. That kind of bravery made him feel weak in comparison, but it also pushed him to be stronger.

In his nightmares, Belinda blamed him for her injuries, but in real life, her kind heart had never placed the weight on his shoulders.

But she should have—he was to blame.

His hubris, his smug belief that Lorenzo couldn't leverage his compliance, had cost Belinda her future in surgery.

And yet, she never blamed Dante.

Dante carried a different kind of guilt; sometimes, he didn't think he'd ever be free of its weight.

He'd decided that his penance would be to hear her voice when he checked on her progress until the day she managed to recover her hands like before.

But the doctors had been honest about the slim chance of that happening, which meant his reprieve would likely never be granted.

Grabbing his cell, he dialed the secret number, knowing it would be close to bedtime in Switzerland.

Belinda picked up on the second ring. "Dante?"

Her voice, soft and soothing, remained the same, despite her situation. "I'm sorry to call so late. I wanted to check in before time got away from me. How are you feeling? How's your therapy?"

"I'm fine, therapy is progressing. You needn't worry. I'm safe."

He didn't know that. He would never make that assumption again. "Do you need anything?"

"My needs are well cared for," she assured him. "How are you? Are you sleeping?"

*Always thinking of others...some things didn't change.* It was now six months since the attack. "How do the doctors feel about your progress?"

"Dante, you need to stop blaming yourself," she admonished gently. "I will be fine. And even if I never operate again, there are plenty more things I can do with my expertise. I am safe and that's what matters—because of you."

No, he was why her life was unrecognizable from before the attack. "If I could go back in time—"

"Stop. Thoughts like that are a useless expenditure of energy. You cannot change what happened, only what happens as we go forward. I refuse to look at my life as cut short. It's simply going to be different. You need to get to that place as well."

"He won't stop until I return to the fold, and I refuse to do that."

"You will find a way to beat him at his game and when you do, you must promise me that you'll get on with your life."

Her belief in him only stung more. Their romantic relationship had died in the attack, but he would never forget what they'd once had.

Still, even at their happiest, Dante had never felt with Belinda the way he felt with Frannie, which only deepened his fear of losing her.

"I've met someone," Belinda shared, surprising Dante with her admission. "I think you would like him."

"Who?"

"My physical therapist. His name is Sven. He's kind and compassionate but very funny. I like how he makes me laugh."

Belinda deserved all the laughter in the world, and if this Sven could give it to her, he had Dante's blessing.

"You don't need to call and check up on me anymore," Belinda said warmly. "I'm well cared for. I will be safe. All I need to know is that you're safe, too."

He couldn't make that promise, and he didn't want to burden her with the information he was struggling with.

"I'm happy for you, Bel," he said, his voice thick with emotion, "I really am. You deserve the best life has to offer."

"So do you."

He wished he could believe that.

"Good night," he murmured.

"Good night, *dolcezza.*"

They clicked off, and Dante spent a good minute staring at his phone, wondering how this all ended.

Did it end with him finally free of his uncle's grip, able to live as he chose?

Or did it end with Lorenzo dragging him back into the fold, yoked to the Santoro family until he died?

He didn't have the answer.

He only knew one thing for sure. He'd do anything to keep Frannie safe—even if it meant walking away from her forever.

# Chapter 14

Frannie's gaze strayed to the lovely lilies, only a little bothered by the mystery. She liked to believe that sometimes nice things happened for no reason. Her brother Fletcher might say that was naive, but she preferred to look at the world with hope in her heart rather than a sour expectation that everyone was out to screw each other.

Although her aunt Jessie was challenging that worldview at the moment.

*No, not going to waste the energy on that woman today,* she vowed, drawing a deep breath, determined to shake off the dark thoughts, but it wasn't easy.

After lunch with her mom, she couldn't stop thinking about what it must've been like for her, knowing her sister had coveted her husband even before discovering this level of betrayal.

What happened to the "girl code"? She couldn't imagine even looking cross-eyed at Darla's soon-to-be husband or, for that matter, her sister's husband (RIP to that amazing man). Even thinking of such a thing made her physically ill.

Was Aunt Jessie a sociopath? Was that genetic? Did it run in families, lurking in the genetic code to pop out when you least expected it, like daisies in a field?

Maybe she ought to read a few books on sociopathy.

Darla blew in like a tornado, sucking up all the oxygen

in the room as usual, her cheeks flushed from the heat and whatever crisis she was running from.

"Please tell me you've started serving liquor from your little café because Lord help me, I need a margarita, heavy pour on the tequila, please!"

It probably wasn't funny, but Darla's theatrics were always amusing. "Sorry, still no liquor license and I don't know that I'll add that to my list of things to do."

"I think you're missing out on an untapped revenue stream. Wine and books always go together. Who doesn't sip on their chardonnay while reading a spicy book at the end of a long day?" Darla quipped as she flopped into a chair with a long-suffering exhalation. She opened her mouth to start again but saw the flowers and stopped, straightening abruptly to gesture at them. "And what the hell is that?"

"Last I checked, flowers," Frannie answered.

"I see that. And from whom? A certain Italian stallion, perhaps?" she asked coyly.

"Um, funny story about that…no. I have no idea who sent them but they sure are pretty. My favorite, too."

Darla's smile faded with confusion. "What do you mean you don't know who sent them? That bouquet looks expensive. People don't just send pricey flowers to strangers out of the goodness of their heart."

Frannie disagreed. "That's not true. I read the other day of someone who received an anonymous donation of $500 to their GoFundMe for medical expenses to help cover cancer treatments."

"That's not apples to apples," Darla said. "Did you post a GoFundMe for flower deliveries to the shop?"

"Of course not," Frannie said with a chuckle. "But someone wanted to do something nice, and I think it's lovely. I mean, maybe it's a condolence for losing my father? Who knows. The universe works in mysterious ways."

"And so do murderers," Darla warned.

"You watch too much true crime."

"So do you, which is why I'm baffled why you aren't freaked out by this. Honestly, it's weird. I think you should throw them away."

Frannie balked. "No way. They're gorgeous and they add a certain something to the lobby. Makes it more inviting."

"Yeah, they're beautiful but honestly, it's kinda creepy if you ask me."

"You worry too much," Frannie said, waving off Darla's paranoia. "So, what's the crisis for today? I'm assuming it's wedding-related?"

Darla scowled, not ready to let it go. "What does Fletcher or Max think about these mystery flowers? Or Dante for that matter?"

"I didn't tell Max or Fletcher. They have busy lives doing their actual jobs. I'm not going to clutter up their head-space with something as silly as this. That'd be like calling 911 because you got a sliver. It's just flowers. No big deal. As for Dante, well, he was a little jealous, actually. It was kinda hot to see him get all riled up but then, once he realized the flowers weren't from another date, he got kinda quiet, maybe even a little protective? It was really sweet."

"Yeah, because he knows it's weird, too."

Frannie shrugged, ready to be finished with this conversation. Why everyone wanted to make a federal case out of a rogue delivery was beyond her. The world had bigger problems."

"So you're really not going to chase this down and figure out who sent them?"

"I tried. It was called in using an internet web service

for flower delivery but there was no way to trace who made the purchase unless I wanted to have a forensic accountant come in and request the company's purchase logs. Which, honestly, isn't going to happen with the very little information I have. It's not like there was a threatening note or anything attached to the delivery. It was just the flowers and I love them, whether they were mistakenly sent to me or sent to me by someone who just thought I'd benefit from a little cheer in my life."

At that, Darla softened. "Your family has been served up a terrible hand as of late. I'm sorry. My head's been so full of wedding stuff that I haven't been a great friend when you need it. Is there anything I can do?"

Frannie appreciated Darla's offer, but there was nothing anyone could do but ride out the storm. "No, everything's in the lawyer's hands right now. I talked with my mom yesterday, and that's pretty much her attitude and while it sucks, she's right. My aunt isn't going to suddenly grow a conscience overnight, so we'll have to trust our lawyers know their stuff. Can you believe she's going around town saying she was more of a wife to my dad than my mother, his *wife*?"

Darla grimaced. "She's got a brass set of balls on her, that's for sure. Your mom is practically a saint."

"I wouldn't go that far but compared to my aunt Jessie, yeah, she's definitely leagues ahead on the 'decent person' track." Frannie sighed, hating the entire mess. "But it is what it is, I guess."

"You're a better person than me. I would be tearing every strand of hair from the woman's head before we even stepped foot in court. That reminds me, I ought to make sure Tom knows that if he cheats on me, I'll turn him from a rooster to a hen real quick and then I'll redecorate his prized truck with my keys."

"All of that is illegal," Frannie reminded Darla with barely suppressed laughter, "but I approve."

Darla jumped to her feet, helping herself to a bottled water from the fridge. "Okay, so enough about that, tell me about your man."

"He's not my man," Frannie corrected her with a subtle blush. "We're keeping it casual."

"Ha! You don't do casual."

"Well, I'm trying something new."

"Good luck with that. Well, how's it working out?"

Frannie pursed her lips, admitting, "Confusing."

"Go on."

"Well, I really want to ask him to go to the lake with me, but I don't know if that's overstepping our boundaries in this whole casual setup because when I'm with him, it doesn't feel casual at all."

"What does it feel like?"

*Dreamy. Perfect. Exciting. Passionate.* "Um, well, it's good."

"Good?"

"Better than good, amazing."

"And he feels the same?"

"I think so?"

Darla frowned. "You don't know?"

"He's hard to read. Sometimes I feel like we're totally on the same page and then the next, I feel he's shutting me out and keeping me at a distance."

"The dreaded hot/cold dance. Hate to break it to you but that's not a good sign."

"What do you mean?"

Darla's expression didn't bode well as she explained, "That's guy code for, 'I'm just not that into you, but you'll do for now.' I should've known he would be a player. He's international, for crying out loud. Too sophisticated, too handsome, too 'not Owl Creek' material, you know what I'm saying?"

Those were precisely the reasons Frannie adored him. "I think he's been hurt in the past. He doesn't like to talk about his past relationship."

"Another red flag."

"Darla, people can have things they aren't comfortable talking about. Doesn't make them red flags."

"You've had sex, right?"

Frannie blushed. "Yeah." *Multiple times—and each time was better than the last.*

"If he's truly not a player, by this point, he should be able to share some intimate details about his life before you. It's not asking too much. If anything, you're not asking enough."

Frannie digested that advice. Was it true? Was she being too accommodating and ignoring her own needs? She wanted to know more about Dante, even if he wasn't interested or available to stick around; she wanted to learn more about him as a person.

"So I should ask him to the lake this weekend?"

"Hell yeah, and his answer will go a long way toward showing you who he is as a man."

What if he turned her down? Was she ready to walk away from Dante if it turned out he was exactly as Darla feared?

Better to know now than later.

Because at this rate? She was going to fall head over heels in love with the man.

If she hadn't already.

Frannie was coming over tonight. She'd called about an hour ago, asking if he wouldn't mind some company, and while he should've made some excuse and declined, he couldn't stop his mouth from saying yes.

He rationalized that she was safer in his house with him than anywhere else, but it was a flimsy attempt at justifying his actions.

*Just say it,* a voice taunted. *You can't stop thinking about her, and you'll take any opportunity to be with her.*

Even if doing so put her in danger.

He growled under his breath, irritated at the useless circular nature of his thoughts. Striding to the kitchen as if he could outrun the guilt on his heels, he turned his attention to putting together a quick dinner.

He enjoyed cooking for Frannie. For one, she was open to trying anything—even though she was lactose intolerant and should avoid dairy—and truly loved his efforts. It was as if everything they did together fit like they were made for each other. He didn't consider himself a great romantic, but since meeting Frannie, he understood why poets created sonnets, even if he'd never have that level of talent.

Plus, there was something sensual about cooking for someone he cared for—the level of intimacy was something he'd never experienced before.

Belinda had been too busy with her work to spend too much time in the kitchen. They'd always eaten separately or ordered in, but at least their kitchen was always immaculate.

Mainly because they were rarely home at the same time.

Looking back, it was easy to see how they'd become affectionate roommates who'd occasionally passed each other in the night, enjoyed a smooch or two, and then went about their routine as usual.

It'd been a comfortable routine but lacking a certain level of passion that he hadn't realized he needed.

Until Frannie.

The attack had irrevocably changed their relationship, but now he realized their romantic life had died long before.

A knock at the front door told him Frannie had arrived. He wiped his hands and put the eggplant lasagna into the oven. He'd even made it with dairy-free cheese, though they'd have to wait and see if it turned out as good as the original recipe.

If it bombed, he had a mini dairy-free charcuterie board waiting in the refrigerator.

When he opened the door, Frannie smiled, holding up a bottle of wine. "I brought the beverage," she announced, lifting on her tiptoes to kiss him as if he were her favorite person.

His chest warmed and his groin tightened, and he was immediately tempted to scoop her into his arms and carry her to the bedroom for a little loving before dinner, but he restrained himself and accepted the wine with an appraising smile. "Ahhh, let's get this chilled so it's ready by dinner."

"You're the chef," Frannie said as she sank into the sofa with a happy sigh. "Have I mentioned how I love this sofa? I'm having sofa envy. It's so much better than the one I have. But to be fair, I did purchase it at a thrift store, and it may have enjoyed a full life in a frat house prior to moving in with me. Not that you would know that because you've never actually been to my house."

"Well, now that you've revealed that your sofa might've been involved in college adventures, I'm not sure that's a glowing endorsement."

"It does kinda smell, too," she grimaced. "But think of the character it has. The stories it could tell."

He grinned. "You're unlike anyone I've ever known."

"You're not the first person to say that," she said with cheek. God, she was beautiful.

He drew in a short breath, feeling as if his chest were being compressed, resisting the urge to tell her everything about his past, his family, and the trouble that was no doubt following him, but he bit down on his tongue and went to the kitchen to chill the wine.

When he returned, she patted the seat beside her. She didn't need to—it wasn't as if there were any other place he'd rather be. Dante slid in next to her, catching a whiff of her shampoo and the lingering scent of her coconut lotion, and he almost forgot why it was wise to keep things casual between them.

"So, I was thinking…how'd you like to spend a day on the lake with me this weekend? I could pack a picnic and show you some of the secret spots that the locals enjoy. We could rent a canoe and paddle to a secluded beach to each lunch."

A secluded beach? On the surface, the offer sounded terrific, but immediately he thought of all the ways that would make them vulnerable to attack if, by some chance, his uncle's men were watching and waiting for the best moment to strike, and his enthusiasm faded.

*Make an excuse, say you already have plans.*

It was the smart play, but he saw something in her eyes that told him saying yes was far more important than following his good sense, and he didn't dare risk turning her down.

The stakes felt so much higher than a simple outing together.

As if their future somehow rode on what fell from his mouth at that moment.

"Sounds like a perfect day," he finally answered, unprepared for how she squealed and climbed into his arms as if he'd just agreed to cosign a loan for her. "Whoa! Wild girl," he chuckled, holding her close.

"I'm so glad you said yes," she admitted, sealing her mouth to his. "We're going to have a great day on the lake!"

"Any day with you is already the best," he murmured against her lips.

He just hoped no nasty surprises were waiting for them.

# Chapter 15

Frannie's heart was filled with sunshine as they slid the rented canoe into the water at the launch point. The weather was incredible, the skies blue without a cloud in sight, and she was excited to show Dante a piece of her hometown that felt personal.

"Summer days spent on Blackbird Lake were an important part of my childhood growing up in Owl Creek," she shared, hopping into the canoe and dipping her paddle in, encouraging Dante to do the same. "We're going to paddle away from the congested areas and head over to my favorite beach. You're going to love it."

"Are you trying to get me in a private place so you can have your way with me?" he teased.

She tossed him a mischievous look from behind her shoulder. "You should be so lucky."

He laughed at her sass, and they continued paddling. Soon enough, they were away from the tourist-friendly areas and heading down a calm channel where the water was barely waist-deep but crystal clear.

"So, this stretch of the river goes on for about three miles and because of the gentle current, it's great for canoeing or paddle boards. During the summer my mom and Uncle Buck used to rent paddle boards for all of us and we'd spend the entire day on the water. Some of my best memories were made on this lake. Sometimes we even got to see a moose on the shore. Of course, we left the moose alone because we valued our lives but one time my brother Fletcher got the bright idea to try and get closer. Thankfully, Uncle Buck didn't let him follow through with that idea. Otherwise, I might've been less one brother."

Dante chuckled. "Young boys often need someone smarter than them to keep them alive." But he realized she'd mentioned an uncle and not her father. "Your father didn't accompany you on these lake days?"

"My dad was always too busy. I don't think he enjoyed all the ruckus created by the kids. He was happy to let my uncle Buck handle the heavy lifting. Plus, now that I look back on the memories, I think my mom and Uncle Buck got along a lot better. I don't remember them bickering at all."

"They were close?"

"Yeah, they became close after my aunt Jessie bailed on the family and left Uncle Buck with the kids to raise." Frannie frowned. "I don't know my new alleged siblings but I kinda feel bad for them having to grow up with Aunt Jessie. At least with my other cousins, they were raised by Uncle Buck, and they had pretty good childhoods."

"Your aunt Jessie is unkind?"

Frannie lifted her shoulders, admitting, "I don't know her, but first impressions go a long way. She's kinda awful. I mean, maybe I'm biased because of what she's doing to my family right now, but she has this hard, jaded way about her that doesn't seem real conducive to being a loving parent."

"And your father was the same?"

"Um, he wasn't hard, per se, more like, disinterested. He always had other things to occupy his time. My dad was like a stereotypical fifties-era man—he expected his wife to keep the house and children while he made the money.

I don't think I ever saw my father lift a finger to clean the house, ever, and he sure as hell never cooked a meal for us. My mom did all of that and worked a full-time job. God, the more I think about it, she must've been exhausted. I need to cut my mom some slack."

"It's similar in Italy in many ways. Many traditionalists. For the record, I don't feel that way. I don't agree that the work of a household should be so unevenly split. My father and mother often cooked together. It's one of my favorite memories of when he was alive. They cooked with joy and love and perhaps it's in my head, but I always remember it tasting amazing."

"I think that's a beautiful thing to remember," Frannie said. "So, no brothers or sisters for you?"

"No, it was just me. My mother never remarried after my father's death. So it remained she and I."

"I can't even imagine being an only child, although sometimes I think I wished for it when things were total chaos around my house."

"I always wanted a sibling. Being an only child can be lonely."

"Makes sense. *Lonely* was never a word in my vocabulary. *Irritated, annoyed, frustrated*—definitely in the lexicon—but *lonely*? Nope."

His low rumble of laughter felt like sunshine on her soul.

"Oh! Look over there!" Frannie pointed to the shore on their left. "There's a deer. I know it's common, but I still get excited when I see them. My brothers used to make fun of me every time I got excited to see a deer. They said it was like getting excited to see a potato at the grocery store."

He laughed. "Depending on how hungry you are, the sight of a potato would be very exciting," he said.

"Ha! That's true. I wish I'd had the wherewithal to think of that comeback when I was a kid."

"I'm fairly certain I have the cutest tour guide in all of Idaho," he said, earning a blush from Frannie. "I love that you get excited about things that most people would take for granted. That's a gift."

She didn't know about that, but she felt warm whenever Dante complimented her over random stuff that most people never noticed about her. Dante made her feel seen, as if she'd been overlooked by those who should've been paying attention her entire life.

*Girl, you're falling in love with him.*

Frannie swallowed, knowing it was true. She couldn't seem to help herself. Everything about Dante was addictive. His smile, his touch, his voice—she couldn't picture anyone else as intoxicating.

*Stop. You don't know anything about him. He could be an international felon.*

That was why this day was so important. Today, she'd get to know more about the man.

And he agreed to come, right? That was a good sign. Besides, she wouldn't let anything ruin their beautiful day, not when it was already so amazing. It was possible Dante was very private and didn't enjoy oversharing. Once he realized his past was safe with her, he'd open up—she just knew it.

She saw her favorite beach coming up and gestured for him to paddle in that direction. Within minutes the bottom of their boat dragged through sand, and they hopped out to pull it further from the water so that the lazy waves didn't send the boat floating downstream. Swimming after a retreating boat was an experience she didn't want to repeat from her childhood.

Dante grabbed the picnic basket Frannie had prepared

while she scooped up the blanket and walked up the beach to a shady spot.

"It's not the Italian coast but I think it's pretty damn spectacular," Frannie said with pride as she carefully laid out the blanket and sat down to kick off her water shoes so her toes could dig in the warm sand. Golden sunlight glistened off the water's surface, glinting as if winking to the sky, and the gentle lap of the waves along the shoreline was a soothing sound that never failed to make her smile. If a happy place existed, it was here.

Dante sat beside her, agreeing heartily. "You do not disappoint. It's stunning."

His joy made her happy. She wished she could bottle up this feeling and moment to enjoy it forever.

A flicker of sadness threatened to dampen her joy as her mother inexplicably popped into her head. Knowing what she knew now about Jenny's past made Frannie wonder if there was ever a moment when Jenny experienced that giddy kind of love.

Somehow, she doubted Jenny and Robert had ever been madly in love. Small towns had a way of pushing people together for whatever reasons, but when those reasons expired or lost their luster, circumstances and reasons less than love kept them together. In some situations, obligation, expectation and habit were iron chains around people's necks.

With a frown, Dante caught her subtle shift and asked, "Is everything okay?"

"Oh, I'm fine." She waved away his concern, a little embarrassed to be a Debbie Downer when everything thus far had been perfect. Opening the picnic basket, she said, "I hope you like ham and turkey because that's what I packed. I even packed a few cheeses for you."

"I like whatever you thought to make."

"Stop being so perfect," she teased, leaning over for a quick kiss.

"I hate to disappoint but I'm far from perfect," he warned with a rueful chuckle.

"Hard to tell from this angle," she said, popping open the basket and pulling out the wrapped sandwiches. "Seriously, I think I'm going to need you to share some of your less desirable traits so I know you're human."

The subtle quirk of a grin was adorable, but it didn't escape her notice that he deliberately shied away from the topic. She tried a little harder. "I mean, you can't be perfect, no one is, but at least tell me something that makes you less intimidating. You're devastatingly handsome, an attentive lover, you can cook like a master chef, and you love books. I've never had self-esteem issues, but when I look at you, suddenly, insecurities start popping up like daisies in a field. Help a girl out."

"You're amazing in every way. You should never question your value, no matter who you're seeing."

"Of course, I'm just…okay, so I guess I'll stop beating around the bush and trying to be clever… I want to know more about you. What I can see is nothing short of amazing, but I need to know more. More than just the surface stuff." She traced her finger along his jaw, gazing into his eyes to ask in a throaty murmur, "Who is Dante Sinclair? Who is the real you?"

Dante froze. The urge to pull away nearly ruined everything good about his day. He wanted to be honest, but he couldn't. She wasn't asking anything out of the ordinary. She had every right to know whom she was sleeping next to, but it was the very thing he couldn't give her.

For her own good.

Swallowing, he forced a smile, gently grasping her hand and pressing a kiss to her palm, prepared to lie through his teeth. "Sweet Frannie, you make me sound more interesting than I really am. I'm just a regular guy who got tired of the same scenery and wanted a change. I didn't want to go to the usual touristy places like New York or California. I wanted something off the beaten path so I could rest and recharge. Owl Creek has been exactly as I hoped it would be—even better, I found you—making the trip unforgettable. What more could I ask for?"

Frannie smiled at the praise, but he could see that she wasn't entirely satisfied. The woman was smart. She sensed he was holding back, and the longer he danced around simple questions about his life, the more suspicious she would become.

He'd have to give her something to chew on, or she'd keep digging—and he couldn't afford her curiosity.

"Okay, you want something material…something personal…" At her small nod, Dante straightened and shared. "Well, the reason I needed a change in scenery is a little cliché. I'm a little embarrassed to admit that my last breakup was a bit intense, and it threw me for a loop. I couldn't function without bumping into memories from the past, and I thought the best way to heal and regroup would be to go on an extended vacation. My work is such that I can telecommute for most of it, so I decided to pack up and go find myself."

The way Frannie melted at his admission made him feel like a toad. He supposed it wasn't entirely a lie—he and Belinda had broken up—but after he'd had to spirit her out of the country for her own safety, they decided it would be best for them to go their separate ways. *Being attacked and left for dead by your boyfriend's uncle tended to destroy the romance in a relationship.*

"I had a bad breakup, too, so I totally understand the desire to pack up and run away. If I hadn't had the shop, I probably would've skipped town, too," Frannie conceded. "In the end, I didn't want him to have the satisfaction of seeing me break, so I toughed it out. But I feel like there's no wrong way to heal from emotional pain. We need to give ourselves permission to do what our minds and bodies need without feeling judged by everyone else."

*God love this woman for her kindness and compassion.* Even if he didn't deserve it. "Are you healed now?"

"I'm definitely on the right path. Relationships, good or bad, always leave a mark. I think that's what people mean by 'baggage' from previous relationships because we take a little piece of that relationship and bring it with us when we meet someone new."

"Was he a good man, this past boyfriend?" he asked, curious. "He wasn't abusive or anything like that?"

"Bobby? Oh gosh, no, just a cheater. I mean, that's pretty bad but in the grand scheme of things, not something I can't get over. Shortly after it all went down, I read something that helped put things in perspective. It was a book on healing emotional trauma. I read this part that said, 'People's actions say more about themselves than what they say about you,' and I realized Bobby's decision to cheat on me was a defect in his character, not mine."

"Very wise."

"Well, it resonated, and it really did help put things in their proper place."

"I'm sorry he hurt you."

Frannie sighed, remembering. "Yeah, I was heartbroken when I found out. Embarrassed, too. Felt like the whole town knew and was whispering about it behind my back.

Small towns are big on gossip and when someone's running around on another person, it's just too juicy to pass up."

"How did you discover he was unfaithful?"

Frannie drew a deep breath, wincing as if it hurt to remember. "I found text messages. And pictures. The evidence was pretty incriminating. He didn't try to deny it, and I was glad. I can't say I wouldn't have punched him in the mouth for lying. Growing up with a big family taught me how to throw a good hook. But, like I said, he didn't deny it. I think he was relieved, actually."

"Relieved?"

"Living a lie takes a lot of energy. Once the cat was out of the bag, he didn't have to pretend anymore."

Dante identified with that statement far more than he would've liked. The burden of a sustained lie was heavier than most people realized. Still, he felt no sympathy for this Bobby character. "He lost you. He got what he deserved."

Frannie smiled, seeming to appreciate his compliment. He'd shower her with sweetness every day if it were up to him because she deserved nothing less. She cozied up to him. "Well, sounds like whoever broke your heart got the worst end of the deal because you're amazing, and I don't like to share."

If only that were true. He'd do anything to go back in time and make a different choice, to believe how dangerous his uncle was instead of blowing off his threats. Belinda had deserved far better than she had received. *You deserve to be happy, too.* Belinda's words echoed in his head, but he couldn't take them to heart, just like when Belinda said them. He shook off the dark thoughts and directed attention to their lunch. "All that paddling worked up an appetite… Let's eat."

"Oh, right!" Frannie laughed, good mood returning.

"You'll love this bread. I buy it from the local bakery, and they make it fresh every day. It's my guilty pleasure."

Dante took a bite, appreciating the flavors. "Reminds me of home," he admitted. "In Italy, most everyone buys their bread, fruits and vegetables at the outdoor market for the day. Fresh bread should never be a guilty pleasure, *dolcezza.*"

"*Dolcezza*, what does it mean?"

"It's a term of endearment, such as sweetheart," he explained.

"I like it," she said, leaning toward him. "I like it a lot."

Lunch temporarily forgotten, Dante curled his hand behind her neck and drew her in, sealing their mouths together. She tasted like the promise of a new day with a sweetness no chocolate could ever hope to possess. He didn't deserve any of her love, her compassion or her goodness, but he selfishly craved it.

The kiss deepened, Dante needing to feel Frannie all around him. He didn't care that they were in broad daylight, that anyone could happen upon them and gawk. When he touched Frannie, the world melted away, and it was only the two of them in a tight, safe cocoon.

In those precious moments, he was far from the reality that his uncle would stop at nothing to bring him back to the family. That he held a ticking time bomb in a safe-deposit box and that his uncle would do anything to prevent the ruin of the family.

Nowhere was truly safe. His uncle had the money to chase Dante around the globe, and eventually, he would find him.

But in this stolen moment—it was only he and Frannie. And he greedily enjoyed every second as if it were his last.

Because it very well could be.

# Chapter 16

Frannie was floating on a cloud. The day couldn't have been more perfect if she'd dreamed it up with the power of a fairy godmother. She'd convinced Dante to come to her place for dinner, which was a massive win because he usually talked her into going to his place.

"You have to promise me that you won't judge my collection of knickknacks," she said, unlocking the front door. "I have a thing for collectible plates. I blame my grandmother for the obsession. She bought my first collectible plate when she vacationed in the Netherlands and the tradition stuck."

Dante smiled. "Have you ever been to the Netherlands?"

"Nope. I've never been outside of the United States, but I do have my passport just in case the opportunity presents itself."

Frannie had always wanted to travel, but she was embarrassed to admit that she was intimidated by the idea of traveling too far from home. It was a fear she hoped to conquer at some point in her life, but when she purchased the shop, her opportunities became limited.

Too limited to traipse along the countryside.

So, she purchased plates instead.

Frannie deposited her keys in the ceramic bowl by the door. "Have you been to the Netherlands?" she asked Dante.

"Not yet."

His answer sent shivers tripping down her back like he'd said he would take her to the Netherlands if she wanted to go. It was silly to think that because he hadn't said anything, but she'd felt like he had.

She was overthinking things.

"How about a quick tour?" she asked, shaking off the dizzying thoughts that served no purpose. Her mother had always said she had her head in the clouds most days and lived in a fantasyland. Probably why she loved books. "Again, no comments on the choice. I call it 'boho chic with a touch of French gothic' but my sister Ruby calls it 'thrift store chaos.'"

Afterward, Dante laughed but nodded, saying, "It suits you—and it's perfect."

"I don't know if I should be flattered or insulted," she said as he pulled her into his arms. "But I'll go with flattered for the sake of my ego."

"What's not to love? It's carefree, cozy and inviting—all good things in my book," he said, walking her backward to her bedroom, which was a short walk from the living room because her house was the size of a postage stamp. He brushed a kiss across her lips. "You know what's the best part about your place?"

She gazed up at him. "The antique claw-foot tub?"

"It's nice but no."

"What then? The suspense is killing me."

The back of her legs bumped against her bed. Dante gave her a tiny push, sending her falling back to land on the soft comforter as he followed, towering over her. "It smells like you—and I love the way you smell," he finally answered before descending for another kiss, searing her lips with the passion that bubbled between them.

Frannie wound her arms around his neck, drawing him closer, loving the way he devoured her from head to toe. When Dante made love, he made her pleasure his sole purpose. She'd never known a man so utterly consumed with his goal, and she was completely addicted.

Dante's weight pressed against her as his big hands cupped her face tenderly as if she were precious to him. *Don't you dare fall in love with him*, the voice warned, but she knew it was a pointless demand because she was falling fast.

Like being dropped from the moon and free-falling to the earth.

What they were doing felt the opposite of casual, but what did she know about being in a "situationship," as her younger cousins called it? Nothing. She was a one-guy kind of girl. And she wanted to be Dante's girl.

*Don't ruin the moment, go with the flow.*

"Dante…are you hungry?" she asked breathlessly as Dante lifted her shirt up and off, wasting no time nibbling along her shoulder blade, traveling up her neck. "I could… make some…pancakes."

"All I want is you," he said, pulling his shirt off and tossing it to the floor. He started to unbuckle her pants, but his gaze caught on something, and he stopped to stare with a subtle frown.

Frannie, her lips still tingling, propped herself up on her elbows, confused by his sudden change in demeanor. *Was it the mention of pancakes?* "Are you okay? What's wrong?"

He reached past her to pluck a single lily from the opposite pillow. The same type of lily that'd been delivered to her shop.

Frannie startled, staring as she scrambled to sit up, more confused than ever. "Where'd that come from?"

"It was on your pillow. Who put it there?" he asked.

"I don't know," she answered, biting her lip, bewildered. "I...honestly have no clue."

This felt different than a random delivery to her shop. She hated to admit it, but it gave her a creepy vibe. Someone had entered her house while she was gone and deliberately placed that lily on her pillow. She swallowed, feeling very exposed.

"You are positive no one you know could've left this flower for you?" he asked in a quiet yet hard tone.

She swallowed. "Dante, I swear I have no idea where that lily came from."

Dante swung away and scooped up his shirt, dressing quickly as he went to the window to check for signs of entry. Frannie grabbed her shirt, unsure of his reaction. Was this jealousy? Mistrust? Or was he concerned that someone was stalking her? "You're not staying here," he decided, pointing to her closet. "Gather your things. We're leaving."

Frannie needed a minute to think. Her heart was thundering in her chest, but she refused to be chased out of her home over something that might have a logical explanation. "I don't want to sound like the dumb girl in the movie that gets killed, but I don't want to rush to conclusions either. Let's calm down and think for a minute."

"There's nothing to think about. You're not staying."

That authoritative tone reminded her too much of her father, and she bristled. "No, I need a minute to think. I'm sure there's a logical reason... I need to find it."

Dante was about ready to ignore Frannie's protests, toss her over his shoulder and physically carry her to the car, but he restrained himself, realizing that the harder he pushed, the more she'd dig her heels in.

She didn't know how much danger she could be in, and he couldn't tell her.

How could he convince her to leave when he couldn't be honest about his circumstances?

Sweat beaded his brow. *Okay, think.* Frannie wanted logic. He'd give it to her. Throttling down his fear, he tried a different tactic. "It could be something innocent, but don't you think it's better to err on the side of caution than assuming it's nothing? What if you're wrong? What's one night? How about this…come back to my place for the night, we'll order a pizza, watch some TV, and tomorrow you can run it by your brother to see how he feels about it. If he feels it's nothing to worry about…well, maybe you're right."

"Fletcher is a cop, so maybe that's not a terrible idea, if only to create a paper trail," Frannie conceded, thinking it through. Still, she seemed undecided. "But on the surface, a pretty flower doesn't seem all that threatening. It's not like it was a bloody horse head or anything like that."

Dante wanted to shake her head off her shoulders. Her place felt compromised, and every moment they remained felt like a minute closer to his uncle's hired men showing up for an unpleasant interaction. He tried again, using a different tactic.

"Someone entered your house when you weren't home and left that flower on your pillow. An anonymous person paid for the flowers to be delivered to your shop, which was suspicious enough, but now the flower in your home? You can't see how that's something to be concerned about?"

He was pressing a little harder, desperate to get her to a safe place. Not that he knew his place was any safer, but he doubted Frannie would let him put her on a plane to Switzerland to hang out with his ex-girlfriend, the last victim of his uncle's revenge.

Frannie wavered. "It's weird," she admitted.

"Yes," he agreed, holding his breath with the hope that she was close to seeing his way of things. "If you're wrong, and someone left you this flower as a warning, I can't fathom not doing something about it. Frannie, please. I care about you."

"I know you do, and I appreciate the concern. I'm just worried about making a big deal about nothing. My family has enough to worry about without me crying wolf over strange flower deliveries. Even saying it out loud makes me cringe. Who gets scared over a beautiful flower?"

"If the message, 'I'm going to kill you,' is delivered in calligraphy does it make it any less threatening?"

Frannie blinked at the change in perspective, biting her lip with apprehension. "Oh, that's a good point. I hadn't thought of it that way. When you put it like that, it's very creepy."

Relief flooded him when he sensed he was finally winning the argument. "Can I help you pack?"

Frannie chuckled with discomfort. "It's just overnight, Dante. I'm not moving in."

He smiled, acknowledging her point. "Good. Five minutes? We can pick up the pizza on the way."

He pretended to be switching gears, excited about pizza, but he knew everything would taste like cardboard. His head was swimming with upsetting possibilities, and he felt pressed on all sides by potential danger.

Frannie reappeared with a small overnight bag, and he relieved her of the burden as he walked to the front door. He tossed her bag into the back seat and opened her door, his gaze scanning the surrounding area, looking for anything unusual. Frannie's tiny house wasn't tucked away in the mountains like his place, but the older neighborhood wasn't heavily populated either. A lot of For Sale signs in yards, which he hadn't noticed before. Vacant houses were excellent places to hide for people who didn't want to be seen.

"I didn't realize there were so many empty houses on your street," he said.

She sighed, looking out the window as they drove by. "Yeah, the economy isn't what it used to be and if you're not in the tourist trade, there isn't a lot of opportunity. I wish the city would come up with some kind of incentive to keep locals here, but I suppose their hands are tied, too. The piece of the pie is only so big."

Dante nodded, pretending to be invested in the plight of the local economy, but his mind was elsewhere, moving at the speed of light, processing possibilities, second-guessing every little thing.

God, he wanted to tell Frannie the damn truth!

If he could level with Frannie, she might understand why he was agitated about a seemingly odd but maybe innocent flower mishap.

But c'mon, a flower deliberately placed on her pillow? That screamed malice.

"You know what? I just thought of a wild idea," he said, catching her attention. "What if we got out of town for a few days? Maybe find a cozy cabin near the lake or even head to the city, get dressed up and hit the town? I'd love a chance to pamper the prettiest woman in Owl Creek. Hell, possibly prettiest in the whole state."

"You're laying it on a little thick, but I like it," Frannie teased. But she shook her head, saying, "As much as I love that idea, I can't leave the shop."

"You're the owner, you can make the rules, *dolcezza*," he reminded her.

"Yeah, but not sticking to my own rules...that's how a

business fails. I know my dad wasn't great at the whole father gig, but he was a solid businessman. One of the things he shared with me when I opened the shop was not to fall into the trap of thinking I'm above the rules just because I pay the mortgage."

It was solid advice—but Dante didn't care about that. He wanted Frannie somewhere safe and getting out of town for a few days would give him time to determine if his uncle had people in town. "Sure, that's excellent advice, and I agree. But there's also something to be said for knowing when to enjoy the fruits of your labor. I've seen how hard you work. You deserve a little pampering."

Frannie laughed but otherwise let the offer die, and he took the hint. If he kept pushing, it would cease to be romantic and turn into something weird, which would only backfire.

"All right, I can see you're not on board, I understand," he said with a short smile. "Should we order the pizza to go, or do you want to eat in the restaurant?"

"Oh, to go. I'll go ahead and order so it's ready when we get there," she said, grabbing her cell phone from her purse.

As Dante listened to her order while he drove, sneaking covert looks her way, he could tell she'd already written the flower incident off as weird but harmless, which worried him. He couldn't blame her, though. Before Belinda's attack, he'd been confident he could handle whatever his uncle threw at him, but he'd been wrong.

Fifteen minutes later, they were pulling into the parking lot. "My treat," she told him when he started to exit the vehicle. "I was going to make dinner tonight, remember?"

He grinned, accepting the offer only because it seemed he'd have a moment of privacy while she grabbed the pizza. Frannie smiled and left, giving him a lovely view of her perfect backside that, if he hadn't been riddled with anxiety, he would've appropriately appreciated.

Once she was inside, he picked up his cell phone and dialed his private investigator. When it went straight to voice mail, he left a message. "I have reason to believe my uncle's associates have followed me to Owl Creek. I need you to find out if my location has been compromised. ASAP. No matter the hour, let me know what you find out."

He clicked off just as Frannie reappeared carrying the pizza. He smiled as she climbed into the car. "Smells amazing," he said.

"Tonight, I'm going to splurge," she announced. "I have special lactase enzymes in my purse and I'm going to enjoy a slice or two of this gooey, cheesy pizza. There's only one thing…"

"Which is?"

"Sometimes they make me gassy," she admitted with a short, embarrassed laugh, shrugging as she added, "You know what they say…gorgeous, gorgeous girls have stomach issues."

He laughed, momentarily forgetting about the looming danger. He leaned over to plant a hearty kiss on her perfect lips. "If that's the deal, I think I can handle the terms."

At that, Frannie barked another laugh as if he didn't know what he'd just agreed to, and he realized that she was the kind of woman he'd be lucky to call his.

Except he had no business dreaming of a future with Frannie…or anyone.

## Chapter 17

Even as Frannie had been determined to downplay the flower incident, her private thoughts were in turmoil. She didn't want anyone to worry unnecessarily over something that seemed silly, but Dante had planted a seed of doubt that was quickly germinating.

As she lay beside Dante, her head resting on his chest, it should've been easy to push aside anything unpleasant, but tonight her anxiety was determined to needle her brain, making restful sleep—or sleep at all—impossible.

Usually, when she had difficulty sleeping, a little fresh air helped. Careful not to disturb Dante, she rose from the bed, grabbed a bottled water from the kitchen, and quietly stepped outside to the front porch.

Sighing, Frannie sank into one of the two porch chairs and enjoyed the starry sky with the night sounds all around her. Owl Creek might not be a mecca of modern convenience—no fast-food places or chain restaurants—but there was something special about being nestled in the heart of nature.

Drawing a deep breath, she closed her eyes and let the cool night air caress her nude skin. The best part about Dante's place was that no one was around for miles, so only the wildlife saw her naked on the front porch.

Hannah always accused her of being a closet nudist because she'd always been running around the house with as little clothing as possible, and if they all went swimming in the creek in the middle of the night, Frannie was the first to shuck all her clothes and jump in naked as the day she was born.

The memory curved her lips in a smile.

Then, there were her wild college days, of course. But that was what college was for—making a few mistakes, poor judgment calls, and memories.

Well, that and getting an education.

A subtle frown pulled her brows as she recalled a name she hadn't thought of in a long while. *Allen Burns.* He'd had a mad crush on her, but she'd only seen him as a friend. That'd been an awkward conversation when she'd had to set him straight.

She winced at the memory.

Poor Allen. So shy with the girls. Had he ever figured out the social dance steps required to find a partner?

Frannie always found it interesting that even as evolved as humans were, they were still animals and programmed to respond to certain mating rituals.

Allen hadn't been very good at discerning social cues, which made people shy away from him, but that was why Frannie had gone out of her way to befriend him.

Why had Allen popped into her head when she hadn't seen him in years?

The door opened, startling her. When she saw it was Dante, and he was holding a blanket, she smiled. "Sorry, did I wake you?"

"It's not your fault. I'm a light sleeper," he said, draping the blanket around her shoulders. His constant chivalry tickled her, but the fact that he did things out of concern for her comfort struck a chord deep inside. "Are you okay?" he asked.

"When I can't sleep, I like to go outside for some fresh air and the fact that I can come outside naked is a huge plus. I can't exactly do that at my place."

"Yes, even with all of the empty houses, it probably isn't a good idea," he said, amused.

"Thank you for the blanket," she said, patting the seat beside her. "Sit with me a minute?"

"Sure," he said, settling into the chair. "Why can't you sleep? Is there anything I can do?"

The subtle suggestion in his tone made her blush, but she playfully tapped him on the thigh. "Dante, you dirty boy," she admonished with a laugh. "No, I just needed Mother Nature, and you have the best view."

He agreed. "I was lucky to find this place. It's been exactly what I was looking for. It'll be hard to leave."

Frannie fell quiet, hating any mention of Dante leaving, but she supposed it was healthy to acknowledge that he wasn't planning to relocate to Owl Creek soon. "Do you miss home?"

Dante considered her question, finally answering, "Italy is a beautiful place but lately, I've been asking myself if I want to stay there."

Hope dared to flicker in her heart. "You're open to relocating?"

He hesitated, as if realizing he'd stumbled onto a subject he wasn't ready to talk about, but he offered a noncommittal "Well, I suppose anything is possible," before dropping it.

Frannie took the hint, but she'd be a liar if it didn't hurt. She wanted an open and honest conversation about their feelings for each other, but she was afraid of pushing against an established boundary and losing him altogether.

She winced internally—that sounded pathetic even in the confines of her head. She should be able to be honest. Without honesty, there was nothing. Why shouldn't she be able to come out and say, 'Dante, I have feelings for you. No, actually, I think I'm falling in love with you. And I need to know if you feel the same.'

But she couldn't get the words out of her mouth. Instead, she grabbed her bottled water and took a long swig before sharing, "So, a name popped into my head while I was sitting out here that I haven't thought of in years—a guy who had a crush on me back in college."

"Why'd you think of him?"

"I think because of the flowers."

Dante frowned. "What's the connection?"

"Maybe nothing but I remember he used to work part-time in the horticulture department. I think he was an Ag major. Sometimes he would bring me fresh flower clippings from the greenhouse. A lot of times, they were lilies. It was sweet."

"Did you date?"

"No, just friends. But he did like me a little more than a friend should," she admitted. "However, I set him straight, telling him that I only felt friendship for him. I didn't want to lead him on."

"How'd he take the news?"

"Um, well, he was hurt, of course, but he didn't freak out or anything," she said.

"Does he live here in Owl Creek?"

"No, we met at Boise State. I don't remember where he originally came from, and we didn't keep in touch," Frannie said with a shrug. "I don't even know why he popped into my head. Probably because he was into flowers. Anyway, random stuff goes through my head at three in the morning." A sudden, welcome yawn cracked her jaw, and she said, "See? Mother Nature is better than any sleeping pill. Ready to go back inside?"

Dante nodded and followed her into the house. Climbing back into bed, she cuddled up to Dante, sighing happily until she realized there was no turning back. She was in love with Dante, and she wanted him to stay.

But did he feel the same?

The following morning Dante rose early to make the coffee and prepare bacon and eggs for breakfast. When he'd woken in the middle of the night and found Frannie gone, his heart had nearly stopped.

When he realized she was sitting outside—naked—on the porch, he'd immediately wanted to drag her back inside. A wave of possessiveness washed over him at the thought of anyone else seeing Frannie's beautiful body, and he realized he had to stop thinking of Frannie as his girlfriend.

Even so, he'd brought her the blanket, though she looked like a wild goddess in the moonlight with her hair loose and the pale light kissing her bare skin.

Frannie appeared, wrapped in his robe, and shuffled to the kitchen, her bleary gaze going straight to the coffee. He quickly poured her a cup and pushed the oat milk toward her that he'd purchased specifically for her in deference to her tummy issues with dairy.

For himself, he enjoyed real cream, which he poured liberally into his morning coffee. "Good morning, beautiful," he said, kissing her cheek as she doctored her coffee. "How'd you sleep?"

"Good," she said, sipping her coffee with a pleased smile. "Perfect."

He chuckled, enjoying how expressive she was about

everything in life. She made a sip of coffee seem like time had stopped, and nothing else mattered but that sip. He loved that about her. He didn't blame her college friend for falling for her—how could anyone resist Frannie Colton?

But given everything behind the scenes, he'd feel better if he looked into the guy.

"I was thinking, just to be on the safe side, I should look into this college guy and see if there's anything to be concerned about."

Frannie waved off his suggestion. "Oh, goodness, Dante, surely you have better things to do than do background checks on guys I haven't seen in ages? Besides, Allen was harmless."

"You're right, it's probably nothing. But I'd feel better if I confirmed that fact."

She seemed to realize he was serious, and sobered. "Dante, are you really that worried?"

"About your friend? I don't know. But I am worried about someone breaking into your house and leaving flowers that you didn't ask for."

"I didn't want it to get into my head because it's nothing serious, but I'm a little unnerved about it."

"As you should be," he agreed, relieved she finally saw things from his point of view. "Look, I know it might seem an overreaction but it's always better to be safe than sorry. And when it comes to your safety, I don't want to take any chances."

She smiled up at him, a vision of sunshine and light, and his heart threatened to jump from his chest and land in her lap. Did she have any idea of the effect she had on him? Never in his life had he ever felt this way about a woman. He was out of his depth. The best he could do was make sure she was safe.

"If it makes you feel better about it, sure, go ahead and look into him. Although, I could probably just have my brother Fletcher look into it."

"I want to do it," he said, fighting that wave of possessiveness again. He wanted to be the one to keep Frannie safe. Ironic, seeing as he was the one putting her in danger.

"Okay," she said easily, taking another sip of her coffee. "Plans for today?"

He was waiting on word from his private investigator, but he couldn't mention that. Instead, he smiled and kissed her forehead, saying, "I'm playing detective today. Enjoy your coffee. There's a plate of bacon and eggs in the microwave. I'm going to jump in the shower. Feel free to join me if you like."

"That's not a fair choice. You know I love food, but I'd also like to be naked with you in the shower."

He shrugged. "You could always reheat the eggs and bacon after..."

Frannie considered the option, then hurried after him, taking a final sip of her coffee. "Water conservation is far more important than the inconvenience of reheating breakfast," she rationalized.

Dante couldn't say he was disappointed. She shrugged out of his robe, and he scooped her up, carrying her to the bed first.

"Hey! You said shower..." she said, playfully accusatory. "What are you doing?"

"Making a mess of you, darling," he answered with a dark grin as he pressed kisses down her belly. "Might as well make sure we're making proper use of the shower."

Her delightful giggle switched to moans, and Dante knew he could happily drown in the sound of her pleasure for the rest of his life.

He needed to find a solution to this situation with his uncle, or he'd lose out on any chance of happiness with Frannie.

He'd always known running wasn't a permanent solution, but he hadn't figured out how to keep his uncle off his back for good.

What kind of life was he offering Frannie if they took things to the next level?

He wanted her in his bed every night, not just here and there, like some meaningless hookup with a casual stranger.

*Casual*—that word couldn't possibly describe what he and Frannie shared, but it was what they'd agreed to.

But how could he offer anything else?

He couldn't.

Not yet, anyway.

Maybe never.

All they had was now.

# Chapter 18

Frannie closed the shop and headed for the grocery store, still thinking about the exciting new shipment of books that had arrived that morning. Dante was so good about taking care of the food she wanted to show him that she could throw something together that was not only edible but delicious, too.

She wasn't Emeril but could hold her own in the kitchen. Jenny had taught all her children how to find their way around the kitchen, and it was a small point of pride that even though she had a modest menu of dishes she could prepare, she made them well.

The farmers' market was only a short walk from the shop, so she grabbed her canvas shopping bag and headed toward her favorite fruit and vegetable vendor.

"Frannie! There you are! I knew I'd find you here, sniffing mushrooms and talking about how a mushroom could be a good substitute for meat," Darla said, rolling her eyes. "As if that was actually a thing. I know you're not a vegetarian, but you do a pretty good imitation of one, always pushing those vegetables."

"Technically, a mushroom is a fungus," Frannie reminded Darla, to which Darla grimaced. "I'm just saying...if you want to be accurate. But yes, it all depends on how you sea-son and cook it." She held up a beautiful portobello mushroom. "See? Doesn't that look delicious?"

"No, it smells like dirt and looks like something I wouldn't ever put in my mouth. I'll stick with a porterhouse."

Frannie shrugged with a grin as she put the mushroom in a baggie to be weighed. "Each to their own. What are you doing here tonight? You barely cook, and you don't like crowds." She paid for her purchase, and they walked on.

Darla sighed, nodding in agreement with everything Frannie had said, but she gestured across the street, "I blame him," and Frannie saw her fiancé admiring a handmade wind chime. "He loves the farmers' market. He says it makes him feel good to support local artisans. I didn't have the heart to tell him that most of this stuff is purchased from China and passed off as homemade."

"That's not true," Frannie said, laughing at Darla's sour attitude. "I happen to know for a fact that Stacy Spencer makes her tie-dyed T-shirts in her bathtub—and they're really cute. I might just buy one today."

"You hate tie-dye," Darla drawled, calling her bluff. "You once said tie-dye is the clothing trend that refuses to die and has worn out its welcome."

She had said that—but to be fair, she'd been in a bad mood that day. "A woman has the prerogative to change her mind."

The hairs suddenly stood on the back of her neck, and she shuddered, glancing around to see why she felt like someone had been staring a hole into her back.

"You okay?" Darla asked, noticing her sudden shiver. "You look like a goose walked over your grave."

"Yeah, it was weird. It felt like someone was standing right behind me, staring."

"I didn't see anyone," Darla said, scanning the crowd.

"But I hate when that happens. Maybe a ghost was standing right next to you."

Frannie didn't like that thought at all. "Hey, don't be putting those kinds of thoughts in my head. I sleep alone, you know."

"You big fat liar. I know you're not sleeping alone these days."

Frannie blushed, clarifying, "Okay, maybe not but it's not an everyday thing. It's a casual arrangement, not a relationship and…" Her voice trailed. Why was she even trying to lie when Darla knew her like the back of her hand? *Pointless.* She met Darla's knowing smirk and gave it up. "I think I'm falling in love with him, Darla. How did this happen?"

Darla shook her head as if to say, 'You poor summer child,' and put her arm around her shoulders. "First, there are worse men to fall for—he seems pretty top-shelf. Second, would it be so bad if you were falling for him?"

"Um, yeah, we agreed to keep things casual because he's not planning to stay in Owl Creek, and I have no plans to move to Italy…or wherever he's going next. Also, I don't actually know much about him. Each time I try to get a little deeper, he switches things up and deftly changes the subject. It's a little 'red-flaggy.'"

"Yeah, you mentioned something about that. How'd the day on the lake go?"

"Amazing! Best day of my life. The lake was beautiful, I packed a picnic lunch for the beach, and we…well, we made good use of the privacy, let's just put it that way."

"Mmm, I love lake days like that," Darla said with a wistful expression. "And then what happened?"

"Well, we went back to my place and…do you remember those random flowers that showed up at the shop?"

"The lilies?"

Frannie nodded. "Well, Dante and I were messing around and just as we were about to get serious, Dante saw a single lily—the same kind as the delivery—on my pillow."

Darla's eyes bugged. "Excuse me? On your pillow? How'd it get there?"

"I don't know."

"That's some creepy shit, Fran. Did you report it to Fletcher?"

"No, it seems silly to report something so small."

"Small? No, someone broke into your house and left something there to let you know they'd been there. It's creepy and potentially dangerous. You need to tell Fletcher."

"So, Dante wants to do a little checking on a guy I went to school with at Boise State. Do you remember my friend Allen Burns?"

"The horticulture nerd who always brought you dead weeds?"

"They weren't weeds, they were clippings, and most of the time they were gorgeous lilies."

Darla's gaze widened. "Do you think it was that guy who left the flower?"

"I mean, it seems unlikely, but he popped into my thoughts at three in the morning. It's funny, I hadn't thought of him in years until I couldn't sleep and then, there he was, in my head."

"I remember him being a little on the weird side," Darla said. "Are you sure it wasn't him?"

"He wasn't weird," Frannie protested. "He was just a little on the shy side and maybe awkward but I'm awkward, too, so we got along."

"Frannie, you're quirky, which, paired with your face, is adorable. Pretty privilege goes a long way to smoothing the road for those with unusual personality quirks. If I'm remembering correctly, he didn't have that luxury."

"He wasn't traditionally handsome, but he was very sweet."

"Did you keep in touch after graduation?"

Frannie shook her head, feeling bad about that. "No, we went our separate ways. We really only had a few college experiences to draw us together. After that, our connection wasn't organic but that's the way of college, right? Everyone goes their separate ways after graduation to pursue their careers."

"I'm still not clear why you haven't told Fletcher?"

"Because it seems silly and Dante is looking into it."

"I thought Dante was a lawyer?"

"He is."

"And he moonlights as a private investigator?" Darla's incredulous expression was pretty damning. "Seriously, Fran, props to your guy for wanting to be your knight in shining armor but sometimes we have to leave certain jobs to the professionals. Dante can pitch legal advice about your family situation if he wants to feel useful."

"It's likely nothing and that's why I didn't mind Dante asking around," Frannie said, defending Dante. "Plus, with everything my family is dealing with, I don't want to add some frivolous nonsense to their plate. Whatever this is, I'm sure I can handle it with Dante's help."

"I love your loyalty to a man you barely know. I'm just saying, I wouldn't trust Tom to know what to do in this situation and I'm crazy about the guy."

"You should be," Frannie said. "Clearly Tom hasn't figured out that you're a double shot of irrational and bossy, and for your sake, I hope he doesn't figure it out until after the wedding."

"Ha! You think I don't have the same concern? That's why I wanted to lock that man down sooner rather than later. We could've eloped, and I would've had a ring on my finger by now." They shared a laugh, but Darla saw Tom waving her over, and she had to cut their conversation short, but not before she made Frannie promise to tell Fletcher. "I don't want to find out on the morning news that my best friend—and maid of honor—was abducted in the middle of the night by some stalker that no one took seriously."

Frannie rolled her eyes and waved Darla on her way. "You worry too much. Go catch up with Tom before he buys that wind chime that will definitely keep you up all night with its bing-bonging in the wind."

Darla's expression of horror as she hustled toward her fiancé made Frannie laugh, but a sliver of doubt remained even as her mood had lightened.

Was it possible she'd made a mistake in not telling Fletcher about the flower on her pillow? What were the chances that she had a real stalker? *Here in Owl Creek?* Seemed far-fetched…but not impossible.

She couldn't help another glance over her shoulder as that feeling remained that someone was watching her.

*Stop freaking yourself out. You're surrounded by people you know.*

*No one is watching.*

But just the same, she hurried with her shopping and quickly headed home.

His cell rang as Dante was getting ready to leave his place to go to Frannie's.

Seeing that it was his PI, he clicked over immediately.

"Dante," he answered.

"Hey, it's Nick. I had a contact with the Wisconsin State

Coroners Association pull some strings to send me the confidential autopsy report on your father. It was relatively easy to get the information—probably too easy, they need to really improve their security systems—but I found something I thought you'd like to know."

Dante's stomach muscles clenched with tension, but he was ready. "Go ahead."

"So, I already told you there was alcohol in your father's system when he was killed but there was something else wasn't part of the public record that definitely seems suspicious."

"Which is?"

"Fentanyl—enough to kill him. Someone wanted to make sure your father didn't survive that night. My guess is that your father was dead before his car even hit the tree."

Dante took a minute to digest this bombshell. His father had been murdered. Alcohol might've been easy enough to explain, but fentanyl? If he knew his father hadn't been a drinker, he knew beyond a shadow of a doubt he never did drugs of any kind—much less a drug as dangerous as fentanyl.

"Any chance the coroner shared how the fentanyl had gotten into his system?" Dante asked.

"No, it's anyone's guess. The coroner didn't do a real extensive report. He probably assumed your dad was a drunk and a drug addict and his vices finally caught up to him. I'm sorry."

Dante accepted the man's condolences, fighting the lump in his throat. His memories of Matteo were dim and hazy, but it hurt in ways he couldn't describe knowing that it hadn't been a cruel but impartial twist of fate that'd taken his father from him but a deliberate act by another person.

"Damn it," he muttered, rubbing the moisture from his eyes, trying to regroup. "Anything else?"

There was a brief pause, then Nick shared, "The widow of the cop who wrote your father's accident report? She died yesterday."

A frisson of alarm spiked his blood. "Natural causes?"

"It appears that way, but I'll know more in a few days. It seems real suspicious that days after I spoke to the woman and she told me about the money her husband received around the same time your father was killed, she ends up dying. I was born at night, but it wasn't last night. Could be natural causes—but then, it doesn't take much to silence an old lady either."

Dante felt sick. Had he inadvertently caused that woman's death by asking questions?

"Send me her obituary so I can see if she left donation wishes."

"It's a nice thought but I'd advise against it."

"Why?"

"Because the old lady didn't have any natural ties to you. If you go and offer some pricey donation to this random lady's cause, it could alert your uncle's men as to your whereabouts. Say a prayer in your head and let God decide whether it's enough. For now, my advice to you is to continue to lay low."

It was solid advice. He wasn't thinking straight. Refocusing, he conceded with a low murmur, "You're right. I've got reasonable evidence that my father was murdered but still nothing tying it to my uncle." Not that he'd likely find any, either. Lorenzo wasn't sloppy—he was exact and precise, calculated. He didn't do anything without multiple fail-safes in place in case plan A went awry.

He used to think his uncle was a genius, which he might

be, but now Dante saw him for what he truly was—a murderer with a limitless bank account.

"Keep looking for possible ties. In the meantime, I have something else I need you to look into that's unrelated to my family."

"Yeah?"

"I want you to check out a guy named Allen Burns, attended Boise State University in 2019, possibly an agriculture or horticulture major."

"What am I looking for?"

"Anything. If the man so much as sneezed the wrong way I want to know."

"Sure."

Dante clicked off and sat for a long moment, thinking about his past, present and future. How would he feel if he never found his uncle's ties to Matteo's death? Unfulfilled? Unable to let the past go?

He didn't want that—not for himself and not for Frannie.

He knew he loved her. It was foolish to pretend otherwise. She was the light in his life, the laughter in his soul that made everything else fall away and seem less important.

But how could he drag her into his life knowing that ghosts might chase him without a chance of peace?

He didn't have the answers. All he knew was that he had to keep her safe. Right now, that meant finding out who was sending her flowers—and if they meant her harm.

## Chapter 19

Frannie was still unsettled by the time she reached home. She'd planned to make a summer salad, but her thoughts were anywhere but with her food prep. Before she realized the time, Dante was at her door with a bottle of wine and that adoring smile she'd come to crave at the end of a long day.

After a sweet kiss, she admitted she was behind in making dinner, but he wouldn't let her carry any burden, much less that of sole dinner prep. "What do you still need done? I'm happy to help. You know how I love being in the kitchen. Especially with you as my sous-chef."

"Sous-chef? No, you're *my* sous-chef, you silly goose." She said it with a playful smile but was glad to have his help. She enjoyed cooking with him. Together, they were a seamless team that made light work of any task they set out to do.

Wasn't that the hallmark of most successful relationships? Embracing the concept of "many hands make for light work," as her grandmother used to preach to her grandchildren, as they groaned at having to haul wood, pick blackberries for summer jam, and peel apples to jar as applesauce for the winter.

He chuckled, seemingly accepting her statement as fact without a single protest. The man was nearly perfect. "I don't want to be casual anymore," she blurted, shocking herself and Dante with her outburst. Her cheeks flared with heat, but she couldn't take it back—not that she wanted to—and it was out there, floating between them like a giant ethereal question mark.

She held her breath, afraid of what he might say, afraid of her feelings getting squashed, but she lifted her chin and stood by her declaration, waiting for his response.

Was that fear? Disappointment? Anger? Or was he embarrassed that the young bookstore owner had gone and done the one thing he'd warned her against, ruining an otherwise great thing between them?

"Please say something."

Dante cleared his throat, apparently realizing his silence was becoming heavier by the moment. He reached for her hand and pulled her close. "You're trembling," he said softly.

"Because I think I might've just ruined what you liked most about us," she admitted in a shaky voice.

"That's not what I like best," he assured her. His throaty voice that never failed to send shivers dancing down her spine.

Was it all about the sex? Granted, the passion between them was out of this world, but she'd be a liar if she didn't say that she wanted it to be about more than something physical.

"Frannie…"

No, she couldn't do this. She couldn't hear him try to let her down gently. Her pride wouldn't suffer such a blow. She tried to pull away, but he held her close. "Dante, you don't have to do this. I get what you're not saying… It's my fault for pushing against the boundary we both set."

"It's not that," he said, furrowing his brow with frustration. "It's…complicated."

"How?"

"I—I don't really want to get into it right now, but I need you to trust me when I say that it's better to keep things as they are between us," he said, though he looked pained just saying the words, which confused her more.

"Dante, I can't—that's not good enough—I need more from you. I hardly know a thing about you. It was okay in the beginning, before feelings got involved, but now? I crave more than you're willing to give. Maybe it's not fair but I'm honest to a fault, and I can't hide what I'm feeling."

"And I love that about you," he assured her and kissed her passionately, framing her face with both hands. She could feel the love between them, yet he continued to keep her at arm's length emotionally. It was maddening. It was also starting to frustrate her because her feelings were bruised.

"Stop," she said and pulled away, separating them. She wiped at her eyes. "Look, I didn't mean to ruin dinner, but I suppose this was a conversation that was coming eventually. I know you feel something for me, but maybe it's not equal to what I feel for you."

"No, that's not it," he said quietly. "You're not alone in your feelings."

Hope dared to spark in her chest. "I'm not?"

"No."

"Then why do you pull away from me and then say things like, 'It's better this way,' as if you know that we don't have any kind of future together?" she asked, confused and hurt.

"Because I can't give you what you need and deserve," he admitted bitterly. "And I hate that I can't."

"What do you think I deserve? I don't need a fancy house or anything like that. Is it finances? Are you broke or something? I wouldn't care if you were. Finances can be fixed—but not if you walk away."

"I'm not broke," he answered, shocking her. "I—" He stopped short, leaving his statement unfinished. Shaking his head, he said, "I have more than enough to see to my needs but even if I didn't, I would never allow you to carry the financial burden of my care."

"It's not a burden if you're helping someone get back on their feet," she said, trying to be gentle. She sensed his pride was speaking. Men were so funny about money and where it came from. Her father had always ensured they all knew that no matter how much money Jenny brought in, he still made more.

"Frannie...please. I can't talk about this right now."

She had a choice—let it go and continue their evening as if it had never happened—or hold her ground and expect some answer.

Her heart hurt. For years she'd watched her mother swallow any grievance for peace in the house, and she swore she'd never be like that.

Yet, tears burned behind her eyes at the thought of ending things with Dante over his lack of equal communication. Was it a cultural difference? Or was she making excuses and dancing around the obvious that he was an emotionally unavailable man who'd been content to keep their relationship surface-deep, but he hadn't wanted to hurt her feelings, so he pretended there was more to it.

"Dante... I need more," she said as a tear snaked down her cheek. "And if you can't give that to me, I understand. But I can't allow myself to fall deeper for a man who's ultimately going to break my heart because he never promised me forever."

"What are you saying?" he asked.

"I'm saying, don't ask me to pretend that my needs don't matter because your needs are more important."

There. She'd said it—she'd essentially thrown a gauntlet.

Now, how he responded would reveal the depth of his true character.

*Please, don't make me wrong about who I thought you were.*

The truth burned his tongue. She deserved nothing less than honesty. How could he spill his guts about everything he was dealing with without putting her in more unnecessary danger?

*Just tell her. You're already in the thick of things. More lies will only make it worse.*

Dante turned away from her, needing to get his head on straight. He needed a minute to think. The smart decision would be to take the out—a clean break for reasons that would make sense without too much explanation.

He could easily say he was still torn up about his last breakup, and it wouldn't be fair to her to keep pretending otherwise. It would hurt, but she'd get over it. He would wear the "international asshole" badge for her safety.

But then he'd have to find a way to make peace with the knowledge that someone else would claim her heart, warm her bed and share her future—which made him want to smash things.

In a relatively short time, she'd become such an important part of his life, almost as if she were fused to him, and he didn't know how he'd survive without her.

He wasn't the romantic type—he didn't fall in love easily or frivolously—and he took matters of the heart seriously.

He would never pretend to love someone for sex or emotional warmth.

It was Frannie he wanted—even though the woman's gas could kill a moose when she ate too much dairy—because she was everything he never realized he needed in his life.

If it weren't for the threat of his uncle looming over his future, he would've proposed to the woman already.

"Dante?"

It was the tremulous tone that killed him. It was as if it was taking everything in her not to bawl her eyes out, and she was holding it together by a thread to get the answers she needed.

And he was doing this to her.

It was his fault that she was hurting.

He turned to face her. He needed more time. He would be honest with her soon. But not tonight. Tonight, he had to save what they had because he couldn't fathom letting her think he didn't care for her.

"My mother died in a car accident two years ago—a drunk driver—and I inherited a modest sum from her estate. Finances aren't a problem," he said, skirting around the truth. He had inherited money from his mother, but it was nothing compared to what he had inherited from his father's family trust—and what he'd banked as the family's premier attorney.

Lorenzo had secured Dante's inheritance the moment they returned to Italy—yet another reason he'd believed his uncle had been a good man.

Suffice it to say Dante would never have to worry about money.

Only his head.

Frannie blinked, unsure of how to process that information. "You're…rich?"

"Comfortable," he corrected, but he was obscenely wealthy, though he was less proud of how that money had been built.

His family's legacy was a patchwork quilt of vice that would turn a holy man's hair white.

"So, why are you so reluctant to take our relationship to the next level?"

"Because it isn't finances that keep me from taking that next step. Emotionally, I'm not ready," he lied. "And you deserve better."

Her expression crumpled, but she nodded. "I understand."

*No, you couldn't possibly.*

He needed more time to sort things out. "But I want to be in a position to be the man you need," he said. "I just need a little more time to sort things in my head."

"So, you're open to more, you're just asking for more time to get there?" she clarified, wiping at her eyes.

"Yes."

"I suppose that's fair," she said, though clearly that wasn't the answer she hoped for. He hated that she thought he was asking for more time to figure out if he loved her because he already knew the answer. He was head over heels about her. "I mean, I can't fault you for being honest from the start that you weren't ready for more. It's my fault for hoping for that to change."

"No, things happen," he said, unwilling to let her think it was one-sided. "I didn't plan on feeling this way about you either, but anything worth having is worth exploring slowly. There's no need to rush what is already beautiful."

It wasn't the romantic declaration she deserved, but it might keep her safe while he continued to find the answers he needed to move on.

*Assuming he could move on.*

That was the ugly truth lurking in the background of his thoughts. He was doing all this work, trying to piece together a puzzle, and he had no idea if it would help him. It was possible he'd finish the puzzle, discover how everything came together to create one messed-up picture, and then he'd have to be okay with the knowledge that he was right but couldn't change a damn thing.

Which wouldn't keep him or Frannie safe.

"I accept your offer. But, Dante...I won't wait forever."

*Fair enough.*

Hopefully, he wouldn't have to make her wait much longer. But he had a terrible feeling he was running out of time to solve anything, much less offer her the future she deserved.

# Chapter 20

The following day Dante was running errands in town when his cell rang. Believing it was his PI, he answered without checking the caller ID.

"Dante, what are you doing? Running all over the place, making trouble...it's unnecessary. Come home."

Dante's blood chilled. He glanced at the caller ID, but Unknown Caller was all that showed. "Who is this?" He scanned the street, feeling exposed. "Who's calling?"

The caller ignored his question. The voice sounded altered to disguise identity and gender. Whoever it was didn't want to be recognized. "The family is worried. Such division, such pain. It doesn't have to be this way. People poking their noses in family business..." the person on the other line tsked like Dante was the problem child. "It's an ugly thing, unbecoming of a Santoro."

Was this his uncle calling him? No, if it were Lorenzo, he wouldn't waste time altering his voice; he'd want Dante to know that it was him. So, if not Lorenzo, who?

"Either you tell me who this is, or this conversation is over."

"Trust that I don't want to see you hurt," the caller said. "You're testing your uncle's patience. Come home and ask for his forgiveness. He will forgive you. He loves you like a son."

Unwelcome pain squeezed his heart. He didn't want his uncle's forgiveness, just as he didn't want his "love." He didn't have the proof yet, but he knew his uncle had had something to do with his father's death, possibly even his mother's. Lorenzo was willing to kill to keep the family secrets, which didn't make Dante feel safe or "loved."

But at one time, he'd loved Lorenzo like a father—and it was that pain that he didn't want to feel.

"Like he loved his brother?"

The silence on the other end was damning.

Dante's temper flared and took hold. "I know my father was killed and I'm going to find a way to prove that it was Lorenzo's doing. Cops paid off, alcohol *and* fentanyl in my dad's system when the man never drank, much less did drugs? I'm getting closer to the answers I need and when I find them—"

"Stop it," the caller hissed. "You're fighting a game you will lose. Don't risk everything for something in the past that can't be changed. You're acting like a child. Time to grow up, Dante. You're the heir to the Santoro empire. Don't throw that all away chasing ghosts."

Something about the caller reminded him of someone. Everyone in Lorenzo's inner circle was intensely loyal—out of fear or true admiration—but there was only one person near enough to Lorenzo to know his every move, scheduled his appointments and handled all details of his life.

"Pietro?"

Lorenzo's secretary and right-hand man, Pietro Romano, had been around the family for as long as he could remember. He handled Lorenzo's details and was as close as any family member to his uncle, possibly closer because he doubted Lorenzo would ever hire someone to take out Pietro like he had his brother.

"Did he kill my mother, too?" Dante asked point-blank. If anyone knew, it was likely Pietro. "Why?"

"From the beginning, he loved your mother. He would never hurt her."

Dante stilled at the unexpected information. For a moment, his tongue was tied, and the caller took advantage.

"You're angry, hotheaded, and set on what you believe is a righteous path. What if you're wrong? Your uncle is not a storybook villain."

"My father might disagree," he replied coolly.

"A rift between brothers you can never understand—and it's not your place to understand."

If that statement was meant to put Dante in his place, it had the opposite effect.

"I won't be lectured by a man who condones and supports my uncle's actions. You're just as bad."

"Everyone is a villain in someone's story, Dante," the caller reminded him.

He was done being schooled. "I won't stop until I have answers. He'll have to kill me."

"Dante, you're being foolish," the caller said, disappointed. "I thought you were smarter than this."

"And I thought my uncle was a good man. I guess we're both disappointed."

"Your answer is final? You will not come home?"

"No."

"Foolish boy." The heavy sigh on the other end sent a chill down his back. "Stubborn-headed like Matteo. And destined to end up in the same place."

The line clicked off before Dante could respond.

What did that mean? The same place? Did that mean Lorenzo planned to have him killed, too?

He always knew that was a possibility, and he'd been

willing to take that risk, but now he had Frannie's safety to worry about, too.

Somehow, he had to convince Frannie it was a good idea to leave Owl Creek for a few days.

*A few days?* Hell, he'd need to convince her to run away with him forever. Owl Creek was compromised at this point.

A sense of déjà vu washed over him. He was replaying his childhood. His father had scooped up his little family and run from the Santoro influence, never staying long in one place for fear of being found.

And eventually, that was exactly what had happened.

Was that his fate, too?

Would history replay itself with him and Frannie?

What if she got pregnant? Would Lorenzo wipe them out and take his child to start again with a fresh slate?

Lorenzo had never married and never had kids of his own.

But he remembered Lorenzo being solicitous and accommodating to his mother when they arrived in Italy. He'd been too young and grief-stricken to look beyond the surface values of their relationship to wonder why his mother had been so quick to return to Italy when his father had done everything in his power to keep them far away.

What was that bullshit about Lorenzo loving Dante's mother? But something was disturbing about that little nugget of information that he couldn't quite push away.

His mother, Georgia, had never remarried.

His uncle had never been far from her side.

He'd never seen them act inappropriately with each other but over the years, Georgia had become very familiar with Lorenzo, decorating his home as if it were her own, and Lorenzo had always ensured Georgia had whatever she wanted.

A sick feeling lodged in his gut. Had his mother been having an affair with Lorenzo all those years after his father's death? And had she known that Lorenzo had been responsible for Matteo's death?

No, impossible. His parents had loved each other. But love needed healthy soil to grow, and it was hard to imagine a life such as theirs as anything conducive to nurturing romance.

Perhaps Georgia had grown tired of running, and Lorenzo's offer of protection and wealth had been too much to refuse.

Lorenzo had been kind to Georgia, but was there more than he'd known? A story he hadn't been privy to that started behind locked bedroom doors?

The thought of his mother and uncle being intimate made him irrationally angry on behalf of his dead father. But did ghosts care about what happened after they died?

He pocketed his cell and hustled to his rental. He felt vulnerable out in the open. If Pietro had found him, chances were high that Lorenzo knew where he was, too.

Was he playing with him? A cat and mouse game?

Was Pietro trying to pull on his heartstrings at Lorenzo's bidding, or was it possible that Pietro truly cared and wanted Dante to be safe?

He hated all the mind games. It was one of the many reasons he'd realized being the Santoro attorney wasn't a good fit for him any longer. He loathed manipulating the law to benefit people who were controlling the system for their benefit, no matter who it hurt in the process.

Lorenzo was all about the end game—he didn't care at all about the pawns on the board.

And everyone was a pawn.

Including him.

\* \* \*

Frannie was about to close the shop when Fletcher called her cell. She picked up, ready with a wisecrack about a fictitious book order, *Men Who Are Emotionally Constipated and the Women Who Love Them*, but Fletcher's news killed her good mood.

"Frannie, there's been an accident."

Immediately, her brothers and sisters jumped to mind, but when Fletcher said it was Dante, she almost couldn't process the information. Shaking her head, she repeated, "Dante? What do you mean?"

"He's okay, but his guardian angel must've been riding shotgun because his car went straight into the lake."

Frannie gasped, horrified. "Oh my God, are you sure he's okay? Where is he?"

"Ambulance took him to Connors to be checked out. He's got a bump on his head and the clinic doesn't have a CT machine. They want to make sure he doesn't have a concussion. But honestly, it's a damn miracle he's alive. I know you're not family or next of kin, but I knew you'd want to know."

Frannie was too stressed to appropriately thank Fletcher for breaking the rules for her, anxious to get to the hospital. "Thanks," she said hastily and hung up. She quickly shut down the store and practically ran to her car to drive forty-five minutes to the nearest hospital.

She might've broken several laws driving to Connors, but she didn't care. All that kept running through her head was how Dante could've been taken from her in a blink of an eye. She swallowed the lump in her throat, too terrified to think straight. She needed to see him, to see for herself that he was okay.

What if he had a concussion? What if his brain was swelling? What if when they did the CT scan, they found a tumor in his head that otherwise would've been lurking in his brain until it took him out on a Tuesday?

*Whoa, settle down.* A concussion was manageable. Fletcher said Dante was going to be okay. She screeched into a parking spot, not caring that she was parked like a blind monkey had been behind the wheel. Hurrying into the lobby and to the reception desk, she gave Dante's name and lied about her connection to him. "I'm his wife," she answered when the receptionist asked if she were family. It didn't feel weird or uncomfortable to claim either. She'd unpack that later.

She heard Dante's voice from behind the curtain in the emergency room bay, and relief flooded her to tears. Pushing aside the curtain, she smiled at Dante, his head bandaged but otherwise looking as healthy as ever and even a little sexy in his blue polka dot hospital gown.

"Are you okay, honey?" She asked, hoping Dante caught on so she didn't get tossed for being nonfamily.

"I'm fine. Just a little bump on the head," he answered. He introduced Frannie to the doctor. "This is my wife, Frannie."

She pushed away the thrill the tiny lie caused because now was not the time to get all fluttery about the future. "Give it to me straight…is he really okay?" She asked the doctor sternly.

The doctor chuckled, pocketing his pen. "Your husband is correct. The CT scan came back with no damage to the brain, though he might have a headache for a few days while that bump heals. I'd recommend light duty, plenty of rest, and no heavy equipment operating for a week or so. Other than that, he's one lucky guy. A car into the lake? That's a story to tell your grandkids someday."

Frannie chuckled and murmured thanks as the doctor left

to start Dante's discharge papers. As soon as the doctor was gone, Dante's easy smile disappeared. He started dressing immediately, shucking the hospital gown and pulling his sodden clothes from the personal bag left with him by paramedics.

Alarmed, Frannie stopped him. "What are you doing? You have to be discharged first. You can't just leave and your clothes are sopping wet. I can run over to Target or something and get you some sweats and a T-shirt to change into now that I know you're not going to die."

"A little wet clothes don't bother me. I'd rather leave now."

"Dante, that's not how the American healthcare system works. You have to finish your paperwork so the hospital knows where to send the bill. I know our healthcare system sucks in comparison to Italy's but it's what we have to work with."

"I'll send cash. We need to go. I didn't need a CT scan and told paramedics that but they insisted because I passed out when they pulled me from the water."

"Well, then it was the right call," Frannie agreed, confused why Dante was so hell-bent on leaving before being officially discharged. "You could've been seriously hurt. What happened?"

"I'll tell you in the car," he said, fully dressed. "Let's go."

Before she could stop him, he pulled her after him, and they slipped out the back door reserved for emergency personnel.

*What is going on?* "Dante...wait!"

But Dante was like a man being chased by the cops, and he wasn't interested in having a little chat while they sorted things out.

She swallowed, realizing that a giant red flag was flapping in her face, and she could do nothing but hope she was wrong.

## Chapter 21

Dante couldn't afford to stick around for the discharge papers. His fake ID would only hold up to so much scrutiny. He hadn't planned on ending up in the hospital anytime soon. But if they'd tried to run his information, it would've returned as false, tripping authorities to his fake identity. Another reason why he'd tried to refuse a trip to the hospital.

Frannie was understandably confused. "Is there something you're not telling me? I don't understand why you were so freaked out about the hospital. Do you have some bad memories associated with a hospital stay? Does it have something to do with your dad?"

She was grasping at straws, trying to understand, *bless her heart*, but if he told her the truth, he would look like a criminal and ruin any chance of convincing her to leave Owl Creek with him.

As it was, his task was an uphill battle, but the minute his brakes failed and he landed in the lake, he'd known he was no longer safe in Owl Creek.

It also made his anonymous call—he assumed it was Pietro, but he couldn't be sure—seem much more of a last-ditch effort to get him to heel before more permanent measures were taken.

He felt terrible for soaking Frannie's car seats, but he'd

pay for a full detail later. "Yes, hospitals bring up bad memories," he said, stacking another lie on the pile he was racking between them.

"You'll need to call the hospital to make financial arrangements," she warned, trying to make sense of his actions. "I mean, I suppose as long as they get their money, it's fine, but it seems like it would've been a lot easier if you could've waited ten more minutes before running out—and you were literally *running*. I felt like I was being dragged down the hallway like a character in a movie being chased by bad guys."

"Sorry, I didn't mean to frighten you."

"It's okay, I guess, just weird," she admitted with a troubled frown before returning to the subject of the crash. "What happened? How'd you end up in the lake?"

Here was the real test—how much to share without tripping any internal alarm bells. He feigned confusion. "I have no idea. Maybe a faulty brake line? I took the turn and maybe I was going a little too fast, but when I pumped the brakes, nothing happened and I plunged over the side of the hill, crashing into the lake. I think I blacked out on impact."

"How'd anyone know you'd crashed?"

"A boater coming in saw the car go in and he called 911 on his cell."

"That boater is your true guardian angel," she said.

He nodded, but his mind was racing. There was no way that his new car had faulty brakes. He was sure that someone had cut the brake line, but he didn't want to scare Frannie.

"It seems so," he agreed, shifting in his wet jeans, hating how the damp fabric clung to his thighs, but he didn't want to return to his place. "Hey, I think I left some clothes at your place. Let's go straight there."

"I don't mind stopping," she assured him. "I think all you have at my house are a pair of pajama pants and a T-shirt."

"Honestly, I didn't want to admit it, but I do have a headache. I just want to relax for the night so pajama pants sound perfect."

Frannie softened immediately. "Of course. I'm sorry, I can't even imagine the horror of what you've been through tonight. It's one of my worst fears to drive into a lake. If you hadn't had your window open... I don't even like to think of what might've happened."

*Yeah, same.* "Too close for comfort," he agreed. "I'm grateful for getting through it."

Frannie sobered. "Dante, my heart just about stopped when Fletcher told me. Everything else seemed to fade to the background as unimportant in that moment. I was terrified that you were hurt."

"I'm sorry for worrying you," he said.

"It's not your fault. I'm not telling you to make you feel bad. I already knew how I felt about you, but this just made me realize that I can't fathom life without you. I hope I never have to experience that."

If his life were his own, he'd ask her to marry him right now, but he didn't have that luxury.

"I promise to never drive into a lake again," he said, trying to make her smile. "I confess, it wasn't ever on my bucket list, but I guess I can check it off anyway." Her strained chuckle hurt his heart. He reached over and squeezed her thigh. "They say statistically people are in one bad accident in their lifetime—looks like I just lived through mine. So there's a bright side to losing my rental car."

A tear tracked down her cheek, but she chuckled as she wiped it away. "And who is 'they'? Is that a legal term?"

It was his turn to laugh. "Definitely. I use it in court all the time. Judges love nebulous sources."

"I bet they do," Frannie said, rolling her eyes. They pulled up to Frannie's house, and Dante exited the vehicle so fast his head throbbed, but he ignored it. He couldn't help but scan the street, looking for anything that seemed out of place.

But Frannie noticed. "Are you sure you're okay?"

"Yeah, my head is pounding, though. My plans for the night include you, aspirin and a bed."

"I think I can make that happen," she said, brushing a tender kiss across his lips.

He didn't deserve a woman like Frannie. If he lived through this, he'd make sure she never went a day without knowing how he felt about her.

The only problem? His uncle seemed determined to snuff out his only nephew—and the heir to the Santoro legacy.

Frannie tried not to fret, but there seemed to be a lot of holes in Dante's story and his reaction to being in the hospital. Every time she thought they'd crossed a threshold and reached another level of trust, something made her question everything they shared.

And she hated that she couldn't take his word at face value.

She'd always told herself that she'd never put herself in a position where her partner didn't deserve her trust, because trust was the foundation of a solid relationship. The questions nagged at her brain, whirring in the background, creating noise that kept her grabbing her attention.

Was Dante lying to her?

He didn't seem all that shaken up about landing in the lake.

He hadn't said anything about contacting the rental agency or filing an insurance claim. For that matter, he hadn't said anything about filing a lawsuit against the car manufacturer for the alleged faulty brakes. Nor had he said anything about asking for an investigation into the accident.

It was like he climbed out of the lake with a nasty bump on his head, shook the water from his hair and decided to put it all behind him like a bout of food poisoning from a questionable restaurant.

But he'd landed in a *friggin'* lake!

If it'd been her, she'd still be wrapped in a blanket, shivering and possibly crying over the ordeal.

Wasn't almost drowning considered a traumatic event?

"I can almost hear your thoughts," Dante murmured, half-asleep beside her. "What's keeping you awake?"

She couldn't be honest, not with him recovering from a head injury, so she lied. Badly. "Inventory. I was supposed to get a new shipment and it didn't come, so I will have to check the tracking tomorrow."

"I'm sure it'll show up," he said. "Shipping has been backed up for a while. I think I read something about a strike on the docks or something like that. No one to unload the ships."

"Yeah, probably."

Dante turned to pull her into a snuggle. "You smell like home," he said with a sigh before dropping back off to sleep.

Was it an old wives' tale that you're not supposed to let someone fall asleep with a head injury? She wouldn't know because they'd left before the doctor could give them discharge instructions, including how to care for someone with a head injury.

But Dante was already asleep, dozing as if he hadn't nearly met his maker a few hours ago.

It was wild how people adapted to circumstances in their life, how things became part of their routine, even if it was anything but normal.

For years she'd suspected her dad wasn't faithful, but her mom had been brilliant at hiding any reaction to his infidelity, so as kids, they weren't subjected to screaming fights or relationship drama. Not that it was healthy, but it wasn't in their face.

But then her dad died, her aunt showed up, and all hell broke loose, shattering the illusion that their family was happy, healthy and well-adjusted.

Which made her think of her current situation with Dante.

Something wasn't right.

She was ignoring her intuition because she'd fallen in love with him, which wasn't a great endorsement for their future.

*If* they had a future.

*He's hiding something*, a voice whispered, and she couldn't look away from the facts staring her in the face.

She had this sense, a tingling in the back of her head, warning her that Dante was lying about something big, which should be all the evidence she needed to walk away and cut her losses.

But she couldn't bring herself to do it, which worried her.

A few years ago, she'd decided to purchase her first brand-new car. She'd been saving all year for the down payment, and she'd been ready to sign on the dotted line. She'd asked her cousin Max to go with her so she didn't get bamboozled by slick car salesmen.

Before they walked into the dealership, Max had imparted the best advice, saying, "Okay, the key to a successful negotiation is to be prepared to walk away at any moment—

even if they have the car of your dreams on the lot ready to go, make sure *they* know you can walk away. Desperation makes people sign bad deals and it's their job to make you feel desperate."

Max had been right. She had walked away from one dealership because the deal wasn't to her liking, but the next dealership had met all her terms, and she'd left the place with the car of her dreams—and the best percentage rate for her loan.

Knowing that you were willing to walk away—even if you were in love—was how people saved themselves from staying in a relationship that was bad for them.

A bad deal.

Was Dante a bad deal?

And by staying, was she signing on for something that ultimately was a bad emotional investment?

She didn't know the answer.

And that was the problem.

# Chapter 22

Dante woke up to find Frannie had already left for the shop. His cleaned clothes were folded neatly on the dresser and there was a note on top that said she had breakfast scheduled with her sister Ruby before the clinic opened and that she'd see him for lunch. He was welcome to use her old pickup until he got a new rental.

Damn it, he must've slept like the dead not to realize Frannie was up and moving around this morning. His brain was still banging from yesterday's event, and it took a minute to shake the cobwebs free. Rising, he groaned against the fresh aches and pains that erupted throughout his body after being tossed about like a rag doll in a washing machine, and went to the shower.

Letting the water sluice down his face, he suffered a moment of panic and anxiety as the situation threatened to overwhelm him.

*Too many questions, too many loose threads.*

He'd paid cash for the car, stuck a rental agency sticker on it so anyone looking would assume it was a rental like any other, and paid for the cheapest insurance he could find on the internet using his fake identity, but he wasn't concerned about the car. He could get another without breaking a sweat, but it was more about the situation with Frannie.

If it weren't for his feelings for her, he would've bailed

on Owl Creek the second he started to feel twitchy, but he couldn't leave her behind, knowing he might've put her in danger.

Attachments were a liability, so he'd been careful not to have any until now.

He hadn't seen it coming. Frannie was the contingency he hadn't been able to foresee.

Losing his phone was inconvenient, but he had another burner back at his place, already preloaded with the important numbers he couldn't lose, including that of his PI.

Dressing quickly, he found the keys to the old truck parked out front and locked up before leaving. He needed to go to his place, pack and figure out how to get Frannie to leave with him.

Desperation had some crazy ideas percolating in his head, but short of kidnapping her, he didn't know how he'd convince Frannie to jump in the car and head into the unknown because it wasn't safe here anymore.

By the time he reached his place, he still didn't have the answers he needed, but he went straight for his hiding spot where he kept a thick stack of cash, his burner phones, and two more fake IDs in case his current identity got burned.

Booting up the phone, he sent a quick message to his PI, letting him know his number had changed.

Almost immediately, Nick called.

"I wondered why you weren't calling me back," he said.

"Yeah, my phone ended up in a lake."

"How's this?"

"It was in the car that also landed in the lake."

Nick whistled low. "Damn. Lucky to be alive. That's some *Final Destination* type stuff."

"Seems my uncle is upping the pressure. What you got for me?"

"Not much on your family yet but I do have some information on that person you asked me to look into."

Frannie's potential stalker. "Go ahead."

"Your guy graduated Boise State with average grades and then moved to Connors, not far from Owl Creek. Maybe about a forty-five-minute drive?"

"Yeah, about that," he confirmed. "What does he do for a living?"

"He's a gig driver for various companies—Uber, Door-Dash, you name it, he does them all."

"So he makes his own schedule."

"Pretty much."

Which would leave him plenty of time to drive to Owl Creek to mess with a former unrequited love. "Anything on his record?"

"Nothing criminal. Just a civil complaint from a neighbor that he failed to bring in his trash cans from the street for a week or so after pickup."

"Was it a recent complaint?"

"About a month ago. Nothing after that, though. Seems harmless."

Didn't feel harmless to Dante. No one right in the head snuck into another person's house to leave flowers uninvited. Especially if they hadn't seen or spoken to one another in years.

"Single? Married?"

"Not married but he might've had a girlfriend at some point. I hacked into his credit card and one of the transactions showed purchases at a lingerie store and a jewelry store a few months back. Nothing since, though."

He didn't like it. Dante had a sense about things. It was one of the reasons he'd been so good at negotiations—he could tell when someone was lying, hiding something, or otherwise off. Except he'd missed all the signs with his uncle until it was too late, and he'd been in waist-deep Santoro muck as his soul started to drown.

"Keep digging. I want to know everything."

But Nick had reservations. "Can I be honest?"

"Of course."

"I think you're barking up the wrong tree. This guy isn't anything but your run-of-the-mill awkward type. He doesn't exactly fit in with the usual social scene but that's not a crime. I think you're hypersensitive because of what you're going through with your family and that's making you see motive where it doesn't exist."

Nick made a solid point. Being chased was enough to make the most levelheaded person paranoid, but someone was messing with Frannie, and he needed to know why. If it wasn't this Allen guy, then who?

Dante grudgingly switched gears. "Right before my car ended up in the lake, I was contacted by someone using a voice disruptor. I think it was my uncle's man, Pietro Romano. He tried to convince me to come home and make peace with my uncle."

"Interesting. Did you get the number?"

"It wasn't a number I recognized but whatever it was, it's now gone because it was on the phone currently at the bottom of Blackbird Lake."

"What made you think it was your uncle's secretary?"

"Something in the way he was trying to get me to come home, to play nice for the sake of family. It reminded me of Pietro. Pietro is rigidly loyal to the family, my uncle in particular, but he was always kind to me. Not everyone attached to my uncle was a bad person."

"But he must've known something was coming because he tried to warn you."

"Yeah, it would seem so."

"What do you have in your possession that is dangerous enough for your uncle to kill to have back?"

"Something that would bring incredible shame to the Santoro name—a secret my uncle will do anything to keep hidden."

Frannie was still thinking about the situation with Dante's car as she shelved books and enjoyed the quiet of the empty store. She hadn't shared her concerns with Ruby at breakfast, but her sister had commented on her pensive mood, mistakenly attributing her uncharacteristic reserve to the family situation.

"It's going to be okay," Ruby assured her, reaching across the diner table to squeeze her hand in solidarity. "No matter what, we'll get through it as a family."

Frannie had smiled, appreciating her big sister's thoughtfulness, but felt guilty that her thoughts had been far from the family drama. Still, she'd said, "I know, it's just a lot to take in."

"Yeah, you're right about that. I talked to Chase yesterday and he said that Aunt Jessie is pushing for *half* of Dad's estate."

"Half? Is she serious?"

"I don't know serious, but greedy and self-centered comes to mind," Ruby said, sipping her coffee. "The nerve of that woman is beyond me. How are Mom and Aunt Jessie even related?"

"She's the evil twin, obviously," Frannie joked.

Ruby chuckled. "Amen, sister. But according to Chase, she has a snowball's chance in hell of getting what she's asking for. If anything, she might qualify for a small settlement, but honestly, I don't think she should get a single cent."

"Me either," Frannie murmured, playing with the handle of her coffee mug. "Mom seems to be handling things well."

"That's Mom in a nutshell," Ruby said dryly. "Allowing anyone to see what's really happening behind the curtain is beyond her capabilities. But then, I guess that was the consequence of living with Dad. He wasn't an easy man to love."

"Do you ever wonder why she didn't leave him?" Frannie asked.

"No. For all his faults, she loved him, and I don't know if that's an endorsement for unconditional love or toxic codependency. All I know is that I wish she could've fallen in love with someone better."

"The heart wants what the heart wants, I guess."

"Yeah, no matter how many red flags are flapping."

Ruby paid for breakfast, and they'd parted ways, but Ruby's last statement still echoed in Frannie's head.

Was she being blinded by love the same as her mom had been with her dad?

"Earth to Frannie, are you listening?"

Frannie was startled as Fletcher's voice abruptly popped into her thoughts. She had no idea Fletcher had even walked into the store, much less was calling her name. "I'm sorry, I didn't hear you come in. What's going on?" she asked, her concerned frown matching his dour expression. "Is everything okay?"

"No, it is definitely not okay," he said, gesturing to her office. "Let's go somewhere private to talk."

"I can't just leave the shop unattended, Fletcher," she said in a low tone, but she was worried about whatever was eating Fletcher to put that look on his face. She motioned for him to follow as she retreated deeper into the Self-Help aisle, which was sadly not the most popular book section. "What's going on?"

"You know how you asked me to look into your friend Dante?"

*Her friend.* She swallowed, embarrassed that she'd even asked, but now, given the circumstances, maybe it was wise. "Yeah, did you find something?" *Please say no.*

"He lied to you."

*Oh, God.*

Frannie stared, unable to process what Fletcher had just said. After a long moment, she asked in a strained tone, "What do you mean, he lied to me? About what?"

"His name, who he is…why he's here…the man can't be trusted. I don't want you around him anymore."

This was all happening too fast. "Hold up, what? I don't understand. What's his name and how do you know all this? Are you sure you have the right man?"

She knew she sounded desperate, but her world was collapsing, and she was grasping at straws.

Realizing she was sinking, Fletcher tried to soften the blow, but there was no easy way to deliver a crap sandwich. "I'm sorry, Frannie, but he's up to no good. Only people with something to hide lie about their identity. His name is Dante Santoro, not Sinclair, and he's part of a dangerous Italian family—the kind that gets away with shady behavior because they have enough money to make problems go away. You know what I'm talking about?"

Those red flags that she'd been ignoring…well, they were practically slapping her in the face now, but she couldn't reconcile what she knew about Dante with what Fletcher was saying. It was like he was describing a stranger.

"You have to have the wrong guy," she protested. "I know Dante. He's the kindest, most compassionate person I've ever met." She felt as if she couldn't breathe. "I'm sorry but you're wrong."

"Frannie, I know it's hard to accept but I asked Max for help because he has access to databases that I don't. The FBI has a file on the Santoro family a mile long but because they're Italian citizens, the FBI has no jurisdiction unless they commit a crime here in the States. They're too good to get caught doing something stupid here, so there's nothing they can tie back to the family, but their hands aren't clean. I'm telling you, Dante isn't safe to be around."

*Is that why his car landed in a lake? Is someone after him?*

Frannie drew a deep breath, trying to calm her racing heart. "Wait, wait, I need a minute to think," she said, fanning her face as tears crowded her sinuses. What nightmare was she in right now? Two days ago, she'd been wondering if she and Dante should put in an offer on a house together, and now Fletcher was telling her that the man she thought she knew—didn't exist!

"Are you saying he's part of the mob?" Frannie asked, trying to make sense of everything.

Fletcher exhaled a short breath, clearly hating to be the bearer of bad news but wasn't willing to back down. "Look, according to Max, the Santoro family isn't connected to the mafia but they're just as powerful. They're obscenely wealthy and that kind of money creates power. You've seen the movies about powerful families—they always manage to get what they want because enough money makes every problem go away. And sometimes that means people, too."

She couldn't make her brain connect the dots with what Fletcher was saying and what she thought she knew about Dante. "If he's part of this powerful family, why is he here in Owl Creek of all places? It's not as if our town is a hotbed of international intrigue. It's literally the most May-berry of places on the map."

"Frannie, every place has its dark corners, you know that. Even Owl Creek. We have drugs, crime, you name it."

"Yeah, I know that," Frannie shot back, exasperated. "But Dante doesn't do any of those things. The man goes out of his way to make sure I have food in his fridge that won't send my stomach into a tizzy. He opens doors and is super protective. I didn't tell you because it didn't seem like a big deal, but I had a mysterious flower delivery two weeks ago that came from an anonymous buyer and then another flower placed on my bed a few days later... Dante has been my shadow making sure that I'm safe. Does that sound like a man who's dangerous?"

Fletcher stared. "What are you talking about...what flowers? And why didn't you report this?"

Frannie groaned, shaking her head. "Because it's not that important, more weird than anything else, and I didn't want to bother you with stupid stuff. I mean, it was flow-ers, not anything scary. But that's not the point. The point is, Dante's been by my side, determined to keep me safe, even if it was from imaginary threats."

"Frannie...did it ever occur to you that maybe he's act-ing like there's something dangerous out there because he knows exactly who sent those flowers and it spooked him?"

Frannie stilled. No, she hadn't thought of that possibil-ity, but she did now. It made more sense than her random stranger theory. "I have to talk to Dante."

"No. I'll talk to him. I'll bring him in for questioning."

"For what? He hasn't committed a crime," Frannie balked. "You can't arrest someone for using a different name to rent a vacation house."

"We have no idea what he's doing here, or why. He might be an international criminal hiding out until the heat passes."

"That seems a little far-fetched," Frannie said, but her voice lacked conviction. *Helloooo, his car landed in a lake!* That internal voice was practically jumping up and down, gesturing emphatically.

The fact was...she didn't know what was true anymore.

Dante had lied to her.

That was the only indisputable fact.

And her stupid, gullible heart was broken.

# Chapter 23

Dante walked into the bookstore and felt the unwelcome, hostile chill coming from the police officer standing beside Frannie. He knew something was up.

"Dante…" Frannie looked crushed, and he felt he was at the epicenter of that devastation. "I—"

"Is everything okay?" he asked, feigning confusion.

But the man cut in with a protective stance, his hand resting on his sidepiece as if Dante were a dangerous threat to Frannie. "I'm going to have to ask you to step outside for a minute, *Mr. Santoro*."

They knew his real name.

Dante caught Frannie's wounded gaze, knowing this man must be one of her brothers. Had she asked her brother to look into his background? He'd never had to hide his identity before, and it was a foreign, uncomfortable feeling knowing they were judging him for being deceptive.

He couldn't blame them.

But he couldn't let Frannie think he was a bad person. He ignored the officer for a minute, directing his attention straight at the woman he loved more than anything. "Can we talk for a minute? I'll explain everything."

But the man wasn't having it. "Outside. Now."

Frannie asked him point-blank, "Is it true?"

The time for lies was over. "Yes." But he was oddly relieved. "And I'm glad you know. But you don't know everything. Let me tell you why."

"There's never a good reason for pretending to be someone you're not," the man replied, his tone hard. "Now, we can do this the easy way or the hard way. Your choice, Mr. Santoro."

Frannie held his stare. "How do I know you won't just keep lying to me?"

"Because now I have no reason to lie and when I tell you why I lied, you'll understand."

"Okay, hard way it is," Fletcher said, grabbing Dante's arm.

"Get your hands off me," Dante growled, stiffening against the man's grip. "I'm assuming you're one of her many brothers and I don't want to make things awkward but if you don't take your hands off me, you and I are going to have an issue."

The man seemed to find Dante's threat amusing. "I don't know how things work in Italy, but here in the United States, threatening an officer of the law is going to land your ass in hot water." He pulled Dante's arms behind his back and zip-tied his wrists together. "We'll finish this conversation down at the station."

But Frannie shocked him by intervening. "Fletcher... wait."

The man looked at his sister in frustration, shaking his head. "Frannie, you have no idea who this man is."

"As far as we know, he hasn't broken the law," Frannie murmured, still conflicted yet shooting dark looks Dante's way.

Dante saw his window, speaking directly to Frannie. "My name is Dante Santoro, I'm heir to one of the most influential and ruthless families in Italy. I changed my name because I didn't want to be found…by my family. I didn't tell you because I didn't want you to be involved with anything as ugly as what I'm dealing with. I haven't killed anyone or committed any kind of crime aside from using a fake name and I never would—which is another reason why I left Italy."

Fletcher quipped, "Great story, let's go."

They managed two steps to the door before Frannie said, "Fletcher, let him go."

"Excuse me?"

"Let me handle this. Dante isn't a threat. This is personal between him and me."

"The hell it is. This man is using an assumed identity. That's fraud."

Frannie couldn't argue that point, but he could tell she was weighing the morality of the situation against what he'd shared already, and she was wavering.

"All I need is a chance to explain," he said, pressing his advantage. He needed her to understand that he wasn't the villain he looked to be.

"Every criminal I know has a sob story—and usually, they're lying about that, too." Fletcher wasn't moved. "A trip to the station is all you're getting today."

This time it was Frannie who was exasperated. "Fletcher, you don't have to do that. He hasn't committed any *real* crime and he pretty much just came clean. Also, he's a lawyer, so he knows the law. Don't waste your time processing paperwork that's not going to go anywhere."

"Frannie…" Fletcher stared long and hard at his sister, but he was digesting her information. Finally, he glanced at Dante, exhaled and shook his head, muttering as he snipped the ties, "I swear to God, if you hurt my sister, I'll show you American justice with extreme prejudice."

Dante rubbed his wrists, nodding. "You're a good brother."

"Yes, I am," he growled, pointing to Frannie, "If he so much as blinks wrong, you better call me."

"I will," Frannie assured Fletcher. "I'll be okay. Thank you, though."

With one final stern glare Dante's way, he exited the bookstore slowly, as if reluctant to take his eyes off Dante. Finally, he climbed into his squad car and drove away.

"So that's Fletcher?" he supposed.

"Yes."

"He seems like a good guy."

"Stop it," she ordered, marching to her front door and locking it, flipping the sign to Closed. "You don't get to blow my world to bits and then try to chitchat about my family. I need you to spill your guts right now."

It was time to be honest—and he was ready for it. Lying to Frannie had become a bigger burden than he ever imagined, and he was relieved to finally be able to come clean.

"In the interest of saving time, what do you know?"

"I know enough. Your family is rich, connected and dangerous. My cousin Max works for the FBI, and they have a file a mile long on your family. But they don't have anything they can pin on the Santoro connection here in the States."

"Sounds accurate," he confirmed. "My family legacy is a checkered quilt of vice and infamy—and I wanted no more part of it once I realized the cost to my soul. I wanted out, Frannie. I swear to you, that's my reason for running away."

"Why'd you have to run away? Are you in danger from your own family?"

"Yes."

Her eyes widened as if she couldn't fathom such a thing, and he knew it was a lot to take in, especially for someone like Frannie, who'd never had to walk side by side with the devil.

She narrowed her gaze with dawning fear. "Your car… did your family have something to do with your car landing in the lake?"

"I don't have proof, but I believe so."

She gasped. "I don't understand…why?"

He sighed, levering himself into the oversize reading chair. "You're going to want to sit down," he said, preparing to tell her the whole sordid story. "There's no happy ending to this story."

Frannie's head was spinning, and she felt spun on her axis.

Dante's story was something out of a movie—these things didn't happen to actual people, did they?

Everything Dante had been through—from losing his father and mother to being drawn in by the uncle now trying to kill him—was more than she could process in one breath. She took a long minute to try and sort the facts into manageable cubes, but tears threatened to fall as she failed miserably.

"How are you handling this? My family has its problems, but they seem miniscule in comparison to what you're dealing with. Oh, God, you must think I'm so naive for going on about my family drama when it doesn't even compare to what you're faced with."

"I've never thought you were naive—kind and compassionate—but never naive," he said, trying to make her feel better. "That's why I think you're incredible. That generous heart of yours is a beautiful thing, and your love has made me realize what I needed most in my life."

Frannie wiped at a tear tracking down her cheek. "My biggest fear after my breakup with my ex was finding someone like him who would break my heart by cheating on me." A small bubble of laughter erupted as she realized there were much worse things. "Instead, I fell in love with an international fugitive with a murderous family. I think that's much worse, don't you?"

He fell silent.

She stared at her hands, slipping into a dark place as her heart wept. What was she supposed to do? Break up with him when he needed someone who wasn't trying to kill him? But then, what did that mean for her? Was she in danger, too? "Is that why you kept asking me to go away for the weekend?" she asked.

He looked miserable—and scared—as he admitted, "I'm not sure if either of us are safe here."

Frannie gasped. "What do you mean?"

"I never should've encouraged anything between us, but I did. And in doing so, I selfishly put your life in danger. I can't take back what I've done but I can do everything in my power to keep you safe. I have enough money to take us anywhere in the world and I have contacts that can create a new identity—"

"No!" She didn't want to be someone else. She liked her life here in Owl Creek. "You can't ask me to change everything about my life in the blink of an eye and expect me to skip after you. Honestly, do you really think that's fair?"

"It's not fair at all," he agreed, his eyes flashing. "And I hate having to ask but the thought of you being hurt because of me—it's more than I can handle! I won't have it happen again!"

*Again?* "What do you mean?"

Dante rose sharply from the chair, startling her with the sudden movement. Tension radiated from his solid frame. She'd never seen him so worked up, and it was a little jarring. She'd only ever seen the calm, cool-headed man who always seemed to have quiet wisdom to share. Not this man who seemed eaten up by an internal fire he couldn't escape.

"My ex—Belinda—the one I don't like to talk about… there's a reason I'm putting all my cards on the table so there's no more secrets between us. Are you ready for the full truth?"

"I think so," she answered, wary. *It gets worse?* In for a penny, in for a pound, as her grandmother used to say. "What happened to your ex?"

"Belinda was a top pediatric surgeon. Her skill was in her deft work on tiny babies. She had a gift that drew people from around the world to have her in the operating room. She could've handpicked any hospital on this planet as her primary residency, but she loved her home country and always wanted to remain in Italy."

"She sounds like a superstar," Frannie said, feeling insecure at an inappropriate moment. How could she possibly stack up against a résumé like that? Dante's ex probably looked like a supermodel, too.

Dante must've sensed her insecurity. He immediately soothed it in a way only he could. "She was incredible—but she wasn't you. Never forget that."

In that split second, Frannie felt a hot wave pass between them as if their chemistry couldn't be contained, even in moments such as this when the world seemed to be collapsing. A rush of powerful emotion nearly sent her to her knees.

As far as she knew, no one planned to fall in love—it just happened.

And sometimes, it happened with the person who seemed a lousy bet on paper. All the reasons to walk away were scrawled in big, bold letters, but she knew she wouldn't.

*Couldn't.*

She would stand by him. No matter what happened.

Even if that meant leaving behind everything she'd ever known.

"Tell me what happened to Belinda," she said bravely. "I need to know everything."

Dante nodded, understanding what was unspoken. His eyes watered, but he choked back the tears.

And then he held her hand and unloaded the most horrific story she'd ever heard. His voice broke at times as he recounted how he'd nursed Belinda back to health and then spirited her away when she could travel, leaving her in Switzerland to rebuild. How he'd been chased by the guilt he couldn't dodge.

She saw the pain in his eyes.

Felt the remorse.

And she knew that no matter who his family was, Dante was cut from a different cloth and would never do anything that led him down the same path. His only choice had been running, and she couldn't fault him for that.

Desperate times called for desperate measures, and it was easy to say but harder to follow through. Most people wouldn't have had the strength of character to do what Dante had done to protect himself and his loved ones, but Dante was one of a kind.

There was no way in hell she'd make him walk that path alone.

"I love you, Dante," she said, holding his gaze. "We'll figure this out together."

"Are you sure? Now is the time to cut your losses. I'll help you no matter what."

She heard the desperate note in his voice, battling a war she couldn't possibly understand, and it hurt her heart.

"I'm not going anywhere," she replied firmly. "But I think we should tell my brother and cousin Max. They might be able to help."

Dante shook his head, clearly opposed to that idea. "The fewer people I put in harm's way, the better. We need to keep our circle small. I know you're close to your family, but you have to trust me on this. Please keep this information between us."

Frannie didn't like it, but she agreed. *For the time being.* Everything was too new to start rocking the boat, but she knew Dante was too close to the situation to see that he couldn't do this alone.

Dante, relieved, pulled her close and sealed his mouth to hers in a passionate kiss that they usually reserved for private moments, away from public view.

But it was as if he wanted the world to know they belonged together. Frannie melted against him, loving how well they seemed to fit, but a chill slithered down her spine at the unpleasant sensation of being watched.

Maybe it was because they'd been so careful to keep their relationship private, or perhaps it was because a seed of paranoia had been planted about his family, but she couldn't escape the feeling that someone was watching.

And it scared her more than she wanted to admit.

# *Chapter 24*

It took some doing, but Frannie talked Dante into not doing anything rash until they'd had time to make a plan. For one, she couldn't skip town without making arrangements for her shop and at least talking to her mom about an extended vacation as a cover story.

Dante conceded, but he was understandably jumpy.

Even though she promised to keep the situation between them, Franny knew she would at least have to talk to Darla. Someone in her circle had to understand what was truly going on just in case things went south in a bad way. Plus, Darla was getting married soon, and it didn't seem fair to not let her know what was happening in case her maid of honor disappeared.

Darla showed up at the shop the next day with a frown. "Okay, you're going to have to explain that very cryptic voice mail you left because I can't make head or tail of what you said."

"Sorry about that. I was nervous about leaving too much detail on the message."

"Yeah, see, when you say things like that my anxiety just gets worse. What is going on?"

Frannie drew a deep breath, still unable to believe she was in the middle of something this complicated. She tried to prepare Darla. "I'm going to need you to suspend your disbelief and listen to what I have to say because I can guarantee you, you aren't going to believe me at first."

Darla's eyes widened with interest. "You've got my attention. Shoot."

With something this big, it was probably best to throw it all out there and sort the details later. "Dante is part of a dangerous wealthy family—not the mob—but rich and powerful enough to bend the rules to their benefit, and they're after him. His name is Dante Santoro, and we'll probably leave town soon. I wanted to let you know so that you don't worry."

Frannie realized Darla couldn't process all of that as fact because who could? These kinds of things didn't happen to ordinary people. Particularly people who lived in Owl Creek, a town known for its pristine lake and quaint downtown. Darla proved she was right with her reply. "I'm sorry, what?"

Frannie tried again. "I told you it was a lot. Here's the thing. Dante changed his name so he could get away from his family, but they may have found him already. Dante thinks they're the reason he ended up in the lake. They tried to kill him by cutting the brakes on his car."

"That *actually* happens?" Darla said, incredulous. "I thought that only happened in spy movies. I wouldn't even know how to find a brake line, much less cut one."

"You barely know where to put the gas in your car," Frannie quipped. "But I had the same reaction as you. I'm still having a hard time wrapping my head around everything, but it's very real—and very dangerous."

Even though Dante had asked Frannie to keep details private, she couldn't keep that intel from her best friend.

Frannie shared what had happened to Belinda and how

she was starting a new life in Switzerland, but not as a pediatric surgeon any longer.

Darla stared for a long moment, then snapped out of it and declared, "You have to break up with him."

"I'm not going to do that," Frannie said, shaking her head. "I love him."

"And I love strawberries but I'm deathly allergic and if I eat one, I'll most certainly die a horrible death. Sometimes we have to give up things that are bad for our health."

"It's not Dante's fault that his family is awful. He's trying to do the right thing."

"Yeah, and brownie points for his moral victory. But if you end up dead as collateral damage, I could not care less about his emotional growth. Catch my drift? His exgirlfriend was beaten almost to death and then maimed for life. Dante's got bigger problems than most people and you're too sweet and loving to see that he's going to get you killed—and then if that happens, I'm going to have to go to prison for killing Dante. See how all of that is bad?"

Frannie loved Darla's bold declaration, but she recognized it for what it was—fear. "Nothing is going to happen to me. Dante is determined to keep me safe, which is why we probably have to leave Owl Creek."

"This is ridiculous. What are you even saying? Leave town with a guy who has killers after him? No, let *him* leave and have him send you a postcard when the heat dies down and you don't have to worry about eating a bullet during dinner."

It was sensible, but she knew she couldn't let Dante deal with this alone.

"If Tom were in the same situation, you wouldn't hesitate to do whatever you could to help."

"Tom would never be in a situation like this," Darla

countered, shaking her head. "Tom lines up and color co-ordinates his socks. He would never end up on the run for any reason—and I like him that way. Come to think of it, your situation has me rethinking all the times I called him boring. I like boring."

"Yes, you love Tom. That's the point, Darla."

At that, Darla fell quiet.

"See? We do what we have to for the people we love—and I love Dante."

"Are you sure? You barely know him," Darla returned in a plaintive tone. "This is the premise of a true-crime documentary in the making. No one in their right mind would just leave everything behind for someone who's being chased by dangerous people. What can I do to change your mind?"

"Nothing."

Darla groaned. "This is a nightmare."

"It's not great," she agreed. "But I wanted someone in my circle to know in case things go south."

"Not to sound like a dick, but how are you going to be my maid of honor if you're fleeing the country? And what about your family? It's not like they're going to be fine with you disappearing. Hell, Max will have the FBI chasing after you and then your lover boy will have two people after him."

Frannie laughed, even though it wasn't funny, but it was because it was so Darla. "Yeah, about that... You might want to replace me in your wedding. As for my family, I'll think of something so they don't worry."

"You're irreplaceable."

Darla's deadpan answer was about more than the wedding, and Frannie's eyes teared up. "Nothing is going to happen to me." It was a promise she didn't have the right to offer because she didn't know what the future held, but

Darla needed some reassurance, or she might fall apart. "With any luck, the situation will resolve itself, and this will all be an unpleasant memory."

"Unpleasant is one word for it."

"I don't like what's happening either, but I can't ignore how I feel about him. This is the real deal—the kind of love that only comes once in a lifetime—and I'm not going to walk away. We need each other."

Darla sighed, giving up even though she didn't seem convinced. But at least she didn't keep pressing, and Frannie was grateful. She couldn't fight her best friend and still have the strength to be Dante's support.

The fact that Darla intuitively knew that was why they'd been best friends since the third grade.

They understood each other. They loved each other.

And that love was why Frannie had to tell her.


Dante felt lighter but no less anxious. He had hated lying to Frannie—each time he saw that questioning look in her eyes, knowing she was sensing his dishonesty, he'd wanted to break down and lay it all on the line, but he'd known he couldn't.

Now that part was done. He'd told her everything—down to the grittiest detail—and she was determined to stand by his side, which humbled him in ways he couldn't even put into words.

No one had ever been so steadfast, so loyal, and he vowed to make sure she never had reason to question his integrity.

His phone rang, and he checked the caller ID this time before answering. It was Nick, his PI.

"Dante, I thought you might want to know…that guy you had me watching just got flagged on some suspicious purchases with his credit card. It could be nothing, but it was out of pocket enough to warrant a second look."

"Yeah? What kind of purchases?"

"Zip ties, chlorine bleach, ethanol and acetone, and an industrial-size bag of cloth towels. Purchased this morning."

He didn't like the sound of that. "Why would a gig driver need those chemicals?"

"He wouldn't. Unless he was planning to make home-made chloroform to knock out one of his passengers."

A warning bell went off in Dante's head, urging him to check on Frannie at the shop. "I have to go," he said abruptly, clicking off. He immediately rang Frannie. She picked up on the second ring, and relief followed. "Are you okay?"

"I'm fine," she said, chuckling quizzically. "You told me to act normal, so I'm just doing my usual shelving. Darla stopped by earlier but it's just me now."

"No customers in the shop?"

"No, it's nice and quiet. Gives me a chance to catch up on my paperwork. I was thinking of maybe asking Darla to cover the shop while we're gone on 'vacation.'"

"Yeah, sure, good idea," he said, distracted. He still had a bad feeling. "I think you should close early today."

"I can't do that. I have a shipment coming today."

"Frannie—"

"Oh! I gotta go, looks like someone's heading my way. I'll see you later. Let's have dinner with my mom tonight."

And then she clicked off like danger wasn't pressing in on them from all sides—and some danger she didn't even know was coming.

Frannie placed her cell phone on the counter just as the front door opened and a man walked through. There was a tingle of recognition, but it took a minute for her to realize she was staring at Allen Burns. However, he didn't look like the same guy she'd shared a few classes with in college.

The years had been rough.

His reedy frame had become soft and doughy, his complexion splotchy and uneven, but his vibe threw her off the most.

Where he'd once been shy and quiet, preferring his plants to people, now there was a disordered air of chaos around him, an anger that pulsated beneath the surface of his seemingly approachable veneer.

*Don't be so judgy*, a voice admonished. Allen had spent his life being bullied by people who made assumptions. She couldn't do that to him, too.

"Allen? Oh, gosh, I almost didn't recognize you! How are you?" she asked, trying to be polite and engaging as she would with anyone who entered her store. "I haven't seen you since graduation. What have you been up to?"

"Frannie…it's so good to see you," Allen said, licking his lips and glancing around the shop. "This…uh, your place?"

"Yep. Bought and paid for—well, not exactly paid for yet, but I'm doing my best, despite the economy."

"You always did love books," he said, stepping a little closer in a way that made her twitchy. "Anyone else here?"

During her freshman year at Boise State, the campus had hosted a women's safety course with the cooperation of the local police. During one class, the instructor had brought a convicted rapist to talk about how he would pick his victims. He'd look for a woman alone, with hair in a ponytail or a single braid because it was easier to grab and pull the victim off-balance, and he'd look for someone who didn't make eye contact because it suggested a level of humility that he could subdue. But going above and beyond those practical tips, most of his victims shared a commonality—they ignored their intuition because they didn't want to come off as rude.

Frannie stepped back as if heading to her counter to grab the short stack of books waiting for her to shelve, her mind moving quickly. *Keep him talking.* Someone was bound to walk in at some point, and likely he'd leave. "So, what's new with you? What brings you to Owl Creek?"

"Where you going? No hug? I haven't seen you in ages, and you're treating me like I got the plague." His tone was joking, but there was an odd gleam in his eye, and his left hand had moved to his jean pocket.

"Actually, I've got a little summer cold. I better keep my distance, or you'll end up with the sniffles, too."

His gaze narrowed with cold suspicion. "Oh, I get it. You're too good to say hello to an old friend now that you've got your fancy boyfriend."

Frannie stilled. How did he know about Dante? "Allen… how'd you know I was engaged?" she asked, stretching the truth a bit.

Allen ignored the question and slowly advanced toward her. "You know, I always thought you were better than most girls. Always so nice. You never made me feel like a freak like the other girls. I liked you."

"I liked you, too, Allen," she said, careful to keep her tone soft and calming, but her heart raced. "But I'm confused by how you knew I was engaged. I haven't seen you in years."

"I've seen you."

She swallowed. "Oh yeah? When?"

He ignored that question, too, but added something else that froze her blood. "I know what you like. More than he ever could. I know you, Frannie."

"Allen, you're starting to scare me. Tone it down, okay?"

"You like to sleep naked with the ceiling fan on medium and only a light sheet for when it gets too breezy."

"Allen!" She felt exposed. "Have you been watching me?"

"You like to eat dairy when you know you shouldn't because it hurts your stomach something awful, yet you do it anyway. I get it, I do things I shouldn't, too. But I can take care of you, make sure you stop doing things that aren't good for you."

"I don't need anyone to take care of me. I need you to get a hold of yourself and stop acting like this or I will call the police."

"I can't have you do that," he said, moving with a swiftness she hadn't realized possible to jerk her toward him. She slammed into him with an *ooof*, and something acrid and chemically pungent went over her mouth and nose as Allen held her with an iron grip.

Instinct made her scream, but she realized too late she should've held her breath and stomped on his instep instead. Her head started pounding as the chemical smell choked out her breath. No matter how she struggled, Allen's grip held her tight. Her fingernails dug into his arm, but he didn't waver. Within a few minutes, her muscles lost their strength, her vision started to blacken, and she slumped in his arms, passed out cold.

# Chapter 25

Dante jumped out of the old truck and ran into the shop just in time to see a thick, doughy man grunting with the difficulty of dragging Frannie's inert body out the shop's back door. Sprinting toward them, he caught the man off guard and punched him hard, causing him to drop Frannie and stumble back.

He grabbed the man by his shirt and drove his fist into his face again, breaking his nose. Shaking him like a rag doll, he yelled, "What did you do to her?"

The man glared up at him through the blood, bubbles of red snot dribbling from his nose and mixing with the drool. "She was supposed to be mine," he said with hot resentment. "Not yours. You took her from me!"

"You're a nutjob," Dante said, shoving him with disgust. The man tried to roll away and scramble to his feet, but Dante drove his foot into the man's soft gut and sent him sprawling, gasping for air. "Don't move," he ordered in a thunderous roar, grabbing the first thing he could find to tie the man's hands together. He remembered seeing Frannie stash a roll of duct tape in a utility box beneath the counter. Winding the tape around the man's hands and legs so tight it probably cut the circulation off, he called 911 while checking on Frannie.

She was still breathing, slow and steady. Just as Nick had

surmised, the asshole had made his own chloroform. Dante could only imagine what he'd had in mind for Frannie once he got her loaded into his car. He had to stop thinking about the what-ifs, or else he might do something he regretted.

Picking her up gently, he carried her to the oversize reading chair that was her favorite and gently stroked her face, trying to wake her up.

Within a minute, Owl Creek PD showed up with lights and sirens. Frannie's brother was first on the scene. He quickly saw Frannie unconscious and started yelling, but Dante cut him off. "The man you want is behind the counter, near the back door. I've got him tied up with duct tape. I think he used chloroform on her."

"Get a medic in here!" Fletcher yelled before moving toward the back where Dante had left the man trussed up like a Christmas turkey.

Paramedics poured into the building, and Dante stepped out of their way while they checked her vitals.

"BP is stable, but her oxygen is low. Let's get her loaded up for transport," the paramedic instructed as he fixed an oxygen mask over her face.

Another officer bagged the cloth that the man had dropped on the ground when he tried to drag Frannie's body out the back door, and Fletcher confirmed it was chloroform. "Who the hell is this guy? Is he one of yours?" he asked Dante, glaring with accusation. "I told you if you hurt my sister—"

"He's a guy Frannie went to school with at Boise State," Dante barked to shut Fletcher up, following paramedics as they loaded her onto a stretcher. "His name is Allen Burns. Look him up. I'm heading to the hospital with Frannie."

He didn't explain to Fletcher how he knew. That wasn't his problem, and he sure as hell wasn't staying behind while the ambulance took Frannie away.

When she woke up, he wanted to be by her side.

But Fletcher wasn't finished. "Hold up, where the hell you think you're going? We're not done here."

"The hell we aren't. That ambulance is taking the woman I love, and I'll be damned if I'm going to sit around and wait for your permission to be there when she wakes up. If you want to talk later, fine, but for now, I'm following that ambulance."

The two men had a short stare-down, but Fletcher grudgingly backed down when he realized Dante wasn't playing chicken with him. "Fine, go. But there will be questions later."

"Fine," he growled back, jumped into the truck and chased after the ambulance. All he could say was that if that asshole had somehow hurt Frannie with his bathtub chemistry set, he'd break all the laws to make sure he never had use of his fingers again.

He pulled into the parking lot and sprinted into the lobby, bypassed the registration and went straight to the ER bay. A flabbergasted receptionist hurried after him, screeching about calling security, but Dante wouldn't let anyone stop him from seeing Frannie.

He found Frannie's bed just as her eyes were opening sluggishly. One nurse was finishing a blood draw and another was adjusting her oxygen flow. The doctor, startled by the commotion Dante had created, saw the concern on Dante's face and waved off the security team that had started piling in after him. "I'm assuming you know Frannie Colton," the doctor said.

"Yes, she's my girl," he answered, wishing he could say she was his wife. "Is she going to be okay?"

"Your name?"

"Dante Sinclair," he said, using his fake identity. The fewer people knowing his real name, the better.

Frannie weakly pulled at the oxygen mask so she could speak, and both men swiveled to protest, but she batted at both of them with a frown. "My head feels like it's full of rocks, and my mouth tastes like a stinky sock smells."

Dante's sudden relief was palpable as he leaned forward and kissed her forehead. "There's my brave girl. How are you feeling?"

"Not great," she answered, looking to the doctor. "Hi, Doc, am I going to live?"

The doctor chuckled, shaking his head. "It'll take more than a clumsy chemical attempt to drag you down. We're running some blood tests to check for any other possible toxins, but your oxygen levels are already returning to normal. I think you're going to be fine, aside from a monster headache. We'll get you some Tylenol for the pain."

But Frannie declined, saying, "I think I've had enough chemicals in my body for the day." To Dante, she said, "I'd rather just go home and lie down in a dark room, sleep it off."

"I will happily arrange that," he said, but then people he could only assume were more family anxiously burst into the room.

Two women who looked similar enough ignored Dante and went straight to Frannie.

"Oh my God, Fletcher group-texted us to let us know someone had attacked you in the store," the first one said, shocked. "What happened?"

Frannie sighed, clearly still processing what had happened, but she took a minute to make quick introductions. "Dante, these are my sisters, Ruby and Hannah, and yes,

I was attacked by a guy I used to know. If it weren't for Dante... I don't know what he had planned."

The women spun on their heels to rush Dante, crushing him in a surprise hug that startled him. "Thank you!" Ruby said, squeezing him hard. "You saved our baby sister. You're a freaking hero."

The one named Hannah wiped away tears. "I'm literally in shock right now. How does something like this happen in our little town?"

"He's been watching me for a while, I guess," Frannie said, swallowing. "He...he...ugh, he watched me sleep. I feel so damn violated right now and icky. Like my skin is crawling at the thought."

Dante wanted to punch the man all over again. Speaking of... "I should probably talk to your brother and give him an official statement. I didn't give him an option of holding me at the scene, but now that I know you're safe..."

Frannie understood immediately, nodding. "Yes, please go talk to my brother. Let him know what happened. Ruby or Hannah can take me home. I'll see you back at my place when you're done."

It was a solid plan, even though he hated the idea of leaving her side. However, seeing her with her sisters, he knew she was in good hands.

"All right, but only because I don't want your brother showing up at your place trying to put me in handcuffs for refusing to answer questions at the scene."

"Fletcher can be stubborn like that," Ruby agreed. "Don't worry, we'll get her home safely."

"Nice to meet you," Hannah said. "Though I wish it were under better circumstances."

"Yes, indeed," he murmured. Stealing another glance at Frannie as her sister smoothed the hair back from her crown with such love, he suffered a moment of envy for never knowing what that was like.

*That's how a family is supposed to act with each other.*

Backing away, he left Frannie in the able care of her sisters and headed to the police station.

Frannie loved her sisters, but she was bothered by the odd expression on Dante's face before he slipped out. Before she could dwell too deeply, Ruby was peppering her with questions.

"Okay, I need details. What the hell?"

Frannie knew they wouldn't rest until she spilled the beans, so she drew a deep breath and shared every detail, down to the weird tingle in her gut that warned her that something was wrong.

"It's so strange. At first I was really happy to see him because I haven't seen him since graduation and I thought we were pretty close, but there was just something weird about his vibe, the energy was off. I think it was something in his eyes. I don't know, but I definitely listened to my intuition, and I tried to put space between us. Unfortunately, I did not do so well at remembering to hold my breath when he put the cloth over my face. Within minutes I was blacking out. If Dante hadn't showed up when he did, I don't know what would've happened."

Ruby shuddered. "I don't even want to think about it, but obviously he was up to no good."

Hannah looked disturbed. "Why were you friends with him in the first place?"

Frannie frowned. "Because I don't like it when people are bullied just because they're different. He wasn't like this when we were in school. When I knew him, he was quiet and shy, and really sweet. I don't know what happened to him between graduation and now but he's definitely not the same person."

Hannah nodded but switched gears. "And who is your knight in shining armor? The chemistry between you is obviously not platonic, so…new boyfriend?"

"Um, yes," Frannie admitted. "We were taking it slow so I didn't want to prematurely share that I was seeing someone, but we've recently agreed to make it official." *Right before planning to skip town because his family is trying to kill him.* Better to leave that part out. "His name is Dante Sinclair and I'm crazy about him."

"Well, he saved your life so he's automatically my favorite person right now," Ruby said.

Frannie smiled, wishing they had more time to get to know Dante under better circumstances. "He's really great," she murmured.

"I definitely get a better vibe from him than your last guy," Hannah admitted. "I mean, I always wanted to be supportive but your ex…seemed smarmy from the start. Good riddance to that guy. Tell us more about Dante. That accent is so yummy."

"He's…um, from Italy." Maybe she shouldn't have shared that? It was hard to censor herself with her sisters but denying the obvious would've been a red flag. "And yes, that accent was the first thing to grab my attention. Followed by his obvious good looks," she added with a blush.

"Can't blame you. Who isn't a sucker for a good accent?" Ruby said. "Well, it's official, you have to bring him to family dinner soon. Mom is going to want to meet him, and it sounds like he and Fletcher have gotten off to a rocky start? So, sooner rather than later would be great so we can help smooth out any bumps."

*Rocky* wasn't the word for it, Frannie thought, shifting with discomfort. Fletcher knew the whole truth about Dante, and she hoped he kept that information private.

She was nervous about Fletcher and Dante talking without a buffer, but she could only hope her brother kept a level head and Dante didn't say or do anything to make Fletcher regret trusting him.

# Chapter 26

Dante walked into the small police station, determined to resolve this without creating more problems between himself and Frannie's brother. She was so close to her family he didn't want to become a wedge, even though he knew it was probably inevitable.

They weren't going to be happy when he and Frannie split town. He would look like the bad guy, and there was no getting around that.

But he didn't have to hasten that opinion by creating friction with Fletcher.

He checked in at the front desk, but Fletcher saw him come in and waved him over to his desk.

"You showed up," Fletcher said with surprise, hitting him with the full measure of suspicion he probably deserved.

"I told you I would."

"Well, forgive me if I don't exactly trust your word right now," Fletcher said. "Have a seat."

Dante bit his tongue and levered himself into the uncomfortable metal chair opposite Fletcher. "I'll tell you everything I know."

"You're damn right you will," Fletcher said. "Start at the beginning. How'd you know that guy was at the shop?"

"I didn't." If he told Fletcher that his PI had been following the guy, he'd ask why and that would open a can of worms. Instead, he said, "I usually stop in to see Frannie at some point during the day. It's part of our routine."

Fletcher didn't seem to like any mention of Dante and Frannie's relationship, which made Dante wonder if he'd been this protective when her ex-boyfriend was out there cheating on her or if he was reserving this attitude just for Dante.

"Then what happened?"

"I saw a guy dragging Frannie down the short hallway to the back door and chased him down, punched him in the face and then subdued him. After I realized he wasn't going anywhere, I checked on Frannie while calling 911. Then you guys arrived. That's the long and short of it."

"How'd you know it was a guy from Frannie's college?"

"She'd mentioned him."

"Did you know him?"

"No."

"Then how'd you know it was him?"

*My PI told me.* "A hunch."

"Guess it was a pretty solid hunch."

"Guess so."

"Also pretty lucky."

Dante leaned forward, finished with the tough cop routine when he wasn't the enemy. "Look, we can be enemies if you want but it'll just make things harder on Frannie and I don't think either of us want that. I love your sister. Seeing that asshole try to drag her unconscious body down a hallway made me see red. I've never been a violent man, but in that moment, I was willing to go to hell if he hurt her. I'm just grateful that I caught him in time before he managed to get her into his car."

At Dante's blunt statement, Fletcher stilled, as if the

importance of what mattered just slammed him upside the temple. All this male posturing was immaterial after realizing they'd all come too close to losing the woman they all loved.

That was the thing, Frannie was a gem. She was kind, compassionate, funny and wise—it was hard to find anyone who didn't find her delightful—which made him feel ugly for selfishly needing her to leave with him.

Fletcher exhaled a heavy breath, frowning as he admitted, "I get that you care about my sister. That much I can see is true. But I can't wrap my head around the other stuff. I'm an officer of the law—integrity matters—and when someone's guilty of lying about something big, chances are, they'll lie about something small. And I make it a point to avoid entertaining liars in my life. But when my baby sister loves someone who's admitted to lying…it puts me in a bad spot. Do you get what I'm saying?"

It was the first honest dialogue between him and Fletcher, and Dante sensed taking advantage of the fragile moment was necessary. "I don't blame you. If I had a sister, I'd feel similarly protective. You already know my family is problematic and I was trying to distance myself from their influence. But it doesn't wipe away the fact that I did lie—to many people for many reasons—and I understand your knee-jerk reaction to keep Frannie away from me."

"Great. So at least we understand each other. But where does that leave the situation?"

The situation would resolve itself as soon as he and Frannie left town, but for now, he wanted justice. "How about we focus on the guy who tried to kidnap Frannie? We can figure out the rest later."

"The investigation is just starting but we've got a detective chasing down the man's background, etc. He's in custody and that's where he'll stay until he's arraigned."

"Unless he posts bail."

"Not likely. Frannie used to babysit for the judge's family. Once this case crosses his desk, he'll set the bail as high as possible and I doubt the guy is rolling in a family trust. He can cool his jets in a jail cell until then."

That was good news, at least. Small-town connections could be a blessing at times.

"If you're running from your family, my guess is you're not planning to stay in Owl Creek for long. What happens then? You gonna break my sister's heart when you bail? Or are you trying to talk my sister into bailing with you?"

The man was too clever. He saw more than he shared and used his "country cop" routine to create the illusion of a dull-minded man—which he was not.

When Dante remained silent, Fletcher shook his head. "Look, man, I'll level with you. Frannie is an adult and she's capable of making her own decisions. But her heart is soft, possibly too soft for what you've got planned and I don't want to see her get hurt. Understand? So, if you're planning to leave town…do it when she's at the shop and just go. Let her move on with her life if you can't offer her a real chance at happiness. Because my sister deserves more than scraps from a man who can't offer nothing but pain and heartache."

Dante swallowed, knowing that Fletcher was right. What was he offering Frannie? Asking her to leave everything she knew for an uncertain future as he ran from his family, leapfrogging from one town to another, only one step ahead of his uncle each day? Was that fair?

That was no life for a woman like her. She deserved the best kind of life where she was cherished *and* safe.

"I would never hurt her," Dante said, though the promise tasted hollow.

"Maybe not intentionally, but you already admitted you're on the run. I don't see how this ends any way but bad."

"I never meant to fall in love with her," he said as if that improved the situation. "I tried to keep some distance between us."

Fletcher seemed sympathetic, saying with a knowing glance, "Oh, I know Frannie can be persistent when she gets something in her head—trust me, I know—but sometimes she doesn't know what kind of trouble she's stepping into because she only sees the good in people. It's one of her best qualities but it sure keeps her family on their toes."

Dante chuckled, Fletcher's words giving him a rare glimpse into what may have been young Frannie's life—protected by a wall of siblings, all the while skipping right into trouble without a second thought. "That's probably what drew that creep straight to her," Dante murmured.

"Likely. Frannie always did love championing an underdog."

Was that what he was to Frannie? The underdog in her eyes? Someone she needed to champion?

He ought to be the one being the champion for her.

Again, he was struck by the fear that he was repeating a loop from his parents.

His father had dragged his mother down a path littered with thorns, not realizing how each step left his mother cut and bruised until she was willing to do anything to be safe again.

The desk phone rang, and Fletcher gestured for Dante to hold up a minute, then answered. His expression darkened as he listened, his jaw hardening. "You're kidding me," he said, shaking his head. Blowing a long breath, he said, "Thanks for letting me know, man. Keep me posted." He hung up and turned to Dante. "That was the detective assigned to Frannie's case."

Dante waited, instantly tense. "What did he find out?"

"That was one helluva hunch," he repeated, eyeing Dante with fresh speculation. "The detective just found a fortified room in Allen Burns's house. Looks like he was planning for a reluctant guest."

"What does that mean?" Dante asked.

"It means that man planned on kidnapping Frannie and holding her hostage for a long time. The sick bastard had shackles bolted into the wall and a bucket in the corner. Holy hell…"

Just like Fletcher, Dante reeled from that intel. He wouldn't have known to get to the shop if he'd missed Nick's call. A delay of even a few minutes could have doomed Frannie to a nightmarish hellscape.

"Tell me how you knew."

Dante didn't want to lie to Fletcher. He was walking the razor's edge with the truth, and it didn't matter that he had a good reason—because more lies just made him look more guilty than he already did in Fletcher's eyes.

"Take a walk with me," Dante said, rising.

Fletcher frowned but agreed, motioning toward the back door. He punched in the security code and stepped outside the building. Once alone in the vehicle yard, Fletcher asked, "Okay, what's with the field trip?"

"My dishonesty has only ever been grounded in necessity. The fewer people who know what's going on, the safer they'll be. You're Frannie's favorite brother. I didn't want to put you in a dangerous position, but it looks like there's no way to fully clear the air between us without the full truth."

"Seems about right," Fletcher agreed, waiting. "So what's the full truth?"

"I knew about Allen Burns because I had my PI looking into him when Frannie started getting weird flower deliveries."

"Go on."

"First, it was a bouquet delivered to her shop. She thought they were from me. When I told her I hadn't sent the flowers, we tried to find out who sent them, but they were sent anonymously through an internet company using a local florist. Frannie waved it off, thinking it was a harmless mistake or maybe even from one of her friends who thought it might be funny to prank her. I didn't find the humor and wanted her to report it, but she said she didn't want to put more on your plate given what your family has been going through."

"That's Frannie, always looking out for everyone else."

"Then, after spending the day on the lake, we got back to her place and there was a single flower laid on her pillow, deliberately placed there for her to find. That was the final straw for me. I didn't want her staying alone after that, but she still didn't want to make a report."

"Damn it, Frannie," Fletcher swore under his breath. "Yeah, those were definite red flags. I knew that was a mistake but Frannie can be real stubborn when she wants to be."

"Well, hindsight and all that. Now we know Allen was the one stalking her, waiting for the right moment to grab her."

Fletcher nodded. "So, why the secrecy? Why'd we have to come outside for you to tell me this?"

"There's more."

Fletcher braced himself. "All right, go ahead."

"The reason my PI was looking into Burns was to either confirm or rule him out. The thing is, Owl Creek isn't safe anymore—for me or Frannie. After my brake line was cut—"

"Hold up, there hasn't been a report completed yet about your car. How do you know it wasn't just a faulty manufacturer issue?"

"Because my PI got a hold of the mechanic shop contracted to go over the vehicle and there was a clear cut in the line. It was deliberately sabotaged. There's only one reason that could happen and it has everything to do with my family. They won't stop until they get what they want."

"What do they want, exactly?"

"Either I come home with my tail between my legs and agree to rejoin the Santoro family or die. There are no in-betweens with my uncle."

Fletcher whistled low. "And I thought *my* dad was a prick. Your uncle sounds like a peach."

"Yeah, that's one word for him. But my point is, he won't stop. Not until he gets what he wants."

"What's stopped him to this point?"

"Aside from the fact that I keep staying one step ahead? I have something of great value to him with the power to destroy the Santoro reputation. My uncle will do anything to get that piece of leverage back."

"I'm dying to know what it is that you've got but my sense of self-preservation keeps my curiosity in check. All I'm gonna say is, I hope you have it in a safe place."

"I do."

Fletcher sighed, shaking his head as if unsure what to do with all that information, but at least he'd lost that suspicion in his stare. That was something.

"Okay, here's the deal," Fletcher said after a pause. "I don't know why—and I hope it doesn't bite me in the ass—

but I'll take a chance and trust you're being truthful this time. I don't know how to solve your problem with your family. But I can tell you if you want to have a life with my sister, you'd better find a solution more solid than being on the run until the end of your days, because Frannie isn't cut out for that life."

Dante knew that. God, he knew.

All he could say was, "I'm working on it," because it was the truth, but even Dante knew that wasn't nearly good enough.

## Chapter 27

Frannie finished getting dressed. She was folding her hospital gown neatly when her mother's voice nearly made all three Colton sisters jump like guilty schoolchildren caught sneaking candy from the teacher's desk.

"Francesca!"

"Mom!" Frannie's hand flew to her chest to keep it from plopping from her sternum. "You scared the crap out of me."

To her shock, Jenny pulled Frannie straight to her for a tight hug as if she were terrified to let go. "I just heard what happened." She released Frannie only to glare at her other two daughters. "And why did I have to hear about it from Hettie Long, the biggest gossip in town, while picking up a package at the post office? Hmm? Neither of you could've picked up the phone and let me know what happened to my youngest daughter? Honestly, shame on you both."

"Mom, it happened so fast… I was going to call but I thought maybe it was something Frannie should tell you in person," Ruby said, looking to her sisters for help. "It wasn't like we weren't going to tell you."

Frannie came to Ruby's rescue. "Beyond a nasty headache and the sudden urge to take some self-defense classes, I'm fine. Don't be mad at Ruby and Hannah."

"Yeah, don't be mad at us," Hannah piped in.

"I'm not mad, I'm just...gosh darn it, Francesca, don't you ever worry me like that again!"

And then Frannie saw the misplaced anger for what it truly was—fear. She swallowed, softening. "Mama, I'm okay and the guy responsible is sitting in jail. Don't worry, crisis averted."

A tear escaped Jenny's eye, and she wiped at it quickly, nodding. "Yes, of course. I'm just rattled, is all. Hettie made it sound so..." she huffed a short breath, looking for clarification "...well, dramatic."

"To be fair, it was kinda dramatic," Ruby said. "Some weirdo tried to kidnap Frannie by knocking her out with chloroform."

Frannie swallowed, flushing with the terrible memory. "Yeah, definitely in my top three most horrible experiences. Zero stars—I do not recommend."

"This isn't funny. Don't you dare make jokes," Jenny scolded with an appalled expression. "This kind of thing isn't a laughing matter. Who is this man who rescued you? I need to personally thank him."

Oh, boy, she thought introducing Dante to her mom would go a lot differently, but there was no escaping the moment. "Mom, I would love for you to meet Dante. He's my, um, boyfriend."

Jenny's eyes widened. "Boyfriend? You're seeing someone?"

"That's what she just said," Hannah quipped.

"You pipe down. I'm not in the mood for any sass," Jenny returned sharply.

Hannah shared a look with Ruby and said, "Well, if there's no sass allowed, I'm out because that's pretty much what I'm made of." Despite her statement, she brushed Jenny's cheek with a quick kiss and made her exit. But not before making a telephone gesture to Frannie, mouthing, "Call me," and blowing her an air kiss.

"Good going, Mom, you chased off Hannah," Ruby said dryly. "Are you happy?"

Jenny waved off Ruby's comment, more concerned with Frannie. "Darling, are you sure you're okay?"

"I'm fine."

Ruby looked at her watch. "Mom, if you want to drive Frannie home, I'll go back to the clinic."

Jenny shook her head. "I wish I could but I'm filling in for a night-shift nurse tonight. I have a private patient in Connors."

"Travel nursing now?" Frannie asked, surprised.

"Only here and there. I'm only doing this as a personal favor for a friend. If I could cancel I would. I don't think you should be alone."

"I won't be alone," she assured her mom, returning to the subject of Dante. "My knight in shining armor will be with me and he won't let anything happen."

"He stays the night?" Jenny asked, mildly troubled, as if Frannie hadn't lived with her ex-boyfriend before he became a cheating turd. "Francesca, is that wise? How well do you know this man?"

"I know him well enough to know that he's the real deal and I think I'm going to marry him. Don't worry, Mom, you'll love him. He's terrific."

Jenny looked like she didn't know what to say—caught between gratitude for Dante saving her daughter's life and the discomfort of acknowledging her daughter had an adult sex life—but she accepted Frannie's decision. She looked at Ruby. "You've met this man?"

"Yes. Today, actually. He's really good-looking," Ruby said with an approving wink at Frannie.

"That's the least important thing," Jenny said, dismissing Ruby's assessment. "Character matters more than what's on the outside."

"Yes, because character was what you were most concerned with when you met Dad," Ruby retorted, calling Jenny out for her hypocrisy.

Jenny had the grace to blush as she settled her purse more securely on her shoulder, preparing to leave. "Please take it easy. You've been chemically assaulted. You need to rest."

"I will," Frannie promised.

"I'll expect to meet this knight at Sunday dinner, yes?"

"Can't wait."

Jenny kissed Frannie on the cheek, then Ruby, and left.

Ruby exhaled a long breath, shaking her head. "Will I ever understand our mother?"

"I don't think any of us will. It's part of her charm—the mystery."

"Is that what that's called?" Ruby pretended to consider Frannie's answer, then remarked, "No, I think it's called 'emotionally distant.'"

"Cut her some slack, Ruby. She's going through a lot. Hell, I think we're all going through a lot."

"Yeah, but you officially win with the 'almost kidnapped' thing. No one else had that on their Bingo card. You're so damn competitive," Ruby teased, poking at Frannie gently. "Okay, let's get out of here."

"Sounds good to me. Can we get a milkshake on the way home? I'm craving sugar."

"Anything you want, sissy."

Frannie smiled, refusing to let any bit of sadness pull at her knowing that she had no idea if Sunday dinner would happen. For all she knew, Dante would have them on the road before the weekend hit.

And she had mixed feelings about that.

She loved Dante—but she loved her family, too.

Fate was cruel to make her choose who she loved more.

Dante finished with Fletcher, still at odds at how easily the tables might've turned the opposite way, and the tension cording his shoulders made him want to punch something. The fact that Frannie had been in danger was more than he could stomach.

He loved her more than anyone.

It was an odd thing to love another human being more than yourself. He thought he'd known true love with Belinda, but now, he knew what he'd felt with Belinda had only been a test run for the real thing.

He'd always care for Belinda, but his feelings for Frannie made him want things he had no business daring to dream about.

Marriage. Kids. A home.

None of that was in his future—even with Frannie by his side, he couldn't give her those things.

It wouldn't be fair to any children they might bring into this world.

But Frannie as a mother? His heart stuttered as fresh longing made the pain of future loss worse.

If he weren't such a bastard, he'd walk away now, but he couldn't.

He'd do anything to make her happy, but it would always be temporary, with a life on the run.

What was he doing?

What was he asking of her?

To leave everything she knew? To go where?

He didn't have the goddamn answers, and it killed him that he couldn't offer much more than his body at night and a promise that he would love her forever, even if he couldn't provide the beautiful life she deserved.

Detouring sharply, he ran into the local florist shop and purchased their biggest bouquet. The last time Frannie had received flowers was from that lunatic. He wanted her to have something beautiful from him to wipe away the terrible memory.

His cell rang. He picked up as soon as he saw it was Nick.

"They have him in custody. Thank you," he said with gratitude. "If it weren't for your call..." He didn't like to finish the thought. It tortured him enough. "Anyway, I appreciate your diligence."

"I'm glad it all worked out," Nick said, switching gears quickly. "I got something you're going to want to know. It's about your parents."

"What is it?"

"On a hunch, I did a deep dive into your mother's finances before she died. I found something that you might find upsetting."

Dante braced himself. "Go on."

"I think your mother had a relationship with your uncle long before your father died."

"What do you mean?"

"I found deposits going back two years from an international bank account in an account only registered to your mother. I traced the deposits, and they are registered to an account owned by your uncle. Do you know of any reason why your uncle would be sending your mother money?"

He didn't, but he was beginning to realize his mother had many secrets.

Was there anything from his childhood that rang true anymore?

His father had been troubled, but he always assumed it was caused by the burden of staying on the run.

Now he wondered if his father had known that his wife regretted choosing a life with him.

Adult relationships were complex, but in his young heart, he'd just wanted his parents to love each other as they once had.

Too bad it didn't always work out that way.

With both of his parents gone, only one person could answer his questions—but even when he was on good terms with his uncle, Lorenzo had refused to answer anything about the past.

Particularly about his brother.

Dante didn't know how to think about any of this anymore.

"Thank you," he said, needing to think. "I'll be in touch."

He clicked off and headed to Frannie's.

But as he pulled onto the street, he saw a car he didn't recognize parked in the driveway.

Perhaps Ruby had stayed until he returned?

His gut tingled in warning. Something felt off.

The old truck rumbled to a stop, and he left the flowers behind until he could ensure that all was well.

His paranoia was on full alert.

He couldn't explain it, but each step closer to the front door filled him with cold dread.

It was probably one of her many family members, he tried to reason, but as he opened the front door, he realized his first instinct had been right.

His uncle's men had found him.

And they were screwed.

The situation had just escalated to panic, and he didn't know how to save Frannie.

*Time to find a way.*

# Chapter 28

Frannie waved as Ruby pulled out of her driveway and disappeared. Her stomach was full of vanilla milkshake, and her headache had subsided slightly, but there remained a dull ache that she assumed sleep would take care of.

As she watched Ruby drive away, she noted how right Dante was about her neighborhood. It really was a ghost town of empty houses. She'd never noticed before, but now she felt suddenly insecure. Letting her blinds down, she went to lock the front door, hoping Dante would show up soon.

*Don't be a ninny*, she told herself when goose bumps rioted along her forearm for no good reason. Except…all those times when she'd talked herself down in the past and felt watched, it had been valid because Allen *had* been watching.

She still couldn't shake the heebie-jeebies knowing that Allen had watched her sleep, had seen her naked, peeping through her bedroom window while she slept.

Like she'd told her sisters, the man who'd walked into her shop hadn't been the man she'd befriended all those years ago. What had happened to curdle an otherwise nice man? Human psychology had always fascinated her, but she hadn't wanted to face a genuinely disturbed person like she had today.

Rubbing her arms briskly, suffering a chill even though it was warm outside, she couldn't shake her jumpiness. She headed to the kitchen for a glass of water, her mouth still tasting like she'd drunk a chemical martini. But before she got there, a large, square-shaped man stepped into view, shocking the sense out of her.

Before she could scream, an arm clamped around her throat and cut off her airway like an iron bar was pressing against her windpipe. "No screaming," a voice instructed in a thick Italian accent that left no room for misunderstanding. "I can snap your neck before you take another breath," he warned.

*I'm having the worst day of my life*, she thought desperately. Surely there was some universal rule that you couldn't face mortal peril twice in one day?

"Stop wriggling and I'll let you breathe."

*Compelling offer.* She stopped struggling, and the grip around her neck loosened, allowing her to draw a gasping breath.

The man from the kitchen gestured for his accomplice to bring Frannie to the dining room. She was forcibly shoved into a chair, her hands and feet tied tightly, while he roughly emptied her purse on the kitchen table, pawing through her belongings as if he had the right.

"I don't have any money," she said, pretending to be ignorant of who they were.

He ignored her, grabbing her cell phone and pulling the SIM card to snap it in half before tossing the remnants to the floor.

Frannie cried in outrage, "Hey! That phone is new!" but he didn't seem to care about personal property. As she started to call him out, he pulled a gun from his back waistband, and her rebuke died on her tongue.

He checked his watch as if he had more pressing things to do than terrorize small-town bookstore owners, and asked sharply, "When will Mr. Santoro arrive?"

"Um, who?" Frannie feigned confusion. It was a long shot, but Frannie wasn't above trying every angle she could think of to buy time or delay a truly awful end. "I don't know—"

"Your lover, Dante," the man cut in, annoyed with her clumsy attempt at deception. She'd make a terrible spy. It always looked so much easier in the movies. Also, she wished she'd paid better attention to how to escape a dangerous situation. "We know he stays with you every night. When will he be here?"

"And how would you know that?" she asked, wrinkling her nose. "Are you some kind of pervert? Were you peeping through the windows, too?"

"Answer the question."

"I don't know," she lied, wishing he hadn't broken her phone. Although she wasn't sure how she could warn Dante away, given her current situation.

"Have you ever experienced the exquisite agony of toothpicks shoved beneath the nail bed?"

She felt the blood drain from her face. "Um, can't say that I have. Doesn't sound like something I would be into. You do you, though. I try not to judge."

"You think you can joke your way out of this?" the man asked, unamused.

"Judging by the stone-cold look on your face, probably not," she admitted. "But you can't blame me for trying. Sometimes a good laugh can ease the tension." *And I tend to ramble when I'm nervous.*

"My patience is growing thin. When is Mr. Santoro coming?"

She could play stupid for a few more minutes or just

cut to the chase. "You're… Dante's family?" she pretend-guessed.

A dark brow went up. "Family? No. Hired by the family to bring Dante home. His family is quite concerned about his absence."

*That's a crock of crap.* "In my experience, family doesn't try to force members to come home if they don't want to."

The man shrugged. "Different kind of family."

Frannie bit her lip before asking, "Are you going to kill me?" Might as well end the suspense.

"Depends."

The simple answer belied the horror of the moment. Her life meant next to nothing to this man. She was no more significant than an ant beneath his shoe. *Well, screw him.* If she were going down, she'd go down without begging. Hopefully, the end was fast and didn't make a huge mess. Lifting her chin, she said, "I believe in reincarnation. I plan to come back as something with very sharp teeth and will hunt you down like a monster out of a horror movie. Just letting you know—so choose wisely."

"Either you are mentally unhinged, or you have a lot of spirit. I cannot decide which."

"And I can't decide if that's a compliment," she returned, refusing to be cowed, even though she was trembling inside. The thing about facing down your potential death twice in one day, it did something to you. Maybe she was still reeling from the chemicals in her system, but she felt oddly detached from everything, which gave her a different level of clarity bordering on recklessness. "Dante is a good man. He doesn't want any part of the Santoro legacy. Why can't you leave him alone?"

"Not my business. I was hired to bring him home. Nothing

was said about a plus-one, so either shut up or offer something useful."

"You're a bully," Frannie muttered but pressed her lips together when the man shot her a dangerous look. She sensed she'd end up in a ditch if she pushed her luck any further.

"I'm a businessman," he clarified, going to stand by the window to watch for Dante.

"So, you're in the business of terrorizing people?" she asked.

"I'm in the business of solutions."

"And Dante is a problem that needs solving?"

"Quiet," he ordered, stepping away from the blinds to stand closer to Frannie. "Your lover is here. If you're wise, you'll encourage Mr. Santoro to come quietly without trouble. I'd rather not make a mess that will require substantial cleanup."

*Cleanup.* She swallowed, imagining her insides painting her living room from the close-range impact of the bullet sending her soul into the hereafter. "Yeah, that would suck for you," she murmured caustically. "Or, you could just turn over a new leaf and walk away from a life of soul-stealing crime and spend the rest of your days atoning for all of the terrible things you've probably done under the guise of 'following orders.' Life is about choices—"

The sudden pain of her hair being ripped from her scalp as his associate buried his hand in her hair, yanking it hard, stole her breath. "You were told to be silent," the man reminded her in disgust. "American women do not know when to shut up."

*Son of a bitch, that hurt.* She blinked back tears as her scalp throbbed in time with the fresh pain in her skull. This had to be the worst day of her life.

And then the door opened—and Dante walked in.

"Hello, Mr. Santoro."

* * *

Dante froze, his blood turning instantly to ice as he took in the situation.

"Hi, honey, we have guests," Frannie said with a pained smile, her neck pulled at an uncomfortable angle.

Dante recognized Benito Ricci, the man holding the gun and watching his every move, as one of his uncle's hired men.

"You are a hard man to find," Benito said conversationally.

"Get your man's hand off my girl," he growled.

"You're not in a position to make demands," Benito said. "You've caused much trouble."

Dante held Benito's stare, promising violence without saying a word. After a long moment, Benito nodded to his associate, who released Frannie's hair. "What do you want?"

"It's very simple. Time to stop playing games and come home."

"My home is here."

"Your home is with your family."

"My family died."

Benito looked annoyed at this back-and-forth. "I'm tired of this ugly country—the language, the customs, the mouthy women, the terrible food—all trash. I cannot imagine what you find here more appealing than Italy."

"We're not exactly jumping for joy having you on American soil, either," Frannie muttered. "You're ruining Italian culture for me, buddy. Previously, I was a big fan."

Benito ignored Frannie, returning to Dante. "You will come with us with zero fuss. Your uncle has arranged for a private plane transport in Boise. He is most eager to put all this nastiness behind him, but first, I need you to procure what you stole."

"That's what he really wants, isn't it? Not me."

Benito shrugged as if that didn't matter to him either way. "The job is to bring you and the item you stole, home. That's what I intend to do."

"And if I don't want to return with you?"

"Then, things get *less* civilized," he answered, shifting his gaze pointedly to Frannie, and Dante knew how precarious Frannie's life was in that moment. "Aside from her constant yapping, she's not offensive to the eye. Perhaps with time, she could be trained to be a suitable Santoro wife, but my guess is that it's more efficient to start fresh with a good Italian woman."

"If anyone's offensive, it's you," Frannie shot back, mindless of the danger but making the situation much more difficult for Dante to save her life. "Also, you dress like a B-movie goon. I thought Italians had more style."

"I could cut out her tongue," Benito suggested as if he found that option more enticing by the minute. "Or perhaps a finger…"

Belinda's ruined hands flashed in his memory, and it took everything in Dante not to spring at the man's throat and rip it out with his bare hands.

Frannie's eyes widened as she swallowed, but she wisely remained quiet.

His options were slim for success. If his only play was to do what he could to keep Frannie safe, he'd take it.

He mentally calculated the odds of success if he rushed Benito for the gun in his hand and found them dismally small. He didn't want Frannie to get hurt, but he had a sinking suspicion that Frannie wouldn't leave this place alive if he didn't use his head to negotiate.

Purposefully relaxing his shoulders, he shoved his hands in his pockets as if casually discussing the latest stock news.

"Civilized, eh? Sure, let's discuss how this might enfold if I were open to negotiating terms. Perhaps I'm tired of running and I'm ready to put this all behind me, but not until I know the terms are beneficial."

"Negotiate?" Benito wagged the gun. "Does it look like you're in a position to negotiate? I hold all the cards."

*The hell you do.* "Call Pietro."

Benito narrowed his gaze with suspicion. "And why would I do that?"

"Because you have no authority to make deals—he does."

"No, you'll get your things, and we'll leave as planned or I'll put a bullet in your lover's annoying head."

Dante held his ground. "Call Pietro. Now."

"Or what?" Benito asked, looking bored.

"Just do it."

Benito's arrogant confidence faltered as he met Dante's unwavering stare. The Santoro stare was legendary—Dante had certainly perfected it before discovering how deep his family's corruption went and why the stare instilled fear in anyone on the receiving end. Benito swore under his breath before tucking his gun in his back waistband and punching a number on his cell. "He wants to speak to you," he said when Pietro picked up, then handed Dante the cell.

"Yes?"

"I'll come home on one condition—Frannie isn't harmed, not a single hair on her head, got it?"

"You'll bring the documents?"

The evidence in his safety-deposit box was his only ace and leverage, but he wouldn't let Frannie get hurt over this. "Yes," he answered tersely. "But I swear if anything happens to Frannie…"

"You have my word, she'll be unharmed—as long as

you hold up your end of the bargain. Your uncle is eager to end this."

"Yeah, I bet he is," he growled, hating that his uncle had won, no matter what. "Tell my uncle's men." He shoved the phone back at Benito.

Benito listened, clicking off with a curt, "Yes, sir," his annoyance probably marred with misgiving at leaving a loose end. That was not how things were done in his line of work. "Untie her," he said, shaking his head. "I'll be in the car. Make your goodbyes quick. I want to be on the road in five minutes."

Dante watched them leave, then went to Frannie as she rubbed her raw wrists, scowling even as she jumped into his arms, whispering, "Good thinking! We can slip out the back—"

"No, Frannie," he said firmly, pulling her free to stare into her beautiful eyes, memorizing the sight of her so he'd never forget he'd once been lucky enough to be loved by her. "I have to go with them."

"What? No! That was just a ruse, right? You can't go with them. You said your uncle wants you *dead*. I won't let you go. That's suicide!"

"I love you, Frannie," he said, ignoring her protests. "I always knew it would come down to this, but I never imagined I might fall in love with someone like you along the way. You deserved so much better—"

"No! Stop it, I won't listen to that crap," she whispered fiercely, her eyes tearing up. "I won't let you go. You're not thinking clearly. We can slip out the back…and… I don't know, run to the neighbor's house and call 911 or something."

"Listen to me," he said, gripping her arms and giving her a sharp shake to get her attention. "They will *kill* you and I'll still have to go with them. Don't you understand? I'm out of options. I'm purchasing your safety by leaving with them. It's the only thing I can do to ensure that you're not hurt. Let me do this for you. If something happened to you…I couldn't live with myself. Please, Frannie."

She crumpled at his pleading, wrapping her arms around him as she started to sob. "Please, Dante…please don't do this!"

He knew there was no other way. His uncle played by rules Frannie couldn't even fathom. She was part of a soft and kind world, whereas his was cruel and manipulative.

Dante felt the ticking clock. Gently disengaging Frannie's grip around his neck, he kissed her deeply, then cupped her face, leaving her with firm instructions. "Do not try to follow us, and do not give my uncle any reason to even think of you after this moment. Promise me."

"I can't," she cried, shaking her head.

"You must promise me, Frannie," he said, blinking back his tears. "I can't live with the thought of you being in danger. I need to know you'll be safe. Please do this for me."

Frannie didn't want to, but she slowly nodded with a choked, "I promise."

*Walk away*, the voice told him, and he dragged himself away from Frannie. Turning on his heel, he walked out the door, afraid to look back and see her crushed expression, knowing she might grow to hate him because of this moment, but she'd be alive.

And that had to be enough.

He was returning to Italy.

Time to put an end to all of this.

Once and for all.

# Chapter 29

Frannie didn't know how long she sat in the dark of her living room, reliving the moment Dante had walked away, but her toes were numb from the cramped position, and the crusted salt from her dried tears made her face feel tight and gritty.

Rising with the stiff gait of an eighty-year-old woman with arthritis, she hobbled to the kitchen to rinse her face and drink a glass of water. Her brain wasn't working, but her heart was working overtime. Waves of pain and grief washed over her as she ran headlong into the realization that Dante wasn't coming back.

Worse, he'd sacrificed himself to save her.

Her head throbbed, reminding her she'd been attacked twice in one day, but the physical pain was nothing compared to the emotional anguish crushing her soul.

She didn't know what to do. Dante had made her promise, but she didn't care about promises made under duress. Except she knew next to nothing about Dante's family besides what he'd told her—and that had been as little as possible due to the circumstances.

She knew relatively little about Dante besides how he liked to sleep, how he brushed his teeth and loved to make her feel special and cherished.

A trapped sob threatened to burst from her chest as she

leaned over the sink, bracing herself as she tried to weather the pain.

She had to talk to someone. Damn it, her phone was in pieces, and she didn't have a landline. With shaking hands, she scooped up the spilled contents of her purse, slid them back into her bag, grabbed her keys and left the house.

She could not sleep in that bed tonight when it smelled like Dante. His absence would only remind her that he was truly gone.

Driving straight to Darla's house, she pounded on the front door, not caring that she was a mess and making a racket when everyone else in the neighborhood was trying to sleep.

Tom, Darla's fiancé, opened the door holding a bat, ready to use whoever's head to hit a home run, but when he saw Frannie, he immediately set the bat down and ushered her inside. "Darla!" he called out, adding with concern, "Frannie needs you!"

Darla came around the corner with an anxious frown, wearing a robe, her hair tucked in a silk hair wrap and a mint green face mask slathered on her face. "What's going on?" she asked, collecting Frannie in a hug as she sagged against her.

She smelled of coconut and pinto beans, which was an odd combination and made Frannie think of the time in junior high when they'd tried to tie-dye their shirts using all-natural ingredients instead of the actual dye. It had been a mess, and all they'd accomplished was a muddy mess that ruined two T-shirts.

"He's gone," Frannie sobbed, her body shaking as she let it all out. Tom left the room and silently returned with a washcloth so Darla could wipe away the gunk. There'd be no time for beauty rituals tonight.

"What do you mean?" she asked, casting Tom a grateful look as she quickly wiped her face. "Who's gone?"

"Dante," Frannie answered mournfully.

"Gone where?"

"Back to Italy."

"That jerk!"

"No," she said. "He was practically kidnapped, and there's nothing I can do about it because I promised I wouldn't."

"I'm sorry, run that by me again?"

Frannie didn't have the energy to go into details, so she gave the TL;DR version. "Dante was on the run from his big, scary family in Italy, but they found him and sent two awful goons to bring him back, using me as leverage." She sniffed back tears, which only made her head want to explode. She winced, adding, "Getting attacked twice in one day is overkill in the karma department. I swear I must've done something awful in a past life to be getting served up this plate of doo-doo in this one."

"*Attacked?* You were attacked?"

"Yeah, I was going to tell you tomorrow, but I never imagined that I might be ambushed when I got home. Allen Burns tried to kidnap me earlier today. Dante saved me, it was a whole thing…but in hindsight that was nothing in comparison to what was waiting for me when I got home."

"Are you kidding me right now? I can't wrap my head around any of this." Darla was visibly reeling, and Frannie didn't blame her, but she was too mentally strung out to soften the delivery.

"Me either, but it happened and let me tell you, stuff like this makes for great movies but it really sucks when it happens in real life!"

Tom, who usually left them to their conversations, had returned with a bottled water for Frannie and caught the tail end of her comment. He handed her the water and sat beside Darla. "Are you okay?" he asked tentatively. "Did they…hurt you?"

"No, nothing like that but the one guy nearly ripped the hair from my head and the other one threatened to cut my tongue out if I didn't stop talking. He, apparently, doesn't think much of our country and was really rude about it."

"And Dante just left with them?"

"He didn't have a choice. It was either leave with them, or they'd start breaking parts of me like they did to his ex-girlfriend."

"Geemini Christmas," Darla exclaimed in a horrified tone. "I can't believe this happened to you. Did you call Fletcher and make a report?"

"No, Dante made me promise not to," she said, feeling sheepish for not calling the police at the very least.

"Well, we can rectify that right now," Tom said, grabbing the phone. "How do you know they won't return and finish the job?"

"Because Dante talked to someone in charge and basically told them to stand down or else he wouldn't give his uncle something he wants really bad."

"Which is?"

"I have no idea."

"This is, like, spy shit," Darla said with the tiniest spark of wonder, as if she found it a little exhilarating even though she shouldn't, but Frannie didn't begrudge her fascination. She would've felt the same if she hadn't been living through it. "So, what happens now?"

"I don't know."

Darla grasped her hand and squeezed it. "No matter what, we're here for you."

"I know. I'm sorry I ruined your night. I couldn't stay at the house...not with Dante gone."

"You fell hook, line and sinker for him, didn't you?" Darla asked, shaking her head with sorrow at Frannie's suddenly watering eyes. She nodded, and Darla's expression melted with pure understanding and compassion. "Well, we just have to find a way to get him back."

"How?" Frannie asked plaintively. "Do you know anyone with the power to strong-arm one of the most dangerous families in Italy to return my boyfriend?"

"No, but you do have a cousin in the FBI. I'd start there. They might be interested in knowing what went down."

"But I promised Dante I wouldn't."

"Some promises aren't meant to be kept," Darla said, shrugging. "I know nothing would keep me from trying to rescue this guy," she said, reaching over to rub Tom's arm. "So, that's what you're going to do for your guy. Everything and anything. It might not work but it's worth a try. At least then you can say you did what you could."

Darla was right. She couldn't give up. Not yet.

"I'll call Max," she said, nodding firmly even though she couldn't quite see straight anymore. Fatigue, chemical warfare and emotional exhaustion had taken their toll, and the bill was due.

Darla took control, saying, "Absolutely—first thing tomorrow morning."

Tom rose. "I'll get the spare bedroom ready."

Frannie started to protest, but a yawn garbled her attempts, and all she could do was stare blearily at her best friend as her eyelids felt weighted with cement. "I suppose you're right," she conceded. "Tomorrow is a better plan."

Darla helped her up, and they walked together to the spare bedroom. Tom had just finished turning down the sheets like the most hospitable host at the most exclusive hotel, and she thanked Darla with a look.

And that was all that was needed.

Frannie crawled into the bed and dropped off before her head hit the pillow.

After a twelve-hour flight, Dante was back on home soil, and within the next hour, he was walking into his uncle's stately home.

Even though his eyes burned from lack of sleep, he went straight to his uncle's office, pushing open the door ahead of Benito and his accomplice, leaving them in his wake.

At one time, this had been his home—he'd had full run of the house—and it had been the first time he'd felt safe and secure.

He pushed away those memories and stared hard at his uncle Lorenzo, who, despite the circumstance, seemed pleased to see him.

"You're home."

"Don't," Dante warned.

Lorenzo's expression lost warmth, and he gestured for Benito and his accomplice to leave. Wordlessly, they exited the office and closed the double doors softly behind them.

"You've caused much trouble and strife, Dante," Lorenzo admonished as if he were lecturing an errant schoolboy caught breaking the rules. "I'm displeased with your lack of civility and loyalty to family. Your mother would be crushed to see what you've done."

At the mention of his mother, Dante stiffened, remembering the suspicious deposits over the years to his mother's account. "I need answers," he said coldly. "You wanted me home? Well, here I am. But this time, I want the truth."

"The truth about what?" Lorenzo asked, holding his stare unflinchingly.

"Did you have my father killed?"

"No."

Lorenzo didn't hesitate, nor did he react in a way that would suggest he was lying, but Dante had the evidence suggesting that someone had paid the investigating officer for a doctored investigation. "You're lying," he said to gauge his reaction.

"I'm not." Lorenzo sighed, leaning back in his soft leather chair as if resigned to the long overdue conversation. "Ask the question you're afraid to ask."

Fatigue burned behind his eyes, but he wouldn't leave his uncle's office until he had the answers to the questions eating him alive.

"If you didn't kill him...who did?"

"Your mother."

His world stopped turning. All he could do was stare, uncomprehending yet violently resisting the implication of his uncle's statement.

"No, she would never..."

"I'd hoped that you'd never ask this question. It's not something one should know about their parent. Your mother was a good woman but when pushed to the edge, even good people break."

"What would you know about good people?" Dante asked bitterly, reeling beneath the weight of the information.

"Just because I can't afford the luxury of goodness doesn't mean I don't know it in others," Lorenzo said quietly.

At that moment, Dante remembered how it felt to love this man, believe in him and wish he'd been his father instead of Matteo. After discovering the depth of Lorenzo's crimes, he'd been ashamed of ever wishing such a thing.

Now he didn't know what to think. He dropped heavily into the thick chair opposite his uncle, his brain swimming in a fog. "I don't understand," he said, trying to fit the pieces of this hellish puzzle together. "My mother loved my father."

"She did, but she'd wanted out long before your father's accident. He wouldn't let her. He threatened to take you and run, so that she never saw you again. She stayed for you. Not Matteo."

"My father ran because of you," he shot back, blaming Lorenzo. "He'd wanted a better life, a clean life for his family."

Lorenzo shrugged as if the reasons were immaterial to the outcome. "Whatever reasons he had, Georgia had lost any shared conviction, and soon after, her love for Matteo died. Behind closed doors, Matteo had become abusive—"

"My father wasn't a violent man," Dante retorted, refusing to believe it. Though a hazy memory of his mother crying behind closed doors and his father storming from the house returned to make him question what he thought he knew about his parents. He'd only been a kid—and a kid's memory was colored by the inexperience of their youth and a forgiving love for their parents.

"She wanted to get away from your father, but he kept you on the move so frequently that she couldn't save enough money to make it happen. She wrote me, asking for help."

"So you started sending her money," he surmised.

Lorenzo nodded.

"But why?"

"Isn't it obvious by now?" Lorenzo asked.

Yes, it was now. "You loved her," Dante said, closing his eyes, feeling sick. "You were in love with my mother."

"I could never refuse her anything."

"Did you conspire with her to kill my father?"

"No. There are some lines even I won't cross." He sighed.

"Your mother called me, told me what she'd done, and I helped take care of the problem."

That was the late-night phone call his mother received the night his father died—and why they were on a plane the following morning.

"Have I not given you everything Matteo should have?" Lorenzo asked stiffly, revealing a rare glimpse of his hidden wound. "I loved you as a son, and you betrayed me."

His uncle was right—he'd taken him in, treated him like a son, given him the best education and opportunity—but he'd hidden the true cost of that privilege until it was too late to refuse.

"You used my love for you as a weapon to keep me doing things that went against my conscience.'

To his surprise, Lorenzo conceded Dante's point. "Perhaps." He spread his hands in a conciliatory gesture, "I made mistakes in the moment that I wish I could take back."

It was the closest he would get to an apology from Lorenzo Santoro. Knowing what he knew now, there was no way Lorenzo had anything to do with his mother's accident. A cruel twist of fate had been responsible for the accident that had taken Georgia, or perhaps, karma had come for its due and delivered justice for her part in Matteo's death.

Either way, Lorenzo was guilty of many crimes, but neither Georgia's nor Matteo's death was one of them.

Dante pulled the envelope he'd taken from his uncle's vault and slid it over to him.

Lorenzo glanced at the envelope as if hating the contents but relieved to have it back in his possession, saying, "What happens now?"

Dante knew he couldn't stay. He didn't want the life Lorenzo had created for him, and he could never be like Lorenzo.

His uncle seemed to understand without Dante having to say the words.

Since Dante had left Italy, his uncle seemed to have aged ten years. Lorenzo had always been active and formidable, a robust man for his age. Now he appeared to be a shell of himself. Losing Georgia and now Dante was a blow he couldn't seem to recover from, and he'd lost the will to fight.

"I'm not cut out for the life you wanted for me," Dante said. "I'm not like you and I don't want to be."

"You're the Santoro heir," Lorenzo said as if that should matter to him. "You have an obligation—"

"No," Dante cut in, shaking his head. "Then, disown me. Cut me off. I don't care about the money. I will walk away from all of it, to be free of everything the Santoro name is attached to."

"You really mean that?" Lorenzo asked with a stiff upper lip. "You would walk away from your birthright?"

"Yes. If that's what it takes."

"What if I changed? Would that make you reconsider?"

Oddly, the offer hit Dante in a tender place, perhaps that place where fond memories of his uncle still lived. But he knew that even if Lorenzo's offer was sincere, his uncle was too set in his ways to make those kinds of changes in a meaningful way, and eventually, perhaps slowly, he'd revert to his old ways.

And he couldn't expose Frannie to this life.

"I've met someone. I want to make a life with her. A normal life, one where she doesn't have to look over her shoulder, wary of someone using her as leverage to get to you or me. She owns a bookstore and she's sweet and kind and compassionate—and not cut out for the cost of shouldering the Santoro legacy."

Lorenzo considered Dante's admission, and something

shifted in his expression. Perhaps he was thinking about how Georgia would've handled Dante's request, or maybe he was too tired to put up too much more of a fight to hold on to him.

"I will free you of your Santoro name so you can live your life as you choose," he said sighing heavily. "Your happiness is what your mother would've wanted. And if this is the only way I can give that to you…I will."

Dante swallowed, realizing what his uncle was sacrificing and why.

What may have begun as love for Georgia all those years ago had also changed into love for Dante.

Even if Lorenzo had shown it in ways that weren't all that loving.

*Speaking of.* "What you had done to Belinda…"

"Say no more." Lorenzo waved off any need to continue, shame in his eyes. "I'll ensure she's taken care of. She'll need for nothing. I swear it."

Dante believed him.

There was nothing more to say.

The rage that had lived in his heart for so long had burned away, leaving an empty hole that quickly filled with sadness and grief.

When he left Italy this time, he'd never return.

When he said his goodbyes this time, it was for good.

And they both understood what that meant.

"Thank you, *lo zio.*"

Lorenzo gave an imperceptible nod, and Dante rose, walking away for one last time.

His uncle would never be a good man—but at one time, he'd been the best man in Dante's life.

And for that, there would always be a piece of Dante that loved Lorenzo like the father Matteo should've been.

# Chapter 30

Frannie stared at Max, confused. "There has to be something you can do. Dante was practically kidnapped by his uncle's men, on American soil! Surely that's a crime? You said that the FBI had a file a mile long on the Santoro family. Here's your chance to bring them in, throw the book at them. Show them how America deals with international terrorists!"

"I'm not saying that a crime wasn't committed, but you said Dante went willingly with them. That doesn't sound like he was kidnapped."

Frannie glared. "They *forced* him to leave."

"At gunpoint?"

"No, but one of them *did* have a gun—and the other guy pulled my hair and threatened to cut out my tongue."

Max tried not to chuckle. It wasn't funny, but maybe in another situation, it would've been a little comical. However, there was nothing humorous about it in Frannie's eyes. "Look, you need to call the National Guard, the Army, or call the freaking president, for all I care. All I know is that I'm not going to sit here and do nothing while the future father of my children is being tortured by his awful, villainous uncle, okay? If I have to fly to Italy and find him myself, I will."

"I have no doubt you would try and in doing so, probably get yourself killed," Max said dryly. "Have you tried calling him?"

"I don't have his number and that stupid goon broke my SIM card." She perked up, remembering, "Hey, that's right, he broke my phone. That's a crime! Use that to extradite that jerk."

"Frannie… I can't deport a man for breaking your SIM card," Max said, trying to talk sense into her, but she had long since left rational behavior behind. She was frantic with worry and ready to hop on a plane to do something reckless if someone didn't help her rescue Dante.

"Please, Max…" she pleaded, needing something to calm her brain. "I'm losing it. I'm so worried."

Max relented, saying, "I'll make some calls, okay, but in the meantime, go home, take a long shower or a bath or something, and try to relax. You stewing isn't going to help Dante, okay?"

Of course, Max was right, but logic was not living in her head right now. She wanted action—she wanted the armed forces to storm the shores of Italy and rescue her beautiful Italian man. Yes, it was irrational and not grounded in reality, but she didn't care.

She just wanted Dante back.

"You don't understand. Dante told me what his uncle did to his ex-girlfriend and now she's living in Switzerland— no, *hiding* in Switzerland—trying to rebuild her life after she was maimed by Dante's uncle's goons! Now try and tell me that I'm overreacting."

Max sobered at this new information but was limited in what he could do. "Listen, I believe you. Dante is part of a dangerous family, but he willingly left the country. I can't just call up the Italian government and demand they hand over one of their citizens without a pretty big reason, and as much as I would love to help in any way possible, I don't know how."

"So that's it? I'm just supposed to sit back, hope for the best and basically move on with my life?"

Max tried a different perspective. "Maybe this is a blessing in disguise. Do you really want to be involved with someone who has ties to such dangerous people?"

It was solid advice—and if she were thinking straight, maybe it might've made a difference, but who could say they were thinking straight when they were in love? "Max... I love him, and I'm terrified. Please. Try and help him. I'll never ask another favor again if you do me this one solid."

Max took a long breath, shaking his head, but he agreed. "I'll make some calls, but I don't know if they'll go anywhere, okay?"

Frannie knew that when Max gave his word, he was good for it. She nodded. This was the best she could get. She had to hope it was enough.

Leaving Max's office, she headed back to Owl Creek to open the shop. The last thing she wanted to do was track inventory and smile with customers as if her world wasn't cracking apart, but it would provide a distraction, at the very least.

The practical side of her nature appeared, reminding her that she couldn't afford to let her business fold, no matter how her heart might be broken.

Just as she finished shelving her newest shipment—*How to Be a Boss Babe in 30 Days or Less*—her landline rang.

"Book Mark It," she answered, and smiled as she heard Darla's voice.

"Calling a landline is like being transported back to junior high before we had our cell phones and our parents insisted on keeping their old number for emergency services," Darla recalled with a nostalgic chuckle. "I kinda miss not being at everyone's beck and call. Anyway, any luck with Max?"

"It doesn't look promising. Max says the FBI can't just extradite from another country on the grounds of kidnapping if the kidnappee went willingly."

"Isn't coercion a thing?" Darla asked, incredulous. "Seems like that would be a thing."

"I thought so, but what do I know?"

"Well, if Max is on it, I feel confident he'll do his best."

Frannie agreed, though it felt hopeless. "In the meantime, I'm trying to distract myself with work."

"How's that going?"

"Not great."

"Hang in there, something will work out."

"How?"

"I don't know but it seems like the right thing to say in a situation like this."

Leave it to Darla to coax a reluctant smile out of Frannie when she didn't want to laugh. "Thanks for letting me crash at your place last night. I slept like the dead."

"No problem. *Mi casa, su casa.*"

"Our senior Spanish teacher would be so proud you retained something from his class," Frannie quipped.

"Hey, I also retained a love of chile relleno, so I call that an educational win."

"Stop trying to cheer me up. It won't work."

"It's kinda working. I know you're trying not to laugh."

*Caught.* Darla knew her too well. "Okay, fine. But it feels wrong to laugh or feel any kind of joy right now when my boyfriend could be suffering unimaginable torment at the hands of his villainous uncle."

"Right, of course, but sometimes inappropriate laughter is the only thing that keeps us from running screaming into the streets when all hell breaks loose."

*Fair point.* "What would I do without you?"

"Aside from collapse into a dramatic heap, weeping and wailing, cursing the heavens for the cruel twist of fate? I haven't a clue. Thankfully, you'll never have to figure that out because you're stuck with me—and there is a bright side to all this drama…"

"Which is?"

"Since you're not skipping town and going on the run… you're back on maid-of-honor detail."

Frannie burst into laughter, realizing this was very true. "And what an honor it is," she replied with a roll of her eyes, but Darla was right. Life wasn't going to stop just because her heart was in pieces.

And it wasn't fair of her to ask Darla to put her life on hold because Frannie had fallen in love with a man who'd never been in a position to offer his heart.

Frannie ended the call and sat for a long moment, just trying to find her center again. *Breathe in, breathe out.* Calm and rational was her jam.

But one thought kept jamming her chill frequency.

*Please be okay, Dante. Please find a way back to me.*

It took several days for Pietro to finalize details of Dante's disownment, and in that time, he and his father's secretary had long talks about how things would work once he returned to the States.

"You're sure about this?" Pietro asked with a disapproving frown. "There's no turning back once this is done."

Dante knew what he was doing, and he was ready. "I am."

Pietro shook his head but finished putting the paperwork in order. "You will forfeit your inheritance aside from what your mother has already bequeathed, which is substantial but not enough for a lifetime. You'll have to go back to work."

"I don't have a problem with that. I hate being idle."

"Yes, you've always been industrious," Pietro said approvingly. "But why this dramatic move? Your uncle has agreed to change his ways…be the man you want him to be."

"Because it wouldn't last. He is who he is and he's too old to change his stripes—and it's not right of me to ask. Besides, the life I want to build with Frannie…is incompatible with my former life, and I choose her."

"What will you do in this new life?"

"Get my law degree to practice in the States, and maybe go into family law. Something that actually helps people instead of tearing them apart. I'm looking forward to being on the right side for once."

"A little idealistic but then, I suppose, that fits you."

Dante chuckled, but the lingering sadness at leaving everything he knew tugged at him. "You were good to me, growing up," he said. "I'll miss our talks."

"You were easy to be good to," Pietro said, pushing a manila envelope toward him across the desk. "Your new identity, fully vetted and legal. Unlike the documents you created, these should hold up against any search."

Dante opened the envelope and saw a large wad of cash as well. "What is this?" he asked, confused.

Pietro shrugged. "A little seed money for your new adventures."

"That's not necessary—"

"Please, let him do this one last thing," Pietro said. "You're the son he never had and he's allowing you to walk away. You have no idea how much this is costing him but he's willing to honor your request. The old Lorenzo would've found a way to force you to his will, no matter the cost. He is changing, bit by bit."

Dante closed the envelope, accepting the gift. He knew exactly how he'd put the money to good use. "Thank him for me."

Pietro nodded. "I will," he said, shaking Dante's hand. "It's been a pleasure watching you grow up to be a good man. Your plane leaves in two hours. A car is waiting to take you to the airport. I've arranged your final travel ticket. Flying economy…as is appropriate for your new identity."

Dante met Pietro's stare and saw the banked amusement. He grinned. *Cheeky bastard.* A sixteen-hour flight with multiple layovers and zero legroom. He'd done that on purpose. "Can't wait," Dante said.

And then he walked out, leaving behind everything he'd known since he was ten, to make a new life with the woman who'd changed his path forever.

Sixteen hours until he felt Frannie in his arms and vowed never to let her go again.

Maybe he'd see if he could upgrade his flight when he got to the airport—because sixteen hours was too long.

# Chapter 31

Frannie did a final wipe-down of the counters at the café, shut down the machines, set the alarm on the bookstore and locked up. It was a week since Dante had been kidnapped— yes, she was still calling it a kidnapping—and Max had not received news.

Either no news was good news, or Dante was in a ditch somewhere.

She'd returned to some routine, but only by pretending that everything would work out somehow, no matter how unlikely that scenario was.

She spent a lot of time visualizing Dante walking through the bookstore door with a smile and a promise that he would never leave her again and that his family wouldn't keep trying to terrorize them.

What if—

*"Ciao, bella."*

Frannie's heart stopped at the familiar voice behind her. She squeezed her eyes shut as her heart leaped into her throat. Had she manifested so hard that she was hallucinating Dante's voice?

"Frannie?"

No, that was definitely Dante. She whirled around, afraid that no one would be standing behind her and that she was losing her mind to grief.

But it was her beloved Dante, standing there as if nothing had happened, as if he hadn't been carted off by those gangsters, breaking her heart into a million pieces, scrambling her thoughts into porridge as the miles stretched between them.

"Dante?" Her voice broke as she ran full tilt into his arms, squeezing so hard she might've cracked a rib or two, but she was afraid to let go as if he might be a figment of her imagination. "Is it really you? Am I losing my mind? How are you here? Did you escape?" Her eyes widened as she rushed to add, "I kept a bag packed in the car with some cash and clothes in preparation of this very scenario—"

"Frannie," he laughed, swinging her around before setting her on her feet to meet her astonished gaze. "I'm not going anywhere. I'm here to stay. There's no need to run."

"I don't understand...what happened?" she asked, confused. "The last I saw, you were being kidnapped—and I don't care what my cousin says, they coerced you into leaving—and you said...well, your uncle wanted you dead! How are you alive?"

"It's a long, sad story and I will tell you every detail but first, just let me taste you." He brushed his mouth across hers in a tender kiss that stole the strength from her knees, reminding her that she was putty in his capable hands and always would be. "God, I missed you so much. A week was an eternity without you."

She felt the same. "Don't ever do that to me again," she said tearfully with a happy smile. "I don't care what happens in the future, you're not leaving without me."

"My love, you will never have cause to worry about that happening. I am yours and you are mine. And now I can offer you what I couldn't before. My uncle and I came to an agreement and I'm free from my Santoro ties. I'm going to get my law degree to practice in the States and we're going to do it right. I want to marry you, Frannie. Now, if possible, but if not, I'll wait until you're ready. I have some money burning a hole in my pocket and I want to buy the home we'll raise our kids in."

"Did you just propose?" Frannie asked, tears welling in her eyes again.

"In a very clumsy and inarticulate way, but yes," he said, laughing. "Please don't hold that against me. I just can't wait to make a life with you."

"I would never hold that against you," she murmured, rising on her toes to kiss him again. "My answer is yes. I will absolutely marry the hell out of you, Dante. I will marry you so hard it leaves a mark on your soul."

"Perfect," he murmured with hunger in his eyes as he lifted her off her feet, deepening the kiss between them as if they weren't in the middle of the sidewalk, putting on a show for everyone to see, but Frannie didn't care. She wanted everyone to know that Dante was her knight in shining armor—no matter what the world threw at them.

And she couldn't wait to start her new life as Mrs. Dante Sinclair.

Or whatever new name identity he'd traded for his Santoro legacy.

As long as her hand was in his…nothing else mattered.

They'd figure it out.

# Chapter 32

Dante held Frannie in his arms, stroking the smooth flesh of her side as she cuddled against him. The darkness around them was a private blanket of security as he shared everything that had happened when he returned to Italy.

He left nothing out—even revealing the sordid secret that he'd stolen from his uncle. The papers Lorenzo had been desperate to keep hidden.

"I'd always known about the aunt who took her life when she was very young, but when I discovered it was to hide the shame of her child's paternity, I was sick to my stomach. My grandfather was a terrible man. To father a child with his own daughter…well, it was a shameful secret my uncle wanted to hide from the world."

Frannie was understandably shaken but compassionate, as always.

"Family secrets are a cancer," she said. "Discovering my dad had a big secret has made me realize that no one is immune to temptation."

Dante held her more tightly, determined to ensure the Santoro legacy never touched their children. He wanted them to know only love and happiness.

"I'm not legally allowed to practice law in the States yet,

but I'll do whatever I can to help you with your family's situation," he said.

Frannie sighed, her fingers tracing small circles on his chest as she said, "Thank you. We can certainly use any insight you can share. My mom and Chase are heading to court next week to deal with Aunt Jessie's claim. I don't know how that's going to shake out, but I know Mom would appreciate the support. Oh, about that, my family wants to officially meet you this Sunday at family dinner. Are you okay with that? My family can be a lot."

"I can't wait."

And he wasn't just saying that. He wanted the whole experience of what it meant to have a big family, and since he was officially an orphan…he was ready to adopt the Coltons as his new family.

He was all in—and couldn't wait to start.

A mischievous smile curved his lips as he murmured against the crown of her head. "How do you feel about being a pregnant bride?"

Frannie gasped in fake outrage, "Dante Sinclair, are you trying to give my poor mother a heart attack?" She rolled on top, staring at him with an equally flirty smile, looking like a goddess in the moonlight. "However, accidents happen…"

And he knew at that moment his heart would forever be safe with Frannie as his partner in love, life and laughter.

In all things. Just as it should be.

\* \* \* \* \*

Don't miss the stories in this mini series!

# THE COLTONS OF OWL CREEK

**Colton's Secret Stalker**
KIMBERLY VAN METER
*February 2024*

**Colton Mountain Search**
KAREN WHIDDON
*March 2024*

**Guarding Colton's Secrets**
ADDISON FOX
*April 2024*

MILLS & BOON

Dear Reader,

Welcome back to Northern Lakes, Michigan, for another installment in my Hotshot Heroes series with Harlequin Romantic Suspense. I hope you've all been looking forward to finding out more about Rory VanDam and that mysterious plane crash he and Ethan Sommerly survived five years ago. And if anyone can find out the truth, it will be determined reporter Brittney Townsend. But Brittney's quest for knowledge just might get both her and Rory killed as there are numerous attempts on their lives. Being a hotshot has never been more dangerous for Rory.

With so many recent wildfires in areas in Canada and in the US, including the town on which I've based Northern Lakes, hotshot firefighters are being hailed as the heroes that they are when they selflessly put their lives on the line to battle these unpredictable blazes.

I have so much respect for the dangerous job that hotshot firefighters do. They are definitely the perfect heroes. And I love writing about the perils of their careers and their private lives in my Hotshot Heroes series. I hope you've been enjoying the series as well. Or if you've just discovered it, I think you'll be able to jump right in and know what's been going on in Northern Lakes—a lot of danger, betrayal and romance.

Happy reading!

*Lisa Childs*

# DEDICATION

**With great appreciation and respect
for all the hotshot firefighters—the real heroes!**

# Prologue

The hotshot holiday party ended without the bang everyone had been expecting and dreading, no one more so than Rory VanDam. Ever since that reporter dredged up the plane crash that had happened five years ago.

No. Ever since the plane crash.

No. Even before that.

Rory had been waiting for the big bang or the next crash. While he'd been waiting the longest, the other hotshots had begun to expect bad things to happen, too, and not just because of their jobs. Being a hotshot firefighter was more dangerous than being a regular firefighter because they battled the worst blazes—the wildfires that consumed acres and acres of land and everything in their paths. But it wasn't the job that put them in danger lately, it was all the bad things that had been happening to the hotshots. Explosions. Murder attempts. Sabotage.

But tonight, the holiday party ended with an arrest but no gunshots, no fight, not even a fire. The party was over now and the hotshots, who had traveled to their headquarters in Northern Lakes, Michigan, to attend it, were tucked up in the bunks at the firehouse unless they had other places to stay. And, since falling in love and getting into relationships, many of them had other places now. So maybe it wasn't just bad things that happened to hotshots. But for

Rory, to fall in love or have someone fall in love with him would be a very bad thing. He couldn't risk a relationship with anyone ever again.

So, with nowhere else to stay, he was lying on his back on one of the bunks, staring up at the ceiling. Despite that arrest tonight, Rory was still uneasy, waiting for the next bad thing to happen.

The immediate danger was only over for Trent Miles tonight. The person who had been threatening Trent in Detroit, where Trent worked out of a local firehouse when not on assignment with the hotshots, followed him up to Northern Lakes. While the young man had run Trent and his girlfriend off the road the day before, he hadn't harmed anyone tonight. Trent's girlfriend, a Detroit detective, quietly arrested her and Trent's would-be killer. Except for that whole running them off the road thing, Rory was relieved that the killer was the only one who'd followed Trent up to Northern Lakes and not the man's sister again.

Trent's sister, Brittney, was beautiful, with her long curly dark hair and big topaz-colored eyes. But Brittney Townsend was also an ambitious young reporter who would sell out her own soul for a story. Or at least her own brother.

Not that Rory could judge anyone for selling out their soul, not when he'd already done it himself. But it still affected him, leaving him feeling hollow and empty inside and alone even in a bar full of other people like he'd been earlier tonight for the party. His coworkers. His friends. At least he hoped they considered him a friend and not the saboteur.

Who the hell was behind all the damn dangerous "accidents" the hotshots had been having? Broken equipment. Like the lift bucket coming loose with Trick McRooney in it and all of the cut brake lines on trucks that had sent or nearly sent hotshots to the hospital. And the loose gas line on the stove in the firehouse kitchen that had caused the explosion that had taken out Ethan's beard and revealed his real identity as the Canterbury heir.

Rory touched his jaw where stubble was starting to come in again. And his uneasiness grew. His disguise was being clean-shaven and short-haired; something he hadn't been for a while until his hotshot training and his new identity.

His new life. But this new life was proving to be every bit as dangerous as his last one. And he couldn't help but think that this life was going to end, too.

As he lay there, he heard the rumble of an engine and then another and another. The firehouse was on Main Street, but there was never much traffic in Northern Lakes at this hour and especially during the winter. And these engines weren't just passing by, they were running inside the building.

The fire trucks.

Who started up the truck engines?

They hadn't been called out to a fire because the alarm hadn't gone off. It would have woken up everyone in the bunk room if it had. And as far as he knew, he was the only one awake because all around him, other hotshots snored.

Trent Miles stayed behind in Northern Lakes after his girlfriend left. A couple of the younger guys, Bruce Abbott and Howie Lane, stayed because they'd been drinking at the party. And a couple of the older guys, Donovan Cunningham and Carl Kozak, stayed, probably for the same reason.

Michaela was here, too. The female hotshot worked as a firefighter in St. Paul, which wasn't far away, but while she hadn't been drinking, the party ended too late for her to want to make the drive home.

Not everybody staying was a hotshot. Stanley, the kid who

kept the firehouse clean, was sleeping here tonight with the firehouse dog, Annie. Stanley's foster brother, Cody Mallehan, and his fiancée, Serena Beaumont, had recently gotten licensed as a foster home and had taken in a kid who was allergic to Annie. And Stanley didn't like to be separated from the big sheepdog/mastiff mix that had saved his life.

His life wasn't the only one she'd saved, though. She'd rescued many other hotshots and their significant others over the past year since Stanley had adopted her to be the firehouse dog. Maybe she was about to make another rescue because she whined and crawled off the bunk below Rory where she'd been sleeping with Stanley. Then she jumped up, put her paws on the side of Rory's bed, and she whined again, obviously as confused and concerned as he was about those running trucks.

"You hear 'em, too," Rory said, and he jumped down from his bunk. While the diesel trucks didn't emit as much carbon monoxide as gas engines, if all of them were running, like he suspected they were from the sound, the level could get high enough to kill.

The air was already getting thick. He coughed and sputtered, trying to find his voice to wake the others. "Hey..." he rasped out the words. "Hey..."

Annie barked, but it wasn't as loudly as she usually barked. Rory needed her to bark as loud as she had the first time she'd seen Ethan without his beard. He needed her to wake the others, or they might not be able to wake up ever again if the carbon monoxide level rose any more.

And he needed to get the hell downstairs and shut off those trucks. He would pull the alarm in the hall, too, before going downstairs. That would certainly wake up everyone easier than he and Annie could.

But once he stepped through the door to the hall, something struck him hard across the back of the head and neck, knocking him down to his knees before he fell flat on his face. His last thought as consciousness slipped away was: Would he be able to wake up again or was his most recent life ending right now?

# Chapter 1

He was having that dream. The one where he was falling through the air, his arms flailing as he kept reaching and reaching, but just nothingness slipped through his fingers. Nothing.

That was all he had now, all that he was now. He had a new name to replace the one he never wanted to hear again. But he'd lost much more than his old name.

And he was about to lose even more.

Before jumping out of the sputtering plane, he'd strapped on a chute, and the weight of it was pulling at his shoulders. It was supposed to open. He had been trained as a smoke jumper. He knew how to do this. But whoever had sabotaged the plane might have rigged the chute, as well. He wasn't the only one who'd jumped out, though.

At least one other chute had opened. He could see it in the distance. Just as he could see the plane, continuing on its doomed flight, spiraling toward the ground as the engine cut out entirely. He was spiraling, too.

Free-falling...

For a second, despite all of his training, he forgot what he was supposed to do. And he'd been trained by the best in the elite firefighting business: Mack McRooney.

But he forgot more than his training. He forgot who he

was now: a hotshot. Mack's voice echoed inside his head. "Breathe. In and out. Relax. And pull the cord."

Mack, with his bald head and booming voice, demanded total obedience. And this student obeyed. He reached for the rip cord, pulling it, and he waited for the jerk on his shoulders, for his body to go up instead of down.

But there was no jerk; it didn't come. The chute hadn't opened, hadn't rescued him. He kept hurtling toward the mountains, to all the pine trees and jagged ridges. And he braced himself for the impact.

For death.

Jolting awake, he jumped and gasped, trying to breathe. But something had been shoved in his mouth and down his throat. Panic gripped him.

They had found him again.

And this time they would, no doubt, make certain that he died.

*You are being watched, and if you don't drop this story, you will die.*

Brittney Townsend's fingers shook slightly as she held the note she'd just pulled from beneath the windshield wiper of her van. When she'd seen the slip of paper, she figured it was a ticket or a flyer for a restaurant or a food truck. She had not even considered that it would be this: a threat.

After weeks of alternating between feeling paranoid and flattered, she should be relieved that her suspicions were confirmed. She'd had this strange feeling someone was watching her.

It had been easy enough to spot the ones who openly stared at her, some of them because they must have recognized her as the reporter who'd broken the big story, who had discovered that Jonathan Michael Canterbury IV was still alive. Or maybe they'd been staring because they had recognized her from the other stories she did. For the fluff pieces her local Detroit station had hired her to do, like report on gallery openings and concerts and new shops and restaurants.

She hated doing stories like that and figured she got saddled with them because she was young and, as her producer told her, cute. And the way he said it...

She had considered reporting him to HR, but everyone else loved him. So she let the comments go. For now. He was probably harmless enough, and she doubted that he was the one watching her. She also doubted that it was any of the people who'd spoken to her after recognizing her. None of them had given her that uneasy feeling that she kept having.

That creepy sense of foreboding, like whoever was watching her wasn't doing so out of admiration but something else...

Obsession. Anger. Revenge?

Her brother had recently had someone go after him for revenge, because Trent hadn't been able to save that person's loved one from an apartment fire. But Trent was a firefighter. His job was definitely a lot higher stakes than hers.

Except for the one big story she'd done about the hotshots. And that plane crash.

She glanced around now, peering into the shadows of the parking garage. It was late, so the only light was the soft glow from the small overheard fixtures scattered throughout the concrete structure. Was whoever had stuck the note under the windshield wiper out there? Watching her from the cover of the shadows?

Goose bumps lifted on her arms despite the heavy wool coat she wore. She reached for the door handle she'd already unlocked and jumped up onto the driver's seat of the van. She suspected that someone had been watching her when she left the station a short while ago. Because it was late, she was the last one leaving the building for the parking garage. But she'd heard shoes scraping behind her on the sidewalk.

She glanced over her shoulder, but in the darkness, she wasn't able to see anyone. But she knew they were there, just as she'd known all those other times she had that uneasy feeling.

Someone was definitely following her. But her stalker wasn't a new fan like she wanted to believe, someone impressed with her reporting, someone who recognized her talent. No. This was someone threatening her.

*You are being watched, and if you don't drop this story, you will die.*

She really didn't have to wonder what story. Because she knew.

This threat wasn't for her to stop working on any of those fluff pieces. Nobody cared that she covered a gallery showing or the opening of a new restaurant; sometimes not even the owners cared because people didn't watch the news on TV. The read it on social media instead.

No. There was only one story of any interest that she had ever covered. The plane crash from five years ago, which had presumably taken the life of Jonathan Michael Canterbury IV and confirmed his family curse, that all of the Canterbury male heirs died much sooner than they should.

But Canterbury hadn't died. Other men had, though, except for one: Rory VanDam. Like Canterbury, he'd survived for a couple of months in the mountains before the two of them had been rescued. Because both men had refused to give her an interview, she wasn't sure how long each had been on their own before finding one other and then being rescued together. The wreckage of the plane and the pilot and a couple of other men, who'd just completed hotshot training and been on board, too, had never been found.

Nobody knew for sure why and how the plane had crashed. Or what had happened to the others. Canterbury claimed he didn't know for certain, but he'd suspected that it was because of him, because someone had been trying to kill him even before that crash.

But what if he was wrong?

The man who'd been trying to kill him, his brother-in-law, denied any involvement in the plane crash. Of course, he could have been lying, as people so often did. But why admit to everything else but deny involvement in the crash? It didn't make sense. If he wasn't the reason the plane had gone down, why had it crashed?

And what if Canterbury hadn't been the intended target after all?

Those were questions that Brittney had been asking herself ever since she discovered Canterbury alive and working with her brother as a hotshot out of Northern Lakes. She wanted to make sure that whatever had happened with that crash didn't happen again, with her brother as one of the hotshots who didn't survive.

Desperate to keep Trent safe, she'd tried asking other people about what had happened to that plane. Like the Federal Aviation Administration, who should have been able to locate the black box of the wreckage. She'd also tried talking to the director of the hotshot training center that the plane had left before the crash.

And she kept trying to talk to Jonathan Canterbury, who was still calling himself Ethan Sommerly. But he refused to give her a follow-up interview. She glanced at the note. Writing that didn't seem like something Ethan would do even if he wasn't best friends with her brother. He was more direct than this. He would just tell her, as he'd been doing every time she asked him, that he had no intention of ever talking about the crash again.

That left Rory VanDam. She'd seen him in passing when she'd been in Northern Lakes covering that story. The thought of him had her heart skipping a beat, but that was just in anticipation of getting more information out of him. Not because of how startlingly good-looking he was, with short blond hair and very pale blue eyes. She hadn't seen much of him, though, because he kept slipping away before she was able to ask him any questions. And both Ethan and her brother had refused to give her a contact number for Rory. Her brother was barely speaking to her after that story.

A twinge struck her heart with regret and with fear. She'd nearly lost him over the holidays when that person who'd wanted revenge against him had been trying to kill him. No, he'd been trying to kill someone close to Trent.

She still hadn't gotten the full story out of Trent yet, she only knew that person had been arrested. Detective Heather Bolton had made certain of that. She'd saved Brittney's brother's life and had stolen his heart in the process.

A tug at her lips curved them up into a slight smile even as a wistful sigh slipped through them. She wasn't jealous. Not really.

It wasn't as if she wanted a relationship for herself. Not right now. Maybe not ever. Despite everybody thinking she'd been too young when her dad died for her to be able to remember him, she did. She remembered that loss and pain not just for her but for her mom and her brother, too.

And every time her hotshot brother went out to fight a fire, she worried that she was going to lose him next. She nearly had, not to a fire but to someone holding a grudge against him.

Like he was holding one against her.

Would he ever forgive her for investigating his hotshot team? For exposing his best friend's secret and real identity and for, inadvertently, putting him in danger because of her exposé?

Hopefully Trent was out of danger now. But she didn't know for certain. Even though the detective had caught the person after him, Trent had stayed up in Northern Lakes.

Too many bad things had been happening there and not just because of her exposé. The Huron hotshots had been having a run of bad luck for a while now.

That was the reason she'd gone to Northern Lakes and had stumbled upon Canterbury, because she'd known something was going on with her brother's hotshot team, and she'd wanted to investigate all those unlikely "accidents." Too many of Trent's team members had been getting hurt or worse. One member of the team had died, and so many others had nearly died, as well.

Had something else happened?

Was that why Trent had stayed up there? And by doing so, had he put himself in danger yet again? But apparently she was in danger, too.

She glanced around that parking garage again, peering into the shadows. She couldn't tell if that person was out there yet, watching her. Or maybe they figured that leaving the note would scare her off.

If so, whoever had left it didn't know her well at all. Leaving that note only piqued her interest more as well as pissed her off.

Feeling a sudden urge to reach out to one of the people who knew her best, she pulled her cell phone from her purse. Before this whole mess with his hotshot team, she'd thought her brother knew her and would have known that she never intended for anyone to get hurt, least of all him. But she couldn't call her mom and stepdad, who probably knew her and her heart better than her brother did, because she didn't want to worry them. So she called Trent.

"Hey."

The quick reply startled her, making her nearly drop the phone. Trent had been declining her calls for so long that she hadn't expected him to actually answer.

"Brittney?" Trent asked, his voice a little louder with concern. "Are you there?"

She drew in a shaky breath and nodded. "Yeah, yeah. I just didn't expect you to pick up." Especially at this hour. Not that eleven was late for Trent when he so often pulled overnight shifts.

He chuckled. "Then why did you call?"

She froze for a moment. Why had she called? Was she going to tell him about the note? If she did, he would no doubt tell her to back off even though he knew that she wouldn't. Then he would worry about her and try to intervene, playing his usual part of overprotective big brother. And he might get hurt trying to protect her, which was her whole reason for wanting to discover the truth, so that he wouldn't get hurt like the other hotshots who'd been lost in that plane crash.

"Uh…"

"You're at a loss for words?" Trent asked. "That's so unlike my little sister."

"Stop teasing her," another voice chimed in on Trent's end. Heather's husky voice.

"You're back in Detroit?" she asked.

"Yes."

"Why did you stay in Northern Lakes for so long?" With the way he and Heather seemed to feel about each other, she was surprised he'd stayed away from the female detective for five minutes let alone two weeks.

"Ah, and now my little sister is back, too," he said. "Firing her usual questions at me."

Brittney felt another twinge then, of nostalgia, remembering how young she'd been when she'd started questioning everything and everyone around her. Trent had always been the most patient with her back then, even more so than their dad and her mom. He'd always been the best big brother.

But she hadn't always been the best younger sister. "I'm sorry," she said, her voice cracking a bit with the emotion overwhelming her, thinking of how close she'd come to losing him over the danger he'd been in. The danger he could be in again...

"Brittney?" Trent said her name as a question filled with genuine concern.

She forced a little chuckle. "What? Not used to me apologizing?" She had actually apologized a few times, over that story she'd done on his friend, but he hadn't been listening to her then.

Maybe that was because he'd known that she wasn't sorry at all about doing the story and would have covered it again. She was genuinely sorry about putting Ethan and Trent in danger, though.

And she definitely didn't want to do that again. But what if they already were in danger, either because of whatever had been happening with the team or something related to that crash?

And her story... That wasn't going away. It seemed to literally be following her around because, as she peered through her windshield, into the shadows of the parking garage, she noticed a little flicker of light.

The flame of a lighter?

The flash of a cell screen?

Or a camera?

Was someone not just watching her but taking pictures, too? For what or for whom?

She was tempted to grab her camera from her bag and take pictures of her own. Maybe she would be able to develop them with light enough to see who was out there, hiding in the shadows, watching her.

She always carried her camera with her because she preferred taking her own photographs. Hell, she would prefer to be a print reporter instead of a network one, but she'd taken the first job she'd been offered.

"Brittney?" Trent called her name loudly from her cell speaker, like he was trying to get her attention.

She nearly smiled again at the thought of all the times she'd tried to get his while they were growing up and most recently while he'd been ignoring her. Just like she intended to ignore that note.

And because she did, she couldn't tell Trent about it. She didn't want him in danger again and certainly not because of her. But if she didn't pursue the story, something could still happen to him and his other team members. She had to find the source of the threat and stop him or her; that was the only way she and the hotshots would be safe for sure.

Or as safe as hotshots could ever be given the hazards of their career.

"Sorry," she murmured again. Then she drew in a breath and forced a smile that, while he couldn't see it, he might hear in her voice. "So you're home?"

"Yes," he said.

And she could hear the smile in his voice.

"I'm home," he said.

But his home had burned down a month ago. So his home…

Was probably wherever Heather's was. His home was Heather now.

"Good," she said. She was happy for him, even as she felt that little bubble of wistfulness rise up from her heart again, as if she was yearning for what he had.

For love…

But she had no time for that now or ever. All she wanted was the truth despite the risk. But she didn't want it just for the sake of a story or her career.

She wanted the truth so that she was no longer being followed and threatened. After starting her van, she drove slowly out of the parking structure, and as she headed home, she continually checked the rear-view mirror to see if she was being followed again or still. There were other headlights behind her, so that person was probably back there, watching and waiting to see what she would do.

If she'd heed that threat…

She couldn't do it, not if backing away let someone get away with murder. And if that plane hadn't crashed by accident, that was exactly what had happened five years ago. Murders and attempted murder, if either Canterbury or Rory VanDam had been the real target. And if they had been, that meant they were still in danger and could put anyone close to them, like her brother or the other hotshots, in danger, as well.

Superintendent Braden Zimmer should have been relieved that Rory was all right, that after two very long weeks he had finally awakened from his coma. But…

Braden's body shook a little as he leaned against the wall of the corridor outside Rory's hospital room. He wasn't sure it was Rory who'd woken up, at least not the Rory Van-Dam that Braden knew. The head injury was so severe, the mild-mannered man that Braden had known for the past five years had fought the medical staff that had been trying to save his life. He thought they were trying to kill him.

But maybe that was understandable after what had happened at the firehouse. Someone had started up all the engines and then struck Rory over the head when he'd stepped out of the bunk room.

Had Rory been the intended target? Or would whoever had walked into the hall have been struck? And hit so hard that he could have died. That he might still have brain damage from what had happened.

Annie, that untrained, overgrown pup of a firehouse dog, had once again saved lives when her panicked barks woke up the other hotshots who'd been sleeping at the firehouse. If she hadn't woken up everyone…

They could have died, and Rory probably would have if he'd not gotten the medical attention he'd needed as quickly as he had. He might have bled to death or the swelling on his brain that had caused the coma might have killed him. As it was, he still wasn't himself. Not yet.

Maybe not ever.

Braden had to do more to protect his team from…one of his team?

The sabotage had started out harmlessly enough in the beginning. A piece of equipment or a vehicle was damaged, but it had been escalating in frequency and in severity to the point that someone was going to die if the saboteur was not stopped soon.

# Chapter 2

The week since he'd awakened in the hospital ICU ward with a breathing tube down his throat he had spent trying to reclaim his memories. So much of the past had slipped away while he was in the coma.

Or maybe he had lost those memories when he'd been struck so hard.

Maybe that blow had knocked the memories out of his mind so that they returned to him only in his dreams. But having them come back to him that way confused him more because he didn't know what was real anymore.

If he was real anymore...

Hell, at the moment, he struggled even to remember his name.

Rory.

That was what everybody who'd come to visit him called him. Rory VanDam was the name on the hospital bracelet wrapped around his wrist. The chart he'd taken from the foot of his bed had called him the same thing while also chronicling all of his old scars and injuries. But a lot of those scars weren't from injuries *Rory VanDam* had received. Except for the blow to his head.

Had that been intended for him? Or would any other hotshot have been struck as hard had one of them stepped out of the bunk room when he had?

Rory, or whoever the hell he was, needed to figure that out, just as he had so many other things he needed to figure out. Like if it was even safe for him, or for his hotshot team, to stay here anymore. But he couldn't figure out anything from this hospital bed. He'd already spent too much time lying in it, the two weeks that he'd been unconscious except for those disturbing dreams.

Memories…

He had spent the entire past week stuck in the hospital because the doctors insisted on monitoring him, making sure that he was medically all right. He wasn't. His head certainly wasn't and neither was his heart. His blood pressure kept going up, probably as those memories had returned.

But he knew that if he intended to make any new memories, he needed to get the hell out of the hospital and figure out who had attacked him in the firehouse. And if they would try again for him or for one of his team members. Or had it been one of his team members who had attacked him?

The tubes were out of him now. The one down his throat and the IV in his arm were gone. So there was nothing but the blood pressure cuff tethering him to the bed. He slipped that off and swung his legs over the side of the bed. While he had some kind of socks on his feet, his legs were bare, as was his ass when he stood up and his gown flopped open in the back.

Where the hell were his clothes?

His legs shook a little beneath his weight as he stumbled across the room toward a cabinet. He jerked it open as the door opened behind him.

"Sheesh, man, have some modesty," a deep voice remarked.

"Hey, if you got it, flaunt it," he replied before turning around to face the man standing inside the door.

Ethan Sommerly's dark brows rose with surprise.

Rory usually didn't throw back smart-ass comments like the rest of the hotshots did. Usually he ignored any smart-ass comments directed at him. He'd learned, the hard way, that it was smarter to keep his head down and stay uninvolved. That way nobody got to really know him, and he didn't get to really know, or trust, anyone.

But that blow to the head had either knocked the sense out of him or maybe knocked his sense back into him. He really didn't know which.

"Everybody said you were acting a little off, a little less like your usual self," Ethan said, "but I didn't see it until now."

"Probably because you haven't been around," Rory replied, ignoring the little twinge of hurt that today was the first time he'd seen Ethan since the hotshot holiday party.

Pretty much every one of the twenty-member team of hotshots had checked in with him over the past week. Trent Miles had come that first day he'd regained consciousness; then he'd left for Detroit and Detective Bolton. But Ethan hadn't come around to visit.

But then the real Ethan couldn't come around anywhere anymore. He had died in that plane crash five years ago. Or so everybody assumed, since no other survivors and the wreckage had never been found.

But what if Rory and "Ethan" hadn't been the only ones who'd survived?

What if...

"You must have gotten whacked in the head harder than I thought," Ethan said, his tone a little defensive. "Because I've been around."

Rory narrowed his eyes to scrutinize his old friend. Ethan usually told the truth about most things, except for his identity that he'd kept secret for five years. Secret from everyone but Rory, who'd always known since the crash who Ethan really was. But Rory had kept Ethan's secret for the same reason he kept his own, because they would have been in danger had the truth ever come out.

That had certainly been proven when Brittney Townsend revealed Ethan's real identity as Jonathan Michael Canterbury IV. The minute everyone had known the infamous Canterbury heir, as the media had dubbed him years ago, was alive, someone had been trying to kill him.

"When were you around?" Rory asked him. And how could he have forgotten?

Ethan's face got a little pink above his beard, which had grown back but was neatly trimmed now unlike how bushy he used to wear it, as a disguise. The man shrugged. "It's probably been a week or so…"

"You were here when I was unconscious," Rory said. Even as his heart lifted a little with that knowledge, he added, "How the hell could I know that?"

Ethan shrugged again and chuckled. "I don't know. They say people in comas can still hear you talking to them."

"*They* don't know what the hell *they're* talking about," Rory said. "Because I didn't hear you. The last thing I heard, before waking up here with the tube shoved down my throat, was the sound of the engines running and Annie barking—"

"So she did save everybody again like Stanley has been swearing she did?"

His heart lifted even more. "If everybody really got out without getting hurt like Braden swore they did." That was the first thing Rory asked when he'd remembered Braden was his boss after he finally remembered who the hell he was supposed to be.

Ethan nodded. "Nobody else got hurt. Braden doesn't lie. Now, Stanley I wasn't so sure about…"

Did Ethan think that the teenager could be the saboteur? Since Braden had shared with everyone that he'd received a note warning him that someone among them wasn't who they'd claimed they were, everybody had been looking at everybody else with suspicion. But that anonymous note had referred to a member of the team and probably to either him or Ethan, not Stanley. And no matter how many memories he might have lost, Rory knew *he* wasn't the saboteur. He didn't think Ethan was, either. But Stanley?

He seemed like a sweet kid who loved his dog.

"I didn't make it across the hall to the alarm to pull it," Rory said. "So Annie must have woken up everyone else before the fumes got too bad. Stanley's right, then, she saved everybody who was there."

"But you."

"I'm alive," Rory said.

"The doctors weren't sure you were going to wake up again," Ethan said, his voice even gruffer than usual. "And after a week passed, your odds of recovering kept getting worse."

"Is that when you gave up on me?" Rory asked. "But that doesn't really make sense, because you, better than anyone else, should know that I'm pretty good at beating the odds."

Not only had they managed to parachute off the plane before it crashed, they'd also managed to find each other within a couple of days and had survived the next two months in the cold of the mountains before they were finally rescued.

Ethan rubbed his big hand across his beard, along the edge of his square jaw. "We both are good at beating the odds."

Rory nodded heartily in agreement, and pain radiated from the back of his head to his temples. Maybe he wasn't as recovered as he thought he was. But he ignored the pain and remarked, "You beat a curse."

"What did you beat, Rory? You've never told me what it was," Ethan remarked.

He sighed again, a heavier one full of all the pain from his past. "I beat a curse, too, of a sort…"

It hadn't been a family legacy of bad luck like Jonathan Michael Canterbury IV had beaten. It was more like the curse of someone who had sworn a vendetta onto him. Revenge for what he'd done all those years ago. But even knowing what he knew now, he would do it all over again. *The right thing.*

But he hadn't shared any of the details with Ethan because, as he'd told him when they'd been stranded in those mountains and had reiterated again a few months ago, the less he knew about Rory the better. The safer he was.

Ethan pointed toward Rory's head. "I don't think you've beaten it for good."

Had the blow to his head been about that or…

"You don't think it was the saboteur who started all those trucks and hit me over the head?" Rory asked. It had to have been. Nobody else knew he was alive.

Unless…

Had Brittney Townsend's exposé about the Canterbury heir got someone else checking out the plane crash more closely? Someone who now wondered if Rory was really someone else?

Ethan shrugged his broad shoulders. "I don't know. The saboteur hasn't been responsible for everything that has happened to the hotshots."

"No, they haven't been," Rory agreed. "Your past came back to haunt you."

"Is that what's actually happened here?" Ethan asked. "Has your past come back to haunt you?"

Rory VanDam's past only went back five years, to the moment, with the help of a US Marshal, Rory VanDam had been created. But the other man…

The one Rory barely remembered, the one he didn't want to remember, *he* had a past. And that was where it needed to stay, for so many reasons.

But instead of answering honestly, he just shrugged.

"The trooper has been trying to interview you," Ethan said, as if warning Rory.

"Gingrich?" His head pounded harder as a memory niggled at him, something about Gingrich…something sinister…

Ethan's dark eyes widened with concern. "You really have forgotten things. Gingrich is in prison now," Ethan reminded him. "He took a plea deal for trying to kill Luke Garrison and Willow and for his involvement in Dirk's murder."

Rory shuddered as he remembered Dirk's gruesome death. That was even worse than…

He shoved that memory back, unwilling to relive that once again, and focused on his friend. Drawing in a deep breath, he asked, "So what trooper wants to see me?"

"Trooper Wells," Ethan said. "She's been wanting to talk to you."

Rory had done his best to avoid having any conversations with any of the state troopers who had investigated what had been happening with the hotshots. He hadn't wanted to give anything away, any clue to his own past and his real identity. Though right now he wasn't even sure what that was…

"But at least it's just her wanting to talk to you and not that damn reporter," Ethan grumbled.

"Brittney," Rory said with a slight sigh.

Ethan grinned. "You haven't forgotten her."

Brittney Townsend, with her gorgeous eyes, deep dimples and curly dark hair, would be impossible to forget but more so for her indomitable spirit and determination than her attractiveness even.

"No," Rory admitted, "and I haven't forgotten that I need to avoid her."

For so many reasons…

The answers weren't wherever the hell that plane had crashed. The answers to Brittney Townsend's questions were in Northern Lakes, the small town out of which the Huron Hotshots operated. And where Brittney was driving to right now.

Ethan, aka Canterbury, had already told her that he thought his brother-in-law had caused the plane to crash. But if that was the case, why was someone threatening Brittney now to drop the story? Ethan's sister's husband was already in jail, heading to prison for a very long time. He had no way of leaving those notes or following Brittney and no access to funds to hire someone else to do his dirty work now like he had before.

So if it wasn't about Ethan, then…

Rory VanDam had to have the answers she was seeking. He had to know something more about the plane crash and about the victims of it. Had one of them been the intended target? Or had he been?

Unlike the last time she'd tried to interview him, she was not going to take no for an answer. No was definitely not the answer she was seeking. Nor was the second note she received after pressing Mack McRooney, the trainer for the US Forest Service hotshots, for information about the plane crash this past week. Well, she hadn't really pressed, she'd just left more messages for him. And then she'd received one herself:

*You were warned. Now you'll suffer the consequences.*

This note hadn't been typewritten on a piece of paper and shoved under her windshield wiper. This one had appeared on her cell phone as a text message with the contact's information blocked.

So the person had her number and knew about her questioning the US Forest Service. When Mack didn't return her calls, she'd tried talking to everyone who'd picked up the phone at the US Forest Service. Nobody had given her any answers, though. But somehow the person leaving her the notes had found out she was still asking questions. The hotshots worked for the US Forest Service.

Maybe one of them didn't want her asking questions about the crash. Ethan had no reason to threaten her—his secret was already out. But what about Rory? Was he hiding something about the crash? Or about himself?

She'd only met him a couple of times when she'd come to Northern Lakes to find out what was going on with her brother and his hotshot team. The twenty members were quite diverse in looks and personality. There were the younger crew members who were excited about their dangerous career, and there were older ones who were more blasé about it but were still incredibly fit because of the demands of the job.

Then there was the elite of the elite. Like her brother. And his friend Ethan. They were next-level fit and strong and muscular.

The new guy, who'd taken the place of the deceased team

member, Dirk Brown, was like Ethan and Trent. But Trick McRooney had been raised by the man who trained most of the hotshot firefighters to be as accomplished as they were.

She'd tried talking to Mack, too, since that plane had left his training center right before the crash. But he had yet to return any of the calls she'd left for him where he lived and worked in the state of Washington.

Maybe his son, Trick McRooney, or his daughter, the superintendent's arson-investigating wife, Sam McRooney-Zimmer, would be able to convince their father to talk to Brittney about that crash and about Rory VanDam.

Rory wasn't as big and muscular as Trent, Ethan and Trick. He wasn't as loud and silly as Brittney's brother and so many other members of the team. But there was something about him, something even more compelling than the others.

At least to Brittney.

Maybe it was just because he was so different than the others. He was muscular, too, but in more of a lean and chiseled way than the bulky muscular builds of the others. He was also quiet and watchful, with features as chiseled as his muscles. And with short blond hair and very pale, icy blue eyes, he looked like some kind of Nordic prince. Like royalty…

But it wasn't so much his good looks that were compelling to Brittney but what simmered beneath the surface. Secrets. She knew they were there, and that maybe he was so quiet because he was determined to keep them locked inside him.

How far would he go to keep his secrets?

Sending threatening messages? Carrying out those threats?

Instead of being scared off, as the notes had intended,

Brittney was even more fired up to learn the truth. And not just for her sake.

Trent worked closely with Rory. If the man was someone that her brother shouldn't trust or who would put him and the other hotshots in danger, they all deserved to know the truth about him.

And about that plane crash.

What the hell had really happened to that plane that someone was so desperate to make her stop pursuing her story about it that they had threatened her twice?

The closer she got to Northern Lakes, the more her anticipation grew. Not of seeing Rory VanDam.

She wasn't even certain he was still in Northern Lakes after the holiday party. She hadn't dared ask Trent about him because, just like the notes, if he knew about them or her intentions to interrogate Rory, he would try to stop her. To protect her?

Or to protect his fellow hotshots?

She still didn't believe he'd forgiven her for the last story she'd done on them. But while she felt badly about that, she couldn't let whoever was threatening her get away with it. The only way to stop the person was to find out who they were. Hopefully Trent would understand that this wasn't about furthering her career, she was doing it for her safety and for his and the rest of his team's.

Last time she'd come up to Northern Lakes, she'd intended to find out why bad things had been happening to the entire team, but the majority of her story had been about Ethan or, rather, Jonathan Michael Canterbury IV.

While she'd been hounding Ethan and following him and his family around Northern Lakes, Brittney had made a good friend and was looking forward to seeing her again. Tammy Ingles owned the salon in Northern Lakes. She was hip and sassy and genuine. With Brittney's career being so competitive, she hadn't made many genuine friends since becoming a reporter, and the ones she'd had from school and college had drifted away as they got married and started families. Or maybe she'd drifted away because she'd been working so hard, trying to move up to serious news from covering those fluff pieces, trying to be as successful as the rest of her family.

The only friend she'd had for long and that she really trusted was her mom. And now Tammy. They talked often on the phone through FaceTime and texts. But she hadn't told her about that weird sensation she'd been having of someone following her. And she hadn't told her about the note and the text, either. She knew that Tammy and Ethan had promised each other no more secrets. So whatever Brittney told Tammy, she would tell Ethan. And he would probably tell Brittney's brother.

But Tammy wasn't just open and honest with Ethan. She would tell Brittney everything she knew about that plane crash and what had been going on with the hotshots. And if she knew, she would tell Brittney where Rory was.

Even if he wasn't in Northern Lakes right now, Brittney would track him down wherever else he was. Hopefully, though, he was still in Northern Lakes. The roads began to curve more as they wound around all the inland lakes in this northeast region of the Great Lakes state. She was getting closer.

The weather was also getting colder. Snow still covered the road despite what had been proving to be a mild winter. At least in Detroit.

The weather wasn't the only thing that was going to be cold here—with the exception of Tammy, everybody else would probably be as chilly and unwelcoming toward her as they'd been the last time she'd visited Northern Lakes. But Brittney found herself smiling anyway. She was almost there.

Then something struck the windshield. Loudly. Like a gunshot blast. The glass spider-webbed, weaving together to stay intact, but obscuring her vision.

She couldn't see the road. Couldn't see the curve.

She stomped on the brakes and gripped the steering wheel tightly. But it was too late to stop the vehicle, as her van left the road and fell onto its side and then its roof, metal crunching as it rolled and rolled. And Brittney couldn't see where she was going.

If she was up or down…

And she had no idea if she was going to survive the crash, or if, just as that text had warned her, she was about to suffer the consequences of ignoring the threat. If she would die just as it had forewarned if she didn't drop her investigation. If she kept trying to find out the truth.

Was she dead?

The shooter stared through the scope of the long-range rifle.

Brittney Townsend had been warned. She'd just been too stupid to heed the warning. So another one had been sent. But she'd gotten in her van anyway and headed north. And without her even noticing, the shooter, who'd been following her on and off over the past few weeks, had followed her again before passing her.

Once off the freeway, the shooter had found the perfect spot, on the road between the freeway and Northern Lakes, to set up this ambush. Just as they'd set up something similar before.

Those other "ambushes" had proved successful.

Or so the shooter hoped. They kept studying the scene

through the scope, finger posed yet on the trigger. Would they need to fire again?

Was Brittney Townsend going to get out of that wreckage? Could she extricate herself from the crumpled metal?

Or was she, just as the note had warned her, dead?

Sirens began to whine in the distance. Had someone seen the crash? Or had the reporter, herself, called for help?

The shooter lowered the weapon and turned back toward their SUV. They had to get out of here now before anyone saw them. Before they were able to confirm if the reporter was dead.

And would it even matter if she was? Some stupid reporter wasn't the real problem. The problem was the past. It could not come back around, and it definitely could not be reopened all over again. Or too many secrets might finally be discovered and destroy the shooter.

The shooter couldn't let that happen, had to do whatever possible to keep the past in the past. So more people might have to die than one ambitious young reporter.

# Chapter 3

After Ethan left his hospital room, with the promise that he would return and drop off Rory's truck, Rory found some clothes bundled up in a bag in the deep bottom drawer of the bedside table. They must have been what someone had brought him because he hadn't been wearing them that night. Those clothes had probably been cut off him in the ER.

Or by the paramedics who'd treated him at the firehouse. Two of the Northern Lakes paramedics worked with him. Dawson Hess and Owen James.

Someone must have raided his locker for the jeans, boxers, socks and deep green US Forest Service sweatshirt they'd found for him. Because the clothes were his. Well-worn and comfortable, so much more comfortable than that hospital gown he tossed onto the bed. He'd just done up the button of his jeans and pulled his sweatshirt over his head when the door to his room creaked opened.

Hoping it was the nurse coming back with the release papers she'd promised him, he turned with a smile only to let it slip away when he saw the trooper walk into his room. Trooper Wells. While he'd struggled a bit to remember her when Ethan had warned him about her earlier, the memories returned of her looking at him the way she looked at him now, with her green eyes narrowed with suspicion.

A lot of people had looked at him that way when he'd been growing up. Mostly because of the company he'd kept and his family than because of anything he'd ever done himself. For the past five years nobody had looked at him that way until recently. Until the bad things had started happening to the hotshots.

"Where do you think you're going?" the trooper asked him as if he'd been breaking out of jail.

After being in this room, tethered to that bed, for three weeks, Rory had begun to feel a little like he was being restrained in prison.

"The doctor told me that I can leave," he said.

"I haven't told you that yet," the trooper said.

"I didn't know you were holding me here," he said. "And on what charges? Is getting hit over the head some crime I don't know about?" Because he sure as hell knew about a lot of them, probably more than she knew.

"I need to talk to you about what happened that night," she said. "And you've been avoiding me."

He gestured back at the bed where his hospital gown lay crumpled on the tangled sheets. "I was right here this whole time."

"With a gatekeeper who kept insisting you weren't well enough to answer my questions," Trooper Wells said, her voice sharp with resentment.

"Well, for the two weeks I was in a coma, I'm thinking it would have been a little hard for me to hear you." Since he hadn't heard Ethan talking to him, or maybe he had and that was why he'd kept dreaming about the crash.

Or maybe there was something about the crash, something that he needed to remember. Some detail that had kept coming back to him in his dreams…

Only now he couldn't remember his dreams that well.

They were fuzzy and unfocused since he'd regained consciousness. He pushed those blurry remnants from his mind and focused on the trooper.

"And if I couldn't hear you, I wouldn't be able to answer you," he continued. "Though even now that I can hear you, I won't be able to help you. I didn't see anything. I just stepped out of the bunk room doorway into the hall and got hit. I didn't see what hit me, much less who did it." It had all happened so damn fast.

"Why did you leave the bunk room?" she asked.

He tensed. Had Braden not shared with her about someone starting the trucks? He knew at one point Trooper Gingrich had been a suspect in the sabotage. And as Trooper Wells's training officer, Gingrich had worked so closely with her that nobody was certain that they should trust her. That she might have actually been working with Gingrich when he'd gone after Luke and Willow Garrison.

Even if she hadn't been, Rory didn't trust her. He didn't trust anyone. Not anymore.

He'd trusted Ethan for the past five years because they'd both had secrets they'd wanted to keep. But now that Ethan's had been revealed...

Rory couldn't totally trust even him any longer. Hopefully he'd kept his word about dropping off Rory's truck in the hospital parking lot.

"Mr. VanDam," Wells prodded him. "Why did you leave the bunk room?"

He lifted his hand and pressed it against the back of his head while he grimaced. "Ahh, I don't really know. With this concussion I've lost so many memories."

Unfortunately, too many of them had returned. Maybe it would have been better if they'd stayed gone.

"You remember walking out of the bunk room," she pointed out. "You remember getting hit."

He shrugged. "Maybe it's my memory, or maybe that's just because of what people told me."

Braden had had to remind him when he'd first regained consciousness and been in such a panic, over the tubes down his throat and over his jumbled mind.

"So other people have been talking to you since you've regained consciousness?" she asked, her mouth twisting into a grimace.

He shrugged again and pressed his lips into a tight line. He was not about to give up any of the team members' names. He might have already put them through more than they deserved to endure. He could be the reason they'd been in danger.

"What is wrong with all of you?" she asked. "I know, thanks to Brittney Townsend's story, that a lot of things have been happening to your hotshot team. However, none of you have reported any of those incidents to the police. I don't think that has anything to do with some stereotypical rivalry between police and fire departments."

There was a reason that rivalry had become a stereotype. Rory had seen it play out, again and again, in his previous life and career. But he couldn't admit to that because that man, the one he'd been back then, needed to stay dead, or he would die all over again and this time for real.

He sighed and admitted, "No. It has to do with your old boss. With Marty Gingrich and his obsession with my boss and hurting him, and he wasn't above using other people to do that, to get to Braden." He'd slept with Braden's first wife and had an affair with another hotshot's wife, too.

Trooper Wells's face flushed nearly as red as the tendril of hair that spilled out from beneath her tan hat. "I had nothing to do with what *he* was doing."

Rory understood all too well how frustrating it was to be judged by the company you kept rather than who you really were as a person. But because he didn't really know her, he had no idea who she really was. She could be just as complicit and cutthroat as her former boss.

"I'm sorry, Trooper Wells," he said with some sincerity. "But I'm not going to be able to help you. There's still too much I don't remember."

"Then maybe you better not leave the hospital," she suggested.

It wasn't just the hospital he intended to leave, and maybe she knew that, too. "I'm sure they need the bed."

As it was, the door hadn't shut tightly behind the trooper, so he could hear voices raised with urgency and excitement. "The paramedics are on their way in with the patient. ETA five minutes."

Not a lot happened in Northern Lakes to keep the hospital very busy unless it happened to a hotshot.

"What's going on…?" he murmured, panic pressing on his heart. Had someone else been injured? Another member of his team?

Trooper Wells's radio began to squawk in her ear, loud enough that Rory could catch tidbits. *Possible gunshots heard. Crash.*

Something bad had definitely happened. He could only hope that it wasn't to another hotshot. He stepped around the trooper and jerked open the door to the hall.

The hospital was small enough that his room wasn't far from the ER. He had only to go to the end of the corridor. The doors to that restricted area opened as a nurse, probably the one he'd overheard talking, rushed through them. And he ducked between them just as they were beginning to close again.

"VanDam!" Wells called out to him.

He glanced over his shoulder, just as the doors closed on her, shutting her out. He turned back, following the nurse who hurried toward where the ambulance would pull into the bay at the rear of the ER.

The nurse wasn't Luke Garrison's wife. Willow was off on maternity leave, taking care of the beautiful, healthy baby she and Luke had. This was another nurse. Older. And vaguely familiar, probably from all the times Rory and his team had been in and out of the hospital.

They'd been getting injuries treated from things they'd thought were accidents. And also from things they'd known weren't. Like having their brake lines cut, nearly being run down and shot at…

Like the patient on their way to the ER now.

*A crash…*

*Gunshots…*

Had someone been shot?

Who?

As he joined the nurse in the bay, she glanced at him. But she didn't tell him to leave the restricted area. Just as he'd vaguely recognized her, she must have recognized him as a hotshot.

*Oh, God…*

So it probably was one of his team coming in the ambulance. Who?

The paramedic rig, lights flashing and sirens wailing, appeared on the road before careening into the lot. The tires squealed and brakes screeched as the ambulance rolled up to the ER entrance.

Rory drew in a breath, but it was shallow, his lungs compressed from the heavy weight of dread and guilt lying on them. He couldn't draw a deep breath. He couldn't slow his speeding pulse, either.

The rig stopped, and the back doors swung open. Owen James jumped out. The former Marine was a member of the Northern Lakes fire department and Rory's hotshot team.

"Owen, who is it?" Rory shouted to the blond-haired paramedic as the hospital staff rushed out to the rig.

Between them and Owen, they pulled a stretcher from the back. Owen didn't answer him. He was totally focused on his patient, firing off stats to ER residents and nurses.

Having been around paramedics a lot, Rory recognized the stats. The low blood pressure and pulse. The low oxygen level.

This person was potentially in trouble. Rory stepped closer, peering over the nurses to see who had been hurt. A woman lay on the stretcher.

She was neither of the female hotshots. She wasn't a hotshot at all. But Rory recognized her. The curly dark hair, the caramel-colored skin that her eyes would have matched if they'd been open.

But they were closed, her thick lashes lying over the dark circles beneath her eyes. She was unconscious. But even unconscious a certain vitality radiated from Brittney Townsend. She was so bright and brilliant, like a star whose light should never dim. Only get brighter.

"Oh, God, no…" Rory murmured.

While the reporter unsettled him and he'd hoped not to see her again because of her determination to get to the truth, he had never wished her any harm. In fact, he'd wished just the opposite…

Brittney squinted and closed her eyes against the lights that were so bright they threatened to blind her. And the pounding, it was so loud and intense that she flinched with pain.

Who was pounding? And where was it coming from? Inside her head or out?

Earlier there had been the sound of a motor running. Maybe her van's.

Maybe some kind of machinery.

There had also been voices yelling out to each other over that noise. Then someone had shouted her name, his gruff voice full of concern. "Ms. Townsend? Brittney?"

She'd tried to open her eyes. She'd tried to reply to him, but it had taken too much effort. Just as the last thing she'd done, grabbing her cell, calling for help, had taken too much effort.

Had she even managed to complete the call? With the way the van had been rolling, the metal crunching, hadn't she lost the phone?

She couldn't be sure now if she had called 911 or if her cell phone or vehicle had detected the crash and placed the call for her. Had she passed out? And why?

Was she hurt? Was that why the light affected her eyes so much? Was the pounding inside her head?

Her mom had gotten migraines from time to time, and until now Brittney hadn't understood how much pain Maureen Townsend must have endured. Probably because her mom had just powered through it as she had everything else in her life. The honorable judge Maureen Townsend was tough. Brittney tried hard to be as tough, as ambitious, as smart as her mother.

A little fluttery feeling passed through Brittney's chest, making her breathe faster, shallower, at the thought, at the realization that she would probably never measure up to the high standards her mother had set for life. Brittney worried that she would never make her as proud as Trent already had. And Trent wasn't even Maureen's son—he'd just come to live with them after his mother had died a few years after his and Brittney's father had already died during a deployment.

Tears stung her eyes, and she blinked, trying to chase them away and fight them back. She was tough, too. She'd had to be.

She drew in another breath and willed the tears away. As her vision cleared, her eyes focused on the man standing over her bed, his pale blue eyes intent on her face and filled with concern.

For her?

Or for himself?

Was he worried about her being hurt or being alive? And if it was the latter, would he try to do something about it, even right here, in what must have been the hospital?

Brittney opened her mouth to scream for help, but before she could get out more than a squeak, his big hand covered her face, cutting off her scream. And her breath…?

Trent's cell lit up with the name Owen James. And nerves tightened the muscles in his stomach. Sammy, the black cat lying on Trent's bare stomach, stood up, arched his back and sunk his claws into Trent's abs. "Owww…"

Sammy jumped off the bed and ran out of the bedroom. And for some reason Trent felt like running, too. He'd pulled a late shift at the firehouse here in Detroit—otherwise he would have been up already. For some reason, seeing this call come in, he wished he was more fully awake.

But maybe he was just overreacting. His fellow hotshots were friends. Just because one of them was calling him now didn't mean that something bad had happened. Except lately.

Every time one of them called, it was because something bad had happened. He drew in a deep breath, to brace himself, and accepted the call. "Hey, Owen, what's up?" he asked.

Silence greeted him. No. Not exactly silence. Other voices murmured in the background of wherever Owen was. Had the paramedic butt-dialed him?

"Owen," he called out, raising his voice. Maybe his friend couldn't hear him over the noise around him, wherever he was. "Are you there?"

The paramedic released a shaky breath that rattled Trent's cell speaker. "Yeah, I…uh… I…"

"What is it?" Trent asked. No. "Who is it? Who got hurt?" Because he heard just enough of the background voices to catch a medical term here and there, he figured out Owen was at the hospital. As a patient or a paramedic? "Are you okay?"

"Yeah, I'm sorry," Owen said. "She doesn't want me to tell you, but I think you should know. And I probably shouldn't tell you because of privacy laws and such…"

"She?" Heather had gone to work a few hours ago, but the area she covered as a Detroit detective was nowhere near Northern Lakes. And Trent was so close to the female hotshots, Hank and Michaela, that he doubted either of them would have asked Owen to keep anything from him. Then he groaned with another realization. "Brittney."

*Damn.*

He'd wanted her to leave his hotshot team alone, to stop hounding Ethan for that follow-up interview, to not shed any more light on the situation with the saboteur than she already had when she'd reported on their string of unfortunate events. He didn't want Braden losing his job as superintendent, and that was bound to happen if any other hotshot got hurt.

But a hotshot hadn't been hurt. His sister had. "What happened?" Trent asked, fear gripping his heart. "Is she all right?"

"Yeah, yeah, she's in the ER getting checked out, but I think she'll be fine. I didn't detect any broken bones. Probably just a concussion."

"*Just* a concussion?" he asked, his voice cracking. "Rory spent two weeks in a coma from just a concussion!"

"She was pretty conscious."

"Pretty conscious?" Trent asked.

"She was going in and out a bit, but seriously, she looks fine," Owen said. "So you don't need to freak out."

But there was something in Owen's voice, something he was leaving unsaid.

"What happened?" Trent asked.

"She got in an accident," Owen said. "Her van went off the road and rolled over. The roads are still snow covered up here. Icy—"

"That's bullshit."

Owen said, "You were up here just a few weeks ago and went off the road—"

"Because someone pushed me off the road," he said. And into a lake.

"There's no evidence that anyone had tried to force her off the road. There's no damage to the front or rear of her van, except for broken windows, and that probably happened when it rolled," Owen said, and he almost sounded as if he was trying to convince himself as much as he was Trent. "She must have just been driving too fast for conditions."

Even though Owen couldn't see him, Trent shook his

head in denial of the paramedic's claim. Trent had taught his little sister to drive, and she'd learned how in Detroit. Since she was fifteen years old, Brittney had had no problem maneuvering rush hour traffic or snow-covered roads.

There was no way in hell that her crash was an accident. Any more than his crash had been when his truck had been forced off the road and into a lake. He was lucky he and Heather hadn't died in the crash or frozen to death in the lake. His stomach flipped at the thought of Brittney going through something like that alone.

But she wasn't alone. Most of his hotshot team was still in Northern Lakes because they'd been worried about Rory and what had happened at the firehouse with all the engines being started up. Trent had stayed there as long as he could, but he'd missed Heather so damn much. At least he'd had a week with her before having to go back.

He jumped up from the bed that they'd spent a lot of time in over the past week. "I'm on my way up," Trent said.

"That's good," Owen said, his voice even gruffer.

"What is it?" Trent asked. "What aren't you telling me?"

"I don't know for sure. Like I said, nothing at the scene indicated that it wasn't just an accident…"

Trent cursed. "I knew it! You don't believe it was any more than I do. What is it?"

"Somebody said something about hearing gunshots," Owen admitted.

Panic gripped Trent's heart so tightly that he gasped.

"But like I said, there was nothing to indicate that. The tires were intact. Nothing had been shot out. If anybody was shooting, it was probably just some hunter. Maybe the sound of the gunfire startled her."

"She wasn't shot?" Trent asked, his heart beating so damn fast.

"No. No," Owen assured him. "She doesn't even have any lacerations."

He released a shaky breath. But he still wasn't entirely relieved. Something was going on with his sister, something he should have known about.

When she'd called him the other day, he'd heard it in her voice. It had been a little brighter than usual, like she was trying to cover up something. He'd just figured it was because she thought he was still mad at her over that damn story she'd done on the team.

"Can you keep an eye on her until I get there?" Trent asked. "Make sure nothing happens to her and that she's—" his voice cracked "—safe?"

"Rory is in with her right now," Owen said.

Trent snorted. "Yeah, right," he said. "He works harder to avoid her than Ethan does."

And if Rory hadn't already been in the hospital himself, Trent might have suspected he was the reason for Brittney winding up there. If anyone wanted to get rid of the reporter, it was probably Rory. The man was even more intensely private and antisocial than Ethan was.

When he wasn't working as a hotshot, he was a ranger on a mostly uninhabited island in the middle of one of the great lakes. Only campers and hikers ever visited the island, which was a national forest, and none of them ever stayed for long. Only Rory had, and that had been his ranger assignment for the past five years.

Ever since the plane crash.

Was Brittney right? Was there more to that story than had already been revealed? And was her pursuit of that story the reason Brittney had wound up in the ER?

# Chapter 4

He shouldn't have touched her. He'd known that the moment he'd pressed his hand over her soft lips. But when she'd opened her mouth, he'd known she was going to scream.

And that damn trooper was hanging around somewhere.

Ready to finish his interview and probably start one with Brittney. And if Brittney screamed while he was leaning over her bed, the trooper was going to think whatever Brittney must have been thinking…

That he was going to hurt her.

"Shh," he said, peering around the curtained-off area of the ER where her gurney had been rolled. He couldn't see any feet beneath the curtains, at least none close enough that anyone could be listening to them. But because the walls were just curtains, everybody in the emergency room would hear her if she screamed.

And they would wonder what he was doing to her.

They weren't the only ones. He wondered himself what had compelled him to come check on her. Owen told him she'd been in a vehicle accident. But from what Rory had overheard from Trooper Wells's radio, it sounded like this crash might have been very much like the other *accidents* the team had been having. And not an accident at all.

Gunshots.

"Calm down," he cautioned her. "If you have a concussion, you're only going to hurt yourself screaming." And because she had been unconscious since she'd arrived at the hospital, he suspected she did have one. But at least she was breathing on her own. And she'd already regained consciousness.

"I'm not going to hurt you," he assured her. That must have been what she'd thought, or why else had she looked like she was about to scream?

Her beautiful topaz eyes narrowed in a glare.

"I'm not," he insisted, and he pulled his hand away, his palm tingling from the contact with her lips. She was so damn beautiful, which was something he was an idiot to even notice much less react to, like he was reacting with a quickening pulse and that damn tingling skin.

And he wasn't an idiot just because she was a reporter and his team member's younger sister…

He was an idiot because he should have known better than being attracted to another woman who would wind up destroying him. And she would…

It was no doubt why she was here.

"Trent left a week ago," Rory told her. At least that was what Braden had told him, that Trent hadn't left until after Rory had regained consciousness. But even after he'd woken up from his coma, Rory hadn't been exactly clear about who was whom. Hell, he hadn't even been certain about his own identity. "So if you've driven up to see him…"

"I drove up here to see you," she said.

His pulse quickened even more, and it wasn't just with attraction now but with apprehension. "Me? Why? Do you know about the…"

He didn't know what to call it. It hadn't been an "accident." Nobody had *accidentally* whacked him over the head hard enough to put him in a coma for two weeks.

Brittney's forehead furrowed beneath corkscrew curls of her chocolate-brown hair. "About the plane crash? Of course I know about it. I reported on it."

He shook his head. "No, I was—"

"There you are," a female voice said, the tone accusatory, and Trooper Wells jerked aside one of the curtains around Brittney's gurney. The woman was looking at Rory, though, before she turned toward the bed and added, "And there you are. I've been looking for both of you."

"Why?" Rory asked. "I already told you that I don't know anything about what happened in the firehouse—"

"What happened in the firehouse?" Brittney asked, and she struggled to sit up from the stretcher. But her delicate features twisted into a grimace of pain.

"Sit back," he said, and he touched her shoulders, trying to ease her onto her pillows again without hurting her. Then he peered around the trooper, out into the ER. "Where the hell is the doctor? Why isn't anyone treating you?"

The head nurse, Cheryl, must have been hanging around within eavesdropping distance because she popped up behind the trooper. "The doctor saw her and ordered an MRI, and we've just been waiting for an opening to use it. It's available now." She edged around Wells then to approach the gurney. "So I need to bring her downstairs to Imaging for it." She unbraked the bed and began to roll it toward Rory and the trooper.

The trooper stepped back but Rory hesitated for a moment. Seeing Brittney arrive in the back of the paramedic rig had affected him, had brought on all kinds of feelings he didn't know he had about her. Concern. Attraction.

Along with those unwelcome feelings had come the unwelcome memories of what happened to people who got too close to him. He didn't want to make any more memories like that.

Never again.

So with a slight shudder, he moved aside, but when the gurney started past him, Brittney reached out and grabbed his arm, stopping it and him.

"Don't leave me," she said, her voice cracking a bit with a vulnerability he wouldn't have expected her capable of feeling.

"I'm sure Trent will be here soon," he assured in case she was scared of being alone.

She shook her head and flinched at the movement. "I don't want Trent. I want you."

Despite knowing that she didn't mean it how it sounded, he felt a jolt like electricity and shock and something else, something he hadn't felt in a long time. A connection.

But she didn't want him. She just wanted his story. And the smartest thing he could do was get the hell out of there before she, or anyone else, could catch up with him again.

Brittney hadn't missed that look of panic on Rory's face when she'd said that she'd wanted him. But she hadn't meant that the way it had probably sounded. She hadn't, and yet when she'd said it, she'd felt this strange yearning for a connection, to not be so alone.

She'd been so focused on her career that she hadn't noticed how lonely she'd been, or maybe she'd noticed but just hadn't wanted to acknowledge it. Kind of like how she didn't want to acknowledge how damn good-looking Rory VanDam was in that conquering Viking kind of way, with his pale blond hair and pale blue eyes. But he had a shadow on his jaw for once, a dark shadow.

While she was closed in the MRI chamber, she focused on his image in her mind. She should have been focusing on her questions instead, about him and the plane crash and about what had happened on the road that had sent her van tumbling over and over.

But her mind shied away from that, from that fear she'd felt in the moment. When she'd heard…

What had she heard before the windshield metamorphosized into a spiderweb? A gunshot? Had someone shot at her? No. Nobody had known she was heading up north. She hadn't told anyone, not even at the station when she'd requested a few days off. But maybe her producer had figured out that she was determined to follow up on the plane crash story. Or someone had followed her…like they'd been following her.

The MRI didn't take long, and she was wheeled back up to the ER, to that cordoned-off area where she'd awakened to Rory leaning over her. Had he really been concerned about her or about what she might have learned?

And the trooper…

Why had she been looking for Rory? To talk about what had happened at the firehouse?

What the hell had happened?

The questions pounded inside Brittney's head like the pain. She probably had a concussion. With the way the van had rolled and the metal had crunched, she wouldn't be surprised if that was what the doctor told her once the results of the MRI came back.

The nurse pulled open the curtain to where a man sat in a chair that had been beside her bed. It wasn't her brother. Even if someone had called Trent, he wouldn't have been able to drive up within the time frame that she must have arrived at the hospital.

The nurse rolled her bed into place, next to that chair where the man was sitting, and asked Brittney, "Do you need anything?"

"Just answers," she murmured.

"The results should be back soon," the older woman assured her with a smile.

Those weren't the answers she needed, though. She just smiled at the woman and nodded.

The nurse was probably busy because she hurried away, stopping only to pull the curtains closed.

Brittney just glanced at those before rolling her head back toward the man sitting beside her bed. "You didn't leave..." she murmured, surprised that Rory had stayed like she'd asked.

He shrugged. "Trooper Wells probably wouldn't have let me. I feel like she's holding me here under house, er, hospital arrest."

"For what?" she asked. "For whatever happened at the firehouse?"

His lips curved into a slight grin. "Do you never not ask questions?"

"You set yourself up for those questions," she pointed out. But it wouldn't have mattered if he'd said nothing at all, she still would have had questions for him.

He sighed and nodded. "Yeah, I guess I did, but I've already been interrogated once today."

"So why did you stay?" she asked.

He sighed again, more heavily, and shrugged. "I really don't know..."

"No guess?" she teased.

"Because you asked me to," he said, as if he was reluctant to make the admission.

Something shifted inside her, making her heart feel

funny. Maybe she had an injury from the seat belt. The damn airbag hadn't gone off. But the seat belt had snapped tightly around her, holding her in her place while the vehicle rolled. She touched her chest then and drew in a shaky breath.

"You're not okay," he said. "Do you need pain medication? An IV? Why haven't they given you anything yet?" He jumped up from the chair then, but before he could stalk off, she caught his arm again.

"They're waiting for the results of the MRI," she said. "And I'm not in pain." To prove her point, she tried to sit up, but she flinched as her head pounded harder and her stomach ached.

"Liar," he said, but his deep voice was soft and the look in his eyes…

She couldn't be sure but it almost looked like admiration. She wasn't used to seeing that from any of the hotshots. Usually they looked at her with irritation. Especially him.

"Okay, maybe it hurts a little," she admitted.

"I'll get Cheryl or a medical resident," he said, and he started to tug his arm free of her grasp.

But she held tighter to him. "No. I don't need anything. It's not that bad."

He shook his head. "I still don't believe you. You trying to prove how tough you are?"

She flinched again, but the pain wasn't because of her concussion. It was because Rory was probably right. She kept trying to prove herself. No. She just wanted to be taken seriously. To be successful. But that wasn't the reason she was so determined to find out everything she could about that plane crash and about the hotshots; she just wanted to keep her brother safe, or at least as safe as he could be with his career.

"That's not it," she insisted. "I don't want to take anything that might knock me out again." She needed to stay awake and stay alert, so that threat wasn't carried out like it very nearly had been. The windshield hadn't shattered like that by accident. Something, and someone, had caused it.

Rory nodded. "I get that. I spent two weeks in a coma."

She gasped and tightened her grasp on his arm. "What happened?" And why the hell hadn't she heard about it?

"That's what I would like to know," another voice chimed in, and Brittney glanced up to see that Trooper Wells had returned, pulling back the curtain to peer in at them.

Rory's long, lean body subtly tensed next to her. Even though Brittney held only his arm, she could feel that tension in him and inside herself, as well. It was clear that the trooper was not done with them. But the hotshot shrugged and sighed. "I told you, Trooper Wells, I didn't see anything. And I barely remember anything."

"About that night or about anything else?" The trooper asked the question that was burning inside Brittney.

He shrugged again. "I have no idea what I forgot."

"Your boss said you barely recognized him or even knew your own name," the trooper remarked.

Rory glanced down at Brittney and then back at the officer. "Do you think this is a good idea? Talking about this in front of a reporter?"

The trooper's face flushed. But she lifted her chin as if powering through the embarrassment. Brittney recognized the gesture and the sentiment. She'd done it herself several times while she'd been covering something live and something had gone wrong.

But until this afternoon, until someone had tried to kill her, nothing had ever gone as wrong for her as this had.

She hadn't taken anything, but she felt strange, light-headed. Maybe with fear more than pain. She tightened her grasp on Rory's arm, deriving a strange comfort in his closeness. For the first time in a long while, she didn't feel so alone.

"I thought you two were more than acquaintances," the trooper remarked with a pointed look at Brittney's hand holding on to him.

Brittney would have jerked her hand away if she wasn't afraid that Rory would take off and leave her. And after what had happened with her van, she really didn't want to be alone. "He's a friend of my brother's," Brittney said. But she really didn't know Rory VanDam. She suspected nobody did. Yet, for some reason, she felt safer with him here with her.

"Who's your brother?" the trooper asked.

Figuring she could find out easily enough, Brittney replied, "Trent Miles."

The trooper's green eyes widened. "He just had an accident himself here recently. His truck went off the road and into a lake."

"That wasn't an accident," Brittney said.

"Was yours?" the trooper asked.

Brittney quickly nodded, grimacing as a sharp pain reverberated throughout her skull. "Yeah, snow-covered roads...all that..."

"Are you sure? There was a report of someone hearing gunfire in the area."

Brittney shrugged. "I don't know about that." And until she could figure that out for certain, she wanted to be the only one investigating her "accident." She knew that Trent and his team had reason not to trust their local police, after one of the troopers had tried to kill a hotshot.

"You didn't hear gunshots?" the trooper asked.

Brittney probably should have told her the truth, but she didn't know how close this trooper had been to the one who'd tried killing her brother's hotshot team member. Close enough to have helped him?

Clearly Rory didn't trust the woman because he had avoided her questions, but he had also avoided answering Brittney's. Until Brittney was certain she could trust the trooper, she had no intention of telling her about anything that was happening with her. About the gunshots.

About the threats.

"I don't know," she said. "I don't remember."

"But you know the roads are snowy? Is that why you went off in the ditch and rolled your vehicle?"

Brittney shrugged again. "I don't know. I really don't remember." It had all happened so fast. She'd always believed she would be better equipped to handle a situation like that. But that blast and the subsequent shattering of her windshield had startled and blinded her. And she hadn't reacted the way she'd wanted to, with the strength and calm that her mom or Trent would have.

She wasn't used to being in danger, not like the hotshots were used to it. And she didn't want to get used to it, so she had to figure out fast who was behind the threats she'd received.

The trooper stared at her, her green eyes hard. "I can't help you if you don't tell me the truth."

"I can't tell you the truth until I know what it is myself," Brittney pointed out. And that was as honest as she intended to be with the trooper.

"You better let the authorities figure that out," the officer advised. "And don't investigate on your own."

While the trooper seemed young, probably even a year

or so younger than Brittney, she was wise. Or maybe she'd simply heard about her.

Wells turned toward Rory again. "That goes for you and your hotshot team, too. Whatever is going on with all of you, you need to leave it to the police to handle. You might know what you're doing when it comes to fighting fires, but you don't know when it comes to fighting bad guys."

Rory's lips curved into a slight, almost mocking grin, and he chuckled. "Really, Trooper Wells. And being up here in Northern Lakes, you know a lot about fighting bad guys?"

There was something in his tone, something that made Brittney pull her hand back from his arm. He sounded like he knew much more about fighting bad guys than any fire-fighter should know.

Because he'd fought them? Or because he'd been one?

# Chapter 5

"Where are you going?" Owen asked as Rory walked past him, heading toward the exit.

He wished he'd been able to slip past the paramedic undetected, but Owen had been hovering somewhere inside the ER since Brittney had been brought in. Just like Rory had been hovering, but now that he knew she was all right, he was free to leave.

He should have left before now, but he'd wanted to make sure that she wasn't in any immediate danger. So when the doctor had ducked behind the curtain and asked him and the trooper to leave, Rory had hovered, like Owen, but close enough that he could hear the results of her MRI.

No broken bones.

And just a slight concussion.

The pressure that had been on his chest since seeing her lying on that gurney finally eased. She was fine. Physically. For now...

But if someone had fired at her vehicle, if someone had caused her to go off the road, she was still in danger until that person was caught. And what if she was in danger because of him? Because she was so damn determined to find out everything about the plane crash?

The person who'd caused it wasn't going to want their secret getting out, that it wasn't an accident. Just like

Rory getting hit over the head hadn't been an accident. And maybe her going off the road hadn't been one, either, which meant that he might be, inadvertently, responsible for her being in danger.

"Rory?" Owen prodded him, his brow creasing with concern as he studied his face.

Everybody had been looking at him that way since he'd regained consciousness from the coma. With such concern and…confusion.

It was as if they didn't recognize him anymore.

Maybe that was because Rory had not recognized or remembered many of them or even himself when he'd woken up after two weeks of bad dreams and oblivion. But he remembered enough now to know that he was in danger and not just because of that whack on the head.

"I got released," Rory said. "And Ethan dropped off my truck earlier." Or at least he'd asked him to do it and Ethan had promised that he would, that he'd have Tammy follow him to the hospital to drop it off before they left for a much-deserved getaway.

Owen peered around him. "Ethan's here?"

Rory shook his head, and his stomach flipped with the pain radiating from the back of his skull. God, he hoped Brittney's head wasn't hurting like his. And if it was, she was damn tough. "No, Ethan and Tammy were taking off, going someplace warm for a couple of weeks."

Owen nodded. "Oh, that's right. I keep forgetting that he quit the ranger job to stick around Northern Lakes."

"Around Tammy," Rory said. "And it's not like he needs the money." The guy was the Canterbury heir no matter how hard his brother-in-law had tried to take him out.

As hard as someone had tried to take out Rory. And Brittney?

Had she been telling Trooper Wells the truth about the crash? Or was there more to it than she'd admitted?

He suspected there was, and that concerned him, way more than it should. But if she was in danger because of him…

"Somebody needs to stick close to Brittney until Trent makes it up here," Owen said. The radio in his hand squawked. "And I have to go out on a call."

Rory tensed. "Who's hurt?"

"Nobody's hurt," Owen said. "It's a transport from the hospital back to the nursing home for someone who is all right now."

Rory's tension eased. "That's good."

"Yes, and I put it off as long as I can, but Trent is still about an hour away," Owen said. "Can you stick around until he gets here?"

"Why me?" Rory asked, his pulse quickening with the thought of sticking close to Brittney Townsend. But that might be dangerous for both of them…

Owen glanced around. "I don't see anybody else here."

"But somebody else would show up if you'd called them," Rory said. "Or if Trent had called them."

"But you were here at the hospital when she got hurt."

Rory narrowed his eyes and studied his friend's face. "What are you saying?"

Owen held up his hands. "I'm not saying anything. But I think we both know that we shouldn't take any chances right now. You should know that better than anyone else after what you've been through."

Rory sucked in a breath. "What…what do you mean?"

"You were in a coma for two weeks, man," Owen said. "Because someone put you there."

He shuddered. Who had done that? A stranger? Or some-one he knew and should have been able to trust?

"That's why we have to be extra careful."

"We have to," Rory agreed. "But her…"

"She's Trent's sister," Owen reminded him.

Rory groaned. "You know how I feel about her."

"I thought I did, but now I'm wondering if you know how you feel about her," Owen replied. "Or did you forget that like you've forgotten some other things?"

"What do you mean?" How badly had he slipped up in those first days after regaining consciousness?

"You've been sticking close to her since I brought her here in the rig, which surprised the hell out of me since you were so pissed off the last time she came up to North-ern Lakes. You were trying so hard to avoid her then that you spent most of the time she was here hiding out in the woods."

"I like the woods," Rory said. "That's why I'm a forest ranger."

"You remember that," Owen said. "But you seem to have forgotten how much you dislike the reporter."

"I don't dislike her," Rory said.

"I see that," Owen said with a wide grin.

"I just don't trust her." She was determined to further her career with a story that might have already put her in danger and would certainly put him in danger if the truth came out. But then he already was in danger and appar-ently so was she…

"You don't have to trust her to keep an eye on her until Trent gets here," Owen said. "And I need you to do that because I have to go."

As if on cue, the driver from the rig called out to him.

"Owen! Mrs. G. wants to get back to the home before *Judge Judy* starts."

Owen smirked. "She wants to get back to Mr. Stehouwer."

The names vaguely rang a bell with Rory. The older couple had been in a fire at the boarding house that hotshot Cody Mallehan's fiancée had owned. They'd been her boarders until the Northern Lakes arsonist had burned down her house.

Everyone had survived, though. But it was just one more reminder of how precarious life was, probably why Mrs. Gulliver didn't want to spend any more time than necessary away from her Mr. Stehouwer. While being alone was the safest option for him and people around him, Rory missed being around other people, being close to them. He hadn't realized how much until Brittney had grabbed his arm and said she'd needed him.

And if she was in danger because of him, he had an obligation to protect her that went beyond even his duty to his fellow hotshots. Rory sighed. "Damn it. Go."

Owen slapped his shoulder. "Thanks. I appreciate it and Trent will, too."

Rory wasn't so sure about that. As pissed off as Trent had been at his sister, he was still protective of her, protective enough that he hadn't wanted her left alone. But if Trent knew what Rory really thought about his sister, he probably wouldn't trust him to watch over her. She didn't just unsettle him with her questions but also with her attractiveness.

And her touch…

Rory didn't entirely trust himself to watch over her and not want more of a connection with her. But he drew in a breath, to brace himself, and turned back toward where he'd left her behind that curtained-off area.

But the curtains had been pulled back. And her gurney was empty.

His pulse quickened with fear. Where the hell had she gone? He started forward, but someone grabbed his arm. And from the way his skin tingled, even through his heavy sweatshirt, he knew who it was.

She chuckled. "You're not much of a babysitter," she remarked.

Obviously she'd eavesdropped on his conversation with Owen. "No, I'm not," he agreed wholeheartedly. And she didn't even know the half of it. She could never know the half of it or she might wind up like the last woman he'd been attracted to.

Dead. He had to make sure that didn't happen, that he kept her out of danger somehow. He couldn't carry any more guilt than he already did.

"Good thing for you that I don't need a babysitter," Brittney said. "But I do need a ride."

Rory narrowed his eyes.

"Ethan dropped off yours," she said, revealing just how much of his conversation with Owen that she'd overheard.

"I'm not driving you back to Detroit," Rory said.

"I don't want to go back to Detroit."

"You should," he said. "You should go back." If not for her sake then for his. Because if she stuck around Northern Lakes, Rory had no doubt that this wasn't going to end well. For either of them.

Brittney suspected that Trooper Wells had underestimated her. She wasn't the first one who'd made that mistake. And she probably wouldn't be the last.

The person who'd left her that note and sent her the text

hadn't underestimated her, though. They knew that if she kept investigating she was going to discover the truth.

On her own.

But she wasn't alone right now. Albeit grudgingly, Rory VanDam was giving her the ride she'd requested. To the body shop that the state police used as an impound lot in Northern Lakes. Brittney already knew which one it was from when Ethan Sommerly's truck had been blown up.

Hers hadn't blown up, but it didn't look much better than Ethan's burned-out truck had looked.

Rory's breath whistled out between his teeth as he pulled his truck up to the fence behind which the mass of crumpled metal sat. He looked from the wreckage to her. "Are you sure you're all right? Did the doctor actually release you?"

"You really don't trust me," she remarked. She'd over-heard most of his conversation with Owen. "You think I would do anything for a story." Only a console sepa-rated her passenger seat from his driver's seat, and she was tempted to lean across it, to tease him, about just how far he thought she would go. But she was already all too aware of how close he was to her, and something inside her, that she'd ignored for a long time, was reacting to that closeness.

"Wouldn't you?" he asked. "Isn't that why we're here?"

"I would do anything for the truth," she said. And she hoped like hell she wasn't risking her life for it. But if she stood around and did nothing, that didn't mean the danger would go away. The only way she could control the danger was to find out who presented the danger.

While she'd had a few doubts about Rory when she first got that note, Owen had verified that Rory had been in the hospital when her "accident" happened. That was why he'd trusted Rory, over other hotshots, to protect her. She wanted to trust him, too; she needed someone she could turn to…

But she didn't want to put him in danger, either, although it seemed like it was already too late for that.

"When did you get hit over the head?" she asked.

His mouth curved into a slight grin. "Why? Do I need an alibi for something?" Then his grin slid away, and he focused on her face. "This isn't the first thing that's happened to you, is it?"

"Just tell me when you got hit and went into that coma," she persisted. He didn't need his coma for an alibi, though. She just wanted to know if the same person might have hurt him who'd been threatening her.

"The night of the hotshot holiday party."

She sucked in a breath and nodded. "That's why Trent didn't come back to Detroit with Heather."

He shrugged. "He stayed before that happened. He was here that night that…"

"You got struck over the head," she finished for him. "Something else happened that night, didn't it?" And was the person who'd left the note on her van the same one who'd hit him? Or was someone else after him? Or just after any hotshot they were able to hurt?

He grinned that slight grin. "My getting whacked wasn't enough for you?"

He was teasing her, trying to be funny, but she couldn't laugh, not at him getting hurt so badly. Instead, she was tempted to reach across the console and touch him, to run her fingers over his head to find his wound. And…what? Kiss it better?

A sudden urge burned inside her to lean closer, to brush her lips across his. Maybe her concussion was worse than she'd thought. "You were in the hospital for weeks, then?" So obviously his concussion had been much worse than the one she'd gotten in the crash. Maybe that was why he wasn't avoiding her like he previously had.

"You didn't check my medical records while you were in the hospital?" he asked. And he probably wasn't teasing now.

"I would have tried," she said, "but Trooper Wells might've caught me with the way she kept popping up like she was lurking around..." She peered out the windows, looking for a state patrol vehicle. The concrete and metal body shop building and the fenced-in yard behind it were on the western outskirts of town, farther from Lake Huron. Trees surrounded the area, blocking it from the highway and even the driveway that led back to it.

"She didn't follow us," he said.

Maybe she hadn't, but Brittney suspected someone else might have. She had that uneasy feeling again, goose bumps rising on her skin with the sudden chill that rushed over her. And she shivered.

"It's not her you're worried about," Rory said.

She glanced back at him to find him staring intently at her, his pale blue eyes narrowed with suspicion.

"What's going on, Brittney?" he asked her.

"Which one of us is the reporter?" she fired back at him with a smile.

His mouth twitched, as if he was fighting against the urge to smile back at her. His blue eyes sparkled.

Her pulse quickened, and not because of some unknown person watching her but because he was. And he was so much better looking than she'd even remembered. She'd been curious about him before, for the sake of her story, but now she was just curious about him. About how his lips would feel against hers...

How he would kiss her...

How he would touch her…

She blinked, trying to break that connection and focus again on what mattered. On finding out why they were both in danger. "I'll answer one of your questions if you'll answer one of mine," she offered.

If he'd been fighting it, the smile won, curving his lips up at the corners. He chuckled and shook his head.

"Chicken," she taunted him with a smile of her own.

He nodded now. "I am definitely afraid of you, Ms. Townsend."

"Why do I scare you?" she asked. Was he feeling what she was? This sudden attraction? This strange connection?

Was it because they'd both recently survived attempts on their lives? Or maybe whoever had caused their accidents hadn't meant to kill them…

Just what?

Scare them away?

"I'm scared," he said, "because I'm not stupid." Then he sighed. "No. I take that back. If I was smart, I would have taken off and left you alone in the hospital."

"Why didn't you?" she asked.

"It's tough to get an Uber in Northern Lakes at this time of year," he replied.

"And you were worried about me hitching a ride?" she asked. "Or were you worried about my brother? Is that why you agreed to babysit me until he gets here?"

"I thought you didn't need a babysitter," he reminded her.

"I don't," she said. Then she glanced around again and muttered, "Maybe a bodyguard…"

"What's going on, Brittney?" He repeated his earlier question.

She dodged it this time by opening the passenger door and jumping out. But when she approached the fence, she noticed that a chain, secured with a heavy padlock, held the gate together. She turned toward the building, but no lights shone inside, although it was kind of hard to tell with the only glass being in one panel of each of several garage doors.

"It's after five," Rory said. "It must close then."

The sky was already turning gray with a pink rim just below the thick clouds.

She cursed. "I need to get in there. My overnight bag is inside the van." That wasn't all. Her purse was in there, too. She rattled the gate, trying to push the sides of it far enough apart to squeeze between, but she couldn't even get her arm through the narrow opening. She cursed again.

"Even if you could get into the fence, I'm not sure we could get inside the vehicle."

She pointed toward where part of the metal had been peeled back like the top of a tin can. "They got me out that way," she said. "I can get back in that way." She rattled the gate again, but the chain was too thick to give her any more room to squeeze through. So she moved farther down the fence and jammed the toe of her boot into part of the chain links while she locked her fingers into another part. Using her arms, she tried pulling herself up.

Rory chuckled.

"Give me a boost!" she ordered him.

"Yes, ma'am."

Then big hands wrapped around her waist, pushing her up. As she went higher, his hands went lower, over the curve of her hips, along the outside of her thighs and finally, where she'd intended him to boost her, her boots. Her whole body tingled in reaction. She swung her leg over the top of the fence and turned to stare back down at him.

"That wasn't what I meant by a boost." But she wasn't

really complaining. Her skin had heated up everywhere he'd touched her. And as the sun set, the temperature was dropping along with it. The wind kicking up tangled her hair across her face, blinding her.

But then Rory was there, close, as he climbed up the fence to her. He swung his leg over, too, and jumped down, landing lithely on his feet in the yard on the other side, with all the grace of a gymnast landing a somersault.

Brittney hadn't been a very good gymnast. She wasn't all that flexible. She struggled to swing her other leg over the top. But when she did, she lost her foothold with her other boot and dangled from way too close to the top and too far from the ground.

"I'll catch you," Rory said.

"I'm not like a cat or a baby being tossed out the window of a burning house," she said. "I'll flatten you."

"Ouch," he said. "You must think I'm pretty weak."

"Don't say I didn't warn you," she murmured. Despite her words, she tried to hang on and find footholds for the toes of her boots. But her fingers slipped from the chain links and she dropped, not to the ground, but into some strong arms.

It wasn't like catching a baby, though. He didn't cradle her easily in both arms. He caught one of her legs and just half her body, while the other half of her dangled forward, nearly hitting the ground. Then they both hit the ground as he stumbled back and fell. But she was sprawled across him, not the dirt, while he lay flat on his back.

"I warned you," she reminded him as her breasts pressed into his hard chest. His heart pounded fast and hard beneath hers, which probably matched its frantic pace.

"I guess I am pretty weak," he said in between pants for air.

She must have knocked it out of him. She wriggled around, trying to get off him. But his hands caught her hips, gripping them like he had when she'd been trying to get up the fence.

"Give me a sec," he said gruffly.

"Are you hurt? Broken bones?" she asked.

"No. Just that damn concussion."

"Did you hit your head on the ground?" she asked, and she stretched up his long body that was so very tense beneath hers and ran her fingers along his jaw to the back of his head. His spiky-looking hair was surprisingly soft, but then she felt what must have been a ridged line of stitches or staples. Her stomach lurched over how badly he'd been hurt, and how lucky he'd been to survive such a violent blow. "You really were hit hard. That was definitely no damn accident."

"And neither was yours," he remarked.

"How do you know?" She hadn't admitted to hearing those gunshots, but she was damn sure that she had.

He reached out, running his hand underneath her van. And he pulled out a bullet. "It must have fallen out of the wreckage."

She let out a shaky breath.

"You're not surprised," he said. "You did hear the gunshots. What the hell is going on, Brittney? And this time I want an answer out of you."

"I'll give you one," she said. "Just not here."

Because she had that feeling again, that sick, not sixth, sense that she was being watched. Her stomach churned with the fear gripping her. If that person was out there and armed again, she wasn't the only one in danger now. Rory was, too.

He'd already survived what must have been an attempt on his life. Would he survive another?

\* \* \*

Braden Zimmer sometimes got this strange feeling, a forewarning, when a fire was about to start. That feeling had helped his wife catch the Northern Lakes arsonist the year before. Sam McRooney-Zimmer had caught Braden, too, when he'd fallen so deeply in love with the arson investigator. Sam had taken a little more convincing to give him and Northern Lakes a chance.

But since there, fortunately, weren't a lot of arson fires in Northern Lakes, Sam traveled frequently, and she was out of town now. Instead of hanging out in his empty house, Braden usually spent more time at the firehouse.

If only he'd been here the night after the holiday party...

But Sam had been home that night.

Despite all her help and her brother's help, Braden still couldn't figure out who the saboteur was. Or why.

Why do all these things to the hotshots, especially if he or she was one of them? Why hurt one of their own like Rory had been hurt? So damn badly.

He'd been released from the hospital, so Braden expected him to come back to the firehouse, which was another reason he was here. And that feeling...

It wasn't the one he got about fires. It wasn't a forewarning, it was certainty and dread, twisting his stomach into knots. Because he didn't need a sixth sense to know that something bad was bound to happen again. Until the saboteur was caught, bad things would keep happening.

His office door creaked open and Trick, his brother-in-law, poked his red-haired head through the opening. "Did you hear about that reporter?"

Braden tensed, and that dread in his stomach got heavier. "What reporter?"

"Trent's sister. Brittney Townsend."

Braden groaned. "What about her?"

"She's back in Northern Lakes."

He groaned again. "Do you think she heard about Rory getting hurt? Is she here about the saboteur?"

Trick shrugged. "I don't know."

"Is she here now? At the firehouse?"

Trick shook his head again. "She was in the hospital last Owen knew. He brought her there in his rig. She was in a crash."

Braden sucked in a breath. "Does Trent know?"

Trick nodded. "Yeah, Owen called him. He's on his way up. He wanted Owen to keep an eye on her but he had to go out on call."

"Then why aren't *you* watching her?"

"Rory is. He was just supposed to watch her at the hospital until Trent got there. But I checked in on them and they were both gone."

Braden groaned.

"It's not like Rory is going to tell her anything about the sabotage," Trick said. "He wants less to do with her than the rest of us do."

Braden dropped back into his chair, but he wasn't really relieved that Rory wouldn't talk to her. "Maybe we should talk to her."

"About what? Her crash? The roads are still pretty slippery. Even though Trent told Owen it wasn't an accident, I figure it probably was."

"Probably." Braden shook his head. "After everything that has happened, I struggle to accept that anything is an accident anymore."

Trick released a ragged sigh. "Me, too."

"We should talk to her," Braden said. "About what happened to her and maybe even about what's been happening around here."

"But Braden, that could cost you your job," Trick warned him.

He shrugged. "I'd rather lose my job than lose one of the team. Again."

"Dirk's death wasn't your fault. That had nothing to do with the team."

But that didn't make Braden feel any better about the loss of a good man. And he'd nearly lost another one when Rory had been assaulted.

With an axe handle.

A firefighter's axe.

That didn't mean that it had to have been a firefighter who'd attacked Rory, though. Stanley often forgot to lock the doors. Really anyone could have gotten inside that night. And once inside, it would have been easy enough to find the keys for the rigs. But Braden still had that sick feeling in his stomach, that dread that the saboteur was one of his team.

# Chapter 6

Rory had wondered before if that blow to his head had knocked the common sense out of him or back into him. He had his answer now as he followed Brittney Townsend through the door she'd just unlocked to a room at the Lakeside Inn in Northern Lakes. He'd lost all his common sense and all sense of self-preservation, as well. Or he would have dropped her off and run away.

No. He would have left her at the hospital until Trent got there. But she hadn't wanted to wait for her brother or to even let him know where she was.

But no matter what was going on between Brittney and Trent, Rory shouldn't be here. He should be somewhere else, anywhere else where nobody could find him. Hell, he should have stayed missing five years ago instead of coming out of the mountains with Ethan, but if they hadn't banded together during those two months, neither of them would have survived. They'd struggled during the long hours it had taken them to find each other.

And now he kind of felt the same way about Brittney as he had when he'd found Ethan on that mountain. Like they were both in danger and wouldn't make it if they separated. That, together, they were stronger and safer. But Brittney wasn't Ethan. He wasn't sure he should trust her, or if she would take chances that would put them both in more danger than they already were.

"This is a bad idea," he said, hesitating on the threshold to her room.

She reached out and grasped his arm like she had in the hospital when she hadn't wanted him to leave her. And this time, instead of holding him in place, she tugged him inside the room and closed the door behind him. Then she locked both the handle and the dead bolt and leaned back against the wood of the door.

"You're not going to keep out a bullet like that," he said. And another of those old memories surfaced even as he fought to force it back down, to drown it out for good. "You need to call Trooper Wells."

"Do you trust her?" she asked.

He sighed.

"So why do you think that I should?"

"It's the hotshots who can't trust her," Rory said. "You should be able to."

"My brother is a hotshot," she said. "So why would I be able to trust her if my brother can't? If she has something against him, she might use me to get to him."

"I don't think she's had as much to do with Trent as she has other hotshots, the ones who live up here," he said.

"What about you?" she asked.

He shook his head. "The most interaction I had with her was today." Because he didn't technically live in Northern Lakes.

"You didn't seem to enjoy that very much," she pointed out. "Are you sure you want me to call her here?"

"I'll leave." He took a step toward the door, but she hadn't moved away from it.

Now he wondered if she had locked and leaned against

the door to keep out whoever she thought was after her or if she'd done it to keep him inside with her. Was it that she didn't want to be alone again? Was she more scared than she would admit? Or was she feeling the same thing he was? This strange draw to her...

"I'm not going to call Trooper Wells," she said. "You don't have to run off."

"You should run," he said. And he meant it. "After finding that bullet, you know that was no accident." Just like so many of the things that had happened to the hotshots had been no accident, either.

"How can I leave?" she asked. "You saw my van. I'm not driving out of here in that wreck."

"You can take a bus," he suggested. "Or have Trent take you back to Detroit when he gets here. You'll be safe there." He hoped.

She shook her head.

He hesitated to ask the question he'd already asked her twice, the question she'd promised she would answer once they left the impound lot at the body shop. But once they'd extricated her suitcase from the back and her purse from beneath a seat, he'd realized that he might be better off not knowing the answer to this question.

Because if he knew, he might not be able to walk away like he should. No. He should run. Every instinct he had was screaming at him to do that, to run.

But to run away, he had to get closer to her. And when he stepped closer, the ground seemed to shift beneath him like it had when she'd dropped from that fence into his arms. He'd fallen for her then.

No. He'd fallen *with* her.

He could not fall *for* her. Or for anyone else. Not ever again.

\* \* \*

Brittney waited for him to ask that question again. She needed him to ask it, or even just to say something, because the way he was staring at her unnerved her. But it wasn't like that sensation she felt whenever someone else watched her.

She wasn't chilled by Rory's stare. Instead, heat rushed through her, and her pulse quickened. Then he closed his eyes, as if staring at her unnerved him, as well. Could he feel this, too? This attraction that was beginning to overwhelm her with its intensity.

His long, lean body tensed, and he asked, "What's going on, Brittney? Why did someone shoot at you? What the hell has been happening?"

For some strange reason she trusted him and not just because he'd been in the hospital when someone had shot at her van. Because he was obviously in danger, too, and he understood what she was feeling…all the fear and frustration and maybe even the determination to find out who the hell was after them.

"Someone's been following me," she told him. "At first I thought it was just my imagination, or maybe someone who'd recognized me." She shuddered now. "Or even my creepy producer."

His eyes opened, filled with concern. "Your creepy producer?"

She shrugged. "I can handle him. And there's no way he would have shot at me or even followed me up here to Northern Lakes." She creased her brow. "No. They might have already been here because the shot came from the direction I was going, not from behind me."

"Who knew you were coming up here?" he asked.

"Nobody."

"Not even Trent?"

"Especially not Trent," she said. "He's barely been talking to me since I did that story about Ethan."

"About Jonathan Canterbury…" he murmured.

"Did you know?" she asked. "Did you always know who he really was?"

He shook his head, but she didn't know if that was in reply to her question or in denial of answering it. "Ethan's refused to do a follow-up interview with you," he said. "And I refused to do one at all."

"I'm well aware of that," she said. "So when I got this note…" Her handbag was slung across her body, so she reached inside and pulled out the piece of paper and showed it to him.

"'You are being watched, and if you don't drop this story, you will die,'" he read the note aloud, his voice gruffer with each word. "What story?"

"It has to be the one about the plane crash," she said. "Because when I tried talking to Mack McRooney about it, this text came through…" She pulled out her cell, but the screen was black. The battery must have died after the crash, just like she might have died in the crash. She'd been damn lucky. "The text said something like, 'you were warned, now you'll suffer the consequences.'"

He shuddered. "And then you were shot at. Damn, Brittney. You need to report this."

"To whom?" she asked. "Trooper Wells? Why should I trust her when you don't?" And why did she feel like he was the only one she could trust? She didn't know him well or really at all. But since waking up to find him with her in the hospital, concerned about her, she had connected with him on a whole other level.

He sighed. "I don't trust anyone, Brittney. Not anymore."

"Why not?" she asked.

He touched the back of his head, where she'd felt those stitches. And she understood why. "Well, you can trust me," she insisted. "When you were getting hit over the head, I was in Detroit. And you were already in the hospital when I found that note on my windshield."

"When did you find that note?" he asked.

"Two weeks ago," she replied.

"And when did you get that text?"

"Earlier today."

His breath hissed out between his clenched teeth. And he shook his head. "Damn, Brittney. Instead of listening to these threats, or at least reporting them, you headed up here. Why?"

"Because I know the only way to make sure this person stops following me and threatening me is to find out who they are and stop them," she said.

"I hope you don't think it's me," he said.

She had briefly considered it but not now, not when she'd seen how concerned he'd been about her in the hospital and now. He was a good man. Like her brother. And she wanted to keep him safe, too. "Like Owen said, you're one of the few with an ironclad alibi," she said. "You're probably the only person I really can trust."

"That doesn't make it safe to be around me," he muttered the words.

But she'd caught them. "What do you mean? These threats are about you? About the plane crash?" That was her suspicion, especially after the text had come after she'd tried talking to the hotshot trainer. But there had been things that had happened to the hotshots since that plane crash. Many things.

He shook his head. "No. I don't know. I'm talking about that night at the firehouse."

"What happened that night?" she asked.

"Trent didn't tell you?"

She shook her head.

"He was probably worried about you reporting about it, about the hotshots again," he said. "So I shouldn't say anything because maybe that's it, maybe that's the story someone wants you to drop."

"If you don't tell me, I'll find someone who will," she said.

He smiled faintly. "I don't think any of the other hotshots are going to tell you about it, either."

She smiled widely. "Tammy will."

"Damn it."

Obviously Ethan must have shared that Tammy and she were friends. "Does that surprise you?" she asked.

He shook his head. "You saved her life. She owes you."

"Is that why you kept Ethan—Canterbury's secret?" she asked. "Because he saved your life?"

"You ask so many questions," he murmured. "Occupational hazard?"

"I just have so many questions," she said. "I always have."

"So that's why you became a reporter?"

"You ask a lot of questions, too, Mr. VanDam," she pointed out.

He shrugged. "I usually don't," he said. "But I'm interest—no, I'm curious."

She was amused that he'd stopped himself from saying interested. So to tease him, she batted her eyelashes and stepped a little closer to him. "About me?"

"About why someone would threaten you and force you off the road," he said.

"I'm curious about that, too," she said. "It has to be related to the plane crash."

"You ran that story months ago," he said. "And you already covered it. So why would anyone be trying to back you off from what you've already done?"

"Because they know what I know, that there's more to that story," she said. "That there's more to the plane crash."

He shook his head. "It was Ethan's brother-in-law. He was behind everything."

"He swears he wasn't," she reminded him.

"Yeah, because people died in that plane crash," he said. "So of course he's not going to admit to that."

"He's already in prison," she said. "And will be for a long time. So what difference does it make? And how would he be following me and leaving me these threats?"

"He hired people to go after Ethan," Rory said. "Maybe he hired someone to go after you."

She shook her head. "That doesn't make sense, and you know it. You're the one who wants me to leave that plane crash story alone."

"I have an alibi. I was in a coma," he reminded her.

She didn't really believe it but she felt compelled to throw his words back at him. "Maybe *you* hired someone."

He snorted. "With what money and how? I'm not a Canterbury."

"Are you a VanDam?" she asked. "Or did you take somebody else's name like Ethan did?" That hadn't really occurred to her before, but if Ethan had pulled it off, maybe he could have, as well.

He expelled a ragged sigh. "You need to stop, Brittney."

"Why? Am I on to something?"

"You must be *on* something," he said, "if you think there's any more to the story you already covered about Ethan. You must be working on something else that put you in danger."

She snorted. "Gallery and restaurant openings? I doubt that anybody wants me to drop those."

"Maybe the competition to those businesses," he said. "Or maybe the competition for your job."

She nearly snorted again. She didn't even want her job, but she once had. She'd once been desperate enough to take any position that would get her screen time, that might get her noticed by a bigger program or network like her mentor, her idol, Avery Kincaid. Avery had worked at the station Brittney worked at; Brittney had been her intern. Then Avery had covered a story about the hotshots when an arsonist had targeted them and Northern Lakes. Avery had gotten her big break after that article and a relationship with a hotshot. All Brittney had gotten from her story about the hotshots was resentment and the attention of someone who had sent her those threats. Who? And why?

Maybe it was about that, about what had been happening to the hotshots. Obviously someone was after them or Rory wouldn't have been hit over the head.

He clearly wasn't going to talk to her about the plane crash. At least not yet. So she circled back around to another question he had yet to answer. "What happened that night you got hit over the head?"

He shook his head.

"Tammy will tell me," she reminded him.

"Since she and Ethan left town for a romantic getaway, I think you'll have to wait until she gets back," he said.

And she groaned. "That's right." Tammy had texted her a screenshot of a plane ticket that Ethan had bought her for Christmas. "They're going on a cruise."

So she wouldn't get to see Tammy this trip. And if she didn't find out who was after her, she might not be alive to make another trip north.

"Damn it, Rory, please," she murmured, and tears of frustration and probably exhaustion stung her eyes. But she blinked them back.

He stepped closer to her now, so less than a foot separated their bodies. "I got hit when I stepped out of the bunk room to find out why someone had started up all the fire engines."

"Was there an alarm? Why would someone start up all the fire trucks?"

He shrugged. "I don't know. A prank."

"Hitting you over the head wasn't a prank," she said. And she reached up to run her finger over that spot on the back of his head, over his spiky, soft hair and the stitches beneath it. "It must have been bad."

"I really don't remember much about it," he said. "I had no idea what happened. And Trent never said anything to you?"

She bit her lip and shook her head. "He doesn't trust me anymore. Not after I did that story."

"Were you and him that close before the story?" he asked. "He never mentioned you before you showed up in Northern Lakes. And then he didn't even admit you were his sister until after you helped saved Tammy's life."

Had he been ashamed of her even before that story? Or hadn't he wanted her to make a nuisance of herself like she had at the firehouse in Detroit? As she probably had the entire time they'd been growing up, when she'd trailed him everywhere, firing questions at him.

She closed her eyes against a sudden rush of tears.

"God, I'm sorry," Rory said. "That was so damn insensitive. I'm sure he had his reasons. He probably didn't want any of the guys hitting on you."

She shook her head. "I'm sure that's not it."

"None of his coworkers in Detroit have hit on you?" he asked.

Thinking of the catcalls and whistles whenever she'd stopped by the firehouse, a smile tugged at her lips and she opened her eyes. Most of them only made those noises to irritate Trent, but there were a couple of them who had made serious attempts to get her to go out with them. "But that's Detroit."

"What does that mean?" he asked. "You're only hot in Detroit?" he asked.

Feeling that pull, that attraction between them, Brittney gave in to the urge to flirt. "What do you think?" she asked. "Am I hot in Northern Lakes?"

"So damn hot that there won't be any snow left on the ground or ice on the lakes," he said. "Yeah, that must be why Trent didn't mention you. He didn't want any of the hotshots hitting on you."

"You wouldn't hit on me," she said. "You would be more likely just to hit me to get away from me."

"I would never hit you," he said. "And I know I should get far away from you, but for some reason I just can't." He stepped closer now and slid his arms around her waist. His chest touched hers, his thighs brushed against hers, and his body was so hard, so muscular.

She sucked in a breath as that attraction turned to desire. To *need*.

"Rory…" Her hand, almost of its own volition, reached for the back of his head again, to pull it down to hers.

But he resisted, his body going all tense.

"See," she said, releasing a shaky breath. "You wouldn't hit on—"

He pressed his hand over her mouth again, like he had in the hospital. Then he leaned close and whispered, "Listen."

And she heard the heavy footsteps in the hall, too. Then the door handle rattled behind her. Someone was out there, trying to get in.

So she'd been right. Someone had been watching her at the impound lot. And they must have followed them back here, to the hotel. To do what?

Finish what he'd tried to do when he'd shot at her van? Kill her? And was Rory going to get hurt along with her? She'd wanted to stick close to him for protection, but she hadn't realized that she was putting him in danger, too. She didn't want him getting hurt any more than she wanted her brother getting hurt. She couldn't lose anyone else she cared about.

*Damn it, Brittney.*

Why wasn't she answering her cell?

Was it payback for all the times that Trent had ignored her calls? Her texts? Her?

He wished now that he could go back. That he could take every call, answer every text.

The only spot he'd still draw the line was with her questions. He didn't want to answer those because he had a feeling that asking them was what had put her in danger.

Because she hadn't gone off that damn road on her own. The roads weren't even as bad as they'd been that day weeks ago when his truck had been forced off the road.

Brittney wouldn't have crashed like that, not without some help. And she wouldn't have disappeared out of the hospital without some, too.

Rory.

Owen had left her there with him.

"What are you worried about?" Owen had asked when he'd called to yell at him after discovering that they were both gone. "Rory couldn't have had anything to do with her accident. He was in the hospital."

"She didn't have an accident, and neither did he," Trent had told the paramedic. "And because they're both in danger, they're in even more danger when they're together."

And Owen had cursed in acknowledgement that Trent was right. He'd offered to look for them, too.

They hadn't been at the firehouse. Or at the impound lot where her van sat all crumpled up like a wad of paper that had missed the wastebasket.

She could have died. And knowing that, that she was still in danger, Trent had headed next for the hotel. Thanks to her mom and stepdad, Brittney had money. So she'd probably check into the Lakeside Inn.

But the front desk refused to tell him if she had. And so he'd sneaked upstairs to check out the rooms.

As he started down the hall on the third floor, he heard something. Not her voice, like he'd been listening for at every door.

But a soft creak. Before he could turn around, something struck him, knocking him to the ground. He could only hope it wouldn't knock him out like Rory had been knocked out for weeks.

# Chapter 7

Rory had hoped that the bullet might have dropped out of some other pile of wreckage in that impound yard. But he'd seen right away that the windshield had spider-webbed out from a hole in the middle of it. She could have been killed. From that bullet. Or from the crash.

It definitely hadn't been an accident. Then there was the note and the text. The threats.

Was it really about the plane crash? Was that why someone had struck him over the head that night?

Had someone else already figured out the truth that Brittney was so determined to uncover?

So determined that it could cost her her life? He wanted to make sure that didn't happen, especially if it was because of him. So he'd driven her back to the hotel and followed her inside, and then he'd been the one in danger.

With the way she'd looked at him...

The way she'd touched him...

He'd wanted to kiss her so damn badly that there had been a buzzing noise inside his head. So he was surprised that he'd heard the heavy footsteps.

But then there had been no mistaking the turning of that doorknob.

Someone was out in the hall. And, since the old hotel had

doors with no peepholes, he'd headed out the window onto the fire escape. He'd only gone down one floor, in through another window and out into the hall. Then, worried about leaving her alone up there, he'd run up the steps, slowing his pace only to quiet his approach.

He'd drawn in a breath before pushing open the stairwell door to the hall. A big man, his back to Rory, stood near another door, listening.

He was definitely looking for someone, and Rory had a pretty good idea who.

Knowing that the man had been armed out there on the road, when he'd fired those shots at Brittney, Rory didn't take any chances. He snuck up and tackled the man, knocking him to the floor. Then, desperate to knock him out before he could draw his weapon, Rory swung his fist toward the man's face.

His knuckles connected with flesh and bone before his eyes focused and he saw whose face he was striking. Trent's.

His hotshot team member shoved him back, knocking him against the wall. Fortunately his shoulders struck first, but the back of his head followed, hitting the thick wainscoting of the hallway, too. Rory grunted as pain radiated throughout his skull. And he flinched and closed his eyes for a moment.

"What the hell!" Trent yelled.

"What the hell, exactly," Brittney said.

Rory opened his eyes and reminded her, "You were supposed to stay in the room."

Before going out the window, he'd told her to do that, and he'd been so damn tempted to kiss her then. But he'd been more worried about her life than how her lips would taste. And as distracted as he'd been, he hadn't realized she hadn't agreed to stay put.

She stood over them now, a lamp grasped in her hands. "And let you get shot or worse?"

"Shot?" Trent asked the question, his eyes wide with shock. They were the same light brown as his sister's, but now his gaze moved from Rory back to Brittney. "Are you all right?"

"I'm fine," she said.

Rory shoved himself up until he was standing, but when he did, the ground seemed to tilt like it had when she'd fallen off the fence onto him. And he staggered. He might have fallen again if Brittney hadn't rushed forward to slide her arm around him.

She pointed the lamp, which she held with just one hand now, at her brother. "What did you do to him?"

"To him?" Trent repeated, and he stroked his jaw. "He hit me."

"What were you doing sneaking around the hotel, trying to get into rooms?" Brittney asked.

She must have assumed what Rory had, that Trent had been the one trying the doors. Rory hoped he'd been, and since he'd kind of caught him in the act, chances were good that it had been him.

But what if it hadn't been...?

He slid his arm around her and peered down the hall in both directions. No doors had opened. Probably because it was still the offseason in Northern Lakes. Too cold for regular fishing and water sports and too warm for ice fishing and snowmobiling. Or was someone behind one of those doors, watching them?

"You should get back into the room," he advised her. She'd left that door open behind her.

"Why?" She looked around then. "Do you think someone else is out here?"

"It was just me," Trent assured them. "The front desk wouldn't give me your room number. And you wouldn't pick up your damn phone or text me back—"

"Frustrating, isn't it?" she interjected with a glare at her brother.

Trent ignored her and continued, "So I kept calling you and listening at the doors…"

"To see if you could hear her phone," Rory finished for him, and his apprehension eased. Since it had just been Trent, she should be safe in the hotel.

Unless whoever was watching her had followed them back to it.

He was torn. Trent was here now. So he had no reason to stay. Except…

What if she was in danger because of her story on that damn plane crash? Because if that was the case, it was all his fault. So he had a duty to protect her, and maybe she was right, that the best form of protection was to find out who was behind the threats and stop them.

So even though he knew he should take off and get far, far away from her, he let her guide him back into her room, as if he needed her support.

As if he needed her.

And he'd learned long ago that it was too dangerous to need anyone. It was better to rely only on himself, except for those two months in the mountains with Ethan. After the things that had happened to him, the blow to his head and her crash, he felt kind of like he was parachuting out of a plane again and that he needed Brittney to survive.

Brittney was furious with her brother. For so many reasons.

So when he came back into the room with the bucket of ice she'd sent him to get, she glared at him again as she took it from him. Then she wrapped some of the ice into a towel and pressed it against the wound on Rory's head where blood had begun to seep through the stitches. She'd guided him to a chair once she'd gotten him into the room. He'd seemed a little unsteady after hitting the wall, and she wondered if he should return to the hospital.

Concerned and irritated, she asked, "What the hell were you thinking?"

The two men looked at each other, as if uncertain which of them was supposed to answer her. She'd tried asking Rory already, but he'd gone out the window so fast she hadn't been able to say anything or stop him.

But she'd been so damn worried.

When he'd rushed onto the fire escape to find out who was in the hall, he could have confronted a stranger with a gun. But Trent wasn't a stranger. Or he hadn't been until lately, since she'd come up to Northern Lakes. No, even before that he'd been keeping things from her. That was why she'd come up to Northern Lakes, to find out what was going on with him...because she'd known it had something to do with his hotshot team.

While she'd known about them, they hadn't known about her. Why?

"I was talking to you," she told her brother.

"And I already told you, I was worried about you, especially when you didn't answer my calls or texts," he explained.

She snorted. "So now you want to play my protective big brother after weeks of ignoring me? And even before that, you denied my existence."

"What are you talking about?"

"Here in Northern Lakes, with your hotshots, nobody knew I was your sister or that you even had a sister."

Trent turned toward Rory, glaring at him. Obviously he knew who had ratted him out to her.

She stepped in front of Rory, not wanting Trent to hurt his friend for just telling her the truth. "Don't blame him. He's not the one who denied knowing me. What was it? Three times before a cock crowed?"

"It wasn't like that—"

"Not exactly," she conceded. "But it sounds like it was close."

"I didn't deny it, but..."

"You didn't claim me, either," she said. "Why? Are you ashamed of me?"

He flinched.

And she felt a pang strike her heart. "Oh, you are."

"Brittney, it's not you, it's your job—"

"My job is who I am, just like yours is who you are," she said.

Trent snorted. "You can't compare fighting fires to reporting on the stories that you have."

Heat rushed to her face with embarrassment, especially with Rory listening to this whole exchange. But then a surge of self-righteous indignation chased away the shame. "I haven't always covered the most compelling stories," she admitted. Not until she'd found the missing Canterbury heir. "But I am good at what I do, and I'm going to prove it to you and everyone else."

Obviously she was on to something significant, or someone wouldn't have threatened her like they had. But the story wasn't as important as discovering who was behind the threats and stopping them. Then she would prove to Trent that she was good at what she did and she could take care of herself and even protect him and his hotshots, as well. As long as she made sure Rory didn't get hurt in the process.

"You're going to get yourself killed," Trent said.

She snorted now. "You could have died that night that Rory got hurt. You were in the bunk room, too. You could have been the one who got hit over the head and put in a coma. And *you* never said anything to me about it."

"I was fine," Trent said. "Nothing happened to me."

But it had to Rory, and knowing now that he'd been hurt affected her for some reason, some reason she wasn't willing to even acknowledge. Yet. "It could have happened to you, if not getting hit then the fumes from the trucks could have hurt you. I still should have known about it."

"I didn't want you reporting on it," he said. "If there's any more scandal around the hotshot team, Braden will probably lose his job."

She sucked in a breath and nodded. Apparently he cared more about his relationship with his hotshot superintendent than with his sister. "So that's how it is."

"After you did that story on Ethan, how can you expect me to trust you?" he asked.

Tears stung her eyes, but she closed her eyes to hold them in. "I need you to leave right now."

"Britt—"

"Go," she said. "Or I'll call hotel security—"

"The only hotel security here is Rory," Trent said with a chuckle.

She opened her eyes to glare at her brother. "Even with a concussion, he knocked you on your ass." But she didn't want him fighting her brother again, not for her or for any reason. "I'll be safer with him than with you right now." Because Rory understood the danger just like she did, and Trent had already been through too much recently. She didn't want him involved in this, and she didn't want to drive a wedge between him and other members of his hotshot team.

"I would never hurt you, Brittney," Trent said. "You know that."

She shook her head. "You already have, Trent. Just leave, or I'll call Trooper Wells to throw you out."

"Something's going on with you," Trent said. "And I want to know what it is."

She shook her head again. "Nope. You can't ignore me for weeks and weeks like you have and then suddenly try to play my big brother again like—"

"I am your big brother."

"Right now you're trespassing in my hotel room," she said. "And I will call the police—"

Trent sighed heavily. "Damn it, Brittney."

"Just go."

She wasn't sure that he would. But he knew her well enough to know how stubborn she was. Even more stubborn than he was, so he sighed again and turned and walked out the door. She waited until it closed behind her to let out the breath she'd been holding. While she was relieved that her brother had left, that meant that she was alone again with Rory.

And the last time they'd been alone, she had nearly kissed him. Maybe Trent skulking around the hallway had saved her from making a big mistake. But now that she'd made her brother leave, she was worried that she might make that mistake yet. Or one that was even worse…

Feeling as edgy as if he was battling a blaze with no equipment, Ethan paced the airport terminal, walking up and down the wide aisle between the gates. He had been looking forward to this trip until Rory got hurt.

But now everything had changed.

Except his feelings for Tammy. He didn't want to disappoint her. She'd been looking forward to this cruise. But she stepped into his path, and he nearly collided with her.

"You're not this upset about a delayed flight," she said. "What's going on?"

He shrugged. "I don't know." But it felt like something was wrong, and it wasn't just that the saboteur had struck again. It was who they'd struck...

Rory.

Ethan had been through so much with that man, but there was so much he still didn't know about him.

"You've been quiet and tense ever since you dropped Rory's truck at the hospital for him."

He hadn't said much during their two-and-a-half-hour trip from Northern Lakes to Detroit, where they were supposed to catch this flight. If the plane ever arrived.

His stomach pitched as he thought of another plane that had never arrived at its destination. The plane he and Rory had been on, the plane that Rory...

"Ethan?" she repeated his name with a question in her voice and concern in her beautiful hazel eyes. "Are you okay?"

Trying to reassure her, he forced a grin. "I'm always quiet, remember?"

She shook her head. "No. You might have been quiet before, but you haven't been since..."

Since they'd become lovers.

And since Trent's sister had revealed Ethan's secret, he no longer had anything to hide. Except for what he knew about Rory.

"Since you," he said. "You make me want to share everything with you." But he couldn't share this, and not just for Rory's sake, but for hers. The way Rory had told him that it was better that he not know...

"So tell me the truth," she said. "Do you really want to go on this trip?"

"I do," he said. "So badly, especially after seeing those bikinis you packed..."

"But?" she prodded. She knew him so well, so well that she answered her own question. "You're worried about Rory."

"I'm worried about the whole team," he admitted. But specifically Rory.

If it was the saboteur who'd whacked Rory over the head so hard he'd put him in a coma, then that person was getting more and more dangerous. Which meant that everyone was in greater danger than they'd been before.

"And you feel like you're deserting them when they need you most," she finished for him, articulating that sick feeling he'd had in his gut since driving away from Northern Lakes.

That sick feeling that something was going to happen to the people he loved like family.

# *Chapter 8*

Rory shouldn't have stuck around at the hospital. He should have hopped in his truck and driven off without checking on Brittney Townsend, without ever talking to the ambitious reporter. He understood her ambition a little better now, after being a witness to the tense conversation between the siblings.

And while Trent hadn't slammed the door on his way out of the room, it felt like he had because the room was eerily silent after he left. So eerily silent that Rory felt awkward clearing his throat.

He felt awkward about more than that, though. Like that almost kiss…that kiss that he wanted to happen now. But that was crazy. They both had too damn much going on, were in too much danger, to entertain an attraction of any kind. But he was attracted to her. Too attracted.

He adjusted the makeshift ice pack against the back of his head. The concussion had definitely messed him up. That had to be why he was still here, why he hadn't gotten as far away from the reporter as he could get, why he'd started to believe that she was right, that it was best for them to stick together like he and Ethan had stuck together.

The person who'd put the threat on her vehicle could have been the same person who'd struck him over the head that night. Or maybe they'd hired someone. Like Ethan's brother-in-law and so many others in Rory's life had proved, a lot of people would do anything for money.

The towel was wet, the ice melting inside it. With a sigh, he pulled it away from his now damp hair and head.

"Are you okay?" she asked him, and she reached out with a slightly shaking hand and took the towel from him.

"Are you?" he asked with concern.

She nodded. "Yes, but I hate fighting with Trent."

"I'm sorry that you did," he said. "I shouldn't have told you what I did earlier—"

"It was the truth," she said. "And I deserved to know."

"Not when it upset you," he said. "And I am sorry about that." He didn't want her hurting emotionally or physically, and because of that, he had to make himself leave. So he stood up with the intent of heading toward the door. But the room spun for a moment, his head so light that spots danced in front of his eyes.

She grabbed him like she had in the hall, sliding her arm around him, using her body to steady his.

Except the heat and softness of her body unsettled him more. He wanted her for more than support. He wanted her.

He dragged in a breath. "I'm fine."

"You should go back to the hospital," she said. "Hitting the wall like you did might have done more damage than reopening your stitches."

"I'm fine," he repeated. "I just need to get some rest." After three weeks of being in that hospital bed, two of those weeks in a coma, he shouldn't need any more sleep for a while. But being active for the first time in three weeks had taken more energy than he'd thought.

Too much energy to fight this attraction to Brittney. So

he had to leave. Fast. Before he did something incredibly stupid…like kiss her.

"I need to leave," he said more to himself than to her. He had to remind his body that it had to move away from her, not closer. He stepped away from her, and her arm dropped back to her side. His legs heavy with reluctance, he headed toward the door. When his hand closed around the knob, he started to turn it, intent on making his escape.

Though he wasn't sure if he wanted to escape from her or from the temptation of her.

"Wait," she said. "Don't leave."

She hadn't touched him, like she had at the hospital when she'd grabbed his arm more than once. But she didn't have to touch him to stop him.

Just her words did that.

Or maybe it was his own desire to stay that stopped him from leaving her. He could give himself an excuse. That he had to stay to protect her, and he fully intended to protect her…after he got some rest. And he had no doubt that Trent was lurking around outside somewhere. Probably back in the hall, intent on making sure nothing happened to his sister. She didn't need Rory.

She might actually be safer if he left, unless she was right, like that instinct inside him that had had him searching for the other parachuter five years ago. That sticking together was their best chance of survival…

But he wasn't going to be any use to her or himself if he didn't get some rest. So he drew in a breath and forced himself to finish turning that knob. But he couldn't quite bring himself to open that door and walk away.

Brittney curled her fingers into her palms, so that she wouldn't reach for him, so that she wouldn't pull Rory back from that door. While someone had threatened her and apparently tried to shoot her, Rory could have been killed in the firehouse. He was in just as much if not more danger than she was.

"Don't leave," she repeated with concern for him and with something more, that desire for him that made her want to kiss him so damn badly.

His long lean body tensed even more than it had when she'd slid her arm around him to steady him. "It would be a very bad idea for me to stay."

He wasn't wrong about that. If he stayed, Brittney was pretty sure she would give in to that desire to kiss him and maybe in to her desire for more. And he was the last guy she should get closer to, because of that feeling she had, about how much danger he was in.

She wasn't going to fall for someone and lose him like her mom had lost her dad. Sure, she'd found love again with Brittney's stepdad. But Brittney remembered the pain her mom had tried to hide from her. Late at night when nightmares had woken her up, she'd heard crying.

Her mother crying.

And she had been so afraid to hear a strong woman like her mom sobbing with such pain and such heartbreak. Brittney wasn't as strong as her mom was. She couldn't love and risk the loss.

Not that she was at risk of falling for Rory VanDam. She didn't really know anything about him, except that he kept, albeit reluctantly, coming to her rescue. At the hospital he'd made sure she was all right, and he'd taken her to the impound lot. And he'd just taken on her brother in the hallway. But he hadn't known it was her brother.

It could have been the man with the gun. Hell, the man with the gun could be out there now. She sucked in a breath at the frightening thought of that. But surely whoever had fired at her wouldn't take a shot at Rory. Unless Rory was as involved in all of this, because of the plane crash, as she'd previously suspected he was. Maybe his getting hit over the head and the threats she'd received were related because someone didn't want him to tell her what had really happened.

"Where are you going to go?" she asked him. "Back to the firehouse?"

He moved as if a sudden chill had passed through him, his body shuddering slightly.

"You know you're not safe there," she said.

"Because of your brother?" he asked, and he turned back toward her then, touching the back of his head.

She shook her head. "As big an ass as my brother can be, he wouldn't have intentionally hurt you. I believe him, that he didn't know it was you when you jumped him in the hall. And he just instinctively shoved you off."

"I wasn't talking about then," Rory remarked.

And she bristled defensively. "There's no way it was him who struck you at the firehouse. Trent's hotshot team members mean everything to him. He would rather hurt me than hurt any of you."

"He would never purposely hurt you," Rory said. "He loves you."

She sighed. "I know. But just because you love someone, it doesn't mean you like them. And I don't think my brother likes me or respects me very much."

"Is that why you're so determined to report on something big, to earn his respect?"

Her face heated with embarrassment as she remembered what he'd overheard, her conversation with Trent. Replaying it in her head, it all sounded so pitiful now. "I want to report on something big because the truth should always come out."

"Why?"

"Because people deserve to know what's really going on." Instead of hearing her mother cry at night, when she thought Brittney was sleeping, she should have just told her what was going on. How much she'd missed Brittney's dad...

"Not if it puts them in danger," Rory said.

And now she knew, without a doubt, that her suspicions had been right. There was more to the story about the plane crash and about Rory VanDam than he wanted anyone to know.

"It's not the truth that hurts people," she said. "It's the people who are trying to keep the truth from coming out, who are trying to keep secrets, that are the threat. But once the truth is out, there's nothing for those people to try to protect anymore. Getting the truth out is the only way to eliminate the danger."

He expelled a ragged sigh and turned back to her, his pale blue eyes intense. "People don't kill just to protect their secrets," he said. "They kill for revenge. For passion..." As he said that, his gaze lowered to her mouth.

Her pulse quickened. The passion was there, burning so hotly between them. She stepped closer, irresistibly drawn to him and wanting to connect in a way she'd never connected with anyone else. And not just sexually.

This attraction between them seemed deeper than desire. But the desire was there. Too strong for her to not act on it, to not rise up on tiptoe and skim her lips along his jaw. "Tell me your secrets," she urged him in a whisper.

And he grinned, his eyes sparkling now with amusement as he stared at her. "You are..." His breath shuddered out, and then he lowered his head so that his mouth brushed across hers.

It was just the briefest of kisses, just his lips sliding across hers. Once. Twice. But she was suddenly aware of every nerve ending in her body, feeling as if she'd been jolted by something like an electrical current.

But he pulled away and stepped back and said, "You are right about one thing. It's not the truth that hurts people. It's people who hurt people." Then he opened the door and stepped out, pulling it closed behind him.

Leaving her alone with that thought and with her body tingling everywhere from just that brief kiss. Was he leaving because he was afraid that he was going to hurt her? Or that she was going to hurt him?

Or did he know who was behind everything?

The threats, the gunshots, someone hitting him so violently over the head?

But if he knew, why wouldn't he report that person? Even if he didn't trust Trooper Wells, surely there had to be someone he could trust.

Another police officer. Or at least his superintendent at the firehouse.

It would never be her. Since her own brother didn't trust her, she doubted that Rory VanDam ever would. He would never willingly tell her his secrets.

Trent didn't trust this strange alliance between his fellow hotshot and his sister. What the hell were they even doing together? Owen had said he'd had to leave for a call, so he'd asked Rory to keep an eye on her.

But the already injured hotshot had done more than that. He'd brought her here and stayed with her.

Trent didn't care how pissed his sister was at him, he wasn't leaving her alone. But she wasn't alone.

From the shadows of an alley across the street, Trent studied the hotel. Not many of the windows were lit up besides that one. The one that had to be hers, or had Rory booked the room?

After what had happened at the firehouse, he probably wouldn't go back there. And there was no way he could be medically cleared to resume his duties as the ranger on that small island.

But if it was Rory's room, why had he invited Brittney to stay with him? The last time she'd come to town nobody had worked as hard to avoid her as Rory had. Not even Ethan, whose whole life Brittney had blown up. After that, Trent would have expected Rory to avoid her even harder. And yet…

Rory was with her. And he'd done his damn well best to protect her. Trent raised his hand to his jaw, which was beginning to swell from where the guy had struck him. Hard.

Then instead of being mad at Rory, Brittney had gotten mad at him. Like a brother trying to find his younger sister was a crime or something.

The only crimes that had been happening lately had been the work of other people. Billy.

That poor kid who'd gone after Trent and Heather. But Billy was behind bars. He hadn't tried to hurt Brittney to get back at him.

But someone had.

She hadn't driven her vehicle off the road on her own or she and Rory wouldn't have been so damn edgy about hearing him in the hallway.

Something was going on, and Trent wasn't going to learn

about it when everyone else did, when Brittney did her damn story about it.

He was going to learn about it now because Brittney might not get the chance to do that story if someone wanted to harm her.

He lowered his gaze from that window then to the street around the Lakeside Inn. It was the offseason right now, so there weren't many vehicles parked near the building. It had been pretty empty, almost eerily so, like the hotel from *The Shining*.

He shuddered at the thought of that horror film. And the horror he would feel if anything happened to his sister or to Rory.

And that was when he noticed the shadow behind the wheel of one of those vehicles, a long black SUV. He was surprised he could see that much through the heavily tinted windows, but he was pretty damn sure someone was there.

And that he was watching the hotel for the same reason that Trent was.

Because of Brittney...

## Chapter 9

Rory was amazed that he'd been able to walk away from Brittney after that kiss. For one, his legs were shaky, and he couldn't blame it on his concussion. His head hadn't hit the wall all that hard, but it must have knocked some sense into him because he had walked away from her. Even though he'd wanted to stay so damn badly.

He'd wanted to be with her in every way. To protect her and to get even closer to her. For the past five years he'd done his best to keep his distance from people, even from his team, and he hadn't realized until today in the hospital with her just how damn lonely he was. How much he craved to be close to someone...

But Brittney Townsend?

Could he trust her?

He needed time to think about what she'd said as well as the thoughts that had gone through his own head. And he couldn't think when he was close to her. Well, he couldn't think about anything but wanting to be closer to her, to be inside her. Maybe a little distance would clear his head.

But once he stepped out of the lobby doors onto the dimly lit sidewalk, Rory had that strange feeling that Brittney had talked about earlier at the impound lot. That sensation that he was being watched.

But was *he* being watched? Or was *she* the one someone was waiting for out in the shadows? Those threats she'd received might not have had anything to do with him or even with the plane crash. But it might involve the hotshots...

Like whoever the hell had struck him over the head...

He glanced uneasily back at the lobby, making sure that she hadn't followed him out. She hadn't wanted him to leave, but she had to know it wasn't a good idea for him to stay with her. He wasn't exactly great protection for her, especially if that damn plane crash was the reason that someone was threatening her.

No. They'd done more than threaten when they'd fired those shots at her vehicle, when they'd caused her to go off the road and her van to roll over and over. She'd been trapped inside that wreckage until Owen and his crew had used the Jaws of Life to extricate her from the van. Whoever had fired that bullet at her vehicle could have finished her off then, before help had arrived.

So maybe they'd only intended to frighten her away. If that was the case, they didn't know Brittney. All that had been accomplished, with the threats and that gunshot, was her resolve to find out the truth being strengthened. She was even more determined to get the story than she'd been before. She seemed to really believe that it would stop whoever was threatening her from hurting her. But he knew, all too well, how the truth coming out could cause more damage.

Was this really all about the plane crash?

And if it was, then it was his fault.

So he'd been smart to leave her. He would be smart to leave Northern Lakes, too. Maybe even Michigan.

"Rory..."

He barely heard the whisper. Where had it come from?

He glanced back at the lobby again to see if Brittney had followed him out. She hadn't, which was good because Rory had a feeling that the person calling his name was trying to lure him into danger.

"Rory..." the whisper echoed back, as if it was coming from between buildings. It was definitely too deep to be Brittney's.

But it sounded vaguely familiar. And Rory realized who it probably was.

"Trent?" he called back. Of course Brittney's protective older brother would have stuck close to her. Despite her unwillingness to share anything with him, he obviously knew she was in danger.

"Shh..." Trent whispered back from somewhere behind Rory.

He turned and saw the gap between buildings, the alley where Trent was waiting for him. He gestured out of the shadows, waving Rory over toward him.

Why? To pay him back for jumping him in the hallway? To warn him to stay away from his sister?

Trent had probably never figured he'd have to warn Rory away from her. Neither had Rory. But Brittney had made sense about them sticking together in order to protect each other while working together to find out who was after them. Was it the same person? If it was, catching that person would definitely keep them safe and make sure they and the rest of the team stayed that way. Or, while they tried to catch him or her, that person got rid of both of them instead. It was a risk either way, and maybe not just to their lives.

Rory expelled a slight sigh of frustration and resignation, then he walked toward the alley. "Hey," he began. "I'm sorry. I really didn't know that was—"

Big hands reached out of the shadows and yanked him

between the buildings. He clenched his fists. Despite just apologizing to his team member, he was ready to fight him again. If he had to.

"Shh…" Trent said again.

"What the hell is going on?" Rory asked.

"I think there's someone sitting in that SUV over there."

Rory glanced around them. There weren't many vehicles parked on the street, but there were a couple of SUVs. "Which one?"

"The black one with the tinted windows."

The description brought one of his jumbled memories into sharper focus. The last time he'd ridden in one of them…

He shook his head, at the memory and at Trent. "How can you see anyone inside?"

"The windshield looks darker on the driver's side, like there's someone behind the wheel," Trent said, and he pointed a finger toward the vehicle.

So there was probably only a driver inside, not a passenger, unless the passenger was already out and maybe inside the hotel.

He let out a soft curse. "We should go back inside, make sure Brittney is okay." She was right—they were safer together.

Trent sucked in a breath. "What the hell is going on with my sister, Rory?"

"I don't understand what you mean." And he didn't know for certain. Was Trent talking about his sister's crash or about what he'd interrupted when he'd messed with the door earlier?

But Trent couldn't know what he'd interrupted. Rory wasn't even certain Brittney had intended to kiss him then.

But he had damn sure wanted her to, and when she had just now...

Rory had had to force himself to stop at just that brush of his mouth across hers, even though he'd wanted to deepen the kiss. Hell, he'd wanted to do a lot more than kiss her.

But she was off-limits and not just because she was Trent's sister. She was off-limits to him because Rory couldn't let anyone else get hurt because of him.

"You know what I mean," Trent insisted. "Or at least you know more than I do or you wouldn't have jumped me in the hall. You were expecting trouble."

"These days every hotshot should be expecting trouble," Rory pointed out.

"Damn saboteur," Trent murmured. "You don't think that's who's going after Brittney..."

Rory tensed. He hadn't considered it. He wasn't even sure that was who had gone after him. But he actually hoped it had been. He preferred to think they were both in danger because of the saboteur and not because of...

He turned back to focus on that long black SUV, and that sensation raced over him again like a cold wind. Someone was inside. Someone was watching them.

Or watching for Brittney? She'd said she'd felt that way before, like someone was watching her back home in Detroit and at the impound lot. The person must have followed them back here.

How the hell had Rory missed that long black vehicle following them? How had he missed it at the impound lot if it had been parked somewhere in the area? Because the person was a professional...either assassin or...

"You should go back into the hotel," Rory told Trent. "Make sure Brittney is okay."

Just in case that driver hadn't always been alone, just in

case someone else had already gone inside the hotel to try to find her like Trent had.

"Damn it, Rory, what's going on?" Trent demanded to know.

"I don't know." He couldn't be sure. But maybe if he got closer to that vehicle, if he could see who was inside it, he would know if Brittney was in danger because of him, because of the man he used to be. The man he had never wanted to be again.

Guilt hung heavily on Brittney, pulling her shoulders down as she hurried downstairs to the lobby. She shouldn't have let Rory leave. He was still suffering from his concussion, which her brother had probably only made worse when he'd knocked him into that wall.

Rory had bled quite a bit on the towel. She hadn't noticed it until after he'd left. She'd thought the reason the thick terry cloth was wet was from the ice melting. But it was more than water…

It was blood. Rory's blood had stained the fluffy white towel a deep crimson.

He needed to go back to the hospital for a CT scan and maybe more stitches if he was still bleeding. If the towel hadn't staunched the worst of it…

She shouldn't have let him go, not in that condition when he was so hurt and vulnerable. And yet he'd taken down her brother who was a big guy. Trent had always intimidated the hell out of the boyfriends she'd had in the past. Not that she'd had many.

She'd always been more focused on her family and her career. She'd never realized that she might have to sacrifice one for the other. When she'd done the story about the hotshots, she hadn't realized what it might cost her.

Her brother.

And maybe her own life…

And Rory's.

He'd handled Trent with ease. Even hurt, Rory was strong and fast. Not fast enough to avoid a bullet, though. But maybe fast enough that he was probably gone by now.

But when she started across the lobby, she could see his truck parked on the other side of the street, the US Forest Service logo on the door.

He hadn't left yet. Where was he?

Had he fallen? Was he lying facedown on the sidewalk?

She hurried through the lobby, past the night clerk who didn't even glance up from his phone. If something had happened to Rory, the young clerk would not have even noticed.

Brittney pushed open the glass door and stepped onto the sidewalk, which was illuminated from the light from the hotel. Nobody lay there. There wasn't even any blood.

Had he fallen on the other side of the street?

She couldn't see beyond the two lanes to the sidewalk on the other side. The businesses over there had closed for the night and the streetlamp was farther down the block, casting no light onto the sidewalk over there.

Her heart pounding fast with fear for him, she started across the street. And then suddenly light came on. Two headlights, the beams so bright that they blinded her.

And an engine revved.

It wasn't Rory's truck. That was still dark. But another vehicle, one just as big or bigger because the headlights were so high. It pulled away from the curb, tires squealing, and steered straight at her.

"Brittney!" someone yelled her name.

But she couldn't move for a moment, frozen in the beam of those lights. Frozen with shock and fear.

\* \* \*

That reporter wasn't going to stop. That was clear enough now that the warnings weren't working. She wasn't backing off. She'd kept making calls, asking questions, and the more interest she showed the more someone else, like the authorities, might get interested.

She wasn't going away. And if she wasn't going to go away on her own, the driver had to make her go away.

Forever.

The SUV had been parked just far enough down the street to be away from the lights of the hotel and the streetlamps but close enough to watch the entrance. Two men had come out before the woman.

And both of them had slipped away into the shadows.

But as the SUV bore down on the woman, the men were suddenly there in the street with her. She was the only one who had needed to die. But the driver had no compulsion against taking out a couple of more.

# Chapter 10

Rory's heart seemed to stop for a moment as he stared at Brittney standing in the beam of those harshly bright lights, frozen, as the SUV bore down on her. While Trent yelled her name, Rory started running toward her, as fast as he could. He jumped in front of those lights and caught her around the waist. Then he propelled her out of the way, rolling across the asphalt with his arms locked around her just as the SUV passed them.

The SUV was so damn close that Rory's clothes rustled and Brittney's hair blew across his face. With as big as the vehicle was, it probably would have killed her. And maybe him and Trent, too.

Maybe Rory was dead. But if he was dead, his heart probably wouldn't have been beating as hard. And he wouldn't be able to feel the asphalt of the road beneath his back and the softness of Brittney's body lying stretched out on top of his.

"Are you all right?" he asked between pants for breath. His lungs burned with the need for air.

The breath that she must have been holding whooshed out in a ragged sigh, warming the skin of his neck where her face was tucked between his chin and his collarbone. Then she lifted her head, her hair brushing across his cheek, and stared down at him. "Are you all right?"

He closed his eyes for a moment, silently evaluating whether anything hurt more than it should. His head ached, like it had since he'd woken up from his coma, and now his shoulder and hip ached, too, but not so much that anything was broken.

A groan emanated from the darkness, and Rory opened his eyes with surprise. That hadn't been his groan.

"Trent!" Brittney called out with concern as she scrambled up from Rory and the ground. "Oh, my God!"

Rory rolled to his side and looked across the asphalt to where Trent lay a short distance from him. "Damn!" He shoved himself up, nearly dropping back down as his head got too light and his vision blurred. He drew in a breath, steadied himself and rushed over to where Brittney knelt beside her brother's prone body. "Trent, are you all right?"

"We need to call an ambulance," Brittney said. "But I left my cell upstairs."

"Mine's dead," Rory said, and he started toward the lobby. "I'll have the clerk call—"

"No!" Trent shouted. "I'm okay. Just knocked the damn wind out of me."

"It knocked you down," Brittney said. "You might have broken bones." She glanced over her shoulder at Rory. "You, too."

"I don't have anything broken," Rory assured her. He wasn't as certain of Trent's condition. He stepped closer and peered down at his hotshot teammate. "Maybe you shouldn't move—"

"I'm fine," Trent insisted, and he shoved himself up from the ground. "I'm just getting damn sick of nearly getting run down."

"Then you shouldn't have run into the street!" Brittney exclaimed. "Either of you!"

Trent shuddered. "You were just standing there, and it started straight for you…" He shuddered again. "I thought you were going to die. You wouldn't move."

She moved now, throwing her arms around her brother. She hugged him tightly for a moment. And Trent held her just as tightly, and over her head, he mouthed words to Rory.

He narrowed his eyes, trying to tell…

"Thank you," Trent said aloud. "Thank you for saving my sister."

Rory shook his head. "I didn't…"

"You did," Trent insisted. "I couldn't get there as fast as you did. I couldn't save her."

While Brittney had escaped injury this time, Rory suspected there would be another time. And what would happen if he wasn't around to save her? Would she survive?

Or was she only in danger because of him? Would she be safer if he left town, like he'd intended when he'd awakened in that hospital bed?

But even if he left, Brittney wouldn't be safe because he knew there was no way she was going to stop pursuing her story. Whatever story the person threatening her wanted her to drop…about the plane crash or about the saboteur or something totally unrelated…

Some story that she'd done in Detroit. And if that was the case, then Rory hadn't put her in danger, but maybe he could help protect her from it. And if it was the saboteur, Rory had no idea how to handle it. This person had pulled dirty trick after dirty trick on the team and yet nobody had figured out who it was.

Could Brittney? Or would trying to find out get her killed?

Brittney was shaking so badly that Trent and Rory escorted her back into the lobby of the hotel. She wasn't shaking because she was cold, even though the temperature had dropped a lot when the sun had.

But even standing near where gas logs glowed in the lobby fireplace, Brittney couldn't stop shaking, at least on the inside. On the outside, she was trying to act tough. She was trying to be as strong and brave as her big brother had always been ever since they were kids. They'd both lost their dad, but Trent had lost his mom, too, a few years later. And he would have wound up in foster care if not for Brittney's mother and stepfather taking him into their home. They were wonderful, generous people, but they'd probably done it more to appease Brittney's fears than anything else.

Trent had been in the vehicle when his mother was killed, and Brittney had been terrified that she would lose him like they'd lost their dad and him his mom. That terror rushed over her now, threatening to overwhelm her. This was why she'd come up to Northern Lakes the first time, to find out what was going on with the hotshot team, to make sure her brother was safe. But now she was the one who'd put him in danger.

"We need to call the police," Trent said. "To report someone nearly running you down."

"Call who?" Rory asked the question. "Trooper Wells?"

Trent cursed. "I'll call Heather."

"Your detective girlfriend has no jurisdiction in Northern Lakes," Rory said.

"But she brought back that kid who followed you up here, who ran you off the road," Brittney pointed out.

Trent sighed. "She brought him back for the crimes he committed in Detroit. And she had to get special authorization to do that."

Brittney really didn't want Heather involved, anyway.

Because Heather was good enough to get the truth out of her about the notes and the gunshot. But as good as she was, she and Trent had nearly died too many times just recently. Brittney couldn't count on their luck holding out. She couldn't risk losing her brother.

Then she turned around and realized she'd lost someone else. Only she and Trent stood in front of the fire. "Where did Rory go?" she asked with alarm.

Trent turned around then, too. "He's leaving…"

Vehicle lights flashed on again as, across the street from the hotel, Rory started his truck and pulled away from the curb. She couldn't let him leave, not when he was probably hurt. She started toward the lobby doors, but Trent stepped in front of her and caught her shoulders.

"You're not going anywhere," Trent said. "Until you tell me what's going on."

"I have to check on Rory," she said. "You hurt him upstairs, and just now…" She shuddered, thinking what could have happened to him. What could have happened to them both…

Maybe she should let him leave, though. She'd thought he was the reason she was in danger because of whatever he'd kept from her about the plane crash, but now she realized it might be the reverse. But who had struck him over the head?

"Rory's tough," Trent said. "He's survived a plane crash and a coma. I think he's indestructible."

Brittney wasn't so sure about that. Eventually his luck was going to run out. If it hadn't already…

"What if that person who nearly hit us goes after him and he's alone?" she asked.

"I think that person was after you," Trent said. "That vehicle didn't move until you stepped out of the lobby."

She shivered.

"Damn it, Brittney, you need to tell me what's going on," Trent insisted.

"Just like you told me what was going on with you a few weeks ago when your house burned down with the body of a murdered woman inside it?"

"I had received that Christmas card with the threat inside," Trent said. "Warning me that I was going to find out how it felt to lose someone close to me. At that time, the person closest to me was you."

Now it was Heather. Brittney felt a little jab of jealousy over that. Not that Heather had replaced her but that her brother was as strong as her mom, strong enough to love somebody that they could lose.

She also felt a little jab of envy that he'd received a card for his threat, and all she'd gotten was that sheet of paper stuck under her windshield wiper. The thought struck her as funny, but she couldn't share it with him despite being tempted. Gallows humor was how she and Trent had dealt with their losses. And she knew it was how his hotshot team dealt with loss and fear.

The humor fled, her fear for Rory's well-being chasing it away. "Where do you think Rory is going?" she asked. Hopefully back to the hospital, but she doubted that.

"Probably the firehouse."

"The firehouse, of course."

"You're not going there until you and I talk," Trent said, his hands tightening on her shoulders.

"Just like how you didn't want me involved in your drama, I don't want you involved in mine," Brittney said.

"You're trying to protect me?"

She gestured toward the street. "You could have gotten run down just now."

Lights flashed in the street as a police SUV rolled up outside.

"Did you call them?" she asked Trent. He was the only one who had his cell on him. Hers was on a charger upstairs, and Rory had claimed his was dead. Unless...

He'd lied, and he'd called after he'd left the scene.

"I called them," the clerk spoke up from behind the desk. "I saw what happened."

Brittney turned toward him, shocked that he wasn't still engrossed in whatever he'd been watching on his phone. "You called? That wasn't necessary."

Or appreciated.

"That dude deliberately tried to run you down," the kid remarked.

"You saw who it was? You saw the driver?" Brittney asked, her pulse quickening.

He shook his head. "No. The windows were too dark. But it definitely didn't look like an accident."

Brittney was pretty damn sure it wasn't, just like her crash earlier hadn't been an accident, either. Somebody wasn't just trying to scare her off now. They were trying to kill her.

Trent had always known his younger sister was stubborn. But he hadn't realized how stubborn until now. The state trooper who'd shown up at the hotel to take the report hadn't gotten much more out of her than shrugging and head shaking.

If Trooper Wells had shown up, she probably wouldn't have gotten anything else from her. Since he wasn't able to...

As much as Brittney liked asking questions, she disliked answering them even more. And he had so many damn questions for her.

But she'd insisted she was tired and needed her rest.

"You're not getting rid of me," Trent had informed her as he'd booked the adjoining room to hers. And he'd made her open the door between them because he knew her too well.

She was probably going to sneak out the minute she thought he was sleeping. So he wasn't going to sleep.

Not now.

Probably not until he knew she was safe. So he sat up against his headboard, peering through the crack in the door between their rooms. He had a good view of her door to the hall. She wasn't getting past him. Just as she very nearly hadn't gotten past the person who'd tried running her down.

Who the hell could be after Brittney?

His stomach churned with the thought that had occurred to him, the thought he hated to even entertain. It could be a member of his team…if that was who the saboteur actually was. But it almost had to be because he couldn't see how anyone else would have been able to get close enough to sabotage their equipment without being noticed.

He'd always felt like his team was his family. But his real family might be in danger because of one of them. At least he knew it wasn't Ethan or Rory.

But who else could he trust?

He called the one person he trusted the most in the world right now.

"Hey, babe," Heather answered, her voice husky either with sleep or the desire that shot through him at just the thought of her. "How's your sister?"

He sighed.

"Your text said she was okay enough to leave the hospital," she reminded him. "Didn't you find her?"

He wasn't sure if he had. The Brittney who'd turned on him in the hall, yelling at him for shoving Rory into the wall, who'd berated him for not claiming her as family on her first trip to Northern Lakes, that Brittney didn't seem at all like the adoring little sister he knew.

That he'd probably taken for granted for too damn long. He could have lost her. Not just once but twice in one day.

"Trent, sweetheart?" Heather called out to him. "Is everything okay?"

He drew in a deep breath before replying. "For the moment…"

But he had a feeling that moment wouldn't last.

"But?" Heather prodded. "What happened?"

"I cheated on you," he said.

She laughed, and he smiled, loving how much she trusted him, how secure she was in his love and devotion to her. Just as he trusted her and felt so damn safe with her. "How's that?"

"I nearly got run over with someone else," he said.

She sucked in a breath. "Damn. Are you all right?"

"Yes."

"And the other person?"

"People," he said. "Brittney and Rory."

"They're okay?"

"Brittney is," he said. "Rory took off so fast that I'm not sure…"

"I didn't even know he was out of the hospital yet."

He'd told her about Rory's concussion, how he hadn't left Northern Lakes until he knew his fellow hotshot was out of the coma and on the mend.

"He just got released, and Owen had him watching Brittney until I got up here."

"The guy just woke up from a coma," Heather said. "How much protection could he be?"

"He saved her life tonight," Trent said. And he stroked

his fingers along his jaw. "He took me down when he caught me lurking around her hotel room, too."

"You were lurking?" she asked. And he could hear the smile in her voice.

"Damn clerk wouldn't tell me which room she was in or call it for me," Trent said.

"But you found her," she said.

"Yeah."

"So why is Rory protecting her?"

"Owen figured Rory was the only one he could trust since he was in the hospital when her van went off the road."

"So he's assuming the worst about that crash, too?" she asked.

"Because I told him that there is no way Brittney would have gone off the road unless it was the same way we did…"

"Because someone forced us off."

"And tonight, with her nearly getting run down in the street outside the hotel…" Emotion choked off his voice for a moment, making him hoarse as he remembered the horrifying moment that Brittney had frozen in the beam of those bright lights.

"And you don't think that was an accident, either?"

"It's what she told the trooper who came for the report," Trent said.

"But you think she was lying."

"She's definitely hiding something," he said. "She won't answer any of my questions. She won't tell me what's going on."

Instead of commiserating with him, Heather chuckled again. "Payback's a bitch, huh?"

He sighed. "That probably is why she's not sharing anything with me. She's still mad that I didn't share anything with her. But I was just trying to protect her."

"And maybe she's doing the same for you," Heather pointed out.

He tensed with the realization. His baby sister was trying to protect him. "But what is she protecting me from?" he asked.

"I'll see what I can find out from her television station here," Heather offered. "I'll talk to her producers and co-workers, see if they have any idea what's going on and who might be after her...unless you want me to come up there?"

"I don't even know if she's staying here," he said. "So no. Focus on Detroit, on finding out what you can there. And I'll see what I can get out of her."

"You be careful," she said.

He smiled. "Of my sister?"

"She is fierce," Heather reminded him. "She's strong and smart."

He knew that in his head. But in his heart, she was that sweet little girl who'd followed him around, firing endless questions at him, confident that he had all the answers. She'd worshiped him then. Now she had to know that he had no more answers than she did.

Actually she had more than him because she knew what was going on, no matter how vehemently she kept denying that she did. Or if she didn't know for certain, she at least had a better idea than he did.

Because he could think of only one reason. His hotshot team. Why else would she have come up to Northern Lakes? Whatever she was investigating was here...

The plane crash? Or the sabotage?

He had to get her to back off for her sake now. For her safety.

"And, Trent," Heather said, her voice even huskier than

usual as it emanated from his speaker. "No more cheating on me. You know defying death is our thing."

"Yes," he said, and he smiled. "Tell Sammy not to steal my spot next to you in bed."

"Nobody can steal your spot," Heather assured him. "And I'll talk to the people at the station right away and let you know what I find out."

"Thank you. I love you."

"Love you, too."

Love was their thing now, but their relationship had started as a ruse to flush out a killer. Or at least they'd thought whoever had sent Trent that card was a killer.

But there had been more dangers in his life than he'd even realized then. So pushing Brittney away had been the right thing, to keep her safe.

He'd known what to do then. He had no idea how to protect her now. Because he had a bad feeling that the biggest danger she faced was herself and her dogged determination to find out the truth no matter the cost.

Even if it was her life…

# Chapter 11

When Rory had first been cleared to leave the hospital, he had had no intention of staying in Northern Lakes. He'd just intended to stop at the firehouse and grab whatever he'd left in his locker before leaving for good. Or at least for the island where he was the ranger on duty.

Would he be safe there?

Was he really even the one in danger?

Would it have mattered who'd stepped into the hall that night the engines had started? Would whoever had walked out of the bunk room been hit as hard as he'd been?

No. He couldn't be sure that he specifically was in danger or if his entire team was, with maybe the exception of one person...

If the saboteur was one of them...

He hated to think that, though.

Just as he hated to think of Brittney in danger. And she definitely was. All night that image of her standing in those high beams had flashed through his mind like those lights had flashed on—suddenly, sharply, sinisterly. If he hadn't been there, would Trent have gotten to her in time?

Or would they both have gotten hurt or worse?

He'd known Trent had stayed with her after that, and he would have made damn sure that nothing else happened to her. So he'd probably been more protection for her than Rory would have been after that last near miss.

He'd been so exhausted last night that when he'd sat down on a bunk to talk to Stanley, who'd been snuggled up with Annie in another bunk, he must have fallen asleep.

But those dreams...

That nightmare had kept waking him up. And he must have woken up Annie, too, because at some point the massive sheepdog/mastiff mutt had crawled into bed with him. He didn't know if she had needed comfort, or if she'd been comforting him.

Or protecting him?

If only Annie could talk...

She could probably tell them who the saboteur was. She must have seen whoever had struck Rory that night.

He stared at her now from where he was pretty much jammed between the wall and mattress since she was hogging the narrow bunk. "So who was it, girl?" he asked. "Who hit me?"

She whimpered and moved her head closer to his. Then she rolled out her big tongue and swiped it across the side of his face.

He chuckled. "Your kisses do not make it all better," he told her.

But he had an idea whose kisses might make him feel better. Brittney's.

Was she okay? She'd seemed so last night, and after what had happened, how close a call she'd had not once but twice, Trent would not have left her unprotected. He might have been irritated with her for reporting about the team and Ethan, but he loved her.

She obviously loved and idolized her big brother, too.

But she was also proud and determined to take care of herself while getting the truth she was looking for.

Was that his truth?

He knew what had happened to that plane. And why.

And it had nothing to do with Ethan and the Canterbury curse, or even the greedy brother-in-law.

No. That plane had gone down because of him. And guilt had weighed so heavily on him ever since it had happened. But that wasn't the only thing he felt guilty about...

Amelia. Not that she deserved his sympathy after what she'd done. But he'd hurt her.

Annie whimpered again and bumped her massive head against his. The dog was incredibly empathetic, which was probably why Stanley had bonded with her so much. The kid had aged out of foster care with nowhere else to go when Cody Mallehan had convinced their boss to hire the teenager to help out at the firehouse. Stanley had had a rough life, but he seemed happy now.

Rory looked around Annie to the other bunk, but it was empty, the bed already neatly made. "I thought you were the kid's shadow," he told Annie.

She whimpered again and swiped her tongue across his cheek.

"Hey, no more kisses," he said with a chuckle.

"Clearly you're not much of a kisser," a female voice remarked.

"Annie? You can talk?" he asked, joking because there was no mistaking to whom the voice belonged.

Brittney.

Annie jumped up from the bunk and barked, as surprised by the reporter's sudden appearance as he'd been.

"Down, girl," Brittney said. "I'm not trying to steal your man. I can see that what you two have is true love."

Rory chuckled, but Annie's barking probably drowned it out. He had to raise his voice to tell Brittney, "I don't know about that. She didn't save me from whoever hit me over the head."

"Shh," Brittney told the dog. "The two people in this room with you both have concussions."

Rory realized that maybe for the first time since he'd awakened from the coma that his head didn't hurt that much. It was just a dull ache now, like the aftereffects of a migraine or a hangover.

He might have preferred the hangover, though he barely ever drank. He had to make sure that he didn't lose control or get confused and talk too much.

Reveal too much.

Brittney had tilted her head to study the door. Her topaz eyes were narrowed with speculation. "Did she bark like this before you got hit in the head?" she asked.

"Not loud enough to wake everybody up," Rory said. "That's why I went out into the hall. To pull the alarm and to shut off the damn trucks."

Brittney nodded.

"What?" Rory asked uneasily.

"Annie knew whoever hit you over the head," Brittney surmised.

No. Speculated. That could be all that it was. She had no proof that one of his hotshot team members had tried to hurt him. Or kill him?

He didn't want to think that someone he knew could want him dead. Again.

But he shouldn't have been surprised. He was just so damn sick of having no one he could trust. No one who really cared about him.

But to want him dead, that was more than disinterest or distaste. That was hate. Or greed.

Because anyone could succumb to greed, he knew that all too well.

Had someone been hired again to try to kill him? Someone he knew. Someone he should have been able to trust...

He slid his hand around the back of his head, to where the skin had been pulled together with stitches and staples, leaving a thick ridge of flesh beneath his hair.

"How are you?" she asked. "That's why I left my hotel room last night. After I saw how much blood was on that towel that I wrapped the ice in..." She stopped and swallowed, as if she'd been choking on something.

Emotion?

For him?

She swallowed again and continued. "I wanted to make sure that you were okay."

"That's why you were out there? In the street?" he asked. And he rolled off the bunk then to stand in front of her. Annie stayed between them, though, as if trying to protect him from Brittney.

But Brittney was a stranger to the dog.

She must have been right, that Annie knew whoever had hit him.

"I'm the reason you came outside last night?" he asked again.

She nodded. "I wanted to make you go back to the hospital to get checked out."

His stomach pitched at the thought of her getting hurt because of him. He reached out to touch her cheek, sliding his fingertips along her jaw. She was so beautiful. And he wanted so damn badly to kiss her again, to really kiss her this time.

But he couldn't afford that kind of distraction now and neither could she.

"We both nearly went back to the hospital…" he murmured, thinking of how they'd rolled across the asphalt. "And Trent?" He glanced around her then. "Where is he? Is he really all right?"

Her lips curved into a slight smirk. "He's going to be pissed when he wakes up and finds me gone," she said. "He booked the adjoining room and tried staying awake all night. He lasted until about an hour ago."

Rory fought the smile curving his lips and shook his head. "It's not safe for you to go out on your own, not after what happened yesterday."

"What happened yesterday?" Braden asked.

Rory jumped and dropped his hand from Brittney's face. She whirled around to the doorway where his boss was leaning against the jamb.

Braden's dark eyes studied them both, and his forehead was slightly furrowed beneath a lock of dark brown hair. Clearly he wondered what was going on between Rory and Brittney.

Rory wondered himself.

Was she just flirting with him to get him talking? To get the story she was so determined to get that two threats and two attempts on her life hadn't scared her off?

In fact, those threats had just made her more determined to find out what was going on because she thought the truth would protect her, that it would lead to the arrest of the person threatening her. But the truth didn't always lead to justice.

Rory could have corrected that misapprehension. The truth hadn't saved him, it had nearly killed him. But knowing his truth would put her in danger, too. If it hadn't already…

"What happened yesterday?" Braden asked the question. "Owen said you were in an accident. And then something happened at the hotel."

"You heard about that?" Rory asked.

"The police were there," Braden said. "I heard the call over the scanner."

"The police were there?" Rory asked Brittney now.

She nodded. "The desk clerk called them. I didn't think the kid was even paying attention to the lobby, let alone out—"

"What happened?" Braden repeated. "From how you're evading my question, I take it that these things weren't really accidents?"

Brittney shook her head. "Not any more than the things that have been happening to your hotshot team have been accidents."

Braden's face flushed slightly. "Is that why you're here? To report some more nonsense?"

She sighed a heavy sigh as if she was disappointed in the hotshot superintendent.

Rory was a little disappointed, as well. Braden had kept a lot of things from them for a while. The note he'd received that had warned him that someone on the team wasn't who they said they were.

Had that note been referring to Ethan really being Jonathan Michael Canterbury IV? Or had it been referring to Rory? Not many people should have realized that he wasn't who he said he was…

Just him and maybe Ethan. But even Ethan didn't really know for certain.

And there was someone else…

Trick appeared in the doorway behind their boss and his brother-in-law. Trick wasn't just the brother of Braden's wife, but he was also the son of the man who'd trained most of them. Mack McRooney knew the truth. But Mack was the kind of guy who knew what secrets needed to be kept. And why.

So Rory doubted that Mack's son or daughter knew anything about him beyond that their father had trained him five years ago along with Ethan Sommerly and Jonathan Canterbury. The real Ethan hadn't survived that crash. He wasn't the only one who'd died in it, though.

Rory felt that jab of regret for the lives lost. Too many...

He couldn't let Brittney become another casualty.

One minute Brittney was standing with Rory in the bunk room, wondering if he was about to kiss her again. Then his boss showed up with another giant of a man following closely behind him. Within minutes of their sudden appearance, she'd been escorted to the superintendent's office.

And the red-haired man leaned against the door, as if blocking her inside with him and the superintendent. His body was so big that she could barely see the door around him. There was no way she was getting out with him there.

"I thought you guys were going to escort me off the premises," Brittney said.

"We probably should have," the red-haired man said with a pointed look at his boss.

Braden Zimmer smiled. "How did you get onto the premises, Ms. Townsend?"

"Call me Brittney," she said. "We're all friends here."

The red-haired man snorted. He had to be Trick McRooney. Braden's brother-in-law. Mack's son. She actually needed to be his friend, so that he could convince his father to talk to her. She suspected that Mack had to know something more about the plane that had just left his training facility in Washington state before it crashed.

Braden smiled. "Okay, Brittney, how'd you get in?"

"The door was unlocked."

Braden groaned.

"The kid with the curly blond hair had just walked out."

"So you let yourself in," Trick said.

She nodded.

"Why?" Braden asked. "Who or what were you looking for?"

Heat rushed to her face. Rory. She'd been looking for Rory, but not for the reasons Braden might have thought when he'd come into the bunk room and found them standing so close together with Rory's hand touching her face.

She'd wanted to kiss him so damn badly then. She still did. But that wasn't why she'd sought him out.

"I was concerned about Rory," she said.

"Why?" Trick asked. "You don't know him. He's barely spoken to you."

She smiled. "That was last time I was here. This time… he's different." He wasn't avoiding her as hard as he had last time. In fact, he'd saved her life last night in the street.

But only she and Trent knew that. The clerk hadn't realized that Trent wasn't the one who'd pushed her out of the way of that speeding SUV, so he hadn't mentioned a third person to the trooper who'd taken their statements. And neither had she nor Trent.

Rory had already been through too much that day. That month…

And five years ago…

He had survived a plane crash. One that Trick's dad had to know more about.

"I've been trying to get ahold of your father," she told Trick.

He just arched a red eyebrow. "You want to train to become a smoke jumper or hotshot?"

"Maybe I should," she said. "I might get more respect…" At least from her brother.

"But that wasn't your real reason for contacting Mack," Braden stated. He knew.

"No. I want to ask him more questions about that plane crash that happened, the one Ethan and Rory survived."

"Why?" Braden asked. "You know everything about it already."

"I'm not so sure about that," she said. She also wasn't so sure that she knew everything there was to know about Rory VanDam. Could Mack tell her more?

Would he?

Or should she just try harder to get the man himself to speak to her?

"So that's why you're really here?" Trick asked the question. "To get me to talk my dad into talking to you?" He was smirking at her.

And she knew the likelihood of him ever doing that for her was pretty damn low. "That and to talk to Rory," she admitted.

"And he's talking to you?" Braden asked. "About the crash?" He exchanged a quick glance with Trick.

Did they think there was more about the crash to discover? Or was it Rory they were worried about? She was worried about him, too.

"What the hell is happening in your firehouse?" Brittney wanted to know. "How does one of your own almost get killed here instead of fighting a wildfire?"

Braden sucked in a breath and shared another glance with Trick. "I wish to hell I knew."

"You have no idea who's been behind all these things happening to your team?" she asked.

Braden shook his head. "They wouldn't be happening if I did."

A little chill passed through her. Was he saying that because he would have turned the suspect over to the police or because he would have dealt with him or her himself?

"What about that story?" Braden asked her. "Are you working on it?"

"About the sabotage?" she asked. "I've tried, but I haven't gotten any of the hotshots to really talk to me about it." Not even her own brother.

But if these guys thought she was working on it, the saboteur might, as well. Was that who had actually left her the notes? Who'd taken a shot at her van?

And last night...

Was it a hotshot behind everything? Was it another hotshot who had struck Rory so hard that he might have died? Brittney needed to find out for her sake and safety, as well as for the sake and safety of the entire hotshot team, including her brother and Rory.

Or someone could die...

Braden's uneasiness intensified during his impromptu meeting with the reporter.

After letting her out of the office, Trick closed the door behind her and leaned back against it again. "She's still working on the sabotage story."

"I know." And that might have been what had put her in danger if Trent was right and she hadn't just had an accident when her van went off the road.

And what about last night?

Someone trying to run her down?

"Maybe you should follow her," Braden suggested.

"You don't think Trent is following her?" Trick asked. "He rushed up here to make sure she's okay. I doubt he's letting her out of his sight."

"That means he's probably in danger, too, then."

"We're all in danger until the saboteur is caught," Trick pointed out.

Braden's stomach churned with that dread. "I know." He released a heavy sigh. "Maybe it's a good thing she's working on this story. Maybe she'll figure out what we haven't been able to…"

"Who the saboteur is," Trick said. But then he wrinkled his forehead and scrunched up his nose. "That's not the only story she's working on, though."

"The plane crash." Braden shrugged. "That was all about Ethan."

"Ethan wasn't the only one in that crash," Trick said. "Rory was, too." He straightened away from the door. "Maybe I should give Mack a call."

Mack's kids rarely referred to him as Dad. He'd been much more than their father, he'd been their mother, too, after theirs had taken off. He'd also been their mentor and their best friend.

Braden nodded. "I'm going to call Trent," he said. "Make sure he's around and keeping an eye on his sister. I don't want anyone else getting hurt."

But he knew all too well that the chance of nobody getting hurt was extremely low. He could only hope they didn't get hurt badly. Or worse…

# *Chapter 12*

Rory hadn't stopped Braden and Trick from whisking Brittney away from him. He knew that neither of them would hurt her. She was safe with them.

And yet he'd followed them. He'd waited outside the office, listening to as much of the conversation as he'd been able to hear through the door and probably Trick's body. Trick was close to the door, so Rory had heard everything he'd said.

Brittney had tried contacting Trick's dad about the plane crash. God, she was smart. So smart that she was probably going to figure out the truth. And that would undoubtedly get them both killed.

Unless…

He had some insurance. Insurance he'd been holding on to in case this day ever came. He just wasn't sure how to use it because he'd never known who he could trust with it.

Or if he should trust anyone at all.

Could he believe Brittney that she was really looking to stop whoever was threatening her? Or was she just looking for a story? Trying to further her career as if that would earn her brother's respect…

Where the hell was Trent?

He should have woken up by now and discovered that she was gone.

Before the conversation finished in the office, Rory slipped away. He hurried upstairs to the locker room, intent on cleaning out his and leaving town.

But every time he had that intention, something came up. Like Brittney. She was in danger, like he and Ethan had been alone in the mountains. But together they'd protected each other, they'd kept each other alive. Could he and Brittney do that for each other?

She stood in the doorway, watching him. "Where are you going?" she asked.

"I need to get back to work," he said.

"There's no wildfire," she replied. "No reason for the hotshot team to go out."

"That's just part of my job," he said. "I'm a forest ranger."

"You're recovering from a head injury," she said. "You shouldn't be out in the woods on your own."

"An island," he said. "But it is heavily wooded."

"Does anyone else live there?" she asked.

"There are a few cabins on it. But mostly it's national forest land."

"You shouldn't be alone," she said.

"There are plenty of animals on the island," he said. And there they were all of the four-legged variety, not the two like where he'd grown up.

"An animal can't call for help if you need it," she said.

"I probably won't need it since there are no other humans on the island this time of year," he said, and he touched the back of his head and that ridge.

"You should get your stitches looked at," she said. "Make sure the wound didn't open back up last night. You bled quite a bit on that towel."

"Sorry," he said. "Hopefully the hotel won't charge you for it."

"Hopefully they won't evict me," she said, "after the clerk called in that incident with the SUV."

"The trooper didn't come to talk to me," he said.

"Trent and I didn't give him your name."

"Him? It wasn't Trooper Wells?"

She shook her head. "She probably would have realized you'd been there, too."

So it was probably only a matter of time before the trooper came to question him again. "I really need to get out of here," he said.

"Why? You want to avoid the police?"

"I want to avoid being asked things I can't answer," he said.

"Can't or won't?"

His lips twitched with amusement over her persistence. "I can't say who was driving that SUV. The windows were too darkly tinted. And I didn't see a license plate. So can't."

"I wasn't talking about that."

"I didn't see who hit me the night of the holiday party, either," he said.

"If only Annie could talk…"

He smiled then. "We've all wished that."

"She could tell you who the saboteur is." She tilted her head then and murmured, "But I wonder if she would…"

"What do you mean?"

"Maybe she would protect him."

"What are you talking about?"

"Stanley," she said.

Rory shook his head. "Nope. No way. And don't you dare interrogate that kid. He was once suspected of being the Northern Lakes arsonist and it nearly killed him." He'd been hit over the head, too.

"Then tell me who you suspect," she prodded him.

"I don't." And that was the problem. He had no idea who the saboteur was. Which was another reason he needed to get away from the firehouse. He could hardly believe that he'd managed to sleep there the night before. But it had been just him and Stanley and Annie in the bunk room.

And he'd been so damn tired.

Still was. But that was her fault. He'd kept thinking of her last night, and not just that horrific moment when she'd frozen in the path of that SUV. But the moment before that, when they'd kissed. It had been such a light kiss and so brief, and yet so damn powerful, too.

"Where's Trent?" he asked.

She shrugged. "Probably still sleeping."

"He should be awake by now." Rory needed him awake and alert enough to watch over his sister so that Rory could get the hell away from her. She'd already messed with his head more than the concussion had.

Or maybe the concussion was the reason she was getting to him so much, making him want her so badly.

"Trent's not going to tell me who he suspects, either," she said.

"That's not why I asked where he was," Rory said. "And I really don't suspect anyone, least of all Stanley." He was a good kid. Everybody on their twenty-member team seemed like good people. But he knew better than to trust that anyone was really who they seemed to be.

Even Brittney. Maybe most especially Brittney.

The way Rory had looked at her just before he closed his locker door had unnerved Brittney. It was like he wasn't sure what he was looking at. Or whom…

Once he closed the door, he grabbed up his duffel bag and stepped around her, heading toward the exit.

"Where are you going?" she asked, and she stepped in front of him, blocking him from leaving like Trick had blocked her. Rory couldn't be serious about going back to some deserted island, not when he was still recovering from a head wound.

"I'll make sure you get safely back to Trent," he said. "And then I'm leaving."

Something about the way he said it, with such finality, made Brittney wonder if she would ever see him again if he left. Not that she should expect to...

She had only been to Northern Lakes once before, and after what had happened to her since her arrival this time, she would be crazy to want to return.

Crazy to want to see Rory again, too. No. She wanted to do more than see him. She really, really wanted to kiss him and to really kiss him this time, not just brush their lips across each other's. But she wasn't about to do that here, in the firehouse, where anyone could walk in on them like Braden had earlier in the bunk room.

And the way he was looking at her now, with such tension and almost suspicion, Rory didn't look at all attracted to her now. If he'd ever been...

Maybe she'd only imagined that it was mutual. But even if it was, she had no time for this attraction she felt for him. She needed to focus on her story...whichever one the person threatening her didn't want her to do.

Was it about the plane crash?

Or the saboteur?

"I should go back to Braden's office," she said. "And see if he'll give me a list of every member of the team." She knew her brother wouldn't give her one. But Braden...

He hadn't seemed as upset about her reporting about the

saboteur as he'd once been. He might even welcome her help in figuring out who it was.

Or he would if he wanted to keep anyone else on his team from getting hurt like Rory had been hurt. But some of the other hotshots who'd been hurt hadn't been because of the saboteur. The dead man's wife had killed him. And a state trooper had tried killing another...

Then there was Trent, who had someone come after him for revenge.

"What about you?" she asked Rory, voicing her thought aloud.

"I won't give you a list," he said.

"What about your past?" she asked. "Anything or anyone in it that might be coming back to haunt you like it came back to haunt my brother?"

His long, lean body tensed even more than it had already been, and all the color drained from his face, leaving him deathly pale, like he had seen a ghost.

"What is it?" she asked. "Your head? What's going on?" And did she need to call a doctor for him?

Or Owen?

Where the hell was the paramedic?

Rory released a shaky breath. "I'm fine. I'm just...talked out, Brittney. If you want that list of team members, ask Braden."

"So you're not going to make sure I get safely back to Trent?" she asked. She was just teasing him. Really.

But she also wondered...did he care about her? Or would he just try to protect anyone he thought was in danger?

Probably. That was undoubtedly the reason he'd become a hotshot, to protect people from fires.

She wanted to ask him about that and about so many other things. But she could feel the opportunity slipping away from her. She wasn't even sure what island he was talking about let alone how to get to it.

Was there a ferry to it?

Since it was largely uninhabitable, probably not.

"We have to leave now for me to take you back to Trent," he said. "Because I can't stick around any longer."

"Why not?" she asked.

His forehead furrowed as if he was confused. "How can you ask me that after everything that's happened?"

"How can you just run away after everything that's happened?" she asked. "That's not going to stop things from happening, you know? The saboteur keeps doing things, and he or she isn't even making them look like accidents anymore."

"It'll stop things from happening to *me*," he said.

Shocked, she sucked in a breath. "And you only care about yourself?"

He hadn't come across that way to her. He'd seemed like he was genuinely concerned about her safety and about his team. Or else why the hell had he run out in front of that SUV last night? He could have let Trent get to her first.

But Trent hadn't.

Rory was the one who'd saved her. Who'd risked his life to do so. So he certainly didn't care only about himself.

Maybe he didn't care about himself at all. Or he would have gone back to the hospital last night. Maybe that was why he was deathly pale. Maybe he needed to go back there now.

"Before you rush off to the middle of nowhere, you should get a medical checkup," she suggested. "You were bleeding again last night."

He shook his head. "I'm okay. And I'll be even better once I'm out of here."

"Away from me and my questions?" she asked, her pride stinging. And maybe something even more vulnerable than her pride.

Her heart.

"Brittney, you need to look out for yourself," he said.

"Don't worry. I'm not your responsibility," she assured him. "You don't have to walk me back to the hotel. I can take care of myself."

"That's not what I meant," he said, his voice gruff with frustration. "I'm just… I can't stay…"

She stepped aside, out of his path, and repeated, "Don't worry about me. Just go. Run away."

Because no matter what he'd done last night, that was what he was doing now. Running away instead of facing the situation and trying to solve the mystery of the saboteur and whoever the hell was after her.

Were they one in the same?

She intended to find out, but she was disappointed that he had no interest in discovering the truth. She'd been such a fool to be attracted to him at all. And now she was damn glad she hadn't kissed him as deeply and passionately as she'd wanted to. Hell, she'd wanted to do more than that, but she was glad she hadn't, especially when he walked right past her and out the locker room door.

Brittney Townsend hadn't been easy to scare away from the story she was after. And now she wasn't easy to kill. She should have died in the wreckage of that van of hers when it had rolled over and over, trapping her inside it.

Miraculously she'd survived that.

But last night…

It hadn't been a miracle that she'd gotten out of the path of the SUV just in time.

That had been interference of another kind. It certainly hadn't been divine intervention. It had been a man. Brittney's white knight wouldn't be able to save her again, though.

Because the next time he was going to die with her, like he should have the night before. The killer wasn't going to make the mistake of trying to use a vehicle again, especially one that had probably been described to the police.

So that vehicle was hidden for now...

Leaving the driver with nothing to drive at the moment. But that hadn't stopped them from following the reporter when she'd left her hotel earlier that morning.

She was at the firehouse now. Probably asking more of her damn questions.

The killer raised their weapon, peering through the scope into some of the windows. Who was in the three-story concrete building with her?

Her white knight?

The gun barrel focused on the door she'd entered. It would probably be the one she exited.

And when she did, she was going to die.

And if she wasn't alone, whoever was with her would die, too. But the killer would have to wait until they were far enough out of the building so that neither could take cover and avoid being hit, like they'd avoided it last night. This time they had to die.

# *Chapter 13*

Damn her!

Damn her so damn much…

Fury coursed through Rory, making his pulse pound as his blood pumped hotly through his veins as he ran down the firehouse stairs to the main level. But he wasn't mad at her. Not really.

He was mad that she'd spoken the truth.

He was running away again, just like he had more than five years ago. And then after running away, he'd hid out here in Northern Lakes and on Bear Isle.

But if he hadn't hidden like he had, he would probably already be dead. And hiding out hadn't just kept him from getting hurt, it had kept the people around him from getting hurt.

Or so he'd thought…

Maybe the saboteur was after the team because of him. Because of that damn note someone had sent Braden…

*Someone on your team isn't who you think they are…*

Sure, that could have been referring to Ethan, but who, besides Rory and Ethan, had known who he really was?

Nobody had recognized Jonathan Canterbury after those months they'd spent in the mountains before they'd been rescued. He had truly looked like Ethan Sommerly, the hotshot who'd trained with them in Washington state.

That man was gone now. And so was another man…

Rory felt that pang in his heart, that guilt and regret. It was all his fault. And instead of bringing their killers to justice, he'd hid to save his own life. And maybe he'd put other people in danger.

Brittney.

Was it his fault that someone was after her? Was she right, that the only way to stop the bad guy was to find out the truth once and for all?

That wouldn't necessarily protect him from the vendetta against him. From the hit sworn out on him…

But maybe the truth would protect her, like he had to protect her. He stopped at the door to the outside, his palm against the metal. And he closed his eyes and sighed.

A nose rubbed against his other hand, the one wrapped around the straps of the duffel bag. Annie whimpered.

"What's up, girl?" he asked.

She must have been waiting by the door for Stanley to return. The kid had probably gone back to Cody's, and he couldn't bring the dog with him there since the child Cody and Serena was fostering was allergic to her.

"I'm sure he'll be back soon," he assured the dog.

"What about you?" Brittney asked as she stepped off the last step of the stairwell. "Are you running away for good or just until I'm gone?"

"I need to get back to the island," he insisted.

"Why?"

He wanted to go back for that insurance. He hadn't been able to figure out exactly how it would help him, though, or he would have used it long ago. And because he didn't know for certain if it was of any use, he replied, "Because I work there."

"Doing what?"

"Monitoring wildlife, the woods, stopping poachers and trespassers. And enjoying the quiet…"

"You really want to go back there for that?" she asked.

He touched the back of his head. "Seems like a good treatment for a concussion. Silence."

But he really needed to retrieve that other thing, the thing that might be able to protect Brittney at least, if not him. But that was only if the person threatening her to back off wanted her to leave the plane crash story alone. If it was actually the saboteur after her, Rory had no idea what to do about him or her. Or he would have done that long ago.

Like he probably should have used his insurance long ago. But he'd never been able to figure out how to use it because he hadn't known whom he could trust with it… because the insurance itself had proved to him that he could trust no one.

"Why haven't you left already?" she asked, and she pointed at the door he had yet to open.

"Why are you leaving?" he asked. "Aren't you going to ask Braden for that list?"

"We both know he's not going to give it to me," she said.

Rory wasn't so certain. Braden was desperate to find the saboteur, which was why he'd hired his brother-in-law as one of the team, thinking Trick could be more objective than he could. But then Trick had fallen for Henrietta…

And for Northern Lakes. He wasn't going back to his life as a floater for other teams. He was here to stay. Or so Rory hoped, for Trick's and Henrietta's sakes.

"It's not like you to give up that easily," Rory remarked.

She narrowed those topaz eyes and stared at him. "You don't really know me."

"I know you're determined." Too determined. It was probably going to get her killed.

She smiled. "I can't deny that."

"Then why are you leaving?"

She held up her cell. "Tammy texted me. She and Ethan decided not to go on that cruise."

"Did she say why?" Rory asked. Ethan had been looking forward to that trip. Hopefully he hadn't canceled it because of him.

"I'm going to find out now," Brittney said. "I hope Trent didn't ask him to cancel, so he could be my babysitter. I don't need one."

"I'll go with you," Rory said, and he reached for the door handle again. He cared about Ethan, about Trent, about his whole damn team. And he cared about Brittney, too. Too much to leave her unprotected.

"I just said I don't need a babysitter," she reminded him.

"I'm not babysitting."

Annie whined.

"She wants to go, too," Brittney said. "She hasn't been barking at me now."

"She tends to get used to strangers pretty quickly," he said. "Except for Ethan. It took her a while to get used to him without his beard. I really shouldn't let her out. She tends to run off."

"Hmm... Wonder where she gets that from?"

Rory resisted the urge to smile. "I'm not running," he said.

"You did. Last night. To save me," she said. "I shouldn't have said what I did upstairs about you only caring about yourself. You jumped in front of an SUV for me."

And he would do it all over again. He didn't want anyone getting hurt, especially if it was because of him and especially her.

"You're not wrong about me," he admitted. "I have been

a selfish jerk." He'd had to be, or he wouldn't have survived as long as he had.

But maybe survival wasn't enough, not when you had to give up so damn much for it.

"And I am going back to Bear Isle," he said. To get that insurance...

Maybe with her help, he could figure out who to trust with it. But should he trust her? Should he get her any more involved than she already was?

"I thought you were walking with me to Tammy's salon," she said. "That you wanted to talk to Ethan."

"I'll walk you over there," Rory said. "But I don't need to talk to Ethan." He knew what he needed to do.

He pulled open the door just far enough to try to keep Annie from squeezing out. But the dog was fast despite her size. And despite her size, she managed to squeeze through the opening and out.

"Annie!" he called to her, and he jerked the door open the rest of the way. And when he did, gunshots rang out, bullets pinging off the concrete building and the metal door. He dropped, pulling Brittney down with him.

She'd been in the doorway, too. Had she gotten hit?

"Brittney?" he whispered into her hair, which was soft beneath his cheek. "Are you all right?"

"Shh..." she whispered back at him. "The shooter might still be out there."

Rory was pretty damn certain that he or she was. And so was Annie. "Stay in here," Rory advised her. "Lock the door behind me and go get Braden and Trick." He pushed her farther inside so he could get out the door. Then he pulled it shut behind him.

More gunshots rang out, echoed by Annie's barks. She

was going after the shooter. Trying to save everyone like she kept saving them…

But who would save Annie from a bullet?

Brittney screamed, "Braden! Trick!"

They were already running down the stairs, heading toward her. "Who's shooting?" Braden asked.

"Where is it coming from?" Trick asked.

She pointed toward the door. "Rory went after him or after Annie…" She didn't know which, just that once again he'd run toward danger instead of away from it. And he had nothing with him to protect him.

Not a gun. No armor. He'd just rushed off with no thought of his own safety.

Tears stung her eyes as fear for him overwhelmed her. And remorse…

If something happened to him, she would regret so many things. Most of all that she hadn't kissed him like she'd wanted, with all the passion she felt for him. She hadn't really showed him how much she appreciated that he'd risked his life for hers last night, either.

And now…he was risking his again.

Some noise, far-off but familiar, pulled Trent from his dream. Or maybe the sound had been part of his dream.

Or the memory he had of gunfire…

Of someone shooting at him and Heather…

Heather dropping through the fire- and water-damaged floor of his burned house. And him not knowing if she'd been shot…

Was someone getting shot now?

The sound faded away then. It must have just been his dream. Or memory.

But then the sharp wail of sirens jerked Trent fully awake. He should have been awake all along.

He'd never intended to fall asleep.

"Brittney!"

His heart pounding, he jumped up from his bed and headed toward the connecting door. It was closed. She must have closed it. When he touched the knob, it didn't turn. She'd locked it on her side. To keep him out or to keep him from seeing that she'd taken off?

Hell, she might have even checked out. But he doubted that. She wasn't leaving Northern Lakes without her story. But what was it going to cost her?

Those sirens…

He was sure she was wherever the police were heading. He pulled open the door to his room and rushed out into the hall. He didn't wait for the elevator, taking the stairs instead. But he knew that no matter how fast he ran, he might be too late. Like he would have been last night…

Rory was the one who'd saved her then. Was he with her now? Had he protected her again?

But at what cost?

His life?

# Chapter 14

Despite her size, Annie must have been part cat because she certainly had more than one life. Maybe even more than nine. Rory could relate. He'd had more than one himself.

Somehow both he and the dog had avoided getting hit despite all the bullets that had been initially fired at the steel door to the firehouse.

Someone must have called the police, though, and the gunfire stopped with the wail of sirens in the distance. The shooter didn't want to get caught.

So why take the chance of firing at them in broad daylight? How determined was he or she to kill...?

And who was the target?

Brittney or him? He'd been hit over the head, but nobody had shot at him and tried to run him down, at least not recently, like had been the case for Brittney.

He needed to make sure that Brittney was safe. He'd left her back at the firehouse when he'd run after Annie. The dog had kept running into the woods behind the firehouse. Was that where the shooter had been standing?

"Annie!" he called out.

Maybe the would-be killer was still out there. Waiting until he got closer to fire again.

Where had the dog gone?

Despite the unseasonably warm winter they'd been having, there were large patches of snow in the woods yet. There were also big sections of mud where the snow had melted and the ground had begun to thaw. If the shooter had been out here, maybe they would be able to track him through the snow and mud.

"Annie…" He lowered his voice now.

While she'd ignored his shouting for her, she turned now, at his whisper, and rushed back to him. Probably as scared as he'd been, she jumped up on him with her paws on his chest. The sudden weight of her body pushed him back, and he slipped and fell into that mud. At least it was mud and not wainscoting or asphalt like the night before.

But then he heard a gun cock, and he realized the fall and the mud wasn't what he should have been worrying about. And that he damn well shouldn't have assumed that the shooter had taken off with the sound of the sirens.

Because above Annie's big head, he could see the barrel of a gun pointing directly at him.

"Where is he?" Brittney asked, her heart hammering so hard with fear that her chest was starting to hurt. She paced by the door of the firehouse, the door that Trick and Braden were blocking as if they realized she would have run out after Rory by now if they hadn't stopped her. "Where is he?"

Braden shook his head. "The police are here," he reminded her. "They're searching the area."

"For the shooter," she said.

Braden said, "They'll find any victims—"

She gasped and slapped a hand over her mouth to hold back the sob that threatened to escape.

"I don't mean that they will find any, that Rory is one…"

"But he was a victim, not that long ago, in this very firehouse," Brittney reminded him. He'd been hurt so badly that he'd spent two weeks in a coma. He'd had no business running off like he had. After Annie or the shooter? "He doesn't have a gun. No way to defend himself…"

The door handle turned, and everybody whirled toward it. A trooper had been standing on the other side of it, so nobody could get inside to them. And probably so that they couldn't get out. She suspected she wasn't the only one who'd been tempted to run out to find Rory.

The door opened, but it wasn't the trooper who entered. Trent walked in instead. "What the hell happened?" he demanded to know. Then he rushed over to her. He clasped her shoulders and stared down into her face. "Are you all right?"

She nodded. "Thanks to Rory. He saved my life again." Even after how terribly she'd spoken to him…

He definitely cared about more than himself. He probably cared about everyone and everything else more than he cared about himself.

Trent peered around the garage area. "Where is he?" he asked.

She shrugged, knocking his hands from her shoulders. "He went after Annie."

Trent groaned. "I love that dog, but she doesn't have the sense to hide from shooters. Instead she races right toward them."

"Shooters?" Then she remembered the professional assassins that Jonathan Canterbury's brother-in-law had hired to kill him. They'd shot at the firehouse, too.

She shuddered. That had been her fault for revealing Ethan Sommerly's real identity. Was this her fault, too?

Had that shooter been after her or Rory?

"It shouldn't be taking this long to find him," Brittney

said, her voice cracking with the fear that overwhelmed her. Unless they'd found him and were working on him because he'd been shot.

Braden nodded. "We should have gone out after him," he said to Trick.

Trick pointed at her. "She would have gone out there, too."

"Brittney," her brother said, his voice gruff with emotion. "You've got to stop putting yourself in danger."

She held up a hand to stop his lecture. "Don't start. Just don't…"

"This isn't getting us anywhere," Braden said, and he opened the door to the trooper standing outside. "We can help you search—"

The guy touched the speaker in his ear. "Trooper Wells found someone."

Someone. Brittney wanted to demand to know what he meant. The shooter? A victim? The dog?

Who the hell had Trooper Wells found?

Ethan had heard the gunfire and the sirens. And he knew he'd done the right thing. He'd come back for his team. They'd been there for him and for Tammy when his greedy brother-in-law had taken her hostage. Ethan had to be there for them now. But he wasn't allowed anywhere close to the firehouse.

He wasn't the only one being held away from the area, though. Pretty much everyone else had showed up at the scene. Stanley was sobbing.

"I don't hear Annie barking anymore," Stanley said.

Donovan Cunningham, who had two teenagers just a little younger than Stanley, wrapped his arm around his shoulders. "That dog is lucky, Stanley. She'll be fine."

"She's been good luck for all of us," Howie Lane said.

He was one of the newer hotshots and was probably just a few years older than Stanley, in his early twenties.

Howie and Bruce Abbott had shown up together. They were young and worked in the area, when they weren't working as hotshots, as arborists.

Sometimes just being around them made Ethan feel old. They were so young and full of energy.

Carl Kozak slapped Ethan's shoulder. "I thought you were gone on a cruise."

Carl was the old man of the team, but with his bald head and muscular build, it was hard to tell his age.

"I didn't feel right taking off when Rory isn't one hundred percent yet."

"He's the one who went chasing after Annie," Howie said.

"You saw him?" Ethan asked. "You were here when the shooting started."

Bruce nodded. "Yeah, we were just about to go to the Filling Station for lunch when we heard the gunshots. Then we saw Annie and Rory running toward the woods."

Stanley gasped. "Was that where the shooter was?"

Ethan and Donovan exchanged a significant glance over Stanley's curly-haired head. The dog had probably gone after the shooter.

And Rory had gone after her.

Had they gotten hit?

Where the hell were they?

# *Chapter 15*

Rory wasn't sure how he'd gone from lying flat on his back in the mud, staring up into the barrel of a gun, to here…

The shower in Brittney's hotel room.

The gun, fortunately, had belonged to Trooper Wells. Although he'd had a long uneasy moment of staring into the barrel before she'd finally turned it away from him.

Despite the warmth of the water washing away the mud, he shivered. Could *she* have been the shooter? Annie hadn't barked at her, so she could have even been the one who'd hit him over the head.

But why…?

Her former boss, Marty Gingrich, had hated the hot-shots, but she had no reason to, even though she had spouted off at a few back at the firehouse. She'd warned them all to stop trying to investigate on their own or they were going to get hurt.

"Is that a threat?" Brittney had asked the question, of course, probably because it wasn't possible for her to not ask one.

She hadn't asked him back to her hotel room, though. She'd told him he looked like hell and that he needed to come back with her.

With everyone else at the firehouse, he'd been happy

to get away from the noise that had had his head pounding again. Or was his head pounding for another reason?

With fear and guilt?

Annie was fine. She hadn't even gotten as muddy as he had. She wasn't hurt.

But Brittney could have been. Those bullets had come so close to her. And to him…

Instead of coming back here with her, he should have headed where he'd intended earlier. To the island…

To his insurance.

But Brittney, and her quick talking, had gotten them both away from the trooper and her questions. She'd insisted that Rory was too weak yet from his concussion to answer any more questions and that she needed to drive him to the hospital.

But she'd driven his truck back to her hotel instead. Then she'd pushed him into the bathroom. "You need to wash off that mud," she'd insisted. "You're not making me lose my room deposit."

He'd chuckled but complied. The hot shower felt really good. But thinking about walking back out there to her had him cranking the faucet to Cold. He needed the blast of icy water to bring him to his senses. To remind him of all the reasons why he couldn't get involved with anyone. As if getting shot at and nearly run down with her weren't good enough reasons…

After turning off the water, he grabbed a towel and then looked around the steamy bathroom for the duffel bag he'd brought in with him. Hadn't he?

Where was his bag?

His clothes?

After drying off with the towel, he tucked it around his

waist and opened the door to the room, peering out through a crack. "Have you seen my duffel bag?"

He'd dropped it at the firehouse before rushing out the door after Annie. But he'd picked it up before rushing out the door after Brittney when she'd given them the means to escape from more of the trooper's questions.

Wells had already interrogated him when she'd found him in the woods, as if she'd suspected he was the shooter. And when he opened the door and found Brittney going through his duffel bag, he wondered if she suspected the same.

"You were with me when the shots were fired," he reminded her. "You're not going to find a gun in there."

"I'm not looking for a gun," she replied without even looking up at him, without looking at all embarrassed for getting caught rummaging through his things.

"Then what are you looking for?" And he was so glad that he'd stashed his insurance somewhere safe.

"Your cape," she replied.

"Cape?"

"You must be some kind of superhero since you keep saving me," she said.

He shook his head. "I'm no hero. Super or otherwise…" Or so many other people wouldn't have died.

"You've saved me," she said.

He gestured at her going through his duffel. "And yet you still don't trust me. What did you really expect to find?"

She shrugged. "I don't know. Maybe a bunch of passports with different names but your picture on every one of them."

"Now I'm a spy?" he asked, and he managed to keep his voice even so he didn't give away how damn close she was getting to the truth.

"Spy or superhero?" she asked. "Which is it?"

"You didn't find a cape or any passports, so I'm not either of those things," he said. And he wasn't. "But I am getting a little cold." The towel was damp from him using it to dry off, though he hadn't dried off completely. Droplets of water still streaked down his back and chest.

Her gaze seemed to track one of those drops sliding down his chest, and he wasn't cold anymore. Not when she looked up again and her topaz eyes had gone dark, her pupils dilated.

"Can I have my clothes?" he asked, reaching out for the bag with a hand that shook slightly. The way she was looking at him was testing his self-control.

Could he contain the attraction he felt for her?

"You are cold," she murmured, but instead of handing over the bag, she reached over it and touched his chest, pressing her palm flat against where his heart was beating so hard and fast.

He shook his head. "This is a bad idea, Brittney."

"Why?"

"You and those damn questions," he murmured before gritting his teeth.

Her hand still on his chest, she stepped around the chair where she left his duffel bag, and she laid her other hand on him, on his abs. "Give me a reason this is a bad idea," she challenged him.

He couldn't hold back a slight grin at her audacity. "Uh, let's see. We won't have to worry anymore about who hit me over the head, tried to run you down and took shots at you and at us. That's because your brother will kill me. My team members will help him. And yeah, the police could show up anytime."

"The police?"

"Yeah, what do you think Trooper Wells is going to do when she checks with the hospital to see if we're really there?" he asked.

"Well, hopefully the police show up before my brother and the rest of the team kill you," she said, and she was smiling now, her topaz eyes sparkling.

"You are probably more dangerous than whoever is after us," he said. Because she was making him forget all the reasons why he couldn't have a relationship, why he couldn't care about someone…

But it was already too late for that. He cared about her.

He groaned, his body aching with the need for hers. And he hadn't even kissed her. He wanted her so damn badly. But he wanted even more to keep her out of the mess that was his life. He didn't want her getting hurt or worse.

Either the man wasn't attracted to her or he had incredible willpower. Because, despite her hands on his bare chest, Rory didn't wrap his arms around her and pull her close. He just reached around her for his duffel bag.

So she drew in a shaky breath and stepped back, letting her hands drop away from him. "Guess I'm not as cute as my producer tells me I am…"

Rory turned back to her then, and his pale blue eyes were intense as he stared at her. "You're not cute."

"Ouch."

"You're beautiful," he said.

She'd been called that before. Beautiful Brittney. She knew she was attractive, but apparently to a man like Rory VanDam that wasn't enough to attract him.

Then he sighed and added, "Stunning, smart, stubborn, infuriating…"

She smiled. "I'm infuriating?"

He nodded. "And that's why. You can't stop asking questions."

"There are things I want to know," she said. "I won't find out unless I ask…" So she drew in a breath and asked him, "Don't you want me?"

He groaned and closed his eyes. "So damn badly…"

"Then why aren't you kissing me? Touching me?"

He grimaced. "More questions…"

"And you're not giving me any answers."

"I don't want you to get hurt," he said.

"I'm not going to fall madly in love with you," she assured him. Not a firefighter. Not a hotshot…

Not someone she could lose like she'd lost her dad while he'd been deployed.

He grinned. "Good to know. That still doesn't protect you."

"You've been protecting me," she said. "And if I didn't already know how damn short life can be, I would have realized it after the close calls we've had. I don't want to regret not doing this…" She closed the distance between them again and looped her arms around his neck, guiding his head down to hers. Then she kissed him.

The second her lips touched his, her skin tingled and her heart started racing. It was like she was coming under fire again and the vehicle she was in was starting to roll over, to spin out of control. But she wasn't inside anything. There were no airbags to protect her and nothing to hold on to but him.

Then he was holding on to her, too, but he just didn't wrap his arms around, he lifted her up. And she wrapped her legs around his lean waist.

His body was so strong, so hard…so hot.

He kissed her back, his lips nibbling at hers, the tip of

his tongue teasing hers. She parted her lips for him, and he deepened the kiss, making love to her mouth.

Then she was spinning again, or at least moving, as he carried her over to the bed. She pulled him down with her, clinging to him. She hooked her finger in his towel, loosening it until it dropped.

And she whistled in appreciation of all his muscles. The man was perfect. Or he would have been but for a scar here and there, scars like the one on the back of his head. "Rory..." She touched her finger to one on his shoulder.

The bullets had missed him earlier today, but she suspected that one hadn't. At some time...that he had been shot. "Rory—"

Before she could ask the question, his mouth covered hers again, kissing her so deeply that she breathed him in, that his breath was her air. And their hearts beat in a frantic rhythm.

He pulled back and panted for breath. "Let me ask a question," he said, his voice gruff.

Unable to speak for the desire overwhelming her, she just nodded.

"Are you sure?" he asked.

She reached between them and wrapped her hand around his erection. It pulsated against her. "Very sure."

"Then you're overdressed," he said.

And the man moved fast, undoing buttons, lowering zippers, pulling off her shoes until she lay as naked on the bed as he was.

But his gaze covered her, moving over every part of her body. "You are so beautiful..." Then his hands and his mouth moved over her, kissing the side of her neck and the curve of her collarbone.

His hands moved to her breasts now, caressing them,

cupping them. Then he lowered his mouth and kissed one taut nipple before turning his attention to the other one.

She arched against the mattress, her body writhing inside with the tension he was building. The demand for release.

"Rory…" She didn't want to wait.

But he took his time, flicking his tongue across her nipple. Then his hand moved lower, between her legs, and his thumb pressed against the most sensitive part of her body.

Pleasure shot through her with a sudden and small orgasm. It had been too damn long since she'd been with someone. Too damn long since she'd felt this kind of pleasure.

She touched him, sliding her fingers over his muscles and his scars. She would save her questions for later because right now there was only one curiosity she wanted to satisfy. How he would feel inside her…

"Rory…" She wrapped her legs around him again.

"I—I don't have anything…"

"No diseases?" she asked.

He chuckled. "No protection. But yeah, it's been a while, so no nothing else, either…and no control if you keep…"

She rubbed against his cock again. "I have an IUD," she said. "And it's been a while. We're good…"

He parted her legs, lifting them up, over his shoulders as he guided himself inside her.

And she nearly came again at just that, that feeling of him filling her. Then he moved, thrusting his hips against her. She arched up, meeting his thrusts, and they found a fast, frenetic rhythm, one that drove them both to panting and grunting and groaning and madness.

Then finally the tension broke, and her body quivered inside and out. The pleasure was so intense, so unending…

Then his body tensed, and he shuddered as he found his release. And her name slipped through his lips. "Brittney..."

He sounded awed.

She was, too, awed by the intensity of the pleasure and the feeling. Of the connection...

But she knew all too well that it couldn't last. That they only had these stolen moments to enjoy each other because whoever was after her wasn't about to give up.

But she wanted these moments to last, so Brittney reached up and kissed him again. Deeply, passionately, and she felt him move inside her.

He groaned and then chuckled. "Brittney..." He definitely sounded awed.

How the hell had every bullet missed? Sure, the shooter had fired too soon, the minute the door had opened. But with the dog rushing out, running toward them, there hadn't had a choice.

If there had been any hope of hitting the target, the shooter had to shoot fast and then get the hell out of there before someone saw where they'd been standing in the woods.

Did anyone see them now? Where they stood in the shadows outside the hotel?

The shooter might have tried to take them out when they'd left the firehouse, but there had been so many police there. And while the shooter had followed them back here, other people had, as well.

The shooter wasn't the only one watching them. They weren't even sure if they were the only one who wanted them dead. And now the shooter wanted them both dead.

*Him* even more than her...

# Chapter 16

Rory knew Brittney was dangerous. To his secret…and to the life he'd built in Northern Lakes with his hotshot team. But he hadn't realized how dangerous she was to him personally until now.

Even as she lay sleeping next to him, he felt as if he couldn't escape her, that he was connected to her in a way he had never been to anyone else.

Not even Amelia…

Which was strange because he'd trusted Amelia and he knew he couldn't trust Brittney. She cared more about getting her story, or the truth, than anything else. She didn't really care about him.

At least Amelia had pretended to. Maybe she even had, but in the end her greed had been greater than her love. And that greed had proved the end of her…

The twinge in his shoulder wasn't just because of how he was holding Brittney but from an old wound. One that tended to remind him of all the reasons he shouldn't take another chance on a relationship.

Brittney didn't want one any more than he did, though. Maybe less than he did. But instead of reassuring him, that had him panicking now. He wasn't about to fall harder for someone than they'd fallen for him. Not again…

He'd intended to stick with her, to protect her and to figure out the truth together. If the saboteur had come after both of them or if someone else had.

But if it was someone else, someone from his past, then he might get sucked back into it. And she might, too. She deserved to know the truth, but would she believe it…?

Without proof?

He could bring her with him to get his insurance, but he needed some distance, some room to breathe, or he might lose his head and his heart completely. So he slipped out of the bed with the tangled sheets and the sleeping woman. But as he did, he felt a twinge in his heart, and he wondered if it was already too late.

If he was already starting to fall for her…

He had to protect himself now, but he wanted to make sure she was safe, too. Who else would stop Brittney from getting hurt? He dressed quickly and quietly and grabbed up his duffel bag. He'd charged his cell last night at the firehouse, so he had it with him now. Once he got into the hallway outside her room, he would call Trent and make sure that he would protect Brittney better than he had and that he would make sure she didn't slip away again and put herself in danger.

And he'd even wait in the hall until Trent got there, to make sure that she was never unprotected. He didn't want Brittney getting hurt. Not like Amelia had…

As he neared the door, he turned back to the bed to look at her one more time. Her hair had tangled across her face and across the pillow where his head had lain next to hers. He wanted to go back there, wanted to close his arms around her warm body and hold her close.

But it was that desire, that need burning inside him that scared him more than anything else right now. He needed some distance, some time to clear his head, so he could figure out exactly how to finally take care of what he should have five years ago.

He forced himself to resist the temptation of Brittney and turn back toward the door. When he closed his hand around the knob and just started to rotate it, she murmured in her sleep. He glanced back over his shoulder, watching as she settled back against his pillow. Once her body relaxed, as she slipped back into deep sleep, he pulled open the door and quietly stepped out into the hall.

He'd just closed it behind him when someone grabbed him roughly, jerking his arms behind his back, preventing him from fighting.

And if he called out…

Brittney might try coming to his rescue. But she had no gun, nothing that would protect her and save him. He had to figure out some way to do that, but he had a feeling that he was outnumbered this time. It wasn't just one shadow looming over him in that hall but two.

But he'd never given up before. Not when Amelia had betrayed him or when that plane crashed.

He wasn't giving up now. Just like before, he wasn't giving up without a fight. And now he wasn't just fighting for his life but for hers, too.

Brittney jerked awake, her arms outstretched, reaching…

Reaching for Rory, but he was gone. The bed was cold. How long had he been gone?

Snippets of a dream came back to her. Men's deep voices. Sounds of a scuffle…

Had that been a dream?

Or had something happened to Rory?

She jumped up and hurriedly dressed. Then she searched

her room and the adjoining bathroom. Rory was gone, and so was his duffel bag. How long had he been gone?

The light was already dimming outside. How long had she slept?

Had the entire day slipped away from her? Just like Rory had?

A twinge of regret struck her heart. Not over what they'd done. She would never regret that. He was amazing in bed. Had brought her so much pleasure…

She had needed that. She'd needed him. Her regret was that he was gone now. And she didn't think she would find him as easily as she had earlier that day. He probably wasn't going back to the firehouse.

Where would he go?

That island where he was a forest ranger?

Or somewhere else? Wherever he was from?

Did he have a home? Family? He'd never said much about anyone but his hotshot team.

And yet, he didn't seem as close as the rest of them were to each other, either. Rory VanDam was a loner now, but had he always been alone?

Despite having dressed in a sweater and wool pants, she shivered. She wasn't cold so much as she felt alone. And despite the closed door, she had that uneasy feeling, that sensation that someone was watching her even though there wasn't even a peephole in the door.

Then the knob rattled, as someone tried to turn it. "Who's there?" she called out. "Rory? Trent?"

The knob rattled more and so did the door as someone tried to force it open. It definitely wasn't Rory or Trent. They would have answered her. They wouldn't want to scare her like this person obviously did.

But if this was the one who'd fired shots at her and

tried to run her down, this person didn't want to just scare her anymore. They wanted to kill her.

Trent had never felt like killing anyone more than he had Rory. When he and Ethan had caught the man sneaking out of his sister's hotel room, fury had coursed through him. And if not for Ethan stopping him, he wouldn't have killed Rory, but he certainly would have messed him up.

If he could…

His jaw still ached a bit from where Rory had nailed him the night before. Even with a serious head injury, the guy was strong.

And stubborn.

He'd resisted Ethan's efforts to encourage them to go somewhere and talk it out while Ethan stayed behind to protect Brittney. Rory had insisted there was nothing to talk about it.

And even though Rory had finally agreed to go to the Filling Station with Trent, he had yet to say much of anything. Trent wasn't sure what to say, either. He was almost too damn mad to talk.

From the way Rory had looked, sneaking out of his sister's hotel room, he could pretty much guess what had happened between them. That was bad enough, made Trent's empty stomach churn with disgust.

But then to sneak out like the man had…

Like he'd been trying to get away from her without waking her up…

A growl bubbled up the back of his throat, but he didn't want to think about why she would have been sleeping. Why she would have been with Rory at all…

Sure, the guy had saved her life. Twice. That Trent knew of. But what if he was the one who'd put it in danger?

He growled again.

"I don't speak Annie," Rory said. "So if you've got something to say to me, just say it." He squared his shoulders and leaned forward a bit, as if bracing himself.

After how Trent had pounced on him in the hall, he was smart to be wary. But Rory was always wary no matter what.

The first time Brittney had come to town, he'd worked damn hard to stay away from her. Why hadn't he done it this time?

But if he had…

She would be hurt or worse: dead.

He released the growl in a groan of frustration. Then he said, "Thank you."

Rory's forehead furrowed, and he leaned farther across the booth and peered at Trent's face. "What did you say?" he asked as if he hadn't heard it or, if it had, he didn't believe that Trent had said it.

"Thank you," he said. "You saved my sister's life. Twice. I can't thank you enough for that…"

Rory's mouth curved into a slight grin. "But?"

"I know she acts tough and all that," Trent said. "But she's got a really soft heart. She's hurt a lot more easily than you'd think. And she's been through a lot."

Concern filled Rory's eyes. "What do you mean? When?"

"We lost our dad when she was really young," Trent said. "Sometimes I think she doesn't remember him, and then sometimes I think she remembers him too much, that she remembers how hard it was for us to lose him."

"On *all* of you, I'm sure," Rory said with sympathy. "Especially your mom."

He shook his head. "My parents were already divorced when he died. He was married to Brittney's mom then."

A muscle twitched along Rory's cheek, and he cleared his throat and asked, "What happened to him?"

"He was deployed, roadside bomb," Trent murmured, and he felt that hollow ache in his heart.

"I'm sorry..."

The sympathy was genuine. Not for the first time, Trent suspected that Rory knew how it felt to lose someone and maybe not just because of that plane crash.

Trent nodded. "A few years later my mom died," he said. "Moe, Brittney's mom, had remarried by then, and Brittney convinced them to take me in, to foster me. She'll fight fiercely for those she loves, and she loves fiercely."

"Why are you telling me all of this?" Rory asked. "Why are we even here?" He gestured at the food untouched on the booth in front of them. "You should be back at the hotel with her."

"And what about you?" Trent asked. "Where are you going?"

Rory's gaze dropped down to the table then. That was clearly a question he didn't want to answer.

"Does this have anything to do with you?" Trent asked.

Rory shrugged. "I don't know."

"I think you know more than I do."

"You haven't had your detective girlfriend looking into this?" Rory asked.

Trent grinned at just the thought of Heather. Talking about fierce women, there was no one fiercer than her. Not even Brittney or Moe.

"What did Detective Bolton find out?" Rory asked.

"That a certain producer has been creeping on my sister."

That muscle twitched in Rory's cheek again when he clenched his jaw. "The one that calls her cute..." he murmured.

Trent bristled with anger over the thought of some-one harassing his sister. "He's not been at work, either. Brittney's coworkers told Heather about him."

Rory didn't look as convinced of the man's guilt as Trent was.

"What?" he asked. "What do you know that I don't?"

"She got a couple of notes," Rory said. "One was shoved under her windshield wiper. Told her to drop a story or she'd regret it."

Trent groaned. "That would just make her more deter-mined."

"The next was a text that told her she was going to die for not dropping it, or something to that effect, and after she got that somebody shot at her windshield. That's why she went off the road."

Trent cursed and jumped up from the table. "Why the hell didn't she tell me this? Why didn't you?" Then his fury turned back on Rory as he realized why. "The story she's supposed to drop... It's about that damn plane crash!"

"Or about the sabotage," Rory said. "She's still looking into both of those."

Trent cursed again. "Probably the sabotage even more now after what happened after the holiday party. Who the hell is doing this?" And he glanced around the bar all the hotshots frequented. Usually they would have been jammed into the big corner booth, but none of them were there now. They'd been at the firehouse earlier, though, so most of them were still in town.

Because Rory had been hurt? Or because Rory had re-covered? Was whoever hit him worried that he was able to identify him?

"You really didn't see who hit you?" Trent asked him.

He shook his head. "Brittney wanted a list of all the hotshot team members. She intends to look into everyone."

"And I intend to stop her," Trent said. "Are you coming with me?"

Rory shoved his hands in his pockets, and his face got a little pale. "Damn. I must've left my keys…"

"You didn't have them," Trent reminded him. "Brittney drove you back from the firehouse." He wasn't happy that his friend had probably crossed a line with his sister, but it was clear that Brittney had been the instigator. Like she usually was.

But as she was learning from those threats, some people really resented the instigator and would do anything to stop them from meddling.

Even murder them…

# *Chapter 17*

Rory didn't know why his pulse quickened as he and Trent neared the hotel. Was it just because, in order to get his keys, he was going to have to see her again?

After...what had happened between them?

But the feeling churning his stomach was more than anticipation, more even than nerves. It was fear. Not of her but for her.

But Ethan was watching her room from the adjoining one that Trent had booked the night before. She'd locked the door on the other side, though, so all Ethan could really see was the hall through the open door of his room. And if he was focused on the hall, he wouldn't be able to see the fire escape...

The one Rory had gone out the night before when he'd sneaked up on Trent. He glanced up at it now and saw that the window to Brittney's room was open, the curtains and blinds hanging out as if someone had exited it in a hurry.

Or dragged someone out of it?

"Trent!" He grabbed his friend's arm and pointed up. "That's her room!"

Trent cursed and started running toward the hotel. While he went through the lobby, Rory jumped on the ladder dangling down from the fire escape and climbed up it. As he ran up the landings, he looked for blood or for any other sign of a struggle. Because he doubted that Brittney had just opened that window for some air…

Not with as chilly as the wind was now that the sun had dropped. It was cold. Too cold to leave a window open.

The escape swayed beneath his pounding feet as he hurried up the last landing to that open window. He leaned over, peering inside, before sliding his leg over the jamb. "Brittney?" he called out.

The door to the hall stood open, spilling light into her room. Into the empty room…

The door and the window were open? What the hell?

He climbed through the window and checked the bathroom. It was empty, too. And he noticed that the door to the hall hadn't just been opened, it had been kicked in, the wood cracked and the jamb splintered.

Hearing footfalls on the stairs, he stepped out into the hall and nearly fell over a body.

"Ethan!" He dropped to his knees and felt his friend's neck, checking for a pulse. It was there. Strong and steady.

But Ethan didn't move. And Rory was almost scared to move him. Had he been shot? Or stabbed? There was blood on the carpet near him.

"What the hell!" Trent shouted, standing over them in the hall. "Is he—"

"He's alive, but we need to call for a rig."

"And Brittney?" Trent asked, his voice cracking.

Rory shook his head. "She's not in there."

Trent stepped around him and looked inside, too, as if he didn't believe Rory. He unlocked the adjoining door from her side and looked in his room, too.

Maybe she'd gone in there. Maybe she was safe. But Trent walked out of it into the hall. He was shaking his head, and tears shone in his eyes.

He was scared for Brittney, as scared as Rory was. He never should have left her.

But Ethan...

He was so damn big. So indestructible...

Then Rory saw where the blood was coming from, a wound on the side of Ethan's head. Someone had struck him just like Rory had been struck those weeks ago.

He hoped that Ethan recovered faster than he did. The man had already been through too much. The Canterbury curse couldn't claim him now, not when he was so happy.

"Owen, get a rig here to the Lakeside Inn," Trent spoke into his cell. "Ethan's unconscious—"

"He was hit over the head!" Rory said, speaking loud enough that Owen could hear him.

"And Brittney is missing," Trent added. "So we need to get Braden and Trick and whoever else we can find to help look for her."

Rory shook his head.

Trent clicked off his cell and asked, "What? Why are you shaking your head?"

"We don't know who we can trust," Rory said. "Besides you and me and Ethan—"

Trent pointed at Ethan's prone body. "He's hurt, man. And I trust Braden and Trick."

But Rory noted that he didn't add any other names. Not even Rory's...

Rory shook his head with disgust. How could Trent doubt Rory now?

Because of the damn story.

Because of the plane crash.

Was that what this was all about? If it was, Brittney was right about getting the truth out. Keeping secrets certainly wasn't keeping her safe.

He needed to get back to the island. He rushed back into Brittney's room.

"She's not there," Trent said.

But Rory wasn't looking for her now, he was looking for his keys. They weren't on any of the tables or the desk. Not lying on any of the furniture...

He didn't have the keys, so Brittney must have taken them with her. Had she used them to get away? He rushed back to that open window and climbed through it. The fire escape shuddered beneath his weight.

"Rory!" Trent called to him. "You can't leave Ethan alone!"

Sirens were already wailing in the distance. Help was on its way. And there wasn't much Rory could do about Ethan's head injury when he was still recovering from his own.

Ignoring Trent, he continued clamoring down the escape and dropped off the end of the dangling ladder onto the sidewalk. Where had Brittney parked his truck?

Hadn't it been here, close to the hotel? He peered up and down the street and didn't see it.

Whoever had broken into Brittney's room must have taken her and the keys and his truck...

Taken her where, though?

And why? Why wouldn't he or she have just left Brittney in the hotel room like they'd left Ethan lying in the hall? Maybe Trent was right, maybe the person who'd been after her was her obsessed producer.

But then why shoot at her and try to run her down if he'd wanted to abduct her?

"Brittney, where are you?" he wondered aloud as he looked around the street again.

Lights flashed on and off. On and off.

And he noted they were coming from the alley where he and Trent had been standing the night she'd nearly gotten run down. But now there was a vehicle in it instead of two men.

He started down the street toward that alley, stepping in front of it just as the lights flashed on again and the motor revved up. He could see the US Forest Service insignia on the side door.

He'd found his truck.

But was it about to run him over?

Brittney lowered the driver's window and gestured for Rory to hurry around the front. To jump into the passenger's door. But he stepped up to her door instead and pulled on the handle. "Let me drive," he said with a quick glance around.

Brittney had already stayed longer than she should have. "He's probably out here somewhere—"

Rory reached through the window and unlocked the door and opened it. "Slide over, quick," he said.

She scrambled over the console. "I can drive—"

"You don't know where we're going, or you would have left already," he said, and he pulled out of the alley onto the street.

Obviously he knew where he was going.

"I couldn't leave," she said. She'd been so disoriented when she'd awakened *alone.* Had he snuck out after they'd made love? But she hadn't known if she was really alone or if Rory was somewhere else, if he'd heard whoever was at that door before she had. But that person hadn't been him or Trent or they would have answered when she'd called out to them. "I didn't know who was supposed to be *protecting* me and what had happened to them."

She'd been so scared that he or Trent had been hurt. Because how else would someone have gotten past them?

"What happened?" Rory asked.

She shivered as she relived those terrifying moments. "I heard some arguing earlier, but that didn't wake me up fully. I'm not really sure what did, but then I heard someone trying to get in the door. I grabbed your keys and my purse and went out the window onto the fire escape," she said.

"That must have been right before someone broke through that door. Did they follow you?" Rory asked, and he was glancing into the rearview mirror as he drove. As if looking for that SUV...

The person trying to get into her room must have been whoever drove that SUV straight at her the night before and who'd shot at her and Rory at the firehouse.

She shivered again.

So the lock and the door hadn't held, hadn't kept her would-be killer out. She'd been smart to run. But what happened...?

Lights flashed and sirens whined as an ambulance passed them. She knew where it was headed: the hotel.

"Who's hurt?" she asked, her heart pounding.

After going out the window, she'd pulled the truck into the alley, shut off the lights and hunkered down inside. But she'd seen Trent and Rory coming back from wherever they'd been, and relief had surged through her. Now she felt a twinge of guilt.

"Who is it?" She reached across the console and clutched Rory's arm.

It was already tense, like his tightly clenched jaw.

"Who's hurt?"

"Ethan," he said. "He must've gotten hit over the head. He was unconscious."

"Shouldn't we go back?" she asked. "Make sure he's all right?"

He drew in a shaky breath. "I want to," he said, his voice gruff with emotion. "But I don't think it's a good idea."

"Why not?" she asked.

"Because someone is trying very hard to kill you," he said. "And I don't think either of us want anyone else to get caught in the crossfire."

She sucked in a shaky breath.

"I assume that's why you didn't tell your brother about the threats you—"

"You told him?"

"Yeah, why didn't you?"

"Because I knew he would get crazy overprotective," she said.

"Like he's been since your van crashed?" Rory asked. "You think holding back that piece of information worried him any less than he's been worrying?"

She sighed.

"Holding back that information misled him," Rory said.

"What do you mean?"

"He had Heather checking out your coworkers and—"

"What?" she asked. "Not that I care..." After nearly getting killed and knowing that she was still in danger and putting others in danger, Brittney had a different perspective on her career. She still wanted the story, but it wasn't so she would be taken seriously as a reporter. She just wanted to make sure nobody else got hurt.

"She heard a lot of things about your producer, and he's been conspicuously off work since you left," Rory said with a glance across the console at her.

She shivered again.

And Rory reached for the heat, turning it up.

Despite the warm air blasting out of the vents, she was still chilled. "As big a creep as he is, I don't think he would go to all this trouble to hurt me. My career, maybe. But my life…" She shook her head. "And he has no reason to want to stop me from pursuing any stories. He doesn't even know that I've been trying to get enough information to do a follow-up to the plane crash and with the hotshots."

"Who does know?" Rory asked.

"I've tried talking to Mack McRooney," she said. "And I've called the FAA with questions about the flight path and the black box…"

"And?"

She shrugged. "Ethan. I'm always bugging Ethan for a follow-up," she admitted.

"Well, Ethan didn't hit himself over the head."

"He was hit like you? Do you think the same person hit you both?"

He shrugged. "I don't know what to think anymore, but I know this needs to stop."

"How are we going to stop it?" she asked.

He glanced across at her again, his pale eyes glowing in the dim light from the dashboard. Clearly he had some idea, but he said nothing, just kept driving. Rory had saved her over and over again, so he had to be heading someplace safe. But with how tightly his jaw was clenched, how grim he looked, he had obviously realized the same thing she had. No place was safe.

Somebody was pounding. Hammering away at something…

Was it an axe chopping through a door? Or a wall? Or a tree?

Ethan breathed deeply, waiting for the burn of smoke, for the tickle that would make him cough. But it didn't come. There was no burn. Did he have his helmet and oxygen on?

He raised his hand to his face and found a mask over his nose. But not the kind that came with his helmet.

What was the pounding? Where the hell was he?

Ethan opened up his eyes to two guys leaning over him. Owen, with a pinched and serious look on his face, and Trent, who looked even more anxious.

But maybe not for him…

Ethan pulled the oxygen mask aside. "Where's Brittney? Is she safe?"

Trent grimaced, and Ethan reached up and grabbed his friend's shoulder. "What happened to her?" he asked, his voice gruff with concern. Despite her pestering him, Ethan had grown fond of Brittney, and he would always be grateful for her help in saving Tammy's life.

If he'd lost her…

That pounding intensified again, and he realized it was inside his head. He grimaced at the pain.

"We need to get you to the ER for a CT scan," Owen said.

He shook his head and grimaced again. "Where is she?" he asked. Then he glanced around the hotel corridor. "Where's Rory?"

"He went to find her," Trent said, "out the fire escape. The window was open."

The tension eased from Ethan, and he relaxed a bit against the hotel carpeting. "She got away."

Of course she would have. She was smart and resilient, like Tammy, which was probably why the two of them had become fast friends. He emitted a little wistful sigh for their missed cruise. He would have to reschedule once he knew everyone was safe.

"How do you know she got away?" Trent asked, his topaz eyes bright with either unshed tears or hope.

"The guy stepped over me again after he broke the door down."

"You saw him?" Trent asked. "Who was it?"

"I didn't see him when he hit me over the back of the head. I went down, but I didn't lose consciousness right away." But he hadn't had the strength to get back up after that first blow. "I just saw his legs when he stepped over me and headed back down the interior stairs."

"Why didn't he go out the fire escape after her?" Owen asked.

"He probably didn't want anyone to see him, in case someone was walking by, or Rory and I were walking back up," Trent said. "Rory saw that open window right away."

"Rory probably found her," Owen said. "I'm sure they're safe. So we need to get you to the hospital, Ethan."

While Owen was certain they were safe, Trent didn't look as convinced.

"Rory's smart and resourceful," Ethan reminded him. "He'll figure out how to keep her safe."

"What if she's in danger because of him?" Trent asked. "She got threats telling her to stop pursuing the story."

"What story?" Owen asked.

Ethan didn't have to ask. "The plane crash."

"Is there more to that story?" Trent asked. "Something someone else might not want made public?"

The pounding resumed inside Ethan's skull. But he didn't know now if it was because of the blow or because of the pendulum of the past swinging back toward him. He'd made a promise five years ago.

He and Rory both had. Rory had kept his promise all these years. And Ethan had, too.

But now…

He'd kept Rory's promise to keep him safe, but Rory was

obviously not safe any longer. And Brittney wasn't safe, either, because she wouldn't give up the damn story. And Ethan was afraid that it might cost her more than her career.

It might cost her everything.

# Chapter 18

Rory kept glancing into the rearview mirror, looking for lights on the road behind him. Then he would know for certain that he'd been followed. Right now, he just had that uneasy feeling, that twisting of his stomach muscles that made him suspect that he had been.

But maybe he was just paranoid.

But his paranoia was for good reason after everything that had happened to him and had happened to some people who'd been unfortunate to be around him.

He glanced across the console at Brittney. Was he protecting her by taking her with him or was he putting her in more danger than she already was? Because she had something going on with her, too, and was it really related to him? Or was it her producer?

Or that damn saboteur…?

Brittney was digging inside her purse and cursing.

"What's wrong?"

"I must've left my phone on the charger," she said. "Can I use yours to call and check on Ethan?"

He wanted to know how his friend was, too, but he hesitated for a moment.

"What?" she asked. "Did you forget yours, too? I still don't understand what all happened at the hotel, how Ethan was hurt and where you and Trent were coming back from…"

"The Filling Station," he said.

"The Filling Station?" she asked. "Why were you…?"

He was trying to focus on the road, on finding the turn-off to what he was looking for, but that wasn't why he wasn't filling in the blanks for her. Recognizing the bend in the road, he turned onto the two-track road in the middle of the national forest. This was what he'd been looking for…

While she was looking for answers.

And with her life in danger now, she deserved those answers. "I snuck out when you fell asleep," he admitted. "Trent and Ethan caught me in the hall. Trent was probably going to kill me, but Ethan stopped him." And then might have lost his life, as well.

No. His pulse had been strong and steady, just like Ethan. The man was a survivor, like Rory, so he had to make it. He had to be okay.

"And so you two went to get a beer together?" she asked.

"We needed to talk."

"That was when you told him about those threats."

"You shouldn't have kept it secret from him," he said.

"Like you're *not* keeping any secrets, Rory?" she asked. Damn. She was smart. Too smart.

"I'm sorry," he said. If this was all his fault, if people were getting hurt again because of him…

"Don't be," she said. "I made the moves on you. I wanted what happened to happen. You didn't need to sneak out, though, so fast that you left your keys behind."

"I don't regret what happened," he assured her, his heart pounding fast as he thought of how amazing it had been, how they'd fit so perfectly, moved so much in sync and had had such a mind-blowing release. "That's not why I took off like that. It's just…"

"What?" she asked. "What is it, Rory?"

"The last woman I got close to wound up dead."

She sucked in a breath then released it in a shaky sigh. "Well, someone was trying to kill me before we ever hooked up, so I can't blame you for that."

Even though there were other possibilities, he was not so sure.

"So did you leave your phone behind with your keys when you made your fast getaway?" she asked again.

"No, no, I have it," he said. "I just… I don't want anyone to know where we're going."

"Why not?" she asked.

"I'm not sure who we can trust," he admitted. He knew all too well how easily some people could be bought, people he'd believed had cared about him. People he had cared about.

The truck bumped along the rutted path between tall trees, but the lights shone up ahead on a clearing in the forest, then glinted off the metal of a big building.

"Don't worry about me telling anybody where we are," she said. "Because I have no freaking idea…" She leaned forward, peering around, but the sun had slipped away a while ago, leaving the area pretty much in darkness but for the lights of his truck.

He braked the truck next to the service door to the hangar. The overhead doors were on the other side of the building by the airstrip. One of his team would realize where he'd gone soon enough, but maybe by that time, he would have gotten what he wanted off the island and made it back already.

He reached into his pocket and drew out his phone. "I have to get something ready," he said. "You can make the call…"

He would leave it up to her who to trust. He'd learned long ago that his judgment sucked when it came to that, or he wouldn't have been betrayed like he'd been.

So was he making another mistake trusting her?

Because that last woman he'd cared about had nearly gotten him killed.

Brittney watched through the windshield as Rory unlocked the door to the massive metal building in the middle of the forest. But there weren't as many trees around here, like they had been cleared away for this...

Whatever it was.

No, like she'd told him, she had no idea where he'd taken her. Then the headlights of the truck went out, leaving her totally in the dark. He'd shut off the engine, and he must have taken the keys with him.

To prevent her from leaving?

But then she couldn't blame him if he didn't want to be left stranded out here in the woods. She wouldn't, either.

Sitting like she was in the dark, she was very aware of the silence. There weren't even birds or animals making noises now. Then an engine started up, and light shone around the corner of the building and from beneath that door.

There was something in the metal structure that had an engine. So Rory wouldn't have been stranded.

She might be, though.

Something vibrated in her hand, and she jumped, realizing that she'd been holding his phone. She glanced at the screen that was lit up with Trent's name.

She accepted the call. "Hi."

"Brittney!" Trent exclaimed. Then he released a shaky sigh that rattled the phone. "Are you all right?"

"Yes, is Ethan?" she asked with concern. The guy wasn't just her brother's best friend, he was also the love of Tammy's life and a really good man.

"He regained consciousness right away, even before we got him out of the hotel hallway," Trent said.

Not like Rory, who'd spent those two weeks in a coma.

"That's good," she said. Hopefully that meant it wasn't a bad concussion.

"We're at the ER now, so he can get a CT and make sure he's as all right as he keeps claiming he is."

"Is Tammy all right?" Brittney asked. "Is she there?"

"She's here, with him," Trent said. "Where the hell are you?"

"I don't know," she answered honestly.

"You're with Rory, right? You have to be since you answered his phone."

"Yes, he's here," she said. She just had no idea where here was.

"You need to get away from him," Trent said with such urgency in his voice that Brittney shivered.

"What do you mean?" The man had saved her life. He wasn't going to hurt her. At least not physically…

Emotionally. She shut that down, refusing to think about that, about what they'd done and how he'd snuck out when she'd been sleeping.

"You were right," Trent said. "You've been right all along that there was more to that plane crash…"

"What?" she asked, her pulse quickening. "What did you find out about it?"

"Ethan didn't know a whole lot, just that when it first happened Rory was blaming himself…"

"Why would he do that?"

"He was the pilot," Trent said. "He went through hot-shot training with Ethan, but he was also able to pilot the planes they were jumping out of. He already knew how to fly. And Ethan doesn't think his name is really Rory Van-

Dam. Somebody else on that flight, somebody who didn't make it off the mountain, called him something else."

"What?"

"Mario."

Even though Trent couldn't see her, she shook her head. But she had no idea why she would deny it. She'd known there was more to the plane crash story and more to Rory VanDam.

"Mario what?" she asked.

"That was all Ethan heard, and when he asked him about it later, when they were stranded, Rory denied it, said he had to be mistaken."

"Maybe he was," Brittney said.

"You got those threats about dropping a story—"

"And Rory was the one who told you about those threats, and he wouldn't have done that if he'd been the one sending them," she reminded him.

"You should have told me."

"Why? So you could overreact?"

"Someone's trying to kill you, Brittney," he said. "So I'm not overreacting. You're underreacting."

She was scared to death, but she wasn't about to admit that aloud or she might fall apart. And she had to keep it together. The side mirror on the truck caught her attention through the passenger's window. She saw something…a flicker of light. But it appeared to be some distance back down that narrow driveway. But what was the message on the mirror? Objects are closer than they appear.

Someone had been following them.

"Trent, I have to go—"

"Where?"

The door through which Rory had disappeared opened again, and he gestured toward her.

Had he seen that light, too?

"Brittney!" Trent yelled. "You have to get away from him. You can't trust him."

"He keeps saving my life, not putting it in danger," she reminded her brother and herself.

"But your life might be in danger *because* of him, Brittney. You have to get away from him and stay away from him," Trent demanded.

*The last woman I got close to wound up dead...*

Rory stood there, gesturing toward her again, but he wasn't looking at her now. He was looking behind her.

Objects might be closer than they appear.

She pushed open the passenger door and jumped out. Trent might be right, but she didn't have a choice right now. Somebody else was out there, and it wasn't Trent.

It sounded like anyone else she could trust was at the hospital with Ethan.

So the only person left was Rory.

Or Mario...

"Brittney!" Trent called out again.

But she clicked off the cell and dropped it into her purse. And as she headed toward the door to the building, something pinged off the metal.

Someone was out there, and he or she was shooting at them. "Hurry up!" Rory said, and he reached out the door and grabbed her arm, pulling her inside with him. He slammed that door and locked it.

But she didn't know why he bothered—wide and tall doors were open on the other side. And outside, a helicopter sat.

"Come on," he said, and he wrapped his arm around her, nearly carrying her toward that machine. "We have to get out of here." He cursed. "We were followed."

She'd been aware of how often he'd checked in his mirrors because she'd been checking, too. There was no way they would have missed someone tailing them unless...

Someone had guessed where they were going. Like a member of his team. Maybe they weren't all at the hospital with Ethan and Trent and Tammy.

"We have to go now!" Rory said. And he swept her around the helicopter, opened the door and lifted her up into it. Then he jumped into the cockpit or whatever it was called on the other side.

He touched buttons and switches, and the blades began to swish above them. Then he reached for some levers and the helicopter lifted. He pointed toward her belt and a set of headphones.

Her hands shaking, she buckled up and put the headphones over her ears. The sounds were muffled, but the noise was still there.

Even the pings as bullets struck the metal of the small helicopter. But it continued to rise above the metal hangar, above the woods.

The gun must have had a long range because it kept firing at them. And on the ground below, Brittney could see little flashes of light as the bullets left the gun. But she couldn't see the shooter.

As fear overwhelmed her, she closed her eyes entirely and hung on tight, terrified that they were going to crash.

Maybe to reassure her, Rory spoke to her, his voice coming through her headphones. "We're going to be all right," he said.

But she didn't know if he was lying to her or telling the truth...about anything.

Then he muttered, "I am not going to crash again."

\* \* \*

The shooter wasn't really worried about the reporter. Not anymore. Not now.

Because the shooter had finally realized the truth of what had happened five years ago and who Rory VanDam really was. They'd been worried about that damn woman, about the reporter, pushing others to look for that wreckage, to find out why it had crashed.

That helicopter needed to go down, or the shooter was the one who was going to suffer. So the gun kept firing; hopefully a bullet would hit the gas tank and that helicopter would blow up like they did in the movies when bullets hit them.

One of the bullets had to hit the target, if not the pilot then the gas tank. This helicopter had to go down like the plane had five years ago. But unlike that crash, there could not be any survivors this time.

# Chapter 19

The helicopter was going down...

Right where Rory intended to land it, on the section of rock that stood atop the hill on the island. No trees could grow out of the rock, and none of the ones near it were tall enough to stand above it. So this was the clearest place to land. Nothing to catch at the blades, and a solid place for the landing skids to rest.

Once Rory sat it down and shut off the engine, he waited for the blades to stop rotating. Then he turned toward Brittney. Her eyes were closed. He could see her face in the moonlight that streamed through the windows of the helicopter. Her eyes weren't just closed but squeezed tightly shut as if she was bracing herself.

Maybe for a crash.

He reached out and pulled off her headphones, and she jumped and flinched. "You're okay," he assured her. "We're okay." For now. "We're on the ground."

And none of the bullets that had struck the helicopter had caused any damage.

Brittney opened her eyes and peered around them then. "Where the hell are we?"

"Bear Isle," he said, and he opened his door and jumped down to the ground. Then he rushed around to help her out.

When she stepped onto the snow-covered rock, she slipped, and he caught her, closing his arms around her trembling body. Maybe she hadn't slipped. Maybe her legs had been shaking too badly to hold her. "We're safe here," he said.

She swung her head around, staring into the shadows of the trees and rocks. "How do you know that?"

"The only thing we have to worry about here might be a bear or a coyote," he promised her. "Whoever was shooting at us back there isn't going to be able to make it out here."

At least not for a while.

Rory's was the only helicopter within a couple hours' drive of Northern Lakes. And if the shooter tried to come by boat, there were still enough chunks of ice around the island to make it hard to get ashore.

As if on cue, a coyote howled somewhere close. Close enough to make Brittney jump again and to make Rory uneasy. "Let's go," he said, and he helped her down from the rock ledge onto the path that wound through the woods to a cabin. His cabin. His sanctuary, really.

"Your hideout," she presumed.

And she wasn't wrong. It probably was more his hideout than anything else. He'd been hiding for a long time. But he had a feeling that he'd been discovered. That the people he'd never wanted to learn the truth knew now that he wasn't dead. He hadn't died in that crash.

Rory opened the door to the cabin and stepped inside, looking around to make sure that it was as he'd left it. Empty. Not just of people but of animals, too. He lit a match to the kindling he had laid in the fieldstone fireplace, and flames flickered to life, illuminating the wood floor and log walls. He turned back toward Brittney, who stood on the outside of the door, hesitating like she had back at the hangar.

"What's going on?" he asked. Then his stomach pitched. "You called Trent. Isn't Ethan…?" He swallowed hard on the emotion suddenly choking him. He and Ethan had been through hell together. He couldn't have lost him, especially now when Ethan was so damn happy. He cleared his throat and asked, "Isn't he okay?"

"He's conscious," she said. "And he's *talking*…"

Rory tensed, waiting for it, because from her tone, there was clearly more to come.

"Mario…"

He could have denied that it was his name, like he had to Ethan all those years ago. And with Ethan assuming another name, he'd had no room to judge him.

Or so he'd thought.

After all, they'd both been afraid for their lives…just for different reasons. Ethan had been convinced that damn Canterbury curse was trying to claim him. And Rory had a curse of his own.

"I'm glad he's okay," he said, then released a heavy sigh of relief.

But she stood there looking all tense yet.

"He is okay, right?"

"They were waiting for a CT scan to confirm it, but he is conscious."

Which was better than Rory had been after the blow to his head. Maybe it hadn't been the same person who'd struck Ethan.

He shuddered, and not just from the cold, but from the thought that there could be two people that cold-blooded in Northern Lakes. But he knew, all too well, that anyone could be cold-blooded, especially when it came to money or their own well-being.

He'd even once been that way himself, when he hadn't

come forward with everything he'd known about the plane crash. When he'd let the people responsible for it escape justice.

But he'd done that for his sake, so that the people who'd wanted him dead had believed they'd succeeded. Playing dead was the only way he'd been able to stay alive.

The door slammed, and he whirled away from the fire toward Brittney. Had the wind slammed the door? Or…

She was bristling, her body tense. "I'm tired of this," she said. "Tired of being in danger. I want to know the truth, *Mario*."

"It's Rory," he said.

"Now. But it wasn't always, was it?" she asked.

He shook his head. "No. But it wasn't always Mario, either."

"So who and what are you really?" she asked. "A hotshot? A pilot?"

"Yes and yes," he said.

"And?" she prodded. Then she sucked in a breath and seemed to be holding it, waiting for his answer.

It had been so long since he'd told anyone the truth. So damn long…

His legs shook a bit, like hers must have from the helicopter trip, and he dropped into one of the big plaid easy chairs that sat in front of the fire. "I was… DEA," he said. "An undercover agent."

In a ragged sigh, she released the breath she'd been holding. She must have been convinced he'd been the criminal, not the cop.

Sometimes, with as deeply undercover as he'd gone, he had felt more criminal than cop. Which had reminded him of how he'd grown up.

"Mario was my undercover identity, my way into the organization," he said. "But I grew up with people like that, so it was easy for me to be Mario. Probably easier than it is for me to be Rory."

"Where did you grow up?" she asked.

"Baltimore."

"And where was Mario?"

"LA."

"And what is your real name?"

He leaned back in the chair and sighed. "When I woke up from that coma, with that concussion, I didn't even know…" He shook his head. "I couldn't remember who I really was. Mario was not my only undercover assignment, my only fake identity. And then there was the Special Forces ops and so many other things that I wanted to forget…"

"The woman?" she asked. "Who was she?"

"Someone who fell for Mario," he said.

"And did Mario fall for her?"

"She seemed sweet. Special. She was also the sister of the guy I took down."

"For drugs?"

"For murder," he said. "My undercover assignment, Mario, was a pilot for a drug cartel. While I was flying their private jet, I witnessed a murder." Remembering that murder, how he'd been unable to stop it, how the whole damn plane could have crashed if he hadn't stayed in control then even as everything had spun out of control around him. "It happened while I was flying, so I didn't have any time to react. I had no idea what was coming. This guy was so cold-blooded, so vicious. He shot this man right between the eyes." He shuddered as he remembered the scene, the blood, the…

But that wasn't even the worst he'd seen.

"Why?" she asked. "Why did he shoot him?"

"Because he thought he was a DEA agent," he said. "He knew someone had infiltrated their organization. He just suspected the wrong man." So that man had died because of him.

She dropped into the chair next to him then as if her legs had given out. "So you're talking about very dangerous people."

"Yes. People who don't forget," he said. "And damn well don't forgive that I arrested the killer and testified against him."

"You were just doing your job," she said. "And why would they go after a DEA agent, especially after you'd already testified and put him in jail?"

"Because the guy I arrested got shanked in jail before his sentencing."

"Then who's after you?" she asked.

"His father."

"I don't understand... You said the woman who got killed was related to them, too. Would the father have killed his own daughter?"

"She set me up," he said. "Got me to meet with her, swore she wanted to leave town with me, start a new life with me, when all she really wanted was to end my life." He rubbed his shoulder, but that wound was nothing in comparison.

"She tried to shoot you?"

He nodded. "She did. And it wasn't just for revenge. Her father had promised her a huge amount of money if she killed me. But a US Marshal killed her before she was able to finish the job."

"The scar on your shoulder?"

He nodded again. "Yeah, she wasn't a very good shot. The Marshal was."

She leaned back in her chair now and closed her eyes, probably overwhelmed with everything he had told her. "I… I don't know what to say…"

"Or what to believe?" he asked.

"It's a pretty wild story," she said. "If I wanted to sell this, I would need proof. Corroboration of the facts."

"So you still want to sell a story?" he asked, his stomach churning with disappointment. "Even though it might cost you your life?" And him his.

He'd started to think there was more to her than ambition, that she genuinely cared about people. At least about her brother. And Ethan and Tammy.

But she apparently didn't care about him.

"I want some proof," she persisted. "Some way to know what the truth really is."

He sucked in a breath now and nodded. "You don't believe me."

"I don't know what to believe," she admitted. "That's why I need corroboration."

He had proof. But for some reason he wanted her to believe him without it. He wanted her to see him for the man that he was, instead of all the different men he'd pretended to be. But how could he expect her to see what he struggled to?

"The person trying to kill us isn't corroboration enough?" he asked.

"Why is that person trying to kill you now?" she asked. "Why didn't that person go after you right after the plane crash?"

"Because the pilot, at least the man who'd been listed as the pilot, didn't survive," he said. "That's what all the reports said. That man was really the US Marshal who had helped set up my new identity."

"People didn't realize he was missing?" she asked.

"He went through the hotshot training with me as my protection. That's why he was on the plane, too, because everybody knew about the hit out on my life," he said. "And after the crash, his presence on the plane was kept quiet. Most people probably believed he'd taken money for killing me and that he'd retired on some Caribbean island."

"But there was coverage of the survivors," she said. "I dug up old articles and news coverage, although you and Ethan both looked pretty worse for wear..." She narrowed her eyes as she studied his face. "And you both did a pretty damn good job of not looking directly at the cameras."

He shrugged. "It wouldn't have mattered. Mario was the disguise. Dark wig, dark contacts, dark beard... I didn't have to wear a disguise for Rory."

"So this is how you really look?"

He shrugged. "Pretty much. I used to wear my hair longer except when I was in the Marines." He rubbed his hand over his short, spiky hair and felt that ridge of a scar beneath it in the back. Where he'd taken that blow.

Had that been the hotshot saboteur or someone who'd started digging a little deeper into the plane crash after Brittney had brought it all back up again? Could someone have realized what he would have looked like without the Mario disguise? Could someone have figured out who Rory VanDam really was? A wanted man?

She stood up and walked around the cabin then, pacing like she was nervous. Or searching? She glanced at the desk in the corner, at the filing cabinet next to it.

"You want to look for that collection of passports you searched my duffel bag for earlier?" he asked.

"Was that today...?" she murmured. "It seems like so long ago."

So long since he'd kissed and held her and made love with her. It seemed like a lifetime ago now. Like a dream that would probably never be repeated because she didn't believe him.

"I don't have any proof, any identification, anything to show I was ever anyone but Rory VanDam," he said. And no one, not even other US Marshals, had known about that identity. He'd created it himself after Amelia had tried to kill him because he'd known there was no one he could trust.

"But you must have something."

"Why do you want it, Brittney?" he asked. And he stood up then because she wasn't going to find what she was looking for without his help. He'd hidden it too well. But then he'd thought he'd hidden well, too, and someone had figured it out.

Or maybe they hadn't.

Maybe they were just trying to hide their involvement in the plane crash. Because that crash hadn't happened due to pilot error. Rory and the US Marshal had discovered a bomb in the cockpit. If they'd tried to dismantle it, it would have exploded. Not wanting to freak the others out too much, Rory had claimed that the engines were failing and urged everyone to parachute off. The timer had given them long enough for everyone to get clear before the plane exploded. But in the chaos, the US Marshal had urged Rory to go before him.

He wasn't sure even now if the plane had exploded. He hadn't seen it go down, and they hadn't found the wreckage. But maybe that was because the bomb had destroyed everything, leaving nothing left for anyone to find.

Except, if Brittney was being threatened to drop her story about the crash, someone must have been worried that the wreckage and the bomb would be discovered. Maybe that bomb could be traced back to the killer.

Rory had something else that could be traced back to him, too. But that crash had proved to Rory that he couldn't trust anyone. Could he really trust Brittney? Because if he or Brittney put his insurance into the wrong hands, Rory had no hope of ever finding a safe place to hide where he wouldn't be found.

He had no hope of staying alive.

Brittney hadn't answered his question. And it wasn't because she was being petty over how many of her questions he left unanswered. It was because she didn't have an answer herself. Why did she want proof?

Because she wanted to sell the story? Could she do that if it would put him in danger?

But then he was already in danger.

He wasn't acting like it now, though. He was moving around the cabin, working in the small kitchenette area, opening soup cans, thawing bread that had been in the freezer. "There's electricity out here?" she asked.

He shook his head. "Power is solar and wind only, but it's enough to run some small appliances and lights."

"Any way to communicate?" she asked as she pulled his cell from her purse and held it up. There was no signal and the battery was draining fast.

He pointed toward a radio on the desk in the corner of the small log cabin. Besides the door to the outside, there was another that opened into a small bathroom. Then the cabin itself had the big stone fireplace with two plaid easy chairs pulled close to it. That fireplace and a king-size bed dominated the space. But there was also a kitchen table and chairs next to the short row of cabinets.

"Are you hungry?" he asked as he carried the food from a small gas stove to the table.

She nodded and joined him, pulling out the chair across from him. He held out a bottle of wine he'd uncorked. And she nodded again, more heartily. But it didn't matter how much she drank, there wasn't enough alcohol to calm her fears or wash away the nightmares she was bound to have.

The only reason she was still alive was because of Rory. He'd saved her twice now. A third time on the helicopter. If they hadn't gotten away, they would have been shot for certain at that hangar in the woods.

No matter what he called himself, he was a good man. Only a good man would have jumped in front of a speeding SUV to rescue her and into the line of fire to save not just her but the firehouse dog, too.

She took a sip of the red wine, which was just a little sweet and a little dry. Kind of like the man sitting across from her, ladling stew into bowls.

"I trust you," she said.

He pushed the bowl across to her. "I didn't poison the soup or the wine," he assured her, his mouth curving into a slight grin.

"Not just about the food," she said. "I trust you about your story."

"It's so wild that it does sound like something made up," Rory acknowledged. "But I don't have a big enough imagination to make it up."

"You lived it," she said. She'd seen the scars on his body. But the real scars, she suspected, were deeper than his skin. They were on his heart. In his mind...

"And you trusted me with this information," she said, awed that he could trust anyone after what he'd been through. "You trusted me with the truth."

He shuddered a bit as if he was cold. The fire was dying down in the hearth. But then he said, "I didn't think I would ever trust anyone again."

"You didn't even trust your team with the truth or Ethan." And he'd been there with him. "Why me?"

"If it's because of me, because of this story, that you're in danger, you deserve to know the truth," he said.

She realized what he meant, that if she died because of this, she should know why.

Braden hated how often he and his team had had to wait out here, outside the ER room, worrying and wondering about one of their own. Dirk was the only one who hadn't survived. But their luck was bound to run out again.

The more times they had to come here, the greater the odds that another life was going to be lost. Was this time because of that damn saboteur again?

"I'm not going to die," Ethan said as he stepped through the doors from the ER. Tammy was under one of his arms, her arms wrapped around him as if she was, with her slight weight, holding up the giant of a man. Ethan lifted one hand to his head and knocked his fist against his forehead. "Hard as a rock."

"More like full of rocks," Trent Miles said. His teasing him seemed like just a reflex. He was preoccupied, worried about his sister and Rory.

Braden was worried about them, too.

Ethan made his way through the crowd of concerned hotshots to where Braden and Trick stood near Trent. Owen had had to leave for another call. Dawson Hess, the other paramedic-firefighter-hotshot, was with his wife in New York City, so Owen was pulling extra shifts.

"Have you heard from Brittney?" Tammy asked Trent,

her voice full of concern for her new friend. Tammy be-friended everyone, she had such a big heart. But she also owed Brittney for helping save her life. She had been the one who'd put it in danger, though.

Trent nodded. "She called. She's with Rory."

"Where?" Ethan asked.

Trent shrugged. "She didn't say."

"The island," Trick said. "I checked the hangar. The he-licopter is gone." A muscle twitched beneath the reddish stubble on his jaw.

There was more to the story. Braden knew it. Trick had already told him. But he must have been leaving it up to him to share or keep it from the others. Seeing the concern on Trent's and Tammy's and Ethan's faces, he was tempted not to share. But they deserved to know the truth, and they all damn well knew how much danger they were in.

"He found bullet holes in the metal walls of the hangar and spent shells."

Trent sucked in a breath. "So someone was shooting at them."

Trick nodded now. "Looks like it."

Trent cursed.

Tammy reached out and touched his arm. "But you talked to her," she reminded him. "She's safe. She's with Rory."

Trent shook his head. "She's not safe with Rory. Rory isn't Rory." He pointed at Ethan. "Tell them what you told me and Owen."

Ethan touched his head again, but he was holding it in-stead of knocking on it. While he was going to be all right, he had a concussion. Fortunately, it wasn't as bad as the one Rory had.

Rory hadn't just had that concussion, though. He'd had other scars. He was a man who'd been through a lot.

That plane crash. Ethan shared that Rory blamed himself for it, that he had been the pilot.

Trick nodded. "I knew he was a pilot from how he flies the helicopter."

"And he stepped in on previous wildfires, flying the plane when nobody else was available," Braden added.

"But he was here, in the hospital, when Brittney had her accident with her van," Tammy said. "He didn't hurt her, and I don't think he would."

"He wouldn't hurt any of us," Ethan said.

But one of them had. The saboteur. "We don't know that any of this has to do with that plane crash," Braden said. "Brittney was also investigating the things happening with our team. And someone hit Rory that night. Maybe Rory saw who it was and doesn't realize it. He's been so out of it since he regained consciousness."

But now Braden understood why the man hadn't even recognized his name at first. Because it probably wasn't his real name.

"Brittney was trying to talk to my dad," Trick said. "Maybe he knows what's going on, too. I tried calling him, but he didn't pick up."

Mack was a busy man, but he usually answered for Braden. "I'll try."

Trick chuckled. "You'll probably get more out of him than I could. I think you're his favorite son now."

"Son-in-law," Braden corrected him. "And it's easy to be his favorite since he only has one daughter."

One amazingly strong woman.

"I only have one sister, too," Trent said to Trick. "And I need to do everything that I can to make sure she stays safe. How can we get out to that island tonight?"

"Rory took the helicopter," Trick said. "So next best

would be a boat, but it's dark and the water's rough with some ice chunks in it. It wouldn't be safe to go out until morning."

But from the look on Trent's face, he was afraid that his sister might not make it until morning. With how the attacks on her and Rory had escalated, Braden was worried about the same thing.

That the next hotshot he lost would be Rory…or whatever his name really was.

# Chapter 20

The wind howled around the cabin, louder than the coyotes had been howling earlier. It would be too dangerous to try to fly back tonight.

Too dangerous for someone to try to fly out here tonight or even to take a boat. Knowing how protective Trent was of his sister and how worried he was about her, Rory pointed to the radio. "You need to talk to your brother," he said. "Make sure he doesn't try to get out here."

Brittney wrapped her arms around herself and nodded. "It sounds like a storm's coming."

"The storm's been here," Rory said. Ever since she'd done that story about Ethan and the plane crash, the storm had been brewing. Then it had just been a far-off rumble of thunder, a warning of what was to come.

The past.

It had come back to get Rory.

He had to make sure that it wasn't out there now. "I need to make sure the chopper is secure." And that nobody had made their way onto the island already. "But first I'll connect you with the firehouse radio where someone should be able to get patched through to Trent's cell," he said. "And I'll give you some privacy."

Brittney narrowed those pretty topaz eyes and studied his face. "Can I tell Trent what you told me?"

He nodded. "It's fine." It was all going to come out, anyway. Because probably the only way to protect her...was to put himself in even more danger...

Once the truth got out, nobody would have any reason to try to stop Brittney anymore. But him...

He still had that hit out on him. So he'd have to go back into hiding, have to leave this life as Rory VanDam and the people in it behind him because he didn't want any more lives lost because of him. "And tell Trent to sit tight on the mainland," he said. "He can't try to get out here tonight. It's too dangerous."

So was staying here with her...

Staring at her across the table as they'd eaten and drunk wine had had Rory hoping that it wasn't just one night, like the aberration making love with her had been.

A one-off.

A dream.

Something he wouldn't be able to repeat...even if he didn't get killed. If his old enemies didn't come for him, Rory was making new enemies among his team. They wouldn't like that he'd kept the truth from them.

And Trent probably wouldn't accept it as easily as his sister had. Hopefully he wouldn't risk his life trying to get out here, though, trying to get to her.

Now if the killer had...

Maybe it would all be over tonight.

Rory turned on the radio and connected it to the firehouse, then he handed the speaker and headphones to Brittney and walked to the door. When he opened it, cold air and icy rain rushed in, soaking him.

"Rory!" Brittney called to him.

But he ducked his head down and headed out into the storm. It was the lesser threat of all the ones he'd recently faced, like his feelings for Brittney. He didn't just trust her, he was beginning to fall for her.

And he couldn't do that…not when they both had so much to lose: their lives.

The door closed behind Rory, but the cold stayed inside the cabin, chilling Brittney deeply. What if that person who'd been shooting at them had managed to catch up to them somehow?

What if he or she was out there, waiting for Rory? He wasn't armed.

As a former lawman, wouldn't he have a weapon somewhere around? Some kind of gun or taser? Something to protect himself, especially when there was a hit out on his life…

No. On Mario's life.

"Brittney!" Trent's voice crackled through the headphones she'd slipped on.

She pressed the button on the microphone and leaned forward. "Trent."

"Stanley said he patched the call through the radio. Are you on the island with Rory?"

"Yes."

"Sit tight. We're trying to figure out how to get there tonight—"

"No!" she shouted, and her voice echoed in her headphones, making her flinch at the volume. "It's too dangerous."

"Why? What's happened? What has he done?"

"Rory hasn't done anything." But save her, protect her, feed her and make love to her.

She sucked in a breath as she realized she was falling

for him. And she had only his word that he was who and what he said he was.

What if she was wrong to trust him?

What if he was lying to her?

But why?

Unless he had been the one responsible for the crash.

"Rory's not even his real name," Trent reminded her.

"No, it's not," she agreed.

"He admitted that to you?"

"Yes, he told me all about his past, and the plane crash," she said.

The headphones crackled. Brittney didn't know if that was just static on the line or her brother trying to talk to her. "What?" she asked. "Are you there?"

"Yeah, I'm waiting for you to tell me what he told you," Trent said.

And Brittney hesitated. Dare she share Rory's secrets?

"Maybe it's better that you don't know," she admitted. For Trent's sake, but mostly for Rory's.

Trent groaned. "If it's that bad, you shouldn't know, either."

"Rory is not the bad guy," Brittney insisted. "But there are some dangerous people after him." She didn't want her brother to be one of them.

"You need to get away from him," Trent said. "Now."

The wind howled so loudly that the windows rattled. Then sleet slashed across the glass. Rory shouldn't have gone out in this, not even to secure the helicopter.

Was that all he was doing?

Or had he taken off and left her here?

"Rory won't hurt me," she said, but she felt a pang in her heart even as she made the claim. He wouldn't hurt her physically, but if he'd taken off, even with the intent of keeping her safe, she was going to be hurt.

He'd already left her once, at the hotel.

And this time they hadn't even made love first.

"The weather's bad, Trent. Don't do anything stupid," she said.

Instead of being offended, he chuckled. "I'm not used to you talking to me like this…"

"Like I'm the calm sensible one and you're…"

"You," he teased.

She wasn't calm and sensible, either. She was scared to death. Not of what she'd learned or even of that killer.

She was scared that something had happened to Rory. He'd been gone for a while. Maybe she needed to go and look for him…

Make sure he hadn't fallen on the rock when he'd gone back up to the helicopter. Or that the killer wasn't out there, that he or she hadn't hurt Rory or worse…

"I need to go, Trent," she said.

"Brittney! You can't go anywhere, either."

"I meant off the radio." But she intended to go somewhere, wherever she had to in order to find Rory.

"Brittney, you need to be careful," Trent said in his best big brotherly voice of concern.

"I'm always careful," she said. But even she couldn't say it without smiling.

Trent snorted. "I mean it. I don't like this, any of it."

"Rory's a good guy," she said. But she wondered now if she was trying to convince her brother or herself.

"Even if that's true, that doesn't mean he's good for you," Trent pointed out.

And it was a valid point.

One Brittney chose to ignore as she'd begun to ignore

most of the unsolicited advice she received. "Stay where you are," she told him. "Don't worry about me."

She wasn't sure how to sign off the radio. But she pushed buttons until the headphones stopped crackling and whatever lights had been lit up went dark.

Just like the cabin had begun to do as the fire died down. She needed to find Rory, make sure he was all right. But she didn't even make it across the room to the door before it opened.

The wind swept into the room along with the hard pellets of sleet and rain. Had the door blown open? Because she didn't see anyone.

Then a dark shadow stumbled across the threshold, his arms laden down with wood. Rory's hair and jacket were soaked, some of the ice clinging to his hair and his chafed skin.

Brittney rushed forward and closed the door behind him, shutting out the wind and rain.

"It's getting cold," Rory said. "We're going to need more wood than this…" He dropped his armload near the hearth and headed back toward the door, as if he intended to go back out into the storm.

But Brittney stood in front of the door, her heart hammering. She'd been so scared that something had happened to him. That he wasn't coming back…

"What's wrong?" he asked with concern, and he slid his cold fingertips along her jaw. "Did Trent upset you? Is he coming out here anyway, despite the storm?"

She shrugged. "I don't know. I tried to talk him out of it."

"Did you tell him about me?"

"I told him you're a good man," she said.

He closed his eyes then and leaned forward, pressing

his forehead against hers. "If I was, I wouldn't want you again like I do…" he murmured, his voice gruff with desire.

Her heart hammered even faster and harder. And she reached up to wrap her arms around his neck, to pull his head the rest of the way down to hers.

He kissed her deeply, and she tasted the beef stew and the wine and her desire. It rushed up, overwhelming her with its intensity.

"I was so worried about you out there," she admitted. "Worried that something would happen to you."

He stared down into her face, his pale blue eyes so intense. "You were worried that I wasn't going to come back?"

She nodded.

"Did you think I'd take off and leave you here?"

"If you thought it would keep me safe, you might," she said.

He nodded, and rain droplets sprayed from his hair to her face. He wiped them away like he was wiping away tears. "I might," he agreed. "But I'm not sure either of us will be safe anywhere until…"

"Until what?" she asked. Then she stared up at him. "You have a plan?"

"Yeah."

She should want to hear it, want all the details, but at the moment, she just wanted him. "Tell me later," she said. Then she rose up on tiptoe and kissed him. She reached for his wet flannel jacket. After unbuttoning it, she pushed it from his shoulders. Then she reached for the bottom of his sweatshirt, tugging it up over his washboard stomach.

He was undoing her buttons and zippers, too, pushing down her jeans, pulling off her sweater…until she stood before him in only her bra and panties.

And even that was too much. She wanted nothing between them. So she unclasped her bra and let it drop onto the clothes that littered the hardwood floor around them. And she slid her panties down her hips.

Rory shoved down his jeans and boxers and stepped out of them and his boots, so that he was as naked as she was.

She shivered, a delicious shiver of anticipation for the pleasure she knew he could give her. But he must have mistaken it as cold because he picked her up and carried her to that big bed.

"Get under the covers," he said. "And I'll add more wood to the fire…" As he threw in a couple of logs, sparks hissed and sprayed back at him.

"Don't get burned!" she said with concern.

"I'm a hotshot," he reminded her as he walked to the bed wearing only a slight grin. The firelight played across his skin, turning it gold, making him look like the painting of some mythical god. "I'm used to playing with fire."

"You jumped out of the frying pan of your old career literally into the fire when you chose your new one, your new identity…" When he neared the bed, she reached for his hand, tugging him toward her. "Why?"

"Fires are more predictable than people," he said with a heavy sigh.

"Trent says that they're anything but, that they can shift and turn at a moment's notice."

"But you know they're always capable of great destruction, of harm," he said. "You can't always tell how badly a person might hurt you, but a fire leaves no illusions." He stared down at her intently, as if he suspected that she would hurt him.

She didn't want to. That was why she hadn't told Trent any of the details yet. Maybe not ever…

This would have been the story to make her career, to

take her permanently off the fluff pieces, but if it cost Rory his life, it wasn't worth it. Nothing was worth that...

But everything was worth this...

Making love with him again. Even though she was putting not just her life but her heart in danger, too.

She tugged on his hand again, pulling him down with her, onto her. His body covered hers, naked skin sliding over naked skin.

"I told you to get under the covers," he reminded her.

"I don't need them," she said. "I need you."

He groaned then kissed her, his mouth making love to hers. And as he kissed her, he touched her, sliding his fingertips in light caresses along her side, over the curve of her hip. He pulled back, panting for breath, and said, "You are so beautiful. So sexy..."

He was the sexy one. She touched him like he'd touched her, just gliding her fingertips along his skin. First it was cold, damp, from the sleet and the wind, but it heated as she touched him.

Then she lowered her hand and wrapped it around his erection, and he began to sweat, beads forming on his upper lip.

"You're dangerous, Brittney Townsend," he said. "You can hurt me more than anyone else."

Before she could ask what he meant, he kissed her again. And his hands continued to move over her, caressing her breasts, cupping them.

He brushed his thumbs over her nipples, and she moaned. The tension was winding up inside her, twisting her muscles into knots. Making her desperate for release...

Then he was inside her, filling her, and they moved together like they'd choreographed a dance. She arched and he thrust. Then finally the tension broke, and the orgasm moved through her with such force and pleasure that she had to cling to him.

Then he called out her name as he came, too. And she knew that he was just as dangerous to her as she was to him because she was definitely starting to fall for him.

And she hadn't ever wanted to fall for anyone, let alone someone in a dangerous career, someone she could lose like she'd lost her dad.

Way too soon...

Way before their time and way before she was ready to let them go...

The killer waited inside the SUV, which rocked and shuddered as the wind battered it. Rain and sleet swept across it so thick and fast that the wipers couldn't keep the windshield clear.

And the driver had to peer through the rain and the darkness to see the dock by which they'd parked, waiting for the boat that was supposed to be coming, that would take them to where the reporter and the hotshot must have gone.

That island, which was part of a national forest, was where the hotshot firefighter also worked as a forest ranger. They'd asked around the bar in Northern Lakes about the helicopter and the man who flew it.

Rory VanDam.

The tall, lean blond guy didn't look anything like dark-haired burly Mario Mandretti. But Mario had been a disguise, a cover for the DEA agent. For the former special ops Marine. With the expert flying and that ability to escape death over and over, Rory VanDam had to be Mario.

The killer had been worried about the wrong thing this whole time, that the reporter's quest to delve deeper into the plane crash would have the FAA and the US Forest Service resuming a search for the wreckage. And DNA had been left behind when the bomb had been planted in the plane they'd known Mario would be flying. They just hadn't realized why he'd been flying it, that he'd gone through hotshot training. That he was a hotshot now.

How the hell hadn't *anyone* known that the DEA agent hadn't died? Why the hell had the DEA agent been hiding out here all this time, posing as some hotshot firefighter?

Why hadn't he gone to anyone? Let the authorities know he was alive?

Was it because he'd realized there was no one he could trust? That the people who wanted him dead were just too rich and too powerful to be stopped?

# Chapter 21

Rory wanted to stay on the secluded island, in the cozy cabin, in that warm bed with Brittney forever. But he'd realized long ago, with the careers he'd chosen and the enemies he'd made, that forever wasn't possible for him.

Especially now.

The sun was shining. The storm had ended with the break of dawn. While the water was calmer now, there was still ice in it that could make it hard to get a boat to the island. But there had been time for someone to get another helicopter.

So they couldn't stay. They had to leave as quickly as they could before the shooter found them. But Brittney seemed as reluctant to go as he was.

She was making the bed that they'd messed up so many times last night, kicking off the blankets, tangling the sheets…as they made love. His pulse quickened just looking at it, at her, and his body hardened.

He grunted and shook his head. "We have to go, Brittney. Now."

She must have heard the urgency in his voice because she stepped back from the bed and pulled on her jacket and hooked her purse over her shoulder. "Okay…"

But instead of heading toward the door, Rory walked over to the desk in the corner. He didn't open any drawers, though.

What he wanted wasn't inside it. He pulled it back from the wall to reveal a small safe between joists in that wall. His hand shook a bit when he twisted the lock and opened it.

There was a gun inside, his old Glock. It had come in handy while he and Ethan had been stranded those months in the mountains. But he hadn't used it since.

And the other thing. The small USB drive beside it, he hadn't used it at all. And he probably should have.

But in order to use it, he would have had to come out of hiding. He would have had to blow up the life he'd made for himself here in Northern Lakes with his hotshot team.

"You do have a gun," she said.

He nodded. "This will do more damage, though," he said as he handed the USB drive to her.

"What is this?" she asked.

"This is the proof," he replied.

"What?"

"This is a recording of the US Marshal who was with me on the plane. He gave it to me when he gave me a parachute to get off the plane before the bomb we found on it went off. He said it was my *insurance*. This will prove what I told you is true. It's the corroboration you need for that big story you've been chasing," he said. "Even bigger than Jonathan Canterbury IV."

She shook her head. "I don't want it."

"What?"

"The big story," she said. "I don't want to put you in danger because of it. If that family is still paying people to try to kill you, you will be in terrible danger."

"If someone is after you because of that damn plane crash, because of me," he said, "the only way to make you safe is for you to tell the story, the whole story. Then there is no reason for anyone to try to stop you anymore."

"But those people, that family, want revenge on you," she said.

"They don't want revenge on you," he assured her. "You won't have to worry about losing Trent, like you lost your dad."

Tears suddenly filled her eyes, either over the loss of her dad or maybe the thought of losing her brother.

"Nobody will die because of you," he assured her.

"You might," she said, her voice cracking. "If I do this story, those people will know you're alive."

He sighed. "Yeah, they won't like that…" But who were they anymore?

He didn't even know what had become of the Falcone family. Amelia's dad had sworn out the hit on him, the vendetta, but he'd already been pretty old five years ago. That was why he'd had his son take over his business interests.

The drugs. Then after Felix Jr. had died, Felix Sr. had promised the empire to his daughter if she killed Mario. He'd thought she was different than her family, like Rory was different from his.

And just as he'd left his family for the service and never looked back, he hadn't wanted to look back at the Falcone family. He also hadn't wanted to draw any attention to his past, to himself. Until now…

"I think it's already too late for that, Brittney. You need to go with your story." He pointed to the flash drive she held. "With that."

Her brow furrowed as she stared up at him. "I don't understand you…" She shook her head. "You wanted nothing to do with me, with the press…and I understand why that was. But why did it change?"

Because he'd fallen for her.

He couldn't tell her that now, though, not when he was

probably going to have to go into hiding again soon. And she wouldn't be able to hide, not with as famous as she was becoming. She was on the verge of the career she wanted, that she deserved. He couldn't take any of that away from her.

"Somebody's trying to kill us," he reminded her. "That's why everything changed, and it's why we have to get the hell out of here."

This time, he didn't wait for her to move. After tucking the gun into the waistband of his jeans, he grabbed her hand and urged her toward the door. As they headed up the path to the rock and the helicopter, he heard another motor.

Someone was coming.

"We have to hurry," he said. If they didn't get away with that tape, Brittney would never get her story. Nobody would probably ever learn the truth about what had happened.

But he wasn't sure that he knew the whole truth now. Maybe there was more going on than he'd even realized. Because was it really some minions for the Falcone family that were after them both?

The threats to Brittney and the blow to his head. Or had the saboteur been responsible for some of the things?

Brittney had been on edge ever since they'd left Bear Isle. He had proof. And he'd given it to her.

The responsibility of it weighed on her, making her bag heavier as she'd carried it from the helicopter to his truck. The entire flight, the entire drive…they'd both been so on edge, so certain that another attack was about to come.

Someone shooting at them.

Who?

Would she find out from playing that flash drive?

"You can play it," Rory said. Somehow, he'd known exactly what she was thinking. But they'd already pulled up to the firehouse.

Other trucks and vehicles were parked in the lot. A lot of the team must have been there. The side door opened and Trent walked out, Trick close beside him. Trick hit his shoulder and looked up, meeting her gaze through the windshield.

"Play it," Rory said.

But Trent was opening her door, pulling her from the passenger's seat into his arms. "Oh, my God, thank God you're all right," he said, his voice gruff with emotion. "I was so afraid I was going to lose you."

"I'm right here," she assured him as she pulled back. His weren't the arms she wanted around her, comforting her, holding her.

But Trent didn't give her a chance to reach for Rory again. Nor did Trick. He was standing by the driver's side. "Braden talked to my dad."

Rory's breath had a catch in it. "Your dad is a good man."

"Mack knew you were more than you were saying you were," Trick said. "He knew because you know my brother Mack. My brother vouched for you with my dad."

Rory's lips curved into a slight grin. "Mack…"

And Brittney didn't know which one had brought out that affectionate smile, the father or the son who were both apparently named Mack.

Trick continued, "My dad said that he kept quiet because Mack told him you had your reasons, whatever they were, for laying low."

Rory turned toward her again. "Play them that recording. That's what's on the drive."

"Recording?" Trent asked.

Brittney pulled the flash drive from her purse with a

shaking hand. "This. His proof... But I need something to put it in."

"Let's use the computer in Braden's office," Trick said. "Let's play it there."

Brittney got swept up between the big red-haired hotshot and her big dark-haired brother. They hurried her toward the firehouse, as if worried that someone might shoot at her again, and once inside, they rushed her to Braden's windowless office. He glanced up from his desk then widened his eyes and released a ragged sigh of relief.

"Thank God you're all right."

She smiled. "I never expected you to be happy to see me."

Braden chuckled. "Well, I am, very happy that you're all right."

Trent, with his arm wound around her, tugged her closer. "Me, too."

"You're not too embarrassed to claim me now," she murmured.

He hugged her now with both arms. "I'm really sorry, Brittney. Very sorry that I've given you a hard time."

"Not just me," she said. But she couldn't see around her to Rory. All she could do was grant his wish. She pulled back from Trent and held out the flash drive to Braden. "We need to play the recording on this."

Braden took it from her hand and pushed it into the side of his desktop. Then he pressed his fingers on the keyboard. "There's just one file on this. An audio file."

Her stomach flipped and dropped. Did she want to hear this? Did she want to know everything about Rory?

"Why do you want to play this?" he asked.

"It's proof." Trick was the one who said it now, not Rory.

She glanced back over her shoulder. But he must have been standing behind Trick. She couldn't see him.

"Proof of what?" Braden asked, but instead of waiting for an answer, he pressed a key and a voice emanated from the speaker on his computer.

"Your DEA agent crossed the wrong family," a male voice was saying. "Felix Falcone is not going to forgive or forget that this Mario whatever cost him his son and his daughter."

"She tried to kill him," another male voice remarked. "She would have if I hadn't been there."

"It wasn't supposed to be you there."

The man gasped. "Who was it supposed to be?"

"Me. I've been paid for this job. To make sure that Mario dies."

"You're a federal agent…"

Brittney held her breath, waiting for a name. But neither of them used each other's.

The federal agent continued, "You can't help him start over with some new identity."

"Why not?"

"Because you're on Falcone's hit list, too, for killing his daughter. The only way for you to stay alive and keep your family alive is to give him up."

"I don't have any family," the man replied.

"What about your life? Don't you care about that?"

"Sounds like I'm a dead man anyway."

"Be a dead rich man. Start over yourself, someplace warm and far away."

The US Marshal sighed. "Sounds tempting…"

Sounded sickening to Brittney, that the people who were supposed to protect Rory had given him up instead. But the woman who was supposed to have loved him had given him up, too. No. She'd tried to kill him herself.

"He's flying you somewhere, isn't he?" the agent asked.

"Make sure that plane goes down and the pilot with it." He chuckled. "Like the captain going down with his ship."

"Do you recognize those voices?" Brittney asked, and she tried peering around Trent and Trick again. "Rory? Do you recognize those voices?"

Trick and Trent both turned around, but Rory wasn't there. He'd slipped away. To go where?

Then she remembered what she'd heard as they'd headed up to the helicopter. The other motor.

But that hadn't been Trent heading toward the island. He was here. So who was there?

"We have to stop him," she said, and she tried to get around Trent to head out the door, too. But her brother held on to her arms, keeping her between him and his boss's desk. "He's going back."

"Back where?" Trent asked. "To his old life?"

She shook her head. "Back to the island. Someone was heading there when we were leaving. It was probably that person who's been shooting at us, trying to stop us."

"The US Marshal or the agent?" Trick asked from behind her brother.

"I think the Marshal died in the plane crash. There was a bomb in the cockpit, and he made Rory and the others parachute out. Before he did, he gave that recording to Rory, maybe so he would know not to trust anyone."

"What do we do with it?" Braden asked. "If we hand it over to the authorities, we risk this agent getting it or destroying it."

Brittney turned around and reached for the USB drive, pulling it out of Braden's computer. "I know what to do."

"This isn't just some story," Trent said. "This is Rory's life."

"Yes, it is, so go after him!" she said. "Don't let him face that killer alone!" She wanted to go, too, but she knew that since her brother wouldn't even let her out the door there was no way he would let her go back to that island, back to danger.

To the danger that Rory was facing alone.

He had a gun. But did it even work anymore? Would he be able to save himself like he had her so many times? Or was he determined to go back and confront the person in order to protect her once and for all?

FBI agent Barry Shelton had a trace on Felix Falcone's landline. But he'd had to get far enough away from the damn island before he got enough reception on his phone to play the call that had come in.

"Falcone? Felix?" a familiar voice said.

"Uh, yeah, this is Felix," the old man replied, his voice weak.

He was weak now. But he still paid. He had no power anymore, but he had money. And nobody to give it to…

"Felix, this is Mario," the former DEA agent told him.

"Mario?"

"Yes, Mario Mandretti," he said. "Do you remember me?"

"Uh, I… I don't know…"

"I was a friend of your son Felix's, and I was close to Amelia, too," he said.

"Felix?" Felix asked, and his voice was muffled, as if he was calling out for him. He chuckled. "I don't know where that boy is off to. Probably down at the basketball courts. And Amelia… She'll be playing with her dolls…"

"Yes," the man replied. "Yes, she will be."

"What's your name again?" Felix asked.

"Mario."

"I don't remember you," he said.

"What about any federal agents?" the man asked. "Do you remember them? Paying them?"

"Paid a lot of them…paid a lot of them…but I don't remember why…"

"I know," the man calling himself Mario again assured him. "I know why, and I know who. I have a recording of his voice. You don't have to pay him any more money, Felix. He didn't earn it."

Barry cursed. A recording.

He'd figured the Marshal might have recorded him. Barry hadn't trusted him. That was why he'd followed him and figured out he was getting on that plane with Mario. So, while they were at that training center in Washington, Barry had planted the bomb in the cockpit of the plane. He'd watched Mario inspect it, and then when he'd gone back inside the building, Barry had acted fast, planting the bomb he'd brought along.

But he'd had to move so fast, he wasn't sure it was going to work. Or what evidence he might have left behind. But when he'd heard about the crash, he'd figured his plan had played out how he'd intended. But the pilot hadn't gone down with the plane.

He was alive.

He was Rory VanDam.

And he had evidence.

It should be gone now, though. If it had been on the island, it would be gone soon.

Unless…

Unless Rory VanDam had already done something with it…

Had already given it to someone?

That reporter. She hadn't dropped the damn story. After she'd run the first story about Jonathan Canterbury, Barry had tapped her phone line. He knew what calls she'd been making, who she'd been trying to contact and question. And she hadn't stopped reaching out, trying to follow up and find out more about the crash.

If she'd gotten that damn recording...

Barry had to do whatever he could to get that recording back. He'd made too much money, but he'd also advanced too far in his career to give it all up for somebody who should have died five years ago.

# Chapter 22

Rory figured the FBI probably still had a tap on Falcone's line. When he'd gone undercover with the DEA, they'd coordinated with the FBI on the investigation.

After talking to the man, who obviously had dementia or Alzheimer's disease, Rory wasn't sure if his calls were still being monitored. But just in case, he'd made certain to mention the recording. But would his plan work how he wanted it to?

Would it flush out the killer toward him or toward…?

Rory sucked in a breath as he realized what he might have done. And his hand slipped a bit on the control of the helicopter, making it dip toward the lake below. Through the windows, he could see the smoke.

The son of a bitch had set the island on fire.

And that had been even before he would have heard that wiretap, if there was even still a tap on the line. The son of a bitch had set Rory's sanctuary on fire.

His heart ached for the animals and the cabin and all the trees and nature. Then he noticed through the window that a boat was heading toward the island.

A US Forest Service boat. His team members were heading out there. They would save what they could.

And Rory had a feeling, since that other boat was already gone, that he had someone he needed to save, too. If he wasn't already too late.

If he hadn't just made a horrible mistake by baiting a murderer...

Brittney was supposed to lock herself into Braden's office and open the door to nobody until Heather got there or the hotshots got back from the island. That was the order that Trent had given her before he left with his crew.

But she'd had things to do.

A promise to keep to Rory.

She should have made him make her a promise, as well. A promise to stay alive.

Where the hell had he gone?

Straight to danger? Or maybe he'd taken off entirely, knowing that his secret was soon to be revealed. It was what he wanted, she reminded herself, as she wrapped up and sent off not just the audio file of the recording but also a video of her coverage of it.

She wasn't sure if her station would play it. But she knew somebody who would. And she didn't even care if she took all the credit for it. Avery Kincaid had done the first story about the hotshots back when the Northern Lakes arsonist had been terrorizing them and the town. Avery had once worked out of the news station in Detroit where Brittney worked. But after that story, Avery had been offered a job in New York City and had moved there. She was Brittney's idol, who Brittney wanted to be. Career-wise.

Maybe even personal-wise.

Avery had married one of the hotshots. Dawson Hess. Not that Brittney intended to marry a hotshot. She just wanted to make sure that a certain endangered one of them stayed alive. And because Avery knew the hotshots well,

Brittney trusted her to do the right thing with the recording and the video she'd sent her. The video she'd taken outside Braden's office but still inside the firehouse, in the conference room on the third floor in front of the podium the superintendent used for hotshot meetings.

While waiting for the large file to finish sending, Brittney walked over to the windows and peered down at the street below. A black vehicle pulled up outside the firehouse. A long black SUV.

A chill rushed over her.

Then a man stepped out of the driver's door. His hair was salt-and-pepper, and he wore dark shades. He just had that look…that federal agent look to him.

Her pulse quickened. Was this the guy who'd tried running her down? Who had shot at her?

She rushed to the door of the conference room, intent on locking it to keep out the federal agent. But then she heard Annie's bark echo up the stairwell from below.

Annie and Stanley were down there, in the garage area. Stanley was polishing the trucks. Maybe the guy wouldn't hurt him. It wasn't as if Stanley understood anything that was going on, he just knew that people he cared about were frequently in danger.

But then he worked in a firehouse, so everyone he worked with put themselves in danger. Stanley hadn't signed up for that job, though. He was just a sweet kid.

A kid that Brittney needed to protect. But how…?

Maybe she was overreacting, maybe this person driving that black SUV wasn't the same one who'd tried running her down, who'd shot at her and Rory.

She slipped out of the conference room and started down the stairs to the ground floor.

Annie's bark got more frantic, and then she growled.

This person was a stranger to her, unlike the person who'd attacked Rory the night of the holiday party. So maybe there had always been two different threats to them.

"I'm sorry," Stanley said, and his voice sounded strained, as if he was wrestling with Annie. "She usually likes everybody."

"I'm not really a dog person," a man replied. And his voice sent a chill running down Brittney's spine. She recognized it all too well from that recording.

She hadn't been paranoid to think he might be that FBI agent—she'd been right. And now she had no idea what to do…

"If you're here to talk to Braden or any of the hotshots, they're not here," Stanley said. "They probably won't be back for a couple of hours."

And Brittney nearly groaned. The teenager had inadvertently let the man know exactly how much time he had before he might be caught. Because she was absolutely certain that he intended to commit a crime…

Especially when he asked, "What about Brittney Townsend, the reporter. Is she here?"

"Uh…"

Annie barked louder, as if the dog knew Stanley shouldn't answer this man's questions.

"She's supposed to be locked inside Braden's office," Stanley said.

The kid was sweet, too sweet to realize that he shouldn't always tell the truth, especially to strangers.

"Why would she be locked up like that?" the man asked with amusement in his voice.

"She's in danger," Stanley replied. "Somebody's been trying to hurt her."

"Why?" the man asked. "Has she been putting her nose where it doesn't belong?"

Had he seen her shadow on the stairs? Did he realize that she was standing there, listening?

Stanley chuckled. "That's what some of the guys say. Rory used to say it the most..."

"I bet he did," the man remarked.

"But now he seems to like her..." Stanley muttered as if he was confused about Rory's turnaround.

Brittney was, too. Had Rory developed feelings for her? Feelings like she had for him?

Where was he?

Had he gone back to the island?

Or was he around here somewhere? Ready to rush to her rescue again?

She couldn't count on that, though. She had to figure out how to save herself and Stanley and Annie, too.

"If he liked her, he wouldn't have let her keep pursuing her story, and he certainly wouldn't have given her what I think he gave her..."

"I... I don't know what he gave her," Stanley stammered. "I... I don't know anything..."

But from the fearful crack in his voice, Brittney knew that he'd figured out that the man he was talking to was not a good man. Annie had already figured it out because she kept barking and growling.

"Shut up that dog!" the man yelled. "Or I will!"

"Annie," Stanley whined at the dog.

And Brittney could hear the struggle between the kid and the animal. He was trying to hold on to her leash. He was getting out of breath, and Annie's nails were clawing against the concrete as she tried to drag him closer to the man.

They needed to get farther away. Out of the line of fire...

Out of the damn firehouse…

Brittney edged down a few more steps until she could peek into the garage area. The big doors were closed, and the man stood between Stanley and the side door he'd entered. It was closed now.

They were all shut inside with this man unless Brittney could figure out how the overhead doors opened. If it was possible there would be witnesses, the agent wouldn't try to hurt Stanley or Annie.

But as she peered around, she saw that the controls were on the other side of the garage. Not far from where Stanley stood. If only she could catch his attention…

But he was focused on his dog, on trying to pull her back from the man. Brittney had caught someone's attention, though, as the man stared up at her. Then he drew his weapon and pointed it, not at her, but at the kid. "You know why I'm here," he said. "So hand it over."

"How…" Her voice cracked. "How do you know about that?"

He smirked. "How do you think?"

Her pulse quickened even more, and she hurried down the last of the steps to join them in the garage area. "Rory told you? What did you do to him?" She wanted to hit him, to shove him back, to shout at him for hurting Rory. Because surely he would have had to hurt him to get him to say so much…

The man chuckled and nodded. "Uh-huh, I was right."

Brittney swore. He'd tricked her into confirming his suspicion. He hadn't known for certain that she had the recording until she'd just admitted it. This was a trick that, as a reporter, she knew and shouldn't have fallen for herself.

"Hand it over," the man said.

She lifted her empty hands. "I don't have it."

He pointed the gun barrel at Stanley, and she edged between it and the kid. Annie jumped on the back of her legs, nearly knocking her down. She turned and pushed the dog back along with Stanley, trying to steer them behind one of the engines, out of the line of fire. And as she shoved, she looked at those controls for the overhead doors, hoping that Stanley would notice what she was looking at...

That he would understand what she needed him to do.

"Get that dog under control or I will shoot it right now!" the man shouted.

And Stanley pulled harder on Annie's leash, pulling her behind the engine.

Some of the tension eased from Brittney. She didn't want them getting hurt. She didn't want anyone getting hurt but this man.

"You damn well have that recording!" he yelled at her. "And you need to hand it over or I will shoot you right in the head. And I'll kill that kid and the dog, too."

"Then you won't find the recording," Brittney said. "I hid it." In plain sight on the third floor, but hopefully he wouldn't make it that far.

At least not before the recording and the video file finished sending to Avery Kincaid.

"You're going to get it now," he said. "And bring it back down here or I'll shoot the kid and the dog."

"You're going to shoot us all anyway," Brittney said. "We've all seen your face. I know you have no intention of letting us live."

Stanley let out a little cry of fear, and Brittney glanced at him to see tears in his eyes. She tried to make eye contact with him before she looked at the controls again. *Please, Stanley, open those damn doors...*

If only he could read her damn mind...

The agent laughed. "You're not wrong, Ms. Townsend. I am going to kill you all. I guess it just matters how you want to die. Slowly and painfully or quick and relatively painless."

She snorted. "I don't want to die at all." And she certainly didn't want Stanley's young life cut short. If only he would move toward those damn doors...

"Get that recording," the guy threatened.

She shook her head. "It's too late anyway."

"What do you mean?" he asked, his body tensing.

"You don't think I would share that kind of bombshell recording the minute I received it? You don't think I got that out to as many news sources as possible to pick it up and run with it?" she asked. "Your voice is going to be played on every news program at every station in the country. It's over for you, Agent. It's all over."

He lowered his brow a bit. "You don't know my name. It's not mentioned on that recording?"

"You don't think someone will recognize that voice as yours?" she asked. "I recognized it the minute I heard you talking to Stanley. You don't think it can be voice matched to yours? That your coworkers and the US Marshals won't start pulling your financials and figure out that you took money to carry out a hit on a DEA agent?" She laughed and shook her head. "Then you're not as smart as you think you are."

"Neither are you, Ms. Townsend," he said. "Because you just pointed out to me that I have nothing to lose. I might as well just kill you and the kid right now." And he raised the gun and moved his finger toward the trigger.

Brittney moved, shoving Stanley and Annie farther back behind the engine as the first shot rang out.

# Chapter 23

He was too late. Rory had known it the minute he'd seen the black SUV parked outside the firehouse. And he'd made a horrible mistake on that phone call.

He'd thought mentioning the recording would get the agent to come out in the open, to come after him, or at least get him to leave Northern Lakes, to leave the whole damn country for one with no extradition. Then Brittney would be safe.

But he should have known that the guy was smart. Or he wouldn't have gotten away with his crimes for as long as he had. So the guy had figured out to whom Rory would have given that recording.

The reporter.

Brittney.

And somehow he'd figured out she was here, at the firehouse. Or maybe he'd just wound up here after checking the hotel and other places in town.

Rory had snuck up to the firehouse, to that side door, since none of the big ones were open. But when he touched the knob, it didn't turn. It was locked. He doubted Stanley had remembered to do that since he rarely did.

And the kid was here. His car was in the parking lot.

And Annie was here. Rory could hear her barking.

She sounded ferocious for once. But underneath that

ferociousness was an element of fear, too. Fear probably more for her people than for herself.

Annie was a protector.

And for years, Rory had been, too. But he hadn't done everything he could have the past five years to protect people. He should have tried to figure out who the hell this agent was earlier. He should have made sure he would never hurt anyone else again.

Rory pulled his keys from his back pocket. Thank God he had one to the firehouse. All the hotshots did. He slid it into the lock now and slowly and softly pushed open the door a bit.

Annie barked louder, but she didn't give him up. Maybe she hadn't even noticed him. She was focused on the man with the gun.

But Brittney stood between that man and the teenager and the dog. She had made certain that barrel was pointed at her, not the kid.

And Rory's heart swelled with more love for her. She was so damn brave. So strong. So smart.

He listened as she tried to talk to the agent, as she tried to buy more time for her and Stanley and Annie. Had she really done with the recording what she'd claimed?

Was it really all over for the agent?

He must have thought so because he flicked off the safety and began to squeeze the trigger. And Rory squeezed his, firing off a shot.

He got the guy in the arm, spinning him around…toward Rory. But when Rory fired again, there was just a click, as either the gun jammed or it was out of ammo.

He hadn't checked it when he'd grabbed it out of the safe. He hadn't checked it once during the nearly five years it had been locked inside the safe because he hadn't wanted anything more to do with guns. He'd wanted to leave that life and that violence behind him and just be Rory Van-Dam, a hotshot firefighter.

But he'd always known that it would catch up to him someday. He'd just hoped that nobody else would get hurt because of him.

"It really is you," the agent murmured as he stared at him. "These past five years, I thought for sure you were dead, just like Mitchell."

"I'm not dead," Rory said. "You didn't kill me the first time you tried, but you killed some other people, some innocent people."

"You think Marshall Mitchell was innocent?" The FBI agent snorted. "He was willing to take bribes. He was willing to kill."

"He only said that because he was setting you up, getting you on that recording," Rory said. "He was going to deal with you once he got me safely established in my new life."

The agent snorted again, then grimaced as he moved his shoulder. But he grasped his gun tightly in his other hand, the barrel pointed at Rory now.

Not Stanley and Brittney...

But had they been hit?

Rory couldn't even see them now. They were behind one of the engines. And all he could hear was Annie whining...

Had the dog been hurt?

Or was she whining because one of the humans with her had been hit?

"He recorded me to get more money out of me," the agent replied. "He probably wanted a bigger cut."

Rory shook his head. "Not everyone is as greedy as you are..."

The agent laughed. "God, you're an idiot. Everybody

has a price. Money. Or fame. With this reporter here…"
He gestured behind him with the gun, but at least he wasn't
pointing at her any longer. But maybe that was because she
wasn't moving…

His heart hammered with fear that she'd already been
hit. That she was lying there bleeding…

Needing help.

Rory had to help her.

"She couldn't wait to send that recording out everywhere," the agent continued. "She used it, used you, just
for her career."

A little jab of pain and doubt struck Rory's heart. Was
the agent right? Had Brittney been using him for her career just like Amelia?

While Brittney's job meant a lot to her, people meant a
lot to her, as well. Her brother…

And even though she didn't know him, she'd put herself
between Stanley and that gun. She'd been doing her best
to protect him and his dog.

The dog continued to whine.

"You're wrong about Mitchell," he said, just trying
to stall for time now. While he couldn't fire his weapon,
maybe he could find one close enough in the garage that
he could use. Like a wrench or an axe. "Why do you think
he didn't tell you my new identity?"

"It doesn't matter," the agent said. "He died. He's gone.
And soon you will be, too."

"Why?" Rory asked. "Felix Falcone doesn't even know
who I am let alone want me dead anymore. He's senile. He
doesn't even know his kids are dead let alone want to
avenge their deaths. You don't need to do this. To do any
of this…"

The agent glanced at his bleeding shoulder and shook

his head. "It's too late now. Too late. She already sent the recording. It's all over, and I'm not going down alone. I'm taking everyone with me that I can."

And he pointed that gun directly at Rory's heart.

Brittney was hurt. But it was more her heart than her body. She would probably have bruises from how hard she'd hit the concrete when she'd pushed Stanley and Annie back and flung herself behind that truck.

The bullet the agent had fired had struck the rear bumper of the rig and bounced back. But another gun had fired, too, the shot echoing so loudly in the garage that it had scared Annie. And Stanley...

While the dog whined, the teenager cried. With his eyes closed, he couldn't see the gestures Brittney was making at him. So she crawled closer, while the two men talked, and she whispered in Stanley's ear.

And finally he opened his eyes and met her gaze. There was fear in his brown eyes but also resolve. He knew what he had to do.

She listened to the men's conversation, waiting for that moment, that distraction that would give Stanley time to get to the controls and get him and Annie out of the garage. And she heard what the agent said about her using Rory just for fame, for her career.

Would he believe that?

Would he think that was all she'd wanted from him, to further her career?

Or would he know that she'd fallen for him?

She didn't dare speak out now. It was better to be as quiet as they could be, so that the agent would forget about them for now. But he hadn't because he said even more, that because she'd sent that recording out nothing mattered anymore.

And she knew in that moment that he was going to kill Rory.

She nodded at Stanley, who moved surprisingly fast toward those controls. He smacked all the buttons, sending the doors up, the motors grinding.

But over that noise, she could hear the gunshots. The bullets pinging off the metal. She hoped that Stanley had followed through with the rest of her plan, that he and Annie had gotten out through one of those big doors.

That they were safe at least. Because she could hear shoes scraping on concrete, could see feet moving toward her. And she knew that she wasn't safe.

And Rory...

She was so damn scared that he'd been hit or worse. That he was dead...

For real this time.

Trent was exhausted from sleepless nights and worrying and that damn futile trip out to the island. He'd seen the helicopter. Rory hadn't even landed. Maybe he hadn't been able to because of the smoke and the flames.

Or maybe he'd realized what Trent had...that Rory's would-be killer wasn't there any longer. He must have set the fire and taken off.

For where?

Northern Lakes.

Brittney was there. Heather on her way. Two of the people he loved most in the world. Two of the smartest, most resourceful people he knew. Surely, they would be all right.

And yet he had this sick feeling, this chill that he couldn't get rid of. He made his team leave early and head back.

And nobody had argued with him, as if they'd all realized what he had.

That something wasn't right.

That people they cared about were still in danger, and it wasn't just Brittney and Heather, but Rory, too. He was the one the killer wanted dead the most, the one he thought he'd killed years ago.

Until Brittney had started digging up the past, pursuing a story that the agent hadn't wanted anyone to pursue.

The closer they got to Northern Lakes, the more anxious everyone got. Braden and Trick kept checking their phones.

Trent checked his, too.

He had no messages from Brittney. But then he wasn't even sure she had her phone or if she'd left it in that hotel room when the killer had been coming for her.

When he'd hurt Ethan...

Ethan was back in Northern Lakes, too, but he was supposed to be resting. Tammy had promised that she'd take care of him, that she would make sure nobody hurt him, including himself.

He smiled a bit at how his friend had met his match in the salon owner. And Trent had met his match, as well, with Detective Heather Bolton.

A text came in from her:

I'm here, heading to the firehouse

She'd sent it several minutes ago, but it probably hadn't come through until the boat had gotten closer to land and cell reception.

He wasn't the only one who'd gotten a message. Trick was staring at his phone and murmured, "I'll be damned..."

"What?" Braden asked.

Hopefully it wasn't something from Trick's significant other. Henrietta "Hank" Rowlins was a hotshot, too, but she and Michaela had been busy at their firehouse up in St. Paul, nearly an hour north of Northern Lakes. Hopefully they were safe.

"I think Mack's in town," Trick remarked.

"Your dad?" Braden asked.

Trick shook his head. "My brother…" There was awe and surprise in his voice, like he couldn't believe it, like he hadn't expected to see him.

Maybe his relationship with that sibling was strained or strange. Trent's relationship with his only sibling had been strained, too. He'd been so angry with her for investigating his team, for running that article about them and Ethan and that damn plane crash.

He'd barely spoken to her lately. And when his life had been threatened, he'd pushed her away instead of pulling her closer. He'd thought he was doing the right thing, protecting her.

Just like she'd tried protecting him when she hadn't told him about those threats. She hadn't even told him about that creepy producer of hers.

That was his fault, that she hadn't trusted him to respect her, to protect her without trying to smother or control her. Not that she'd ever listened to him…

So no doubt she hadn't locked herself in Braden's office like he'd ordered her to do.

As the boat pulled up to the dock, Trent jumped off before even tying it off. He needed to get back to the firehouse, to make sure Brittney was okay.

To find out where the hell Rory was…

And Heather…

Braden and Trick caught up to him, running alongside

him as they rushed toward Braden's truck. They'd ridden with the hotshot superintendent to the dock.

Braden clicked the locks, and they all jumped into the vehicle. The boss must have felt his urgency because he drove fast, making the trip to town and to the firehouse in record speed.

But the lights that flashed weren't behind them. No officer followed him. They were already at the firehouse. Lights flashed on police cars and an ambulance. And parked alongside one of the curbs was that black SUV that had nearly run down his sister that night, that would have if not for Rory rescuing her.

Trent had been right to be worried. Something bad had definitely happened here. Had he lost anyone he loved? Everyone he loved?

# *Chapter 24*

Rory felt like he was in that coma again. He was caught somewhere between consciousness and sleep. And Ethan was right. He could hear voices around him.

"I'm so sorry, Trent," a female voice was saying. It wasn't Brittney's, though. It was huskier. Heather. The detective. "I got here too late."

Too late?

Too late for what? Was Brittney okay? Had she been shot like he'd feared? Then he'd been too late, too. He hadn't saved her at all.

Where was she?

He dragged his eyes open and peered around. He could see concrete and people's shoes. He was on the ground. He reached out, trying to shove himself up. "Brittney…" he murmured.

Big hands caught his shoulders, holding him down. "Take it easy," Owen said. "You've been hurt."

"Me?" He shook his head. "Brittney…"

Where was she?

He had to find her. She had to be here somewhere.

He turned his head and noticed what he'd missed before. The sheet. There was a sheet lying over someone. Blood stained it. He couldn't see who was under it.

The sheet covered the face of the person. Whoever it was hadn't survived.

"Brittney…" He coughed and gasped for breath as fear and grief overwhelmed him.

"You're aspirating, man. You've got to stop fighting me. Let me treat you."

"Help her…" he murmured, but he could see that it was already too late. Brittney was gone.

Fury coursed through Brittney. She'd never wanted to assault an officer before, not until Trooper Wells insisted on interrogating her instead of letting her go back inside the firehouse to check on Rory.

Was he going to make it?

How badly had he been hurt?

Those were the only questions she cared about, not the ones Trooper Wells was asking her. "Did you see the shooter?"

"What shooter? I saw that agent. He shot at me and Stanley and—" her voice cracked with fear and dread "—and he shot Rory. I need to check on Rory." She tried to step around the woman, but she'd trapped her between her body and the side of her state police SUV. She'd acted like she was going to put Brittney in the back seat and arrest her.

For what?

For trying to see the man she loved? The man who might be dying on that firehouse floor.

The blood had been spreading across his shirt when she'd scrambled over to him. And she'd tried stopping it with her hands, tried helping him. But then other people had rushed in. The police. Owen and another paramedic.

And she'd been pushed and pulled aside, taken away from him. And now he was being taken away from her.

Over the trooper's shoulder, she saw Owen and that other paramedic carrying him toward the open doors of the ambulance.

"They're taking him away," she said. "I have to go!"

"I need to get your statement while everything's fresh in your mind," the trooper insisted.

Was this how people felt about her when she kept firing questions at them that they had no time or inclination to answer?

"I need Rory!" she cried.

But the ambulance didn't wait for her. It sped off, lights flashing and siren wailing. Rory was alive, but they obviously needed to get him to the hospital fast.

And that was how Brittney needed to get there, too.

"Please," she said, her voice cracking with a sob now. "I need to see how he is."

"You can't do anything for him," Wells said. "He's getting the help he needs."

Was she implying that he didn't need Brittney?

Maybe he didn't. All she'd done was turn his world upside down. But it didn't matter if she couldn't help him medically, she still needed to be there for him emotionally.

"I need to be with him," Brittney insisted.

And the woman just stared at her.

And Brittney's fury turned to pity. She understood now why Wynona Wells didn't understand her. "You've obviously never been in love."

Brittney could have said the same for herself until recently. But even before that, she'd known what love was like from watching the people she loved. Her mother and her father had loved each other so much. And her mom and her stepdad...

And Trent and Heather.

They walked up to her now. "You've asked enough questions already, Wells," Heather told the other law officer. "Brittney needs to be checked out, too."

"She hasn't been shot."

Trent pointed toward the torn sleeve of her shirt and her jeans. "She's been roughed up." And his voice was rough with emotion when he said it. "She needs to be checked out at the hospital."

She shook her head. "I need to make sure that Rory is all right."

"I have questions about him, too," Wells persisted. "I don't understand what's been going on here."

Heather snorted. "You're not alone in that, Trooper, but we'll figure it out. Right now, we need to get Brittney to the hospital."

Heather was smart. She knew Brittney wasn't hurt badly, but she must have figured she needed to be at the hospital for another reason. For Rory.

But was Heather's urgency an indication that his condition wasn't good? That he might not make it…?

Tears sprang to her eyes, blinding her. But Trent wrapped his arm around her, guiding her toward Heather's vehicle. And Heather, ever the law officer, put her hand on the top of her head as she helped her into the back seat. Brittney could have felt like a perp again, like Wells had made her feel, but there was affection and understanding in Heather.

She knew how upset Brittney was because she was in love. She understood. Brittney needed to be with Rory for however long he had left.

Braden's firehouse was a crime scene. Again.

Blood spattered the concrete and the side of one of the rigs. Lives had been lost.

At least one…

He wasn't sure about Rory. He'd regained consciousness for a minute, but then he'd lost it and his ability to breathe on his own.

Owen had done something with a long needle and rushed him to the hospital. The man had already spent three weeks there. Had already cheated death recently and then again five years earlier.

Braden stared down at the dead body. A sheet covered him, but his black pants and shoes stuck out from under one end of it. The gun that had been clutched in his hand had already been bagged and taken into evidence along with his badge.

FBI special agent Barry Shelton. His was the voice on that recording. Brittney had verified it to Trooper Wells, but according to the trooper that was pretty much the only question that the reporter had answered.

Braden couldn't blame her. She wanted to be with Rory. Just like Braden wanted to be with Sam.

But she was gone. On a case out west.

He needed her here.

But he had her brothers. Not just Trick.

Mack was here. He'd sent the text to his younger brother, and he'd made his presence known even though he hadn't shown himself yet. Braden gazed around the area. Where was he?

Why hadn't he come forward yet?

He had to be the gunman. The one who'd shot the FBI agent and saved Brittney and Stanley and hopefully Rory, as well. Heather had said she'd gotten here too late.

So why hadn't Mack stuck around?

What was the deal with Braden's mysterious brother-in-law?

Mack knew Rory. No. He'd called him something else when he'd told his dad to talk to no one about that plane crash. But at the time he'd thought the man he knew had died. Mack hadn't been in the country then.

He very rarely was. What the hell was Mack? Not that it mattered much right now. He'd taken out the bad guy. Unfortunately, Braden suspected Agent Shelton wasn't the only bad guy who was messing with his team.

There was still the saboteur among them. Too many things had happened to them, too many things that hadn't been accidents. And Braden doubted the FBI agent had had anything to do with those incidents. He probably wasn't even the one who'd started up the trucks and hit Rory over the head, because he would have made damn certain he'd killed him then.

Stanley rushed up, away from the officer who'd been talking to him. And Braden closed his arms around him. "You're okay," he assured the kid. "You did good."

Annie jumped up, as if wrapping her long legs around them both, as if she thought this was a group hug.

"Brittney told me what to do," he said. "To open the big doors. She thought it would stop the man from shooting us if there were witnesses. But he shot Rory anyway." He started shaking. "He shot him anyway…"

Rory had to make it.

He had to. He'd already been through too much.

# Chapter 25

Rory could hear her voice in his head. She was talking about how a man who'd risked his life for others had had others give up his life for money. How people he should have been able to trust in law enforcement and even in his personal life had betrayed him…

How a hero had had nobody to turn to, and yet he'd continued being a hero, working as a hotshot firefighter. And his name was Rory VanDam.

"Cory…" he murmured. No. Not anymore. Cory was from a long time ago. A few lifetimes ago. Cory didn't matter. Even Rory didn't matter.

Only Brittney did.

That was her voice. She had to be here. But when he opened his eyes, he found himself alone but for the TV. It sat across from the bed where he lay with tubes and machines hooked to him.

"Déjà damn vu…" he murmured, but this time he didn't have a tube down his throat. He was breathing on his own. But his throat was dry as if he'd been asleep for a long time again. How long had he been out this time?

And why?

He felt his head, but he had only that ridge of a scar on the back of it. The stitches were gone now. So his head hadn't been injured again. Then he patted his chest and felt the bandage between his heart and shoulder.

"Damn…"

He must have gotten shot. He remembered the agent raising that gun, pointing it at his chest.

And he remembered the body with the sheet over it.

"Brittney…"

He'd heard her voice earlier. Or had he just imagined that? Then he focused on the TV again and saw her on the screen. She looked to be standing at Braden's podium, talking about Rory, playing that recording…

She had gotten it out just like she'd told the agent she had. Agent Barry Shelton. The reporter covering her, Avery Kincaid, showed his picture and reported about his life and his death.

Rory didn't recognize him, wasn't sure he'd ever met the man until that moment in the firehouse. The moment he'd been afraid the man had killed Brittney.

Was she alive?

That video from the firehouse, of her standing at Braden's podium, had probably been shot before the agent had showed up. Before Rory had.

He fumbled around, looking for a remote, a way to turn up the TV. What about Brittney?

He waited for more coverage but the program switched to a commercial. And he cursed.

"You're awake," a woman said, her voice cracking with emotion.

And he turned to find Brittney standing in the doorway. Was she dead? She looked like an angel with her brown curls and pale brown eyes. She was so beautiful.

Or maybe he was dead and he was just imagining her.

But the machine beside the bed recorded his blood pressure, which seemed to have gone up at just the sight of her.

"Are you all right?" he asked.

"I am now," she said.

He glanced at the TV. "Yeah," he agreed. "You're famous. You're on the national news now."

She had everything she'd wanted. The respect. The career. So what was she doing here? With him...

His heart seemed to shake in his chest, trying to swell, to warm, with hope. But Rory had never had much luck with love or anything else, really. Everybody who'd ever claimed to care about him had betrayed him.

Even a member of his hotshot team was willing to hurt the rest of them, kept sabotaging the damn equipment. So if he couldn't trust them, how could he trust her?

Maybe Agent Shelton had been right. All she'd wanted was the story.

"Are you here for a follow-up interview?" he asked. He gestured toward his door. "Got a camera crew out there?"

Her topaz eyes widened and she sucked in a breath. "Wow. Screw you. I can't believe you listened to what that creep was saying. That all I care about is my career."

He pointed toward the TV. "You got your big story."

"I gave that story to Avery Kincaid. I just did the video to let her know what was going on. I wasn't counting on her to use my part of it."

He sucked in a breath now. "You gave it up? It nearly got you killed. Why would you give it to someone else?"

"Because it didn't matter anymore who covered the story, it just needed to get out there," she said. "The truth needed to get out there."

"And you should be the one getting the credit for it," he insisted. She'd worked so hard that she deserved it.

She shook her head. "I thought you got shot in the shoulder, not the head. But you're not making any sense. First you act like you're mad I did the story, and now you're insisting that I should be the only one getting the credit for it. What's wrong with you? What do you want?"

*You. Just you.*

He wanted to say those words, but he couldn't bring himself to utter them now. He had no damn idea what was going on, how badly he was hurt. And how much danger he might be in now that the truth was out.

But Felix Falcone had dementia. "Is that FBI agent dead?" Was that who'd been covered with that sheet?

She nodded.

"Who killed him?" he asked. His gun had jammed. He hadn't been able to protect her and Stanley or even himself.

She shrugged. "I don't know."

"You haven't been investigating?" he asked.

She cursed again. "I told you that I'm not here for that damn story," she said. "I'm here for you. To make sure that the man I love wakes up."

"You love me?" he asked, and his heart swelled now with that hope as warmth flooded it. Was it safe for him to tell her how he felt about her? Would she be safe if he told her?

She'd been so happy to open that door and see him sitting up in bed, awake. It had been a long week since he'd been shot. And of course, he woke up when she was gone. When she'd finally given in to Tammy and Trent's nagging for her to get a shower and some sleep.

But the way he'd been acting since she'd walked in...

"You really believe what that agent said about me, how all I care about is my career?" she asked, her heart aching. But did she have a right to be upset about that? For so long that was what she believed, too, what she'd wanted to be true. She'd wanted to only care about her career so that she wouldn't love someone and lose them.

Like she'd nearly lost Rory.

Maybe she had.

Not to death but to his own doubts about her. Did he even believe that she loved him?

And if he couldn't believe that, he probably didn't return her feelings. Tears rushed to her eyes, and she turned toward the door but was too blinded to find the handle. She fumbled around, searching for it.

Then strong hands gripped her shoulders, turning her around. She blinked her tears away to stare up at Rory. "You shouldn't be out of bed." He'd dragged some of the machines with him. Hell, he'd dragged the bed behind him in his haste to stop her from leaving.

"I love you," he said. "I love you so much that I don't want to be around you if that will put you in danger." His hands moved from her shoulders to her face now, cupping it. She could feel a tremor in him, moving through him. "I love you so much."

"I love you," she said. "And the only danger I am in is getting my heart broken if you try to push me away."

He pulled her close to him now, wrapping his arms around her. "I'm not going to push you away," he said. "I'm tempted to never let you go. But I know you have your job—"

"I don't care about—"

"I do," he said. "It's your career. And you've worked too damn hard to walk away from it now. Take the credit and the opportunities that come up with that story and know that I will always be here for you."

"What about you?" she asked. "What are you going to do now that the truth is out?"

He shrugged. "The truth was always out that I'm a hotshot and a pilot. That's what I intend to keep being once I'm medically cleared to return to duty."

"You don't want to go back into law enforcement?"

"I think I lost my touch for that," he said. "I haven't figured out who the saboteur is, and I've probably been working right alongside whoever it is."

She shivered as she realized that he and her brother were still in danger. "I don't want you getting hurt again," she said.

"I wish I could promise that I won't, but we both know how unpredictable life is," he said. "It's not just officers and firefighters who get hurt. Anybody anywhere can have an accident or become a victim of a crime, even children. So loving anyone is a risk that you might lose them."

She closed her eyes on a fresh wave of tears. "I know you're right."

"You survived losing your dad," he said. "And you were a kid then. You're strong, Brittney, so much stronger than you give yourself credit for being. You can handle anything."

"Even loving you?" she asked, opening her eyes to stare up at his handsome face.

"Am I worth the risk?" he asked.

She nodded. "You're worth every risk. I love you so very much."

"I love you," he said, and he pulled her even closer to his madly pounding heart.

Hers was pounding hard, too, but with love, not fear this time. She wasn't afraid of falling for him like she'd once been. She knew that he was a survivor, too. He'd already survived so much and was still here. She wasn't worried about loving and losing him. She wasn't worried about anything anymore. Not even the saboteur, because so many people were determined to figure out who he was and stop him, that he wouldn't escape justice much longer.

A while ago the saboteur might have felt guilty over how hard they'd struck Rory over the head. But Rory might have seen them leave the bunk room before the trucks started. VanDam had been the only one not snoring or breathing hard like everyone else.

But the saboteur didn't even feel guilty anymore, didn't feel anything at all anymore except for anger and resentment. And the only time they felt less angry and resentful was when something went wrong or somebody got hurt.

Somebody was going to have to get hurt again.

Soon.

\* \* \* \* \*

# *Romantic* Suspense

## Danger. Passion. Drama.

## **Available Next Month**

**Colton Mountain Search** Karen Whiddon
**Defender After Dark** Charlene Parris

.......................................................

**A High-Stakes Reunion** Tara Taylor Quinn
**Close Range Cattleman** Amber Leigh Williams

.......................................................

LOVE INSPIRED

**Baby Protection Mission** Laura Scott
**Cold Case Target** Jessica R. Patch

Larger Print

.......................................................

LOVE INSPIRED

**Tracking The Truth** Dana Mentink
**Rocky Mountain Survival** Jane M. Choate

Larger Print

.......................................................

LOVE INSPIRED

**Treacherous Escape** Kellie VanHorn
**Colorado Double Cross** Jennifer Pierce

Larger Print

Available from Big W, Kmart, Target,
selected supermarkets, bookstores & newsagencies.
OR call 1300 659 500 (AU), 0800 265 546 (NZ) to order.

Visit **millsandboon.com.au**

# 6 brand new stories each month

# Romantic Suspense

## Danger. Passion. Drama.

# MILLS & BOON

Keep reading for an excerpt of
SECRET AGENT SURRENDER
by Elizabeth Heiter—find this story
in the *Hot Pursuit: Undercover Detail* anthology.

## Chapter One

"This is a bad idea," Marcos Costa muttered as he drove the flashy convertible the DEA had provided him into the middle of Nowhere, Maryland. Or rather, *up* into the middle of nowhere. He could actually feel the altitude change as he revved the convertible up this unpaved road into the Appalachian Mountains.

"It was your idea," his partner's voice returned over the open cell-phone line.

"Doesn't make it a good one," Marcos joked. The truth was, it was a brilliant idea. So long as he lived through it.

The DEA had been trying to get an in with Carlton Wayne White for years, but the man was paranoid and slippery. Until now, they hadn't even had an address for him.

That was, assuming the address Marcos was heading to now actually did turn out to be Carlton's mansion and not an old coal mine where a drug lord could bury the body of an undercover agent whose cover was blown. Namely, his.

"According to the GPS, I'm close," Marcos told his partner. "I'm going to hide the phone now. I'm only going to contact you on this again if I run into trouble."

"Be careful."

"Will do." Marcos cut the call, hoping he sounded confident. Usually, he loved the thrill of an undercover meet. But this wasn't their usual buy-bust situation, where he'd show up, flash a roll of money, then plan the meet to get the drugs and instead of doing a trade, pull his badge and his weapon. Today, he'd been invited into the home of a major heroin dealer. And if everything went like it was supposed to, he'd spend the entire weekend there, being wined and dined by Carlton.

Because right now, he wasn't Marcos Costa, a rising star in the DEA's ranks. He was Marco Costrales, major player in the drug world. Or, at least, aspiring major player in the drug world, with the kind of money that could buy a front-row seat in the game.

Pulling over, Marcos slid the car into Park and popped open a hidden compartment underneath the passenger seat. Ironically, the car had originally belonged to a dealer down in Florida, and the compartment had been used to hide drugs. Today, Marcos turned off his cell phone to save the battery and slipped it in there, hoping he wouldn't need it again until he was safely out of the Appalachians.

This was way outside normal DEA protocol, but Carlton Wayne White was a big catch, and Marcos's partner was a fifteen-year veteran with a reputation as a maverick who had some major pull. Somehow, he'd convinced their superiors to let them run the kind of op the agency hadn't approved in decades. And the truth was, this was the sort of case Marcos had dreamed about when he'd joined the DEA.

"Let's do this," Marcos muttered, then started the car again. The dense foliage cleared for a minute, giving him an unobstructed view over the edge of the mountain. His breath caught at its beauty. He could see for miles, over peaks and valleys, the setting sun casting a pink-and-orange glow over everything. Carlton Wayne White didn't deserve this kind of view.

Then it was gone again, and Marcos was surrounded by trees. The GPS told him to turn and he almost missed it, spotting a narrow dirt trail at the last second. He swung the wheel right, giving the convertible a little gas as the trail got steeper. It seemed to go on forever, until all of a sudden it leveled out, and there in front of him was an enormous modern home surrounded by an ugly, electrified fence.

Most of the people who lived up here were in that transitional spot between extreme poverty and being able to eke out a living to support themselves. They had a reputation for abhorring outsiders, but rumor had it that Carlton had spread a little cash around to earn loyalty. And from the way the DEA had been stonewalled at every attempt to get information on him, it seemed to have worked.

Marcos pulled up to the gate, rolled down his window and pressed the button on the intercom stationed there. He'd passed a major test to even be given this address, which told him that his instincts about the source he'd been cultivating for months had been worth every minute. "Hey, it's Marco. Here to see Carlton. He's expecting me."

He played it like the wealthy, aspiring drug dealer they expected him to be, entitled and a little arrogant. His cover story was that he came from major family money—old organized crime money—and he was looking to branch out on his own. It was the sort of connection they all hoped Carlton would jump on.

There was no response over the intercom, but almost instantly the gates slid open, and Marcos drove inside. He watched them close behind him and tried to shake off the foreboding that washed over him. The sudden feeling that he was never going to drive out again.

Given the size of his operation, the DEA knew far too little about how Carlton worked, but they did know one thing. The man was a killer. He'd been brought up on charges for it more than once, but each time, the witnesses mysteriously disappeared before he could go to trial.

"You've got this," Marcos told himself as he pulled to a stop and climbed out of the convertible.

He was met by his unwitting source, Jesse White. The man was Carlton's nephew. Jesse's parents had died when he was seventeen and Carlton had taken him in, provided him with a home and pulled him right into the family business. Unlike Carlton, Jesse had a conscience. But he was desperate to prove himself to the uncle who'd given him a home when no one else would. Marcos had spotted it when he'd been poring over documents on all the known players. He'd purposely run into Jesse at a pool bar and slowly built that friendship until he could make his approach.

"Hey, man," Jesse greeted him now. The twenty-four-year-old shifted his weight back and forth, his hands twitching. He was tall and thin, and usually composed. Today, he looked ready to jump at the slightest noise.

*Please don't get cold feet*, Marcos willed him. Jesse didn't know Marcos's true identity, but that didn't matter. If things went bad and his uncle found out Jesse had brought an undercover agent to his house, being a blood relative wouldn't save the kid.

Marcos tried not to feel guilty about the fact that when this was all over, if things went *his* way, Jesse would be going to jail, too. Because Marcos also saw something in Jesse that reminded him of himself. He knew what it was like to have no one in the world to rely on, and he knew exactly how powerful the loyalty could be when someone filled that void.

In Jesse's case, the person who'd filled it happened to be a deadly criminal.

Marcos had gotten lucky. After spending his entire life in foster care, being shipped from one home to the next and never feeling like he belonged, he'd finally hit the jackpot. In one of those foster homes, he'd met two boys who'd become his chosen brothers. He wasn't sure where he would have wound up without them, but he knew his path could have ended up like Jesse's.

Shaking off the memory, Marcos replied, "How's it going?" He gave Jesse their standard greeting—clasped hands, chest bump.

"Good, good," Jesse said, his gaze darting everywhere. "Come on in and meet my uncle."

For a second, Marcos's instinct was to turn and run, but he ignored it and followed Jesse into the mansion. They walked through a long entryway filled with marble and crystal, where they were greeted by a pair of muscle-bound men wearing all-black cargo pants and T-shirts, with illegally modified AK-47s slung over their backs.

One of them frisked Marcos, holding up the pistol he'd tucked in his waistband with a raised eyebrow.

"Hey, man, I don't go anywhere without it," Marcos said. A real aspiring dealer with mob connections wouldn't come to this meet without a weapon.

The man nodded, like he'd expected it, and shoved the weapon into his own waistband. "You'll get it back when you leave."

Marcos scowled, acting like he was going to argue, then shrugged as if he'd decided to let it go. The reality was that so far, things were going as expected. Still, he felt tense and uneasy.

Then Jesse led him down a maze of hallways probably meant to confuse anyone who didn't know the place well. Finally, the hallway opened into a wide room with a soaring ceiling, filled with modern furniture, artwork and antiques, some of which Marcos could tell with a brief glance had been illegally obtained.

From the opposite hallway, a man Marcos recognized from his case files appeared. Carlton Wayne White was massive, at nearly six-and-a-half-feet tall, with the build of a wrestler. His style was flamboyant, and today he wore an all-white suit, his white-blond hair touching his shoulders. But Marcos knew not to let Carlton's quirks distract him from the fact that the drug dealer was savvy and had a bad temper.

"Marco Costrales," Carlton greeted him, appraising him for a drawn-out moment before he crossed the distance between them and shook Marcos's hand.

Marcos wasn't small—he was five-nine—and made regular use of his gym membership, because he needed to be able to throw armed criminals to the ground and hold them down while he cuffed them. But this guy's gigantic paw made Marcos feel like a child.

"Welcome," Carlton said, his voice a low baritone. "My nephew tells me you're in the market for a business arrangement."

"That's right. I'm looking—"

"No business yet," Carlton cut him off. "This weekend, we get to know one another. Make sure we're on the same page. Things go well, and I'll set you up. Things go poorly?" He shrugged, dropping into a chair and draping his beefy arms over the edges. "You'll never do business again."

He gave a toothy smile, then gestured for Marcos to sit.

That same foreboding rushed over Marcos, stronger this time, like a tidal wave he could never fight. He could only pray the current wouldn't pull him under. He tried to keep his face impassive as he settled onto the couch.

Then Carlton snapped his fingers, and three things happened simultaneously. Jesse sat gingerly on the other side of the couch, a tuxedo-clad man appeared with a tray bearing flutes of champagne and a woman strode into the room from the same direction Marcos had come.

Marcos turned to look at the woman, and he stopped breathing. He actually had to remind himself to start again as he stared at her.

She was petite, probably five-four, with a stylish shoulder-length bob and a killer red dress. She had golden brown skin and dark brown eyes that seemed to stare right inside a man, to his deepest secrets. And this particular woman knew his deepest secret.

Because even though it wasn't possible—it couldn't be—he knew her.

"Meet Brenna Hartwell," Carlton said, his voice bemused. "I can see you're already smitten, Marco, but don't get too attached. Brenna is off-limits."

It *was* her. Marcos flashed back eighteen years. He'd been twelve when Brenna Hartwell had come to the foster home where he'd lived for five years. The moment he'd seen her, he'd had a similar reaction: a sudden certainty that his life would never be the same. His very first crush. And it had been intense.

Too bad a few months later she'd set their house on fire, destroying it and separating him from the only brothers he'd ever known.

After all these years, he couldn't believe he'd recognized her so instantly. He prayed that she wouldn't recognize him, but as her eyes widened, he knew she had.

"Marcos?" she breathed.

And his worst nightmare came true. His cover was blown.

# NEW RELEASE!

## Rancher's Snowed-In Reunion

The Carsons Of Lone Rock

Book 4

**She turned their break-up into her breakout song.
And now they're snowed in…**

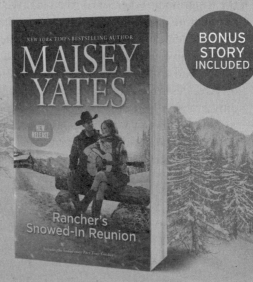

**BONUS STORY INCLUDED**

Don't miss this snowed-in second-chance romance
between closed-off bull rider Flint Carson and Tansey
Sands, the rodeo queen turned country music darling.

In-store and online March 2024.

## MILLS & BOON

millsandboon.com.au

# Subscribe and fall in love with a Mills & Boon series today!

You'll be among the first to read stories delivered to your door monthly and enjoy great savings.

## MILLS & BOON SUBSCRIPTIONS

### HOW TO JOIN

**Visit our website**
millsandboon.
com.au/pages/
print-subscriptions

**Select your favourite series**
Choose how many books. We offer monthly as well as pre-paid payment options.

**Sit back and relax**
Your books will be delivered directly to your door.

# MILLS & BOON

## —— JOIN US ——

# Sign up to our newsletter to stay up to date with...

- Exclusive member discount codes
- Competitions
- New release book information
- All the latest news on your favourite authors

Plus...

get $10 off your first order.

*What's not to love?*

Sign up at **millsandboon.com.au/newsletter**

**f** @millsandboonaustralia  🐦 📷 @millsandboonaus